Pucking Mad About You

By K.C. McDermott

ISBN (paperback): 979-8-9898117-8-6
ISBN (eBook): 979-8-9898117-9-3

Book Cover and Hartford Hydra Logo
by Mick Estabrook

1st edition 2025
10 9 8 7 6 5 4 3 2 1

Content Advisory

This book includes mature (18+) themes and potentially upsetting situations that include stalking (not by the MMC), kidnapping, attempted murder, claustrophobic conditions, and multiple explicit depictions of sex, including some non-traditional sexual practices and proclivities like light BDSM.*

*For more details on tropes & trigger see https://karencpmcdermott.com

HARTFORD HYDRA

Book 1

Prologue

Two Years Ago
Ash

I tromp through the tunnel after the game, the blades of my skates feeling springy on the rubberized floor. Or maybe it's the spring in my own step after extending my goal-scoring streak to five games tonight.

My shot didn't come until the last two minutes. Rather than pass to my wing, I managed to shake my defender and get within a few feet of the goal. I faked a shot left, then did a literal pirouette on the ice, pulled the puck all the way around, and barely slid it in the right side as the goalie lunged left. Michelle Kwan would've been envious of the spin.

Maybe I was selfish not to pass, but I really wanted that five-game goal streak, so I held onto the puck, and it paid off. My teammates swamped me against the boards in celebration as we pulled ahead out of the tie we'd been stuck at for a period and a half.

After that, our goalie held off several desperate attempts by the other team to score in those waning moments, and we claimed victory.

I've already been interviewed twice out on the ice about my streak, and Coach told me to get out of my gear quickly and into the press room for some follow-up.

"Good job, Gun," my linemate says as he claps me on the shoulder on his way to his locker. He doesn't seem offended that I didn't pass to him. As long as I score, he's fine with it.

"Thanks," I say as I fish out my cell phone. There's a message from Grace, and I smile.

Grace

Yay! Congrats on the win and the streak! I miss you.

Ash

Thanks. Miss you too. I'll call later. Press conference.

I put the phone away and start to pull off my kit.

I met Grace about a month ago when we were in LA for a game against the Kings. We both thought it would be a one-night stand, but she reached out to me later, and I was glad she did. I'd been thinking about her, and now we're dating long-distance. She's come down to Florida once since then, and I made it back out to LA a week ago for a hurried twenty hour-visit where we barely left the bed.

Grace is an actress and stunningly beautiful. She's just my type, too, with long, light brown hair, a slim figure, and plump lips that make it look like she's perpetually pouting.

More than that, she's confident and driven. I have a thing for women who know what they want in their careers and go after it.

Just as long as they know I'm in charge in the bedroom.

Grace mainly does guest spots on crime procedurals, but I know she'll make it big soon. She's up for a small but important role in a movie that would film partly in Miami, and I'm crossing my fingers she gets it. It would put her much closer to me for at least a few months, and it would do a lot for her career.

We're heading into the playoffs soon, and once hockey season is over, I'll have some down time to see her. It may still be a couple months, though, since I intend to make it all the way to the Cup.

"Gunnarsson! Let's go!" Coach calls into the locker room.

I pick up my pace as I finish taking my pads off, then sit down to remove my skates. I can leave everything else below the waist on for now until after the press conference. I can't keep my public waiting.

They want to talk to the hottest thing on the ice right now, and I'm here for them.

Chapter 1

Present

Ash

My mouthguard goes flying as I hit the boards like they're a concrete traffic barrier. Pain shoots through my cheek as I bite down on it, and I taste the metallic tang of blood when I swipe the cut with my tongue.

Fucking Lapointe. He's been homing in on me tonight like he's a heat seeking missile and my ass is on fire.

"My left ball dangles better than you, Gunnarsson," Lapointe throws out before pushing off me to catch up with the puck.

"Real original, asshole!" I shout back before swiping up my guard and shoving it back in my mouth. Not my best comeback, but the verbal game was never my forte.

I can handle Lapointe's hits. The bigger issue is he hasn't stopped chirping at me since we got on the ice.

Or maybe he's been 'quacking,' since we're playing the Ducks?

Regardless, I've already missed two easy shots – or easy for me – and it's pissing me off.

It's only preseason, but clearly no one has forgotten how last year ended for me, and they're not planning to let me forget it either. Especially not Lapointe.

I streak down the ice and get back in position. We've got the puck, and Bouchard is trying to find a shot. I'm wide open, and he glances my way but passes to Cote instead. Cote tries to flick the puck into the top left corner, but it bounces off the crossbar and the goalie smothers it when it hits the ice again.

"What the fuck?" I say to Bouchard as I skate by him. "I was open."

"Sorry, didn't see you," he says. "Next time."

Fuck that. He saw me. He didn't trust me to make the shot.

I pull my mouthguard out and spit blood onto the ice.

"Looks like you're bleeding," Lapointe says as he skates up, getting in my face. "Don't worry. I've got you covered."

His glove is off, and he grabs the front of my jersey to shove something down the collar. I push him away and reach for whatever he just put down my shirt. I feel a small lump, but I can't grab whatever it is. I take off my glove and reach into my jersey to pull out…a tampon.

I'll fucking kill him.

I wheel around to find Lapointe and take off as I spot him. He's laughing, but his face turns serious when he realizes I'm not stopping.

I slam him back against the boards as he swings at my head. The blow glances off my helmet, and he opens his mouth to yell at me, but I shove the tampon into his open trap and clamp my hand over it to hold it in as I pin his head to the glass. His eyes widen, and he throws another punch that dislodges me before he spits the tampon onto the ice.

"Motherfucker!" he shouts.

Lapointe and I punch each other wildly, each trying to land something. Kelsier and Petruck join the fray along with a couple of the Ducks, then the refs are on us, pulling us apart.

One of the refs picks up the tampon by its string.

"Match penalty, number seventeen," he tells me. "You're outta here."

"He's the one who brought it!" I yell as I gesture at Lapointe, who's smirking at me. "I was just giving it back to him."

"Out! Now!" the ref repeats as he directs me toward the tunnel.

I go, swearing like a sailor the whole way.

"PMS is a bitch, right?" Lapointe calls to me, and Kelsier has to block me from turning to go after him again.

"Take it easy," Kelsier says. "You've already been kicked out. Don't make it worse."

He's right. How did I let things get this bad?

Ash

Two hours later, I'm showered, dressed, and on my way up to see the big boss – the owner – who asked to see me after the game. And when I say 'asked,' I mean that in the same way my mother used to ask me to take out the trash.

"Go right in, Mr. Gunnarsson. He's waiting for you," Mr. Kaladin's assistant says as I approach her desk.

"On a scale of one to atom bomb, how pissed is he?" I ask her.

She only smiles encouragingly, and I sigh before I knock a couple times and open the door.

"Ah, Mr. Gunnarsson," Max Kaladin says from behind his desk as I peek inside. "Come on in."

The desk is huge and sits at the far end of an office that I'm sure is bigger than my first apartment. There's a God damn fireplace and sectional in one corner of the room, for Christ's sake.

"It is Gun-arsson and not Guuh-narsson, right?" Kaladin asks as I step inside and close the door.

"Yes, sir," I say as I head toward the desk. "My parents Americanized it when they moved here. Everyone mispronounced it anyway."

He nods. "Well, it's good to finally meet you."

He's smiling, and I feel like this has to be a trick. The man spent a lot of money to bring me here, and not only am I sucking ass in the preseason, I got ejected from one of our last games before the regular season starts.

I stop in front of the desk, and Kaladin reaches out to shake my hand. I meet it reluctantly.

The owner of the Hartford Hydra is in his mid-thirties with hair that's a shade of red I've never seen a man pull off well until now. I expect to tower over him, but he's only an inch or two shorter than me, and he seems fit, like he works out.

Max Kaladin has his hands in just about every industry you can think of. He was already filthy rich when a pharmaceutical company he owned developed a weight loss drug that, for a change, actually worked, and he became *'buy his own continent'* rich. For some reason, he decided to use some of that money to start a new NHL team.

"Sir, just let me apologize-," I start, but he waves me off.

"Have a seat," he says. He gestures to one of the chairs in front of his desk as he sits in the plush leather one behind it.

"Tell me what happened," he says when we're both settled in.

I hesitate. This still feels like a trap. The owner of my last team would've been turning purple by now if I'd pulled the shit I did tonight, but Kaladin sounds perfectly calm as I wait for the other shoe to drop.

He looks expectantly at me, and I launch into the short version of everything that happened between me and Lapointe from the time we took the ice until I got ejected. He listens patiently, nodding at all the right times, and I dare to think he might not boot my ass.

He's quiet for a long while when I finish, so I add, "That's it."

He nods again. "So would you agree we have a problem here, Mr. Gunnarsson…Ash? Can I call you Ash?"

He can call me whatever the fuck he wants. Just please, dear God, don't let him kick me off the team.

"Ash is fine," I say. "And just so I'm sure we're on the same page, can you specify what problem you're talking about?"

A smile ticks at the corners of his mouth. "I'm talking about how you implode whenever someone gets in your head," he says. "The problem is you can't handle a little trash talk."

Can't handle a little trash talk? He's right, but it sounds both condescending and accusatory, and I feel instantly defensive.

"It was more than a little trash talk," I argue. "The asshole put a tampon down my jersey." I pause. "Pardon my language, but Lapointe crossed a line. I don't appreciate that kind of misogynistic BS."

He nods. "Yes, and I'll see about getting him disciplined as well, but you can't deny this has been a problem well before tonight."

He's right about that too, but he knew that when he signed me. It's why he was able to get such a great deal on me. I'm damaged goods.

"I know I fall apart when guys start chirping at me, but-"

"You understand that's part of the game, right?" he asks.

Is it, though? That's debatable, but I'm not about to argue with a man who has more money than God and who's also my boss.

"I'll work on it," I promise.

"Did the Lightning have you working with a sport psychologist?"

"Yeah, but it didn't help. And if you'll excuse me for saying so, the guy you've got here is even worse."

Kaladin cocks his head at that before he picks up a sheet of paper and hands it to me. I take the paper and skim it before frowning.

"What's this?" I ask.

"Hopefully, the answer to our problems."

I raise a brow. "*Our* problems?"

He leans back in his chair. "Ash, do you know why I signed you?"

I thought I did, but his question makes me second-guess myself.

"I'm a former Rookie of the Year and a hell of a goal scorer when I keep my head in the game?" I suggest. I mean it as a statement, but it comes out as a question.

He waves a hand. "You're a fucking amazing goal scorer when you've got your head in the game, but there are plenty of other great players out there I could've signed."

"I was the least expensive?" I say, trying to keep the bitterness at bay.

He shrugs. "That didn't hurt, but part of the reason I signed you is *because* of your little trash talk problem, not in spite of it."

I stare at him. "What?"

"I'm trying to build a brand new hockey team in a very small state where there's lots of competition for fans," he says. "There's a dedicated fan base here that will embrace the Hydra because they're still pining for the Whalers, but there aren't enough of them to fill an entire stadium."

The Hartford Hydra is Connecticut's only professional men's sports team, and its first NHL team since the Whalers moved to North Carolina in 1997 to become the Hurricanes. The state never quite let go of the team, as evinced by the Whalers merchandise that sells alongside Hydra gear on game days. Even the Hydra's colors – navy, silver, and white – are a subtle nod to the last years of the Whalers.

"Do you know what fill stadiums?" Kaladin asks.

"Winning games?" I guess.

"That's one thing," he says. "The other is drama. Spectacle. People come to a hockey game expecting a good fight, and they're disappointed if they don't get one."

"You…want me to fight?" I ask.

"Sometimes," he says. "But more than that, I want you to be able to take your anger and channel it into scoring goals rather than falling apart."

His words are a knife to my gut, and I lock my jaw.

"Look," Kaladin says, leaning forward over his desk, "you have name recognition because of what happened last year."

My jaw tightens even more, and he hurries on.

"It may not be the kind of name recognition you want, but you have it," he says. "People will be watching. You can either implode again and end your hockey career…"

My stomach bottoms out as he confirms my worst fear.

"Or you can turn things around and show people what you're made of," he goes on. "You gained a reputation as someone who's affected by trash talk, and some people will come to watch you fail, but more people will come to see you use that as fuel to kick ass. And when we win the Stanley Cup this year, they'll stay and become fans."

I blink at him. "You…think we can win the Stanley Cup?"

"I know we can," he says, pounding a fist on the desk for emphasis. "We have the best goalie in the league. Our defensemen are freight trains on skates, we have some of the top rookies in the country, and I have a player who – until the end of last year – was arguably the best center in the NHL." He gives me a meaningful look. "We have the talent. We just need to put it all together and make it work, and that starts with you getting your head on straight. I need you to be a leader on this team."

So no pressure.

"How exactly do I get my head on straight?" I ask.

He gestures toward the paper. "Go see this woman. If she agrees to help you, put in the work and do what she says. Hopefully by the end of the season, you'll have figured out how to ignore the chirping."

"She's not a psychologist," I point out.

"No, but the psychologists you had didn't help. It can't hurt to try something different, and this woman is at least an expert."

I look at the paper, then back up at Kaladin. "Sir, I'm not trying to pass the buck here, but wouldn't it be better for you or your people to reach out to her? What incentive does she have to say yes to me?"

"I'm making you do this because it's your issue, and you need to prove you're willing to take steps to fix it," he says. "I won't make you contact this woman. You need to decide what you're willing to do to help yourself. That's why you need to be the one to reach out."

I nod. "That's fair. But what I mean is…um…" I search for the right way to remind him people don't work for free, but he's ahead of me.

He picks up a business card and hands it to me. "When you're ready to discuss terms with her, have her call that number. I'm sure she'll find our offer more than generous."

I look at the card. It's for someone in HR.

"Is…that all?" I ask. I still don't believe I may get out of this office without him tearing me a new asshole.

"That's all for me," he says. "Go see Cedric in PR before you leave, though. He needs to discuss how to handle the media questions about tonight's incident."

I groan inwardly. I knew it wouldn't be that simple, but in all honesty, I'm still getting off far easier than I should.

I rise. "Thank you, sir. I won't let you down."

He nods. "I knew we'd have some work to do when I signed you, Ash, but I only give so many chances."

He says the words calmly enough, but I hear the ultimatum.

Get my head on straight or prepare to be cut loose.

Chapter 2

Gray

I've been staring at my computer screen for fifteen minutes. I know because it's set to go to sleep after that long, and it just went blank.

The empty document reappears and stares judgmentally at me when I jiggle the mouse, each blink of the cursor a finger tap on the desk.

I wanted to start writing a book based on my recent research study today, but it's not happening, and I grimace at the waste of time.

It's the fourth week of classes, and it's that sweet spot between the first few weeks of the semester, when there's a constant stream of students coming by for signatures to add a class or to ask questions that are answered in the syllabus, and the sixth week when students realize they're not prepared for their first exam. For the next week or two, my office hours will be sparsely attended, so I need to use them productively.

I type the word "The." I have no idea what comes next, but lots of sentences begin with the word "the," so I'm playing the odds.

I'm about to delete the word when a tall form fills my doorway. The young man in the threshold must be almost six and a half feet tall, and his shoulders are so broad they nearly touch the sides of the doorjamb. He wears loose jeans and a hoodie with the hood pulled over his head.

I assume he's a football player, and I mentally scan the room in my Introduction to Communication course, trying to picture who this could be. I'm good about knowing the names of the students in my smaller seminar classes by the end of the first week, but I'll be lucky if I remember half the faces in my three hundred-person COMM 1000 lecture before the end of the semester.

The young man steps into the room, filling it with his presence, and I feel a tingle up my spine. It's that tingle a woman gets when she's facing a strange man, and instinct tells her to run while years of social grooming tell her not to make a scene. There's something oddly…overwhelming about this guy.

I close my laptop and smile up at the young man, social grooming winning out. "Can I help you?"

"Dr. Mackey?" he asks, only half looking up.

"Yes."

"I was wondering if I can have a few minutes of your time."

I raise a brow. Maybe a bit too polite for a football player? His voice is soft and deep, and something about it soothes my worries.

"That's what my office hours are for," I say. "Have a seat."

The kid glances down either side of the hall before coming in and closing the door behind him. The closed door puts me on edge again, and I consider reaching into my purse to thread my keys through my fingers, just in case. The guy seems nervous, and that sets off alarm bells.

When he finally pulls his hood back, I have to suppress my shock.

He's older than I thought, a man, not a kid. He's likely in his twenties, but closer to my age than to an undergrad. He has a broad forehead and a strong, clean-shaven jaw that narrows into a pointed chin. His deep-set eyes look hazel, but the light in my office isn't great, so I can't be sure.

"Thanks for seeing me," he says as he sits in the chair across the desk from me. It looks laughably small beneath him.

He runs a hand through soft brown hair that's several inches long on top. It falls back around his face in a way that gives him a slightly unkempt look, which – now that I'm no longer on edge – is sexy as hell. The hair would easily cover his eyes if he combed it forward, but it's only long enough to cover his neck further down. Somehow the whole package is both boyish and rugged at the same time.

I guess he's a graduate student, or he wants to be. Potential grad students often visit professors they want to study with before applying to a school, but I pray he's not here to ask me to be his research advisor.

I recently published a study on trash talk that catapulted me into the spotlight as an 'expert' on the subject. Since then, students have asked me about working on similar studies, but if that's what this man wants, I'll have to turn him away. There's no way I'd be able to work with him and not have filthy, sinful thoughts that would risk getting me fired.

As it is, I hate myself for caring that my hair is hastily thrown up into a messy bun today or that the florescent lights in this office make it look dirty blonde rather than golden like it is in the sun. I'm also wearing a shapeless cardigan over an even more shapeless skirt.

The man eases back in his small chair, trying to get comfortable, and I note the way his long legs stick out in a manspread.

"Dr. Mackey, I'm Ash Gunnarsson," he says and pauses.

I cock my head, waiting for more. It seems like he expects me to know the name, but honestly, it sounds made up.

I nod. "Good to meet you, Ash. What can I do for you?"

"You…study trash talk, right?"

"I do."

He pauses. "Do you know who I am?"

I frown, and now I'm worried. Please don't let him be the son of the dean or the president of the university. I don't have tenure yet, and I'll be fired before the end of the year if I have to take him on as a student.

"No," I say. "Should I?"

He looks relieved. "It's probably better you don't," he says, "and I need you to keep this visit confidential."

My frown deepens. "Confidential? Why? Who are you?"

He looks at me for a long moment. "Confidential, right?" he asks. "There's some law or something about that, isn't there? You can't tell anyone what I tell you?"

I smile. "This isn't a confessional, Mr. Gunnarsson, and I'm not a priest. The law you're talking about is FERPA, the Family Educational Rights and Privacy Act. It's a federal law that protects student educational records. It means I can't tell people things like your grades without your permission, but it only applies to students, and I have a feeling you're not a student here."

His face falls, and I have mercy on him.

"That being said, I have no desire or reason to tell anyone your business, so why don't you just tell me what you need."

He eyes me, obviously weighing if he can trust me or not. At this point, my curiosity is piqued enough that I need to know why he's here.

"I'm one of the centers for the Hartford Hydra," he says finally.

It takes a moment for my brain to make sense of that, but then it hits me. He's a professional hockey player on Connecticut's new team. Or their relatively new one. If I recall, the team was formed last year and didn't have the most auspicious start.

Trying to get a new sports team off the ground in Connecticut is an uphill battle. We're a small state, and we're wedged between Boston and New York, two professional sports powerhouses, both with their own NHL teams. The Hartford Hydra's owner, billionaire Max Kaladin, seems to have more money than brains, though, so good luck to him.

"New to the team?" I guess.

"Yes," Ash says. "Mr. Kaladin brought me on this season to help turn the team around, but I have a problem we…I hope you can help with."

My brow furrows. "How exactly can I help?"

He hesitates. "I'm a great player," he says. "Probably one of the best centers in the league if I put modesty aside, but I have a problem staying focused when guys are chirping at me."

My brows pinch deeper. "Chirping at you? As in…"

"Trash talking," he clarifies. "I get rattled. I was able to keep it under wraps for a few seasons, but it just got worse until it came to a head at the end of last season, and…things didn't end well."

"I see."

"Do you follow hockey, Dr. Mackey?"

I shake my head. I don't watch as many sports as a person who studies sport communication should, and hockey was never at the top of my list.

"So then you don't know how my last season with Tampa Bay ended."

"No."

He exhales deeply. "Long story short, I imploded in the playoffs. My contract was up, and they decided not to renew me. Since then, word has gotten around about my issue, and other teams are reluctant to pick me up. Only Mr. Kaladin was willing to take a chance on me, and I can't disappoint him. He's the one who gave me your name and suggested I contact you."

"Suggested?" I ask.

"He said it was my choice to put in the work or not. He wants me to take responsibility for the issue, so here I am."

"I don't understand what you need from me," I say. "I'm a Professor of Communication. I'm not a sport psychologist. I'm not even a regular psychologist. I have no clinical background. Surely you have a sport psychologist on staff who can help you with this."

He scoffs. "We do, but he has no idea how to help me. Everyone knows trash talk happens, but their attitude is to suck it up and ignore it."

"So exactly what do you want me to do for you, Mr. Gunnarsson?"

"You know how trash talk works. Can't you…" He waves a large hand in the air as if he's flourishing a magic wand. "Fix me?"

I let out a small laugh. "You want an intervention."

He frowns. "You mean like…you'd get all my teammates together and have them tell me how much they need me and shit?" He closes his eyes. "Please just don't tell me we all have to hug, because there's no way I'm hugging Mack or Kingston."

"No, nothing like that," I say. "An intervention in social science is when we design a strategy or action to adjust a behavior that addresses a problem. Essentially, it's an attempt to intervene and alter an existing dynamic. We deal in inoculations and interventions. If we want to prevent a certain behavior from starting, we inoculate against it. If we need to stop or alter a behavior that's already happening, we design an intervention."

His face scrunches as he tries to wrap his head around my scholar-speak. "So…it would fix me," he says finally, interpreting my words.

I open my mouth to say it's not that simple but decide against it. "Sure. If successful, an intervention would fix you," I say instead.

He brightens, and for the first time since he arrived, he looks almost as if he's about to smile.

"Great. So when can we do this?" he asks. "How long will it take?"

I sigh as I realize he's misunderstood.

Despite its pervasiveness in competitive activities, trash talk is understudied. I found precious few scholastic articles on it when I did my study. Only philosophers had a lot to say about it, and most of that was an attempt to argue the immorality of the practice.

My own study really just established what most people already knew: trash talk can negatively affect the performance of its target. There were a few other key points, but that was the primary one, and thanks to my university's stellar PR department, I became big news.

None of this qualifies me to psychologically treat a professional athlete, though.

"I'm sorry," I say, "but you misunderstand. I don't have an intervention for you. Interventions have to be designed and tested. They can take months at minimum, if not years. There's no intervention that currently exists for dealing with trash talk."

His face falls again, and his eyes go soft. "Please," he says, holding out his hands as if to make me see reason. "You have to help me. Hockey is my life, and I'm in danger of losing everything I've worked for."

My heart twists, and I feel like I just kicked a six-and-a-half-foot puppy. I want to take it all back and promise to fix him.

"Even if I had something that could help you," I say, trying to hold on to my resolve, "the semester just started. I have classes, advising, and university service. Do you have any idea how many committees I'm on?"

He doesn't, and I'm sure he doesn't care, but I'm trying to convince myself more than him that I don't have time for this.

He leans back to fish in the pocket of his pants, and I'm treated to a view of his groin thrusting my way, which is just cruel. He pulls out a business card and hands it to me.

"Call this number," he says.

I take the card. It has a name, title, phone number, and the name of the company on it. Kaladin Global Group.

"Mr. Kaladin told me to give you that and have you call," he says.

Fine, I'll bite. I pick up the landline on my desk and dial the number. It rings twice before a male voice answers.

"Hello, this is Dr. Gray Mackey," I say. "I'm here with Ash Gunnarsson from the Hartford Hydra. He gave me this number and…"

I listen as the man on the other end starts talking, and my eyes widen as he lays out the absurdly generous compensation package Mr. Kaladin has approved for my work with his player. It includes a staggering amount of grant funding for both myself and my department if I actually succeed in curing Ash of his trash talk issue.

"I'll send over the contracts for you to sign," the man says after more-or-less telling me I won the lottery.

"Hold off on that for now," I say. "I have to talk to the head of my department before I agree to anything."

There's a beat of silence on the other end of the phone that's pregnant with incredulity after the numbers the man just gave me.

"I'll email you the contracts anyway," he says. "Show them to your department head and the university's lawyers if you want."

"Fine," I agree. I start to give the man my email address, but he assures me he has it.

I hang up the phone and catch Ash's eye. He looks so hopeful, but I'm not sure I can agree to do this. I don't actually know how to help him.

On the other hand, developing inoculations and interventions was ultimately my goal when I decided to study trash talk, and this may be just the opportunity I was looking for to see what works and what doesn't. I hate to make Ash my guinea pig, but if there's a chance I can find something that helps both him and me, maybe it's worth it. It's not exactly good science to do it this way, but for the money Kaladin is offering, maybe I can bend the rules this once.

Better yet, if I document my process and do this as by-the-book as I can, I might be able to publish the results. I'd need to go through the proper channels and get Ash to sign off on participating, but…

I look again at the gorgeous specimen of male athleticism sitting in front of me and my stomach drops. Nope. It's my original problem all over again. Working closely with this man would be a hockey season of wet dreams waiting to happen, and I don't have enough extra money floating around to buy the amount of lube it will take to make it until…When does hockey season end anyway?

Then I recall I'll have plenty of extra money if I agree to help.

This is also the opportunity of a lifetime, and I'm not even talking about the funds. Having access to a professional athlete on a project like this is the goal of just about any researcher doing sport-related scholarship. Passing this up would be stupid.

That's assuming I don't screw Ash up or make him worse.

"So you'll help me?" he asks.

"What I told the guy on the phone stands," I say. "I need to run this by my department head before I can agree to anything. I'll need to see if she has any concerns I haven't thought of."

And she will. I'm sure of it, so I'll let her be the 'bad guy' and nix this.

Ash nods. "Okay. No problem."

I'm treated to another thrust of his groin as he roots in his pocket again, this time to pull out his phone.

"What's your number?" he asks.

"I can just email you when I have an answer," I say.

He looks at me, thumbs poised over the phone screen, and I'm a hundred percent certain I'm the only woman who's ever tried to avoid giving him my phone number.

I sigh and give him my cell number.

He enters it in his phone, and seconds later, my cell pings on my desk with an incoming text from an unknown number. I pick it up and read.

Unknown

Looking forward to working with you, Doc.

"I haven't agreed to anything yet," I remind him.

He winks at me. "No, but this way I'm all set when you do," he says with a grin, and – God help me – he has dimples.

Thankfully I still have half an hour until class because I'm sure there's now a wet spot on my skirt that will need to dry before then.

Ash stands, and I do as well. I'm 5'7" – not exactly short – but even from across the desk I can tell he towers over me. He extends a hand, and I shake it.

"It was nice to meet you," he says. "Regardless of whether you end up working with me or not, text me if you ever want to attend a game, and I'll set you up with a couple tickets."

"Thank you. That's really sweet of you," I say, careful not to promise anything on either count.

He flips the hood back over his head and turns to leave. I'm not sure how many people will recognize him on campus, but better to be safe.

It occurs to me I don't know why he doesn't want to be recognized.

"You don't want anyone to know you came to see me because…," I say, inviting him to fill in the blank.

He shrugs. "It's probably moot at this point, but our PR guy doesn't want anyone to know I'm working with you. Or *could* be working with you," he corrects. "He says that will only confirm for people how big the issue is, and he doesn't want word getting around more than it already has. When they send over those contracts, there will be an NDA clause that prevents you from talking about anything that happens between us."

So much for getting a publication out of this.

"Understood," I say, and he opens the door to leave.

Now that I know he's not a student, I allow myself a quick once-over of his physique. I can't tell a lot with his baggy jeans and hoodie, but I see enough to know he's probably ripped under all that clothing.

It's been about a year since I've had sex, and it must finally be getting to me because I'm ready to text him right now and take him up on that offer of hockey tickets.

Ash turns down the hall, and I give him a good ten seconds before I sit back down and google him. I've reached a new low, but I don't care.

Ash Dagur Gunnarsson. His family moved to the US from Iceland a few years before he was born, then they moved to Canada when he was five. He came back to the US when he was drafted by the Tampa Bay Lightning. He's twenty-seven years old now, three years younger than me, and at 6'4", he's one of the taller forwards to play in the NHL, since forwards are typically the smaller players on a hockey team.

I look up news about him and find half a dozen articles that blame him for Tampa Bay losing their chance at the Stanley Cup last year. As Ash suggested, he started out playing great, but he played more and more erratically as the season went on, and he imploded by the end. The Lightning were up three games to one in the semi-finals, but Ash seemed to lose steam, and the other team crept back in. He rallied in game seven to score a goal in the first period, but then he did nothing for the rest of the game and spent a lot of time in the penalty box. The Lightning lost that game, 3-2, and with it, their chance at the Cup.

I'm not sure it's fair to blame Ash for the loss, given that there were plenty of other players on the ice that could've done their part, but maybe I'm missing some context. I don't know enough about hockey to judge how his loss of focus might've affected his teammates.

I scroll further but regret it as a gossip article about him dating an actress named Grace comes up. She's not an A-lister by any means, just a woman I've seen play a one-off character in the law dramas and buddy-cop shows I watch. She's beautiful, though, and Ash looks happy as he poses for pictures with his arm around her.

The article is from a year and a half ago when he was still in Florida, but I can't find any recent mention of whether or not they're still together.

By the time I finish nosing around the internet, it's almost time for my class. I forward the contracts from Kaladin Global Group to my department head, Melinda, with a quick note that I need to talk to her, then shut my laptop down and mentally prepared to go lecture.

I generally enjoy teaching, but I'm an introvert at heart, so I have to psych myself up to face a room full of three hundred undergrads. Teaching is like a performance in a way, and it takes a lot out of me. I much prefer to do my research, but that's not my primary responsibility at the university.

I sigh and stand to go to class. I'm counting on Melinda to veto the idea of working with Ash because part of me *really* wants to work with him, and that alone tells me this isn't a good idea. I don't make good decisions when it comes to men.

I text my best friend Celena on my way.

Gray

Free tonight? I need wine.

I get a text back seconds later.

Celena

What did your students do now?

Gray

Nothing. Ash Gunnarsson. Familiarize yourself and be prepared to discuss.

I'm aware it took me less than an hour to break my promise to Ash about not telling anyone he came to see me, but there's no official NDA in place yet, and I'm pretty sure BFFs are exempt in situations like this anyway. I have to tell someone, and Celena can keep a secret.

A minute passes before my phone pings again with her reply.

Celena

Oh my.

Oh my is right.

Chapter 3

Gray

"Let me get this straight," Celena says as she cradles her glass of Chardonnay later that night at the local wine bar.

I want to explain that wine glasses have stems for a reason — so the heat from her hands doesn't warm the wine — but I bite my tongue. I'm an admitted wine snob and also what they call in the wine world an ABC drinker…Anything But Chardonnay.

"A tall, gorgeous professional hockey player just walks into your office today," she goes on, "asks you to fix his trash talk problem, and offers you an obscene amount of money to do it?"

"Technically the HR guy offered me the obscene amount of money," I correct, "but otherwise, that's the gist of it."

Celena takes a long gulp of her wine before setting the glass down.

"I hope you bought a lottery ticket before you got here," she says, "because the stars must be aligned."

"No lottery ticket. I still haven't accepted it happened."

"Have you told your boss yet?" she asks, leaning forward. "Don't you have classes and shit?"

"I did, and I do, but Melinda tentatively okayed it. I still have to teach classes and advise, but she agreed to suspend all my other university obligations, and she all but promised me tenure if I make this happen. The funding they're offering is too good to pass up. She just wants the university's lawyers to look at the contract to see if we can negotiate around the NDA so I can publish any results that come out of the…I'm not even sure what to call it."

"Do you get to go to games?" Celena asks. "Will you meet the rest of the team? Ooo! Can you get me an autographed jersey?"

She gets more excited with each question, but I have to burst her bubble.

"I'm not even sure I'll agree to it yet."

She looks at me like I just told her the beehive hairdo is coming back in style and I'm thinking of getting one.

"Gray, why wouldn't you agree to it?" she asks incredulously. "Between the money and the opportunity to work with a professional athlete, this is a no-brainer. And have you seen the man, for God's sake?"

"Oh, I've seen him. That's the problem," I counter. "How the hell am I supposed to work with a man like that for the next few months?"

"How the hell can you not?" she shoots back.

I sigh and take a sip of my Malbec. I opted for the heavy stuff tonight.

"Look, that's not the main reason I'm wavering," I say. "If I have to, I'll give myself a few orgasms before I meet with him, then put on my big girl panties and do what I can to help him. My bigger problem is that I don't actually know *how* to help him. All my work is theoretical. He needs a practical solution, and I don't have time to research and test one for him. Best case, I may be able to put a bandage on the problem. Worst case, I exacerbate things, he'll be kicked off the team or sent back down to the farm league, or whatever they do in hockey, and I'll have wasted thousands of dollars of Kaladin's money and pissed off not only a billionaire, but the entire state of Connecticut."

Celena stares at me, then takes another healthy sip of her wine. "Or," she says, holding up her forefinger, "you could succeed in finding a solution and pioneer a psychological treatment that turns him utterly trash talk-proof. He, in turn, helps the Hydra win the Stanley Cup, and the entire state of Connecticut rejoices and re-embraces professional hockey. Both Ash Gunnarsson and Max Kaladin are so grateful that the three of you become a throuple, and you live happily ever after with your billionaire and hockey star husbands, which I swear I saw in a novel somewhere."

I roll my eyes. "Polygamy is illegal. I could only marry one of them, and how on earth would I choose?"

Celena lets out a long groan. "Jesus Christ, Gray. How does your brain always fixate on the one negative in a sea of positives?"

Celena is the ever-optimist to my little cloud of doom. Give me any situation, and I can tell you the ten different ways it can go sideways. Celena, on the other hand, is still convinced she'll one day take that flight into space she's always wanted.

"I'm sorry," I say, "but this could derail my whole career if it goes wrong. I'm just getting traction, and I can't do anything to jeopardize it."

My phone pings with an incoming text, but I ignore it.

"You're writing a book, aren't you?" Celena asks. "Can't this be like a case study or something? Just take lots of notes about working with this guy, then turn them into a book."

"I can't do that unless the university's lawyers get the NDA thrown out, or at least changed."

Celena considers this. "Okay fine, but I think our first step here is to get you back on a dating app."

I blink at her. "What? Why is that our first step?"

"If you're going to work with this guy, you'll need a boyfriend. You need to be getting sex from somewhere because, let's face it, that man puts some models to shame."

I deflate. She has a point. Regardless of how things work out with Ash, it may be time to put myself out there again, but I'm not excited by the idea. I dread it.

Aside from my introversion, there's also the way my last relationship ended. The one that turned me into a paranoid stalker by the end. The one where I spent the entire day before a date in a state of raw-nerve anxiety until the guy, Drew, inevitably canceled on me at the last minute, and I fell apart.

My phone pings again with another incoming text, and I swipe in the pattern to open it. I frown as I see who the texts are from.

"I've got two messages from Ash Gunnarsson," I tell Celena.

Her eyes widen in excitement. "What do they say?"

I open the texts, and there's a short message as well as…

"Holy shit!"

"What is it?" she asks, peering over my phone to see the screen.

"He sent me a God damn dick pic."

"What!" Celena grabs the phone out of my hand, and her eyes blow wide as she looks at the screen.

"Holy fuck," she says. "That's…that's a really nice dick."

I grab the phone back from her and read the texts. The first came in about a minute ago.

Ash

> I was thinking about you. We should get together.

That message sits above a picture of an erect cock that lays across a toned stomach. It's hard to tell its exact size from the picture, but I'd guess it's above average both in length and girth. There's a slight upward curve to the shaft, and the base is nestled in a short smattering of curly brown hair. The message attached to the pic reads, "In case you need some incentive to think about the offer."

I force myself to click the phone screen off.

"Gray," Celena says, "if you needed a sign from the universe about what to do, I'm not sure it can get much clearer than that."

"It's a sign alright. A sign I should run for it." I shove the phone back in my purse before taking a big gulp of my wine.

Celena sighs, downs the rest of her Chardonnay, and clunks the glass onto the table. She takes one of my hands in both of hers.

"Honey," she says, "I'm not sure where you got this fear of life, but I'm telling you now that, as your best friend, I'm not letting you turn down this opportunity. I don't know what prompted this man to send you a dick pic less than six hours after meeting him, but whatever happens with that is incidental compared to the opportunity you're being given to work with a professional athlete. Let's not make assumptions just yet. Maybe the pic was a mistake."

I blow out a long breath. I suspected the same. He must've meant to send the pic to someone else. The thought eases my mind in some ways but not in others.

"You're probably right," I say. "He's drunk, and he sent a booty call to the wrong person."

"Exactly. Just disregard it for now. In the meantime, we need to update your dating apps and get you back out there."

Gray

Later that night in bed, I scroll through one of the dating apps Celena put me on. It's a new one where you can search through potential partners based on a set of criteria and then, for each result, you tag the person with up to three categories. The categories range from "Cross to the other side of the street" to "Good for a one-night stand" to "Dear Future Husband." The more people you tag, the more the algorithm learns what you like and curates a list of people you may wish to reach out to. If you and another person select at least one of the same categories for each other – all except for the cross the street one – the app will notify you both that your goals match. The name of the app is InSync.

Celena also has me on one of the older, more established apps as well. She wanted to put me on four or five dating apps, but I don't have time to check them all, so I limited her to two.

Celena also created my profile for me. I'm listed as a teacher, because I learned that listing my occupation as "professor" intimidates men. According to my profile, I like sports, talking dirty, and drinking wine.

The picture of me she chose was taken at the beach this past summer. She's cropped out of it, and I look pretty good in my bikini. My breasts are a C cup, and they're decently perky in this top, but I worry about the message the picture sends to the men on the app. I'm not looking for just sex. I want an actual boyfriend.

I look over the profile of one guy who works in finance and likes to take his boat out on Long Island Sound during the summer. He's decently attractive and a couple years older than me. I tag him as "Let's have coffee" and "Down to have dinner," then shut down the app.

It's late and I have one of my early classes tomorrow, followed by two back-to-back ninety-minute committee meetings. I can get out of at least one of those meetings in the future if I start working with Ash, but I have some serious concerns about accepting this project, not the least of which is having to see the man whose dick pic still sits on my phone.

I stare up at the ceiling.

I will *not* look at the dick pic. I will *not* look at the dick pic…

I grab my phone and open it to pull up the dick pic. I really need to delete it, but I can't bring myself to do it. If I were a different kind of person, I'd be on the phone with the tabloids auctioning it to the highest bidder. Fortunately for Ash, I'm not that kind of person.

Unfortunately for him, I *am* the kind of person who's going to pull out my vibrator and masturbate to the pic before bed.

Celena was right. I need to get laid.

I reach into the second drawer of my nightstand and pull out my vibrator and a dildo. It usually takes both to get me off, and I take one last good look at the picture of Ash's cock before setting the phone aside, turning on the vibrator, and laying back on the bed.

I press the vibrator to my clit to get things going, and when I feel myself get wet, I slide the dildo in. I haven't used it much lately, so it fits tightly, and I can't help but wonder how Ash compares. I think he's bigger than the dildo, but I can't tell for sure from the pic.

I start to rock against the toys, and the sensation builds quickly. I imagine Ash above me, moving between my legs as I grip his shoulders and rock my hips into him.

What would he be like in bed? He's a hockey player, so aggression must be in his nature, but he's also got that boy-next-door look about him. Would he be a gentle lover, or would he take me hard and fast?

I always tell myself I want the former, a man who'll make love to me slowly, but it's the thought of the latter that sends my body into overdrive.

I come as I imagine Ash driving into me while he tells me what a great fuck I am. I cry out as I hold the vibrator to my throbbing clit, and my muscles spasm around the dildo.

When I finally come down from my orgasm, I shut the vibrator off and lie there to let my breathing return to normal.

A minute later, I pull my phone off the nightstand and google, "When does the NHL season start?" Opening night is October 7 this year, a week and a half from now.

I do a search on the Stanley Cup playoffs. Those start in April and go anywhere from mid-June to late June, depending on how many games have to be played. Each round is the best of seven games, so teams might play only four games, or they might need all seven.

Six to nine months. That's how long I could potentially work with Ash if I agreed to do this.

Six to nine months to come up with an intervention that will 'fix' him.

Six to nine months of having to look him in the eye after masturbating to the dick pic he almost certainly sent me by accident.

I sigh and reluctantly delete the pic from my phone. If I'm going to do this, I need to start with a clean slate. No more fantasizing about him. I had my one lapse, and now it's time to be professional.

I shut my phone down and plug it into the charger. I'll double check with Melinda tomorrow that I'm okay to do this, then I'll email Kaladin's people. They can tell Ash. There's no way I'm texting him, since I don't want him to think his dick pic was a deciding factor.

I grab my toys and head into the bathroom to wash them off. My clean slate starts with rinsing the evidence of my shame down the drain.

Chapter 4

Ash

I feel like my head is weighted down with lead balls the next morning. The alarm clock on my nightstand makes three different sounds of increasing urgency when it goes off, and it's on the last one of its cycle, which tells me I've been out of it through the first two.

I hit the off button and reach for my phone. I unlock the screen, pull up my text messages…and I'm immediately presented with a picture of my own dick.

Fuck me sideways. Who did I send a dick pic to last night?

I had trouble falling asleep and took one of those high-powered sleep aids they warn you not to take when you need to drive or operate heavy machinery. I don't use them anymore regularly, but I have a few left over from the last time I filled the prescription, and I was desperate.

I squint at the screen. My just-waking vision is still blurry, but as soon as I make out the G-r-a at the top of the text message screen I groan. I sent the pic to Grace, my ex-girlfriend.

I consider sending an apology text with an explanation, but in the end, I just delete the text messages and pray she doesn't respond. The last I heard, she was dating someone from one of those superhero franchises, but I don't remember which one. I'm not even sure if it's Marvel or DC, but it doesn't matter. Hopefully Grace has enough…well, grace, to just delete the pic and pretend I never sent it.

Our breakup was amicable, so I'm reasonably sure the pic won't show up on TMZ, but I broke a cardinal rule of PR by sending it. Maybe I can plead diminished capacity with Cedric if something happens.

I shut down the message app and sit up. I'm groggy and can feel my heartbeat in my head. I remember now why I stopped taking these pills.

I swing my legs out of bed and head to the shower. I need to be at the rink in an hour for weight training, so I better get my ass moving. Unfortunately, I have a raging case of morning wood I need to take care of first. I don't remember dreaming last night – I never do when I take those pills – but something clearly has me hot and bothered this morning.

Half an hour later, I've jerked off, I'm dressed, and I have my protein shake in hand as I head out the door.

I couldn't tell which way Dr. Mackey was leaning yesterday when I left. She was clearly reluctant to help, but I swear I saw her start to crack when I turned on the puppy dog eyes. They're my superpower. I didn't check to see if she's married or not, but that look works on all women.

I understand why she doesn't want to work with me. She's afraid she can't help, and she doesn't want to let me down. What she doesn't understand is that she's my last hope. The sport psychologist at Tampa tried to help me and failed miserably. We tried everything: visualization, ignoring the trash talk, positive reinforcement. Nothing worked.

When I got to Connecticut, Kaladin immediately set me up with the sport psychologist here, but that guy was even more clueless than Tampa Bay's doc. He tried to convince me I was being overly sensitive and told me I just needed to toughen up.

I'm not crazy about the idea of letting yet another person try to fix me, but I'm out of options. I don't know anything else but hockey, and if Kaladin cuts me loose, I'm not sure what I'll do with my life.

Honestly, the fact Dr. Mackey is so reluctant to help is almost comforting. If she agrees to work with me, maybe she'll be willing to try some out-of-the-box ideas rather than sticking to the old psychological standbys. I don't know why, but I have a good feeling about this.

Well, I do this morning anyway. Last night I was stressed and anxious enough to take one of those pills, and now I'm praying Grace just rolled her eyes and deleted the dick pic I sent her.

It's not like I want her back. She and I had a good year together before we started fighting, and it all went downhill from there. Trying to make things work long-distance was a strain on us both, and it was a relief when our relationship ended. Why my drugged-up brain decided to send her a pic of my cock, I'll never know.

I get to the rink with minutes to spare, park in the garage, and double-time it up to the locker room.

"Hey, thought you were gonna miss weights today," Kelsier says as I dump my bag on the bench.

"Overslept," I say. "I feel like I got hit by a train."

"Heard from that professor yet?" he asks.

Zane Kelsier was the first guy to come over and welcome me to the team when I joined the Hydra this year, and we hit it off right away. He's my best friend here and the only person I told about my meeting with Dr. Mackey. He's a defenseman, an inch taller than me and a year younger.

"Not yet."

"But you think she might be in?"

I shake my head. "No idea. I heard how much money Kaladin offered her, and I can't imagine anyone turning that down, but who knows."

He pauses. "What are you going to do if she doesn't agree?"

"No fucking clue."

Kelsier's been trying to help me out by chirping at me on the ice whenever he gets the chance, but it's just not the same as when the opposing team does it. There's no real sting to it, and half the time he just makes me laugh.

"Kelsier! Gunnarsson! Get your asses in the weight room!" the strength coach shouts as he pokes his head into the locker room.

Kelsier and I snap to attention and hurry to follow him.

"What's the professor like?" Kelsier asks as we hurry after the coach.

I shrug. "I don't know. I didn't get much chance to talk to her. She seemed a little annoyed I was there."

"She hot?"

I shrug again. "Not really. I mean, I guess she was pretty enough. She looked young, but she was dressed kind of frumpy."

Kelsier frowns. "No tight pencil skirt? No black stilettos? Not even a blouse where her breasts are straining against the buttons, begging to be set free?" he asks, his tone growing more disappointed by the word.

I chuckle. "Dude. No, none of that. You got a teacher fetish I don't know about, Kels?"

He cocks his head. "Let's just say I had a professor in college that made me want to come to class every day and sit in the front row."

"Let me guess," I say as we enter the weight room. "You got an A in that class."

"Fuck no. I got a C," he says. "I couldn't stop imagining her lips around my dick. I didn't hear a word she said all semester."

Ash

Two hours later, Kelsier and I are done with weights, and we're showered and ready for lunch. We're just heading out when I hear a voice call my name.

We turn to see the PR guy, Cedric, hurrying toward us. He's a slim black man with closely buzzed hair and a chinstrap beard. He's wearing a suit with just the vest and not the jacket.

Cedric stops in front of me and Kelsier, and we look down at him. Normal people always seem so small after I've been in a room full of pro hockey players. Our defensemen average 6'3", and Kingston, our starting goalie, is 6'7". The shortest forwards on the team are 5'10".

"What's up, Cedric?" I ask.

He looks uncertainly at Kelsier, and I assume he has news about the doc that he's wary about sharing in front of others.

"He knows about the doc if that's what this is about," I tell Cedric.

He frowns but then nods. "We heard back from Dr. Mackey," he confirms. "She agreed to work with you. We're just waiting for her to return the signed contracts after the university's lawyers look at them, then you can go ahead and meet with her."

My heart soars at the news. I know she hasn't done anything yet, but just the thought she might be able to help makes me feel lighter than I have in days. Shit, it's like the girl I just asked to the prom said yes.

"Awesome, man," Kelsier says, giving my arm a light punch.

"Wait, is she supposed to come here, or should I go to her office?" I ask Cedric. "I assume I still shouldn't be seen in public with her?"

Cedric sighs. "There's only so long we'll be able to keep this under wraps, but for now try to stay out of sight. Going back to the university isn't a good idea. Maybe go to her place or yours first? If she insists on somewhere public, you can meet her here, but be discreet. The more people who know about her, the more likely the story is to get out."

"Will do," I say, and Cedric hurries off.

I pull out my phone and text the doc.

Ash

Heard you agreed to work with me. Thank you.

Ash

PR dude says we should stay out of public places. Come to my place Thursday night after dinner? Is 7pm too late?

I text her the address, and I see the three dots jump around as she types out a reply. They stop, and I wait, but no text comes through. They start up again for a few seconds then stop. Still no response.

"She reply yet?" Kelsier asks.

"She's typing, but she hasn't sent anything yet."

"Maybe she's rethinking her life choices," he jokes as I shove the phone back in my pocket, and we head for the food court.

"Fuck you," I say with the hint of a grin.

My phone pings, and I pull it out again. It's not Dr. Mackey, though. It's my sister, and I shove it back in my pocket.

"What did she say?" Kelsier asks.

"It wasn't the doc. It was Inga. She wants me to call her."

"And you're not going to?"

"Fuck no. She just wants to ask me if I'm bringing someone to her wedding, and if I say no, she's going to try and set me up with one of her friends." I pause. "Or she heard about my fight with Lapointe and wants to ream me out. Either way, I'm not calling her."

"And she's going to let you ignore her?" he asks.

"Of course not. But that's a problem for Future Me to deal with."

Kelsier chuckles. "Future You is gonna be pissed at Past You."

I roll my eyes. "What else is new?"

My phone pings again, and I swear as I pull it out. "If she thinks-"

I cut off my rant as I see who the text is from.

"It's the doc," I say. "She agreed to come to my place Thursday."

Kelsier claps me on the shoulder. "Congrats, man. You're on your way to recovery."

I feel a strange mix of relief and trepidation. I'm relieved Dr. Mackey is on board, but I'm uncertain she'll be able to help, and if she can't…

No, I can't think like that now. Dr. Mackey will fix me.

She has to.

Chapter 5

I sit in my car in the circular drive of the beach-front, stone-façade house at seven o'clock on Thursday night wondering what the hell I was thinking. When Ash asked me to come to his house rather than the stadium, I wasn't sure how to take it. I typed, deleted, then re-typed several responses to his invitation, starting with, "I don't think that's a good idea," and somehow ending with, "Okay."

Other drafts in between included messages like "WTF" or "Should I bring wine?" but I decided not to read into the invitation.

I finally convince myself to stop being a baby and get out of the car to head up to the house. I pause at the front door, hand poised to knock, but I notice the doorbell is one of those high-tech ones that takes video and notifies your phone if someone is outside. Ash likely knows I'm here already. Indeed, just as I'm about to knock, the door swings open.

I'm not prepared for how good the man looks. He's wearing a forest green Henley with the buttons undone and loose jeans that fit just snuggly enough to show he's got really nice thighs.

I silently curse myself again for agreeing to this.

"Hey, come on in," Ash says, opening the door for me to pass.

His mouth quirks up on one side to give me half a smile, and the dimple there makes a brief appearance before ducking back undercover.

I try to smile back, but I'm more convinced than ever this is a bad idea. "Thanks," I say as I step inside.

I purposely wore black yoga pants and an oversized sweatshirt tonight to make myself feel as plain as possible. I considered dressing up to show him I could be more than a nerdy academic type, but I decided to lean into the dullness to remind myself, and him, why I'm here.

"Can I get you anything?" he asks as he leads me through the foyer of a gorgeous, spacious house. "Water? Coffee? Beer?"

He doesn't mention wine, so I don't bother asking.

"Water would be great. Thanks," I say.

He leads me into an open kitchen-living room area, and my eyes widen at the wall of windows that overlook the Sound. I can't see if there's a beach directly behind his house, but lights from a marina dot the view a couple miles down the shore to the left.

The team may be called the Hartford Hydra, but they're not actually based in the capital, which sits in the middle of the state. Instead, Max Kaladin – perhaps wisely – built his stadium down near the shore, close to the casinos. It's not surprising then, that high-earning players like Ash found housing on the water.

"Have a seat," he says, gesturing to the plush sofa in the living room, and I head over to sit down.

Ash veers off into the kitchen, which looks like something out of a *Modern Home* magazine. It's sleek and simple with clean lines and lots of granite and stainless steel, and I wonder if he actually does his own cooking. He grabs a glass out of the cabinet and starts to fill it from a watercooler, then stops and checks the jug on top.

"Dammit."

He puts the glass down and disappears for a second into another room before he comes back holding a new five-gallon water jug by the handle. Even from the couch I see the muscles and veins in his hands and forearms flex as he replaces the empty container with the new one.

"Sorry, the water won't be cold just yet," he says as he grabs some ice cubes from the freezer to add them to my glass before retrying the cooler. "I can get you some more when the new water chills enough."

"It's fine," I say.

He fills a second glass and brings both over, handing one to me before thumping down into the loveseat next to the couch. He sits in the middle of it and manspreads, which once again emphasizes how long his legs are.

I'm surprised to see him drink water instead of beer, but then again, he's an athlete, and I'm sure they're on strict diets.

"So how does this work?" Ash asks, looking at me expectantly.

I huff a laugh. "Good question. Like I said, I'm not a clinical psychologist, so I don't have this all worked out, but I can tell you what my study found, and we can go from there. Does that work?"

He nods. "Sounds great."

"I assume you didn't read the article on the study?" I ask as I settle back and cross one leg over the other.

His eyes widen, and he looks like I just told him there's a pop quiz he didn't study for.

I wave a hand. "Never mind. I was just curious, but I can tell you everything you need to know."

"Yeah, I'm sorry, I didn't-"

I wave my hand again. "Really, don't worry about it. I'm sure you've been busy with practice and training. I shouldn't have put you on the spot, and, honestly, unless you have a background in statistics, half the article won't make sense to you anyway."

His shoulders ease, and I feel like a jerk for having asked now.

"What I found was fairly simple," I say.

I stop, stumped at where to begin. Yes, the study was simple, but that's provided you have some basic knowledge of social scientific concepts and theories. I'm not sure how to explain this to a layperson.

It's not that I assume Ash is a dumb jock. I learned long ago not to buy into that stereotype, but the sheer amount of background information I could give him paralyzes me as I collect my thoughts.

"Alright," I say, regrouping. "I looked specifically at mental and emotional effects. The results suggested at first that trash talk mentally distracted participants when they engaged in a competitive activity, but when I separated those results out by gender, they broke down. Women were mentally distracted by the trash talk, but men weren't, presumably because they're used to hearing it, so they find it easier to filter out."

He's frowning, and I realize I probably could've left all this out since it doesn't apply to him anyway.

I grimace. "Sorry, it's not relevant, so forget I brought it up. The part that's relevant to you-"

I stop again.

"Excuse me for not asking earlier, but you do gender identify as male, right?" I ask. I'm sure I would've heard about it in the news if he didn't, but better safe than sorry.

His eyebrows shoot up. "Do I not look male to you?" he asks.

Fuck me. He looks very, very male to me, but that's beside the point.

"I've learned not to assume anything," I say, trying to recover. "What you look like to me doesn't matter."

"So I don't look male to you?" he presses.

I see the hint of a smile on his lips, and I know he's trying to tease me, but it's more complicated than he realizes.

"What does male and female look like?" I ask. "For someone to *look* female, does she have to wear a dress and have long hair like the icon on bathroom doors?"

He shrugs. "That's a good place to start, isn't it?"

"So should I assume someone who wears pants, has short hair, and has non-existent breasts is male then?" I ask, and his expression falters.

"I know this may seem nitpicky," I go on, "but you run into problems when you identify gender based solely on extremes of masculinity and femininity."

He nods slowly. "It's the hair that's throwing you then," he says as he runs a hand through the longer locks on top of his head to push them back from where they've fallen into his eyes.

He's still teasing, and I decide to let him have this one.

"A little bit," I say.

I'm dying to run my fingers through his hair. Getting myself off before

I came did nothing to help the situation between my legs, and I'm ashamed at how weak I am for lusting after him right now.

Ash considers the idea a second more, then shrugs. "Yeah, I consider myself very male," he says with a grin. His eye crinkles the tiniest bit so I'm not sure if it's a wink or not, and now I'm wondering if he's alluding to the dick pic he sent me.

I almost ask him but talk myself out of it. He doesn't seem the least bit self-conscious about sending it, and I'm not bold enough to bring it up just yet. Maybe when I know him better.

"Alright, so we'll stick to the results of the study as they relate to male participants," I say, trying to regain control of the conversation. "The part that's important to you, then, is the emotional effects of trash talk."

He frowns. "Emotional effects?"

"Everyone experiences emotions," I say quickly before he can deny he has them. "But how and when we express them can vary. I specifically looked at anger and shame because they're often related."

He looks at me as if this is news to him, which it probably is. The shame-rage connection is well-documented in social science, but I wouldn't expect someone outside the discipline to know this.

"Experiencing shame can often lead to anger and vice versa," I explain, "and that's exactly what my study found. Participants experienced both of these emotions when subjected to trash talk, but the interesting thing is that the order in which they experienced them varied by gender. Women got angry, then experienced shame."

"They felt ashamed for feeling angry?" Ash asks, and the question is clarifying rather than doubtful.

"Exactly," I say. "Anger often isn't an acceptable emotion for women to display, so they're conditioned to feel bad for expressing it."

He nods. "Women do tend to take more shit for expressing anger than men," he says knowingly.

I stare at him as his observation throws me for a second.

He shrugs. "I have two sisters. The sins of the patriarchy are a common topic of conversation at holiday gatherings."

I blink, then smile. "And what do they think of your hockey career?"

He smiles back, and I'm transfixed by his dimples.

"You mean my job where I play a sport that epitomizes the inherent violence of athletics and encourages problems to be solved through physical altercations?" he says, clearly quoting someone. He cocks his head. "They're so proud."

While I agree with the description in principle, I feel bad his sisters view his career that way. Ash has achieved a level of success many people only dream of, and his family doesn't appreciate it.

"I'm sorry," I say seriously.

He waves a hand. "It's fine. They are actually proud of me, but I think they tell their friends I play professional tennis or something."

We've gotten way off track, and the more depth this man shows me, the worse my crush on him gets. I need to refocus.

"Anyway," I say, "that doesn't apply to you either. The part of the study most relevant to you found that men experienced shame in reaction to trash talk, and that, in turn, made them angry. They had the opposite experience as women."

He frowns. "Why?"

"The data doesn't really tell us why," I say, "but we can posit a few theories based on the literature. Basically, we experience shame when our ideal image of ourselves is challenged or shattered. For men, that image often involves success in competition, so most likely their experiences in the study somehow made them question that image. In short, they were affected by the trash talk enough that their performance suffered and they felt shame. This, in turn, led to anger-"

"Then anger led to hate, and that led to suffering?" he asks, paraphrasing Yoda from one of the *Star Wars* movies.

"That was outside the scope of the study," I quip with a grin.

"Sorry," he says. "I couldn't resist."

"Technically you're not far off," I say. "A few researchers have suggested the shame-rage cycle is a large part of what drives misogynistic groups like incels."

He looks surprised, but I don't want to go down a research rabbit hole or I'll be here all night.

"Your issue with trash talk, then," I hurry on, "could be that you've let your opponents make you question your ideal image. That makes you ashamed, which makes you angry, and that makes it harder to focus."

He raises his brows. "You think I'm ashamed of myself?"

I open my mouth, but realize my mistake. Fuck.

"Shame is a harsh word," I say, trying to backtrack. "It's more about undermining your ideal image. Let me give you an example."

He nods at me to go on.

"In 1997, Scottie Pippen told Karl 'The Mailman' Malone that the mailman doesn't deliver on Sundays in an NBA finals game, and that line is widely credited with helping the Chicago Bulls win the game. Are you familiar with it?"

"I know the line, but I'm not sure of the details around it," he says.

"Picture this, then," I say. "There are 9.2 seconds left on the clock in the game, and the score is tied at 82. Malone, normally a really good free throw shooter, is awarded two free throws. In most cases, Malone will make those shots, and then the best the Bulls can do is tie to send the game into overtime. As it happens, though, it's a Sunday night, and Scottie Pippen leans over to Malone, who's known as 'The Mailman' because he always delivers, and says to him, 'The mailman doesn't deliver on Sundays.'"

Ash smiles. "It's a great line."

"It is," I say, "and so appropriate you can't help but marvel at the cleverness. In fact, the best lines of trash talk are often the ones that are exceptionally bold, brutal, or clever, and this one is exceptionally clever."

"The line worked?" he asks.

I nod. "Malone missed both free throws, the Bulls rebounded, and Michael Jordan hit a jump shot at the buzzer to win the game."

"And it worked because Pippen undermined Malone's ideal image?"

"Theoretically, yes," I say. "We'll never know for sure what was going through Malone's head during those shots. Maybe he just cracked under pressure and would've missed those shots regardless, but the story that he missed because of the trash talk is just too good not to consider."

I take a sip of my water and lean forward. "Think about it. Malone has a reputation as a player that always delivers, so he's been given the nickname The Mailman. That's his ideal image. But there's one time mailmen don't deliver mail, and that's on Sundays. It's a Sunday. At the very least, Pippen created doubt in Malone's mind. The line was too clever to ignore, and chances are that it at least made Malone pause. It presented him with a flaw in his ideal image, and he missed the first shot."

"And now Malone is really doubting himself," Ash says.

"Exactly," I say, not surprised he's caught on so quickly. "Missing the second shot is almost a self-fulfilling prophesy at that point. Pippen created the doubt, and Malone's own miss anchored it. Prior to the first free throw, the line was just a clever piece of trash talk. After it, the idea that The Mailman might not deliver on a Sunday is becoming a reality. Malone's ideal image of himself has been shaken."

"And then he misses the second shot," Ash says.

"Yes," I confirm. "And it's not hard to envision that after that first shot, Malone might feel ashamed of himself for buying into Pippen's trash talk. He's angry at himself for missing."

Ash nods along, and I dare to think I've salvaged this lesson.

"I understand," Ash says.

"So…what do you feel when opposing players are trash talking, uh, chirping at you?" I learned earlier today that chirping is the common term used in hockey for trash talking.

"You mean, do I feel ashamed or angry?" he asks.

I realize my mistake. I shouldn't have told him the results of the study. Now he's going to try to shoehorn his emotions in to fit them.

"Not necessarily," I say. "Those are the two I looked into, but there could be others. I want you to tell me what *you* were feeling, even if it doesn't fit my results."

He leans back and extends his long arms across the back of the loveseat. I try not to be impressed by his arm span and fail.

"I guess I did feel a little ashamed the other night," he says. "Lapointe made sure I was bleeding, then he stuck a tampon down my jersey. I know it shouldn't have upset me, but it did."

My eyes flare. "Someone shoved a tampon in your jersey?"

He nods.

"So you felt…emasculated?" I venture.

He shrugs noncommittally. "Maybe."

"Trash talk often includes gender or sexuality-based comments. Implying someone is womanish or gay is common in trash talk, even though leagues often have rules against it." I pause. "What did you do when this guy shoved the tampon in your jersey?"

His look turns distinctly deer-in-headlights. "I…don't want to say."

I cock my head at him and give him my best '*Out with it*' look.

He sighs. "I went after him and shoved the tampon in his mouth. Then we tried to beat the shit out of each other."

My jaw drops open before I can think of how to respond. "Alright. Well, the good news is that your reaction suggests you're within the bounds of the shame-rage dynamic."

"And that's good?"

"Actually, yes. If we know what we're dealing with, it should be easier to come up with some strategies to help you. If you were experiencing different emotions, we'd have to pinpoint those first before proceeding."

"Alright," he says, leaning forward and interlacing his fingers. "For once I'm just like everyone else. So what do we do now?"

Good question.

Chapter 6

Ash

"How did it go with the doc last night?" Kelsier asks as we step onto the treadmills the next day. "Did she fix you?"

"She gave me fucking homework," I say as I turn the machine on and the belt begins to move.

Kelsier looks like he's about to burst out laughing, and I give him a *'Don't you fucking dare'* look.

He purses his lips and suppresses the laugh before he asks, "What kind of homework? You got an essay due already?" A smile tugs at the corners of his mouth again.

"No, she wants me to make some notes before I see her again on Sunday," I say.

"What kind of notes?"

"I'm supposed to reflect on my 'ideal image.'"

Kelsier stares at me. "What?"

I wave a hand as we bump the treadmills up to a fast walk. "The doc says trash talk can make people feel shame and rage, and shame happens when a person's ideal image of themself is threatened. She wants me to decide what mine is and think back to the times I got angry over guys chirping at me. She wants to see if they," I put up air quotes, "'challenged my ideal image.'"

Kelsier continues to stare at me before giving an *'Okay, whatever'* shrug. "How's that going to help?"

"Not sure yet," I say. "I think it's one of those things where I can maybe handle the chirping better if I know why it affects me?"

"And the rage part?"

"We haven't gotten that far yet. She said something about looking into anger interventions."

"Like anger management?" he asks.

"I guess so."

Kelsier nods, and we increase the treadmills to a light jog.

"I looked her up on the university's website," Kelsier says. "She's pretty. I thought you said she was frumpy looking?"

"She was dressed that way the first time I saw her, but she looked nice last night." I shrug. "I suppose she was cute."

I think back to my meeting with the doc. I couldn't help noticing her legs in her yoga pants. I normally go for really slim women, but there was a shapeliness to the doc's thighs, a roundness, that appealed to me. Like they'd be something to hold onto when…

I shake the thought away. Clearly my body is trying to tell me it's been too long since I've had sex if I'm thinking of the doc that way.

Kelsier chuckles. "We'll get you hot-for-teach yet. You should bring her in to meet the team."

"And why the fuck would I do that?"

"Maybe she can figure out more pieces of the puzzle if she sees all the knuckleheads you work with," he suggests. "Plus, I want to meet her."

"I can't bring her here. No one is supposed to know I'm seeing her."

Kelsier scoffs. "Did you think you were going to keep that a secret? The whole team knows already."

"What?" I glare at him. "What the fuck, Kels!"

He holds up his hands. "Don't look at me. I didn't tell anyone."

"Then how the fuck does everyone know already?"

"Cote's sister goes to the university and saw you come out of Dr. Mackey's office the other day," Ryan Petruck calls from two treadmills down. He's a 6'6" defenseman we call "Mack" because he's built like a Mack Truck, and getting hit by him feels much the same.

"Fuck," I say.

"Cote kept it off the group chat," Mack goes on, "but it made the rounds anyway. When coach overheard, he swore us all to secrecy. Anyone who blabs outside the team gets benched for two games."

"And no one bothered to tell me everyone knew?" I ask indignantly.

"Nah," Mack says as he continues to lumber on the treadmill. The poor machine strains under his solid weight. He was a competitive lifter in his high school days before he decided to focus on hockey.

"We've all got bets on how long it takes you to fuck her, by the way," Mack adds. "Kels is right. She's cute."

I frown. "Jesus Christ, Mack. She's not a bunny. She's a professor."

"So?" Mack says. "You don't think some of those puck bunnies have big, impressive jobs?"

"I'm not interested in her," I say.

Mack looks at me like I just said Wayne Gretzky is overrated. "Dude, if you don't want her, bring her by and let the rest of us try our luck."

An unexpected twinge of something plucks in my chest at the thought of introducing the doc to the team. She's pretty enough, but I'm not attracted to her. I mean, there was the way she bit her lip when she stopped to think, but…

I shake my head. I need to cut those thoughts off right now. Dr. Mackey is my…therapist? My psychologist? My…trash talk guru?

Whatever. I'm not sure how long we'll be working together, so getting involved with her is a bad idea regardless.

"Why would I want to subject her to all you idiots?" I ask Mack.

He waves a '*To hell with you*' hand at me as he increases the speed on his treadmill, and it groans in protest.

"What can it hurt to bring her by?" Kelsier asks. "Since everyone already knows."

I frown at him, but he gives me an unapologetic look as we bump the treadmills up again.

"Hey, coach!" Mack calls across the room. "Gunny wants to bring his doc by to meet the team. It will help her figure out why he's such a headcase or something. He was afraid to ask you."

Kelsier and I whip our heads around to see Coach Davis and one of the trainers huddled over a tablet on the other side of the room. Coach glances up briefly to acknowledge Mack.

"Yeah, sure," Coach Davis says. "Whatever helps." He goes back to his discussion with the trainer.

"I didn't-," I start to protest, but Kelsier cuts me off.

"Thanks, Coach!" he yells before I can get anything out.

I turn and glare at him again. "What the fuck?"

He shrugs. "Sorry. I really want to meet her."

"Yeah, but she's not just going to meet you. She's going to meet the rest of these assholes too."

"Asshole and proud!" Mack says, pumping a fist in the air as he jogs.

"I'm gonna fucking beat the shit out of you both," I grumble.

Mack chuckles. "Good luck. I'll even give you the first swing."

He's right. I'd only hurt my fist on his jaw if I tried to hit him, and then he'd pound me into the ground.

"Looks like it's a done deal," Kelsier says, grinning at me. "When can we expect to meet her?"

"When hell freezes over," I tell him.

"Man, don't make me steal your phone and text her," he says, and he bumps his treadmill up again to a run. "This is happening."

I follow suit and turn mine up. There's still a chance the doc will turn down the invitation, and I cling to that slim hope. I'm not sure why I don't want her coming here – the guys aren't that bad – but for some reason, I don't want to expose her to them.

Maybe I like having the focused attention, and I'm worried about losing that if she comes here and meets everyone else.

Maybe I just don't want to share her.

Ash

Later that night, my finger hovers over the 'Send' button on my phone as I watch TV. I've typed a message to the doc, deleted it, and retyped it about three times now. Each version of the message makes the invitation more and more my idea.

Ash

> Hey, so Coach was thinking maybe you should come meet

Delete.

Ash

> I've been telling the guys on the team about you, and they

Delete.

Ash

> Would you be interested in coming by the rink to meet the rest of the team? It could give you an idea about the vibe among the guys. You said you didn't know much about hockey.

My finger is nearly touching the screen, and I've almost decided to delete this message and try again when my finger accidentally brushes the 'Send' button.

And now it's on its way. Fuck.

I stare at the phone, TV show forgotten, as I wait to see what happens. It's almost a minute before the app indicates the message has been seen, and I hold my breath, watching for the three dots that show the doc is typing. They stop, and when I don't see them after a minute, I force myself to put the phone down.

I wasn't sure how the invitation would be received, and now I worry the doc is reading into it. But this is all business. If meeting the guys gives her insight into why I react to trash talk the way I do, then let her come.

It's almost twenty minutes before my phone finally pings with an incoming text.

Gray

I can come if you think it will help.

It's not an enthusiastic acceptance, but neither was my invitation.

Ash

I'm not sure it will, but one of my teammates thought it might, so I figured it couldn't hurt.

A pause before the dots bounce again.

Gray

When were you thinking?

Ash

The season starts next week, and we're away for the first two games. How about when we get back?

Gray

Sounds good.

I wonder if I should text her back with an exact day and time, but the dots bounce again, and I wait to see what she's typing.

Gray

Am I still coming by your place on Sunday?

Ash

Yeah that works.

A pause before the dots appear again.

Gray

Have you been doing your homework?

I smile. Her tone seems playful, and I decide to be a smartass.

Ash

I did, but my dog ate it.

Gray

I don't recall you having a dog.

Ash

My neighbor's dog ate it?

Gray

Gray

It's a good thing you have time to redo it before Sunday.

Ash

I'm a procrastinator.

Suddenly I feel bad for giving her a hard time. She must deal with this bullshit all the time from her actual students.

Ash

Sorry. Just kidding. Do your real students act like this?

Gray

You have no idea.

The dots bounce for a bit longer.

Gray

Don't get me wrong. Most of my students are great. There's always just a couple each year that make you reconsider your life choices.

I send a laughing emoji.

Ash

I was probably one of those students in high school. I got my act together more in college to stay eligible for my hockey scholarship.

Gray

On behalf of your college professors, thank you.

I snort.

Ash

What are you doing now?

Suddenly I'm curious about her and what she does.

Gray

Almost done grading homework. Then I need to plan my lesson for Monday, work on a research proposal, and maybe do some more digging on anger interventions.

My brows arch as I look at the time on my phone.

Ash

Holy shit doc. It's already 9pm.

Our neighbor when I was a kid used to complain that teachers got paid for a whole year while only doing nine months of work, but it seems like they cram a whole year's worth of work into the nine months.

Gray

And only three more hours of work to go. 

Ash

At least you get summers off?

Gray

Not really. That's when most faculty catch up on research. If they don't teach a summer class.

God damn.

Ash

And why did you choose this career again?

Gray

For the prestige. Or the children. I forget.

I chuckle. She's snarky, and I like it.

Gray

If you didn't play hockey, what would you be?

I think for a minute. There was never really a time I considered doing something other than playing hockey, and luckily, I was always good enough that pursuing a career in it was a viable option. Now that my future in hockey is threatened, though, maybe I need to start considering alternatives. The thought makes my gut clench, and I shake it away.

Ash

I went through a dinosaur phase when I was young, so there was a brief period I wanted to be a paleontologist.

Ash

Actually, I wanted to be a dinosaur trainer, but when I learned that wasn't an option,

She sends a laughing emoji.

Gray

I respond with my own laughing emoji.

Ash

Her crying emoji comes through.

Ash

I don't get anything back for almost a minute, then her 'thumbs up' emoji pops onto the screen. It feels anticlimactic, but I put the phone down and go back to watching TV. For some reason there's a small thrill building in my chest at the thought of seeing the doc again…but also a small dread at bringing her to meet the team.

Chapter 7

Gray

I scroll back up to the top of my text conversation with Ash and reread it, second guessing everything I wrote. I was surprised to get his invitation to meet the team, and I had to powwow with Celena before answering. A voice in my head told me that, for a pro athlete, meeting his team is akin to meeting his parents, so Celena and I spent almost twenty minutes vastly overanalyzing the implications.

I look at the messages one more time and decide I played it cool enough. Hopefully I didn't give Ash the wrong impression. I was aiming for politely interested but not eager. Of course, then I insisted on getting personal with him by teasing him about his homework and asking about his childhood dreams.

Jesus, Gray. Thirsty much?

I also overplayed the '*I'm a busy person*' card. Yes, I'm still grading, and I should look over my lesson plan for Monday before bed, but the research proposal will have to wait for Saturday, as will looking into anger interventions.

I was also carrying on two other text conversations at the time. One was with Celena and one was with ManOfYourDreams89 from that InSync dating app Celena signed me up for.

I assume the username is tongue-in-cheek. Or at least I hope it is. The guy seems normal enough, if nothing exciting. But normal is a good start.

He and I both selected "Down to have dinner" because I got a notification earlier today that we matched. He sent me a message a couple hours ago, but I only had time to answer just before Ash texted. At one point I was juggling conversations with ManOfYourDreams89 as well as Celena and Ash and praying I didn't mix them up.

I also need to message back ShadowDaddy55, who I'm guessing is a reader, so at least he has that going for him.

My phone pings.

Celena

Where did you leave it with Ash?

Gray

We'll discuss the details of meeting the team on Sunday.

Gray

And he's still salty he never got to ride a T-Rex.

There's a long pause before Celena sends a GIF of someone looking completely confused.

Gray

He wanted to be a dinosaur trainer when he was a kid.

There's a pause before the dots bounce.

Celena

Did he volunteer that info or did you ask?

I sheepishly type out my answer.

Gray

…I asked.

I practically feel Celena's judgement in the dancing dots.

Celena

Oh honey. You didn't.

Gray

I did and I'm not sorry.

Celena sends a laughing emoji.

Celena

You're supposed to be flirting with the dude from InSync, not your hockey player.

Gray

I'm meeting that guy for dinner on Sunday before I go to Ash's. That way if the date is bad, I have an excuse to leave.

Celena

 Glad to see you're giving him a chance.

Gray

Sorry. Just having a hard time feeling excited about all this. I'm starting to remember how much I hate online dating.

Celena

Would you rather go to a bar and pick up drunk guys?

Gray

The last romance novel I read involved a woman falling in love with her stalker. Why is that not an option?

Celena

Because in real life we call that a 'red flag' sweety.

Gray

Whatever.

The InSync app on my phone dings with a message notification, and I switch over to it.

ManOfYourDreams89

Looking forward to seeing you on Sunday. What's your address?

I frown.

Gray

Why do you need my address?

There's a short pause before his answer comes through.

ManOfYourDreams89

So I can pick you up.

Oh hell no.

Gray

I'll just meet you at the restaurant.

A longer pause.

ManOfYourDreams89

A gentleman should pick a lady up.

Um, no. I switch over to my message chain with Celena.

Gray

InSync guy is saying he should pick me up because 'A gentleman should pick a lady up.'

Celena sends a GIF of a woman reacting in horror.

Celena

Seriously? Was he born in the 50s?

Gray

I feel like this is more of a red flag than the stalker thing. I'm canceling.

Celena

Don't overreact. Just tell him no.

Gray

I did. He's trying to insist.

Celena

Tell him again.

I switch over to the app and respond to ManOfYourDreams89.

Gray

I appreciate the offer, but I'm going to drive myself.

If he doesn't take the hint this time, I'm canceling, no matter what Celena says.

Seconds pass before his answer comes through.

ManOfYourDreams89

Okay. See you there.

I let out a long breath. Part of me was hoping he'd insist so I had an excuse to get out of this. The other part of me feels bad about my piss-poor attitude. It's hard enough to make connections online as it is, but what hope is there when I'm already expecting – even hoping – for that connection to fail?

I resolve to give ManOfYourDreams89 a chance.

Gray

Two days later, whatever shred of optimism I had about my date tonight with ManOfYourDreams89 – or Barry, as I learned his name is – has fled entirely.

To make matters worse, I slept wrong last night and woke up with pain shooting down the side of my neck. It hasn't helped that I spent the day hunched over my computer, first to work on my research proposal, then to look up anger interventions for Ash.

I turn to unbuckle myself in the car and immediately regret the motion as my neck and shoulder twinge painfully. I rub the area, but that hasn't helped all day, and it doesn't do anything now either.

I get out of my car and head into the restaurant.

I still feel like I should've called the date off when Barry tried to insist on picking me up, but part of me is still hoping things might work out with him so that I don't shamelessly drool over Ash later tonight. I convinced myself Barry genuinely thought he was being nice by offering to pick me up and that he wasn't actually an axe murderer who wanted to know where I lived so he could hack me to death in my sleep.

Some men don't understand the things women need to consider when online dating. For instance, one of my male friends complained that women he met online never wanted to do anything fun on a first date. It was always dinner or coffee. He was an athletic and outdoorsy guy, tall and husky, but an absolute teddy bear, and he asked me in frustration once why women would never agree to go on a hike with him on a first date.

I told him it was because no woman in her right mind would ever walk into the woods alone with a man she just met. That stopped him short, and all he could say was, "Oh. Right."

I walk into the lobby of the restaurant, and a man stands to greet me.

My heart drops. He's easily ten years older than his profile picture suggests, and while I don't mind an older man, his boy-next-door quality has suddenly turned to '*I still live in my parents' basement*' vibes.

"Barry?" I ask tentatively, holding one last thread of hope I'm mistaken about this being my date.

The man smiles widely. "Gray. It's wonderful to meet you."

I hold out my hand to shake his, but he takes it and kisses it. I force myself not to yank it back out of surprise. Sweet lord, this is going to be a long date.

We check in with the hostess, and she shows us to a table. Thankfully it's a booth, because I'm pretty sure this guy would try to pull out my chair for me if it was a table.

Okay, maybe I'm being a bitch about this. There are still certain niceties I appreciate from a man, like holding a door open for me. Pulling out a chair wouldn't be so bad, but this guy's insistence on trying to pick me up tainted his behavior for me, and I can't help seeing him as too old fashioned now.

I look at the menu the hostess leaves. The wine list is at the front, and they have one of my go-tos.

"So you're a teacher?" Barry asks. "What grade?"

I look up and see he's got his menu closed and is looking raptly at me.

"College actually," I say. "Technically I'm a professor."

His face falls, which I'm used to by now, but it still makes me angry.

"Sorry, I guess we were both a little inaccurate in our profiles," I say.

He cocks his head in confusion. "What do you mean? Where was I inaccurate?"

I blink at him. "I...It just looks like the profile photo you used might be a few years old," I say, although 'a few years' is generous.

He shrugs. "Yeah, a few, I guess. But I look pretty much the same, don't I?"

I sigh inwardly. "More or less."

He brightens. "So a professor then. What do you teach?"

"Communication," I say. He still hasn't opened his menu, and I point to it. "Do you already know what you want?"

"I usually just order what my date is having," he says.

I stare at him for several seconds before angling my head in question. Then I wince and grab my neck as it twinges. Barry doesn't seem to notice.

"Can I ask why?"

"To be polite," he says.

I'm stunned into silence again. For the life of me I can't conceive of why eating the same thing as your date would be polite. I understand avoiding especially pungent or garlicky food, especially if you're hoping for a kiss later, but ordering the exact same thing as your date?

"Please, feel free to order whatever you want," I say. "I'd prefer you order something you like instead of what I like."

He looks uncertain for a moment but finally smiles sheepishly and opens the menu.

Gray

An hour later, I've barely managed to make it through dinner. I was afraid Barry might be a serial killer — and maybe he still is — but it's more likely he's just a sweet, socially awkward man who's probably still a virgin and is desperate to do what it takes to please a woman.

The problem is that I'm already a teacher by day. I don't have the time or energy to instruct a man on what I want or need after hours as well. I want someone who knows what he wants and is willing to take the initiative to learn what I want on his own.

Barry walks me all the way to my car and hovers near the door as I get in. I assume he's hoping for a kiss, but it's not happening.

"I had a great time," he says. "Maybe I can pick you up next time."

Fucking hell. I can't believe he's still on that. For that matter, I can't believe he thought this was a good date. The conversation was stilted at best, and I didn't feel any connection whatsoever. Not that I plan to tell him that now.

"We'll see," I say. "Good night."

He doesn't move, and I can't close the door without hitting him.

"I'm sorry, I really have to get going," I say. "I still have a lot to grade before class tomorrow."

His smile falters, but he nods and steps back. "Yeah, no problem. I'll text you."

"Sure," I say with a smile as I close the door. My neck twinges from the motion, and I rub it as I start the car.

I back up and drive out of the parking lot as quickly as I dare, keeping an eye on Barry in the rearview mirror while he heads to his own car. As soon as I turn out of the parking lot, I call Celena.

"Date over already?" she asks, her voice coming through the speakers.

"I'm surprised it lasted as long as it did," I say. "It was awful."

There's a pause. "Okay, I'm just going to ask, and I'll believe whatever you say," Celena says. "Did you at least give him a chance? You weren't exactly excited to go on this date earlier."

"And I still wasn't right up until I got to the restaurant, but C, the date was objectively bad," I say before filling her in on the discrepancy with his picture, his belief it was polite to eat whatever I was eating, and the several other odd things Barry said and did throughout the meal.

There's silence on the other end of the line when I'm done.

"Shit," Celena says finally. "That *is* bad. Did he at least pay for dinner?"

"I insisted on paying for my own," I say. "There's absolutely no way I'm going out with him again, so I didn't want to feel obligated to him in any way." I pause. "Actually, I expected him to argue with me about that given his insistence on trying to pick me up, but he didn't."

"What does he do for a living again?" she asks.

"I don't think his profile said, and I forgot to ask."

"At least you get to go see Ash now," Celena says. "That should make the rest of the evening better, no?"

"Are you serious? I just had a horrible date, my neck hurts, and I have to go stare at a gorgeous athlete all night that I have no hope of dating."

"What makes you think you have no hope of dating him?"

I wish she could see how hard I roll my eyes at that question.

"His last girlfriend was an actress," I say. "You do the math."

"Whatever," Celena says. "One of these days you'll stop selling yourself short in the looks department."

"I'm not," I say. "I'm pretty, but let's be real. I'm not date-a-hockey-star pretty. Besides, it's not just about looks. It's a classic case of jocks don't fall for nerds. We have nothing in common. I plan my vacations around academic conferences. He travels around North America in a cloud of testosterone and spends his nights surrounded by puck bunnies."

"I'm hanging up on you now," Celena warns. A pause. "Wait, I thought you weren't meeting Ash until eight o'clock."

I sigh heavily. "I'm not. I have to go kill half an hour before I can head over to his place."

"Text him to see if you can come early," she suggests.

Part of me wants to cancel with Ash altogether. The date with Barry drained me, and I'm not feeling up to this tonight, but I made a commitment, and I plan to see it through.

"Alright, I'll text him," I say. "But if he says no, then I'm stopping somewhere to get a drink."

"Are you okay?" Celena asks me.

"I'm just really tired and frustrated right now," I say. "I want to date again, but I forgot how much mental and emotional work it is."

"I know, hon," Celena says gently. "Hang in there. It will get better."

"Thanks. Good night."

"Good night. Text me tomorrow about how things go with Ash."

"Will do."

Chapter 8

Ash

"Hey, come on in," I say when I open the door for Doc Mackey. She texted a little while ago to see if she could come early, and I told her to head on over.

Her eyes travel down and back up my body briefly before her jaw sets. She mutters a thanks as she walks past me into the house. I look down at the gray sweatpants and black v-neck t-shirt I'm wearing, and frown. My feet are bare as well, and I wonder if she's angry at me for not dressing more professionally.

It was a long day at practice, and I wanted to be comfortable. She'll have to deal.

The doc herself is more dressed up than the last time she came over. She has on a black skirt, tighter than the one she wore the first day I met her, but not so tight it looks like she's trying to show off her body. The sweater she wears hugs her torso, so I see she has a nice figure, with full breasts and hips that give her an hour-glass shape.

"Can I get you anything to drink?" I ask as we head to the living room.

She flops onto the couch after setting her laptop on the coffee table. Her mouth works silently as if she wants to say something before she finally decides on, "Water is fine."

I go to the water cooler, fill a glass, then go back to the couch and hand it to her.

"Now tell me what you really want to drink," I say as she's about to thank me.

Her mouth hangs open in surprise as I call her on the lie.

She sighs. "I don't suppose you have any wine?"

I consider what's in my cabinets. "Does it have to be good wine?"

"No. I'll take Two Buck Chuck at this point," she says.

I'm not entirely sure what that is, but the name says it all, so I head back into the kitchen and open the cabinet that contains a built-in wine rack. I keep some on hand for entertaining, even though I don't drink it myself. I pull out a bottle and hold it up.

"Robert Mondavi Cabernet Sauvignon?" I ask.

Her face eases. "That's better than I was expecting."

I'm not sure how to take the comment, but I let it go and fish in the designated kitchen gadget drawer for the corkscrew. I find it in the back and open the bottle.

"Tough day?" I ask as I open cabinets, trying to remember which one contains the half dozen wine glasses I own, again, purely for entertaining.

Not that I ever actually entertain. But maybe someday.

I find the glasses and pour her some wine. I look at her when she doesn't answer and find her staring out the large windows that overlook the water.

"Dr. Mackey?" I ask as I walk over and hand her the wine.

She snaps out of her daze, then winces as she looks at me. Her hand goes to her neck to rub it, and I wonder if she just pulled something.

"Don't call me that," she says, and there's an edge to her voice. I raise a brow, and her face falls.

"I'm so sorry," she says. "I didn't mean to snap at you. I…I was on a first date earlier in the evening, and it didn't go well. But that's not your fault, so I shouldn't take my bad mood out on you."

The words come out as a whoosh of breath, and she deflates in front of me as she takes a big gulp of her wine.

That same twinge I felt days ago is back at the mention of her date, but I ignore it.

"Do you want to talk about it?" I ask as she winces again.

"Absolutely not," she says. "I'm here to help you, so let's focus on that. Just do me a favor and call me Gray." She sips her wine again. "I normally insist my students call me Dr. Mackey for professional reasons, but you're not really a student, and it feels odd to have you use my title while we're sitting in your living room."

I shrug one shoulder as I sit across from her on the loveseat as before. "Fair enough…Gray. So where do we start?"

"Let's start with your homework," she says. "What did you decide your ideal image is?"

I lean back and think a moment. I've been considering this for days, and I'm still not sure I have a complete picture.

"I guess my ideal image isn't that much different than Karl Malone's," I say. "I imagine myself as the guy the team can depend on. The guy who can deliver a goal when we need it. But that's gotta be the ideal image of most athletes, right?"

Gray shakes her head once but stops on another wince. "Not necessarily," she says. "You see yourself in relationship to your team. Your ideal image is dependent on how they view you. Not all athletes are that way. Many — too many — want the glory. They're happy to be in the spotlight while their teammates see them as the star. You want to be the guy 'who can deliver a goal when *we* need it.' Not just you. The team."

I nod as I mull this over. The truth is, the 'We' guy in me has only come about in recent years. If I'm brutally honest with myself, I was very much that 'I' guy in my first few seasons in the NHL. The last couple years have been humbling, though, and my team approach has apparently changed because of it.

"So what does that mean for me?" I ask.

"I'm not sure yet," she says. "What else can you tell me about your ideal image? If I were to ask your teammates what they thought of you as a player, what would you want them to say?"

"What I'd *want* them to say and what each one of them *would* say are different things," I argue. "I'd want them to say they respect me and know they can count on me to do my job. And maybe that's what Kelsier would say, but Kingston, our goalie, would probably say he wants me to be a scoring machine. The more goals I make, the more pressure it takes off him to keep the puck out of the net."

Her brows pinch in thought. "You're right," she says. "Your teammates will have their own hopes for you based on their personal priorities and outlooks. So what should you take away from that?"

I just look at her. "Um…"

"If everyone wants something different from you…," she prompts, and her point clicks into place.

"I can't please everyone," I say.

"Exactly," she says. "It's not wrong to want your teammates to be able to depend on you, but maybe you're letting your desire to be what everyone needs overwhelm you. Maybe the trash talk is getting to you because you're afraid of letting everyone down."

I think for a moment. That's a possibility.

"So what do I do about it?" I ask.

"About that part, I'm not sure yet," she says. "In the meantime, I've been looking into anger management techniques we can work on." She opens her laptop and boots it up before opening a document. One hand goes to her neck again as her other runs across the mousepad, and she grimaces as she rubs near her nape.

"Are you alright?" I ask. "You keep rubbing your neck."

She starts to shake her head but stops. "I'm fine. I just slept wrong and strained something. That's what started the whole day out like shit."

"Do you want-"

"Stress inoculation," she says before I can finish the thought.

"What?"

"Stress inoculation," she repeats, looking at the document on her computer. "Basically, we'll develop a toolkit of responses to trash talk for you, and you'll practice using them so your go-to response isn't anger or frustration."

"You want me to practice trash talking back?"

"No, by 'response' I mean more of an internal response," she explains. "For example, when someone says something offensive to you, you'll have a store of happy memories or funny thoughts you automatically think of that might help even out your mood. Your homework for next time is to-"

"Create a list of happy memories and funny thoughts?" I cut in.

She smiles. "You're a fast learner."

Her phone pings, and her head jerks toward it, which immediately causes her to put a hand on her neck and start rubbing again.

I can't take it anymore, and I get up off the loveseat to sit down next to her. She looks at me in alarm.

"What are you-"

"Turn around," I tell her. "I'm tired of watching you wince. Let me massage your neck for you."

Her eyes flare wide, and she starts to shake her head before she remembers that will hurt. "No, I-"

I hold up my hands in innocence. "I promise I won't do anything inappropriate," I say. "It's just obvious you're in pain, and I want to help. I studied Kinesiology in college. I know what I'm doing."

Maybe that's a stretch. I'm not actually a massage therapist, but the mention of my college study seems to persuade her. I see surprise and maybe interest in her eyes. I notice they're a light golden brown with rings of dark gray around the irises.

"Turn around," I repeat.

There's indecision on her face, but after a few seconds she gingerly shifts on the couch to give me her back.

"Right side?" I ask.

"Yes."

Her long blonde hair is pulled back in a ponytail, so I reach up and sweep it over her left shoulder. I think I feel her shiver.

I start massaging her neck and shoulder, but her sweater bunches under my fingers, and I have to keep adjusting my grip.

"What are you wearing under this?" I ask. "Can you take it off?"

Her body stiffens. "I…have on a bra and camisole," she offers hesitantly, and my brain searches for what a camisole is.

"That's like an undershirt?"

"More or less."

"Would you mind taking off the sweater? It would make this easier."

She hesitates for several seconds before grabbing the hem of the sweater and pulling it over her head. Surprise freezes me for a second as I'm treated to the sight of large tattooed feathered wings that stretch across her shoulders and halfway down her back into the camisole.

"Wow. I wasn't expecting those."

She doesn't say anything as I push her hair over her shoulder again, then reach up without thinking to trace the arch of one wing. Her shiver is obvious this time, and I pull my hand away.

"Sorry," I say. "They're just really beautiful."

"Thank you," she says softly.

We wait in silence another few seconds, but when she doesn't say more, I go back to massaging her neck and shoulder. The muscles are all in knots, probably from tensing around the injured area, and she flinches occasionally when I hit an especially sore spot. It's several minutes before I feel the muscles loosen up, and I knead hard when I find one stubborn knot that won't let go.

The doc lets out an involuntary noise as I dig in, and I'm a hundred percent certain it's one she makes during sex. We both go still.

"I'm-," she starts to say, but I cut her off before she can apologize.

"This one's tough. I should've warned you before I went after it."

I see her throat jump as she swallows.

"Just let me get this one loose, and you should feel better," I say.

"Alright," she says, the word barely a sound.

I go back to working on the knot, but I'm now hyperaware of everything about the woman in front of me. There are goosebumps on her arms, and when I inhale, the scent of something floral winds its way around my brain. I'm not familiar enough with plants and flowers to recognize the scent immediately – Lavender maybe? Jasmine? – but whatever it is resets my senses.

I'm leaning in close enough to flutter the wispy hairs at her nape with my breath, and I have the sudden, inexplicable urge to kiss the back of her neck. I lean back quickly.

I refocus on the knot and start to work at it again. My other hand holds her opposite shoulder to keep her steady, but she remains quiet this time. Finally, I feel the knot release.

"Got it," I say, letting go of her, and she breathes an audible sigh.

I scooch back a few inches to give us some room, and the doc pulls her sweater back on before turning to me.

"Thank you," she says. "That does feel better."

"No problem." I pause, and the air is thick with something unspoken before I break the silence again. "We get back into town late Thursday night, well, technically Friday morning, and then we'll have practice that afternoon. Can you come by to meet the team?"

"Yeah, sure. I usually have Friday afternoons free."

She looks like she's about to say more but stops herself.

"What is it?" I ask.

She shakes her head. "It's nothing. Never mind."

"Just tell me," I say.

She sighs heavily and looks down. "It…It's about those texts you sent me the night we met."

My brows furrow as I search my memory for what texts she could be talking about.

"I'm not sure what your expectations are, but I think we need to keep this professional," she goes on.

I frown deeper. "What?"

"I mean, I don't want to assume why you sent the picture," she says, "but I think we can both agree that letting things get…personal would make working together entirely too awkward."

"Picture?" I ask, completely confused. I don't remember ever sending her a picture, and certainly not one that has her this flustered and flushed.

What she's talking about finally hits me a second before she speaks.

"The dick pic you sent me," she says.

My eyes blow wide. "Oh fuck." I shoot off the couch as I run my hand through my hair. "Fuck, fuck, fuck."

I feel the doc's eyes on me as I start to pace, but I can't bring myself to meet her gaze as the significance of the G-r-a I saw on my phone that morning hits me. Not Grace…Gray.

I run my hand through my hair again. I almost put her in my phone as "Doc Mackey" that day we met, but I decided to just use her first name instead, and the result of that simple decision slaps me upside the head.

"Doc, I'm so sorry. I mean, Gray," I say, turning to her. "That text wasn't meant for you. I thought I sent it to my ex-girlfriend Grace."

Her mouth hangs open a second. "Oh. Of course. I…I suspected it wasn't meant for me." She pauses, then asks, "Had a few too many beers that night?"

I huff a small laugh. "High-powered sleeping pill. I was anxious about whether you'd agree to help and was having trouble falling asleep. I guess between the pill and thinking about you, the signals got mixed up in my brain…and on my phone."

She lets out a breath that contains a laugh as well. "That's a relief."

Strangely, she doesn't sound relieved.

We stare at each other, and the implications of this sink in.

"So…uh…You've seen my dick," I say, trying to keep it light.

Her cheeks pinken and she looks away. "I did, but…"

Her head snaps back as her eyes lock with mine, and she winces at the movement, her neck still not a hundred percent.

"I deleted the pic," she says quickly. "You can check my phone."

She grabs the phone off the coffee table and thrusts it toward me.

I put my hands up. "I believe you." A smile quirks up one corner of my mouth. "But admit, you took a good long look at it."

Her face flames this time, and I have my answer. I shouldn't tease her, but I kind of like doing it. The flush of color on her cheeks makes her even prettier, and I can't help wondering what she'd also look like with tendrils of her hair sticking to the side of her sweat-sheened face after…

I shake the thought away again. Nope. Don't go there. It's been a few months since I've had sex, and my body has clearly been trying to tell me something lately, but the doc is right. She and I need to stay professional.

"I couldn't really help looking at it," she says defensively.

I frown as something occurs to me. "Wait, so you thought I sent you a dick pic that night, and the next day you agreed to work with me?"

This time her face drains of color.

"No!" she says. "I mean, yes, that's the sequence of events, but that's only correlation, not causation. I didn't agree to work with you *because* of the dick pic. I agreed to work with you *in spite of* it."

I eye her like I don't buy it.

"I swear," she says. "I almost turned down the offer because of it."

I give her a look of exaggerated offense. "My dick isn't *that* bad-looking, is it?"

The doc closes her eyes, realizing she's not going to win this discussion. When she opens them again, she's gotten her bearings.

"It's a lovely dick," she says, "and my life has been enriched for having seen it, but it didn't influence my decision to take this job."

I smile. "Not sure it's ever been called 'lovely' before, but thank you."

There's a stretch of silence before Gray rises from the couch.

"I should probably go," she says.

I hold up a hand. "No, please. I'm sorry," I say. "I spent my childhood getting under my sister's skin, and old habits are hard to break. I couldn't resist teasing you, if only to mask my own embarrassment."

Her face softens. "No apology needed. I'm sorry if I made you uncomfortable."

"It's fine," I say. "I'm a big boy."

Her eyes flare, and I know she caught the unintended innuendo.

"Can we start over? Forget about the pic?" I ask.

She nods. "Of course. It was an honest mistake."

I nod back. "Thanks for not sending it to the tabloids."

She smiles. "It was touch-and-go for a hot minute, but my fear of karmic retribution won out."

I return the smile. "Well, it's good to know which way your moral compass points."

I motion for her to sit back down, and we retake our original places.

"So where were we?" she asks.

"I think you were going to vaccinate me against trash talk or something?" I say.

Her brows furrow a second before she understands. "Ah, inoculate. Right," she says. "We were talking about stress inoculations."

I bite back a comment about being fine with that as long as I don't have to take it in the ass. That would only send the conversation spiraling back in the wrong direction. As it is, the thought alone has me wondering if the doc likes anal.

God damn it. I need to get laid.

Chapter 9

Gray

A few weeks ago, I didn't expect to be sitting on my couch on a Tuesday night with a glass of wine, waiting impatiently for the NHL season to start, but here we are. Celena came over for support.

There's a minute and a half to puck drop, and my knee bounces uncontrollably so the wine in my glass threatens to slosh over the edge. Celena finally puts a hand on my knee to hold it down.

"Relax, lady," she says. "You'd think you yourself were playing with how nervous you are."

"I have no idea why I'm this anxious," I say. "I've only been working with Ash for about a week and a half, so I don't expect anything has changed with him, but who knows."

"It will be fine," she says. "Do you even know anything about hockey?"

I shrug. "I've been watching YouTube videos about the rules, but I assume I'll pick up more as we watch the game. I'm counting on the announcers to explain what the hell is happening."

"Icing is a thing, right?" she asks.

"Yeah, it has something to do with sending the puck down the other end of the rink, but I'm sketchy on the details," I say before taking a healthy sip of my wine. Tonight I'm drinking a right-bank Bordeaux red.

The players line up at center ice, and I lean forward.

"What number is he?" Celena asks.

"He's seventeen," I say, "but he's not out yet. They play in shifts, and he said the coach was still deciding whether to put him at second or third line. He won't be starting regardless."

Celena looks at me blankly. "Okay."

"They only stay on for like a minute at a time or something crazy like that, then they switch off with the next shift," I explain. "Hockey has unlimited substitutions. Ash told me he was almost always first line before his trash talk issues started, but the coach has him playing further back until he gets a handle on the problem."

Celena nods, but it doesn't look like she fully understands. I only barely understand it myself.

On TV, the referee drops the puck and the players all surge into motion. The other team gets control first, and I struggle to follow the little black puck. Hockey is a fast game, and my eyes aren't used to the speed of the action yet. I read that goalies often warm up their eyes before a game by looking back and forth in preparation to track the puck.

About a minute later, the action stops for a penalty.

"What the hell just happened?" Celena asks.

"Some kind of penalty," I say. "Tripping, I think."

"It says 'power play,'" Celena says, pointing to the screen.

I look and see that one of the Hydra is in the penalty box already. Shit.

"We have to play down one man for the next two minutes," I say.

We. Listen to me talk like I'm part of the team.

I take another sip of wine as play resumes, and I once again try to keep up with the piece of rubber bouncing all over the place. I have no idea how the players keep track of the thing while also on skates.

The penalty ends, and the Hydra have survived their first power play as the next shift of forwards comes onto the ice.

"There's Ash," Celena says, and I look where she's pointing.

Sure enough, number seventeen is on the ice, and I can't take my eyes off him. I never thought of tall men as particularly graceful, but Ash is surprisingly quick and smooth on skates for someone who's nearly six and a half feet tall.

It seems like he's on the ice for a ridiculously short amount of time before he heads off again, but he hasn't gotten into a fight yet, so I'll take the small victory.

The first period ends about forty minutes later with both teams still scoreless. Even for a newbie to hockey, I can tell our goalie has been nothing short of spectacular. The other team took more shots on goal than us, and Kingston made some incredible saves, once even managing to throw himself from one side of the net to the other in time to make a diving save on a puck that seemed all-but destined to go in.

"Goalies are really flexible," Celena says as if channeling my thoughts.

"Agreed," I say. "My knees hurt just watching that. Joints were not meant to bend that way." I hold up the empty wine bottle. "Another?"

"How long is the game?" she asks.

"Two more periods."

"Three periods?" she says. "That's weird. Yeah, I'm up for another."

I head downstairs into my cellar, grab a Châteauneuf-du-Pape off the rack, and bring it back upstairs. Might as well stay with French red.

"How's it going with Ash anyway?" Celena asks. "Did seeing him make up for the bad date?"

I down the last few sips of the wine in my glass and start working on the cork of the new bottle.

"He gave me a neck massage," I say as I pop the wine open.

Celena's brows shoot up. "Oh? And what brought that on?"

"I slept wrong and had a crick in my neck. He convinced me to let him work on it."

Celena waits for me to go on. "And?" she prompts when I don't.

"And not only is the man gorgeous, he has magic fingers," I say. "And he convinced me to take my sweater off, so he's seen my tattoos." I take a big swig of the wine I just poured myself.

"What did he think of them?" Celena asks.

I sigh. "He said they were beautiful."

"And somehow you don't seem happy about that," she observes as she pours herself some of the new wine and takes a sip.

"Why would I be happy about that?" I ask. "The man is off limits, but he's sweet, and he becomes more interesting every time I talk to him. It's not fair." I take another drink.

"Remind me why he's off limits again?" Celena asks.

I look at her incredulously, then count reasons off on my fingers. "I need to be professional, I'm older than him, he's insanely hot and I'm-"

"If you say you're not, I'm going to slap you," she interrupts.

I give her a frustrated look, but I don't finish the thought. "Look," I say instead, "aside from the fact I was hired to help him with a problem and shouldn't be lusting after him, he's out of my league."

"Why is he out of your league? Because you're a couple years older than him?"

"Three years."

She waves a dismissive hand. "First of all, the years mean nothing. You look young. Second, as I've told you multiple times, you're beautiful. Stop suggesting you aren't. Even if you're not supermodel gorgeous, do you think he's so shallow he can't find you attractive?"

"He doesn't seem interested," I argue, not bothering to address the individual points.

"He called you beautiful."

"He called my tattoos beautiful."

"He asked you to undress for him."

"So it would be easier to massage my neck."

She smiles triumphantly. "Aha! He found an excuse to touch you."

"He saw I was in pain, and, nice guy that he is, he offered to help."

Celena throws up her hands in defeat. "Fine. I give up. Spend the next few months torturing yourself by lusting after him in secret rather than opening yourself up to the possibility he might actually like you."

She swipes up her wine glass and marches off to harumph down onto the couch. I sigh heavily and pick up my glass to go join her.

"I'm sorry," I say as I sit down next to her. "I know my pessimistic streak drives you crazy. I just can't help it sometimes. I've let too many men undermine my confidence, and I don't know how to pull up out of this nosedive now."

My eyes start to prick, but I force back the moisture. I won't let them have any more of my tears.

Celena puts an arm around my shoulders. She's always there to pick up the pieces when my dating life inevitably goes to hell. When I couldn't stop crying after a particularly bad breakup years ago, she came over and brought me to her house to spend the night so I wouldn't be alone.

I rest my head on Celena's shoulder. "Thank you."

"You can thank me by keeping an open mind," she says. "I just have a good feeling about this guy, and I don't want you to dismiss the possibilities because you're afraid of being hurt again." She pauses. "What about the dick pic?"

"A mistake. He meant to send it to his ex, Grace."

"You asked him?" she asks, and I nod. "Well, that's disappointing."

"Tell me about it," I mumble.

"What?" she asks.

"Nothing."

Ash

The second period is about to start, and I'm feeling okay. I'm not playing too bad, and no one has chirped at me yet.

It's our opening game, and everyone is a little nervous, so maybe they all have better things to worry about than getting on my case.

The game is scoreless so far, but not for lack of trying. Both goalies have been putting on a clinic, so it's been hard to get anything past them. I had a great shot toward the end of the first period, but Cote couldn't get his stick out of the way fast enough, and it barely deflected the puck so it hit the post instead of going in.

The shot gave me some confidence, though, and I feel like I'm settling in. Coach has me at second line, and I'm excited as the puck drops to start the next period. When my shift comes around, I'm chomping at the bit to get out there, so I practically fly over the boards.

I skate like a madman down the ice, and for the first time in a while I feel like myself. I check someone hard and take control of the puck. I streak back down the ice the other way, but they're already on me. I pass to Bouchard, but two seconds later, he passes it right back to me.

I don't think. I just shoot.

The puck somehow slips past two defensemen and between the goalie's knees. Elation shoots up my spine as I score my first goal of the regular season.

The away crowd gives a collective groan as my teammates swamp me.

"Fuck yeah!" Bouchard shouts as he claps me hard on the shoulder. "That's more like it, Gunny!"

We all skate past the bench for congratulatory fist bumps, and then it's time to reset. I end my shift half a minute later, but I'm jazzed now.

When I get back on after we cycle through again, though, something has changed. Fig and Mack got into it with a couple of Leafs during their time on the ice when Toronto scored a goal that nearly took out Kingston, so now there's extra tension. More than that, I'm a target for having scored that first goal. On my next possession, I get crunched against the boards so hard it knocks my skates out from under me, and I fall forward onto my knees.

"You look good on your knees, Gunnarsson," the guy who hit me says as he skates away.

The chirping has started, and my anger flares. I surge to my feet, ready for a fight.

By the end of the second period, we've had two good brawls, and the Leafs have kept up a steady stream of trash talk whenever they get the chance. I've missed three more shots on goal, at least one of which I should've made, and I'm starting to lose my cool.

As we head into the locker room for the second intermission, I'm barely holding it together. Whatever confidence I had before is long gone, and I'm pissed at myself for falling apart.

Alright fine. I'm *ashamed* of myself for falling apart, and that's pissing me off. Apparently the doc was right about the whole shame-rage thing.

"You okay, Gunny?" Kelsier asks when we're back in the locker room.

"Yeah, fine," I lie.

His look says he knows that's bullshit.

"Hold it together, man," he says. "We're in this. We need you to find some of that mojo you had at the beginning of the period."

We need you.

The words hit home as my last conversation with the doc about my ideal image flashes through my mind. I want to be the guy they can count on, but I'm letting them down.

Chapter 10

Ash

A few days later, I head down to the guard station at the administrative entrance of the arena and training center to meet Doc Mackey. The guard just called to tell me she was here, and I snuck out of the locker room while Mack and The Don were having an argument over whether jock itch was a fungal infection or a bacterial one.

It's not an argument I need to witness, nor one I want to know why they're having.

I turn the corner and catch sight of the doc waiting by the metal detector. She told me to call her Gray, but I'm still having trouble getting that to roll off my tongue. I always called my professors in college "Professor" or "Doctor," so wrapping my brain around calling her by her first name will take some getting used to.

It also doesn't help that she's wearing a suit today, although I notice it looks really good on her. It's navy blue and tailored perfectly to her body, so it shows off her curves. The skirt reaches just above her knees, and she's wearing a pair of low, red heels that accentuate the arc of perfect calves. Her hair is tied back in a jaunty ponytail that looks like every hair has been assigned its place and told not to move.

I feel like I've met three different Gray Mackeys so far – the frumpy professor, the casual academic, and the consummate professional – and I'm curious to know which is the real one.

"Doc, I mean, Gray," I say, heading toward her. "Glad you could make it." I turn to the middle-aged guard she's been talking to. "I'll take her from here, Ben."

"Thanks, Mr. Gunnarsson," the man says before heading back inside his office. I've told him at least twice to call me Ash, but for the first time I understand his reluctance to use my first name.

Ben offered to have someone bring the doc up, but I figured it would be better to come get her and introduce her to everyone gradually, rather than throw her directly into the lion's den. I'll take her up to see the coaching staff first, and afterward I'll have Kelsier meet us somewhere. Once I've eased her in, I can bring her to see the rest of the guys.

"You look great," I say. "I like the suit."

She gives me a small smile. "Thanks. I wasn't sure what to wear, but I decided business was the way to go."

She really does look good, and I foresee the guys checking her out. The thought annoys me, until I remember Kingston, and then my insides go downright cold.

Kingston is a notorious playboy, and it's grudgingly accepted on the team that if he wants a woman, anyone else will step back until either Kingston decides he doesn't want her anymore, or the woman makes it abundantly clear she doesn't want him. I wasn't here last year, but according to Kelsier, no woman has ever turned him down.

A twinge of fear shimmies up my spine. Goalies can be some of the most squirrely, superstitious players on a hockey team, so other players often go out of their way to keep them happy. At least, that's the way it was on most of the teams I played for. The last thing a team wants is a goalie with the yips.

Kingston is one of the less quirky goalies I've played with, but the rumor around the locker room is that he needs to have sex before a game to help him release pent-up energy so he can focus. I suspect Kingston himself started the rumor, but regardless of its origin, the bottom line is that if Kingston wants a woman, everyone else steps aside.

The thought of letting Kingston have Doc Mackey, even though I'm not interested in her, makes my whole body feel…unsettled.

"We'll meet the coaches first," I say as we head toward their offices.

"Great," she says, smiling politely.

I eye the doc as we walk, trying to decide if she's pretty enough for Kingston. She seems to get prettier every time I see her, but Kingston has particular tastes, and I don't think the doc fits them. For one, she's too tall. She's on the high side of average in height, but most of the women I see Kingston with are tiny.

Really big guys who like especially tiny women never made sense to me. At just under six and a half feet myself, I hate having to stoop or arch my neck too far to kiss a woman. It's uncomfortable.

The size difference also limits your sexual positions, and I like a little flexibility. Figuratively and literally.

Grace was on the taller side, and that's one of the things I liked about her. She was also gorgeous, even by Hollywood standards, but it always took a lot of work for her to get ready. She could spend an hour on her makeup alone, and it seemed like such a waste of time to me.

I glance at the doc to see if she's wearing makeup. It looks like she might have a little on around her eyes, and her lips look glossy, but she's not wearing anywhere near what Grace used to put on.

I shake myself mentally, not sure why I'm so concerned with how the doc looks. She's here to help me with my mental game, not audition to be my next girlfriend.

We reach Coach's office, and I knock.

"Yeah, come in," he calls from inside, and I open the door. Doc Mackey follows me inside as Coach looks up.

"Coach Davis, this is Dr. Gray Mackey," I tell him. "She's the one helping me with my chirping issue."

Coach stands and shakes hands with the doc.

"Dr. Mackey, nice to meet you," he says, then gestures to me. "Looks like you've got your work cut out for you."

He's smiling, but I still grimace. The criticism stings, although it's not undeserved. Other than my moment of brilliance in the second period of game one, our opening road trip was a shitshow. We lost both games, and

I think I spent more time in the penalty box the second game than I spent on the ice, which cost us two goals during power plays.

Doc Mackey smiles back at Coach, but it seems forced. "Well, trash talk has been used for centuries for a reason, Coach Davis," she says, "and we don't currently have a viable intervention against it, so it's going to take some time to find something that works. I'm sure you didn't expect Mr. Gunnarsson to be fixed after a couple games, right?"

The question sounds innocent enough, but I hear the edge to her words. Coach must hear it too because he's speechless for a moment before he finds his voice.

"No, of course not," he says with a bit of a laugh.

I'm not sure if the doc's defense was more for me or for her, but I'm grateful to her for managing Coach's expectations. More than that, the subtle way she had him on the ropes for a second was…kind of sexy, and now I'm seeing the doc in yet another new light.

Fuck me. I can't let myself think of her that way.

Most of my frustration in game two was self-directed for not having corrected my issue yet, but Doc Mackey's words put things in perspective. This isn't going to be a quick fix, and I have to manage my own expectations as much as Coach needs to manage his.

We chat with Coach a little more before I take the doc in to meet the assistant coaches and the trainers. Then I text Kelsier to meet us near the weight room. He's already there when me and the doc come around the corner a couple minutes later, and I groan inwardly at the shit-eating grin on his face. I give him a look that begs him not to be an ass.

"Is this the doc I've heard so much about?" he says as we approach.

I flash him another warning look that he ignores.

"Doc, uh, Gray, this is Zane Kelsier," I tell her. "Or Kels as most of us call him. Kels, this is Dr. Gray Mackey."

Kelsier and the doc shake hands as he grins the entire time.

"Kelsier is one of our defensemen," I say.

"It's great to meet you," the doc says to him. "Ash has mentioned you. It sounds like you're good friends on the team?"

Kelsier throws an arm around my shoulders, nearly putting me in a head lock. "I'm his best friend," he tells her.

"For now," I say, prying him off me. "We'll see how the rest of the day goes."

"Tell me, Doc," Kelsier says, ignoring me, "what kinds of treatments are you using on my boy here to fix his problem? Have you had to start the electroshock therapy yet?"

Doc Mackey smiles at him, and this time it looks genuine. "That would certainly make things easier," she says, "but unfortunately I'm not licensed to conduct electroshock."

Kelsier grins wider and leans in. "I won't tell anyone if you try anyway," he says in a loud whisper.

She laughs. "Have you played together long? Did you know each other before the Hydra?"

"Nah, we only met a little while ago when Ash joined the team," Kelsier says. "He kind of latched onto me, and I didn't have the heart to push him away."

"Uh…who approached who first?" I ask indignantly.

"Well, I came over to introduce myself first," Kelsier admits, "but only because you made those lost puppy dog eyes at me, and I can't resist a stray." He winks at the doc.

I scoff and roll my eyes. "He's so full of shit," I tell her.

"You sound like me and my friend Celena," she says, smiling.

"Who has she met so far?" Kelsier asks me.

"Just the coaching staff and trainers," I say. "Where is everyone?"

"Most of the guys are in the locker room getting ready for practice."

"Is…Kingston there?" I'm not sure how to ask without letting on why I want to know, but Kelsier guesses.

"No, it's safe," he says. "The goalies are down on the ice for their own pre-practice."

The doc looks between us questioningly. "Safe?"

"Kingston can be…hard to deal with sometimes," Kelsier tells her. "He has what one might call a 'high maintenance attitude,' so it might be best to save meeting him for your second visit."

He's not wrong, and I'm grateful to Kelsier for giving the doc a reason to steer clear of Kingston. In addition to being a playboy, Kingston can also be an arrogant ass.

The doc's brows rise at Kelsier's explanation, but she shrugs. "Alright. Lead the way then."

We head down the hall to the locker room, and Kelsier holds up a hand to halt us when we get there.

"Let me check to be sure everyone is decent," he says before opening the door and poking his head inside. "Hey," he calls in. "Gunny's professor lady is here. Is everyone dressed?"

There's a chorus of eager voices from within as Kelsier looks around the room.

"Jesus Christ, Mack," he says after a second. "Put some fucking pants on. Your jock strap doesn't count as being 'dressed.'" He looks back at me and the doc. "It will just be a minute."

The doc looks at him as if she's trying to decide if he's serious. Knowing the guys as I do, he is.

Finally, Kelsier opens the door fully, and we follow him in. There's another chorus of greetings as Doc Mackey enters, but I sigh as I take in the sight before us. Everyone is dressed, but just barely. Half the guys have their shirts off. Mack only has compression shorts on that leave nothing to the imagination, and Fig is wearing his shirt with only his boxer briefs underneath. Assholes.

"Guys, this is Dr. Gray Mackey," I say to the room at large. "And that's Dr. Mackey to you," I clarify as Mack opens his mouth to say something. "She's here to see what I have to put up with from you lot."

There's an uproar of protests, and I hold my hands in a *'Don't blame me because it's true'* gesture.

"What the hell, Gunny?" Fig says. "We're a fucking delight."

Gray looks at me. "Gunny?"

I shrug. "Just about everyone has a nickname," I say. I jerk a thumb toward Fig. "This is Connor Figuin, or Fig for short."

The doc nods at him. "Nice to meet you, Fig." Her face goes serious. "I'm sorry. Can I call you Fig, or is that just for teammates?"

"You can call me whatever you want, Doc," Fig says, smiling widely at her. He steps forward, but Kelsier stops him.

"Hey! Stay back," he tells Fig. "Don't make me get the spray bottle."

I glance at the doc, but she's got a faint smile on her lips, so I go on.

"This is Remy Bouchard, Alexi Samsonov, Matt Cote, Jon Novich," I say, pointing around the room in order. "Aksel Nilsen, Anders Aasgaard."

"They're our Norwegian twins," Kelsier cuts in.

"We're not twins," Aksel says in annoyance.

The two of them do look a little alike, but they're not related.

"They're twins," Kelsier assures Doc Mackey.

"Fuck you," both Aksel and Anders say at once.

Kelsier gives the doc a knowing look. "See?"

"Moving on," I say before the Norwegians can respond, "This is Ryan Petruck, or Mack as we call him."

"Mack?" the doc asks in confusion.

"As in Mack Truck," Kelsier clarifies, and the doc nods. Mack needs no further explanation.

"Teach!" Mack greets her with a mock salute.

"That's Donatello Archer," I go on quickly. "You can call him Don if you're talking *to* him, or The Don if you're talking *about* him."

The doc raises an eyebrow.

I give her a *'Just go with it'* look and introduce the last of the players in the locker room. There are a few other guys missing aside from the goalies, but this is a good start. No need to overwhelm her.

"You staying to watch practice, Doc?" Fig asks.

She looks at me questioningly. "I'm not sure. Am I allowed?"

"Yeah, of course," I say, not sure why the thought of her staying to see me...see *us* play gives me a small thrill. "If you want to."

"I'd love to," she says. "My knowledge of hockey is a bit subpar, so I welcome the chance to learn more."

"I'll get you set up on the bench," I say.

"Forget practice," Mack says, stopping us as I turn to lead the doc toward the rink. "When are you going to come hang out with us?" he asks her. He turns to me. "You're going to invite her out the next time we go to the club, right?"

The doc looks at me nervously, and I'm not sure if she's afraid to be put on the spot, or if she's nervous that Mack put *me* on the spot. Either way, I give her a reassuring look.

"Yeah, of course," I say, keeping my eyes on her. "It may be a few weeks, but I'll definitely let you know when we're going to hit the club, and you should join us. Just don't, under any circumstances, agree to dance with Mack if you value your toes."

"Hey," Mack protests. "At least I get out there and bust a move occasionally. That's more than you can say, Gunny."

The doc's face eases into a smile. "You don't dance?" she asks me.

"Not usually," I say. "The dance floor is always so crowded. I like to just sit back and listen to the music."

"You'll dance, right, Doc?" Fig asks. "Show Gunny how it's done?"

She smiles indulgently. "We'll see."

"We'll get you out there," Fig promises. "In the meantime, it's a date. You're coming with us the next time we go out to the club."

He grins at me like a fucking Cheshire Cat, and I decide to check the shit out of him during practice today. Fig is one of our smaller forwards, but I'm not above crunching him to make a point. If he thinks he's going to make a move on the doc, he needs to think again.

Gray Mackey is off-limits to him and every other one of these assholes, and I'll make sure they know it, one way or another.

Chapter 11

Gray

Almost three weeks later, the Hydra have somehow managed a 50/50 record, even with Ash's continued issues on the ice. After losing their first two away games, the team squeaked out a win in overtime at their home opener, and that gave them some momentum for a while until things started to fall apart again.

I haven't seen much of Ash since I met the team. I'm in the middle of midterm exams at the university, so I've been underwater with grading and helping my grad students with their research and teaching responsibilities. The break Melinda promised me from my service activities has only partially materialized, and I'm exhausted.

While Ash and I haven't seen much of each other, we text constantly. I know when his practices and games are, and he knows when I teach, so there are periods of silence between us, but when our free time lines up, especially on nights he doesn't have games, we text for hours.

The small thrill I get when my phone dings with an incoming text from Ash is reminiscent of the way I used to feel with Drew in the beginning of our relationship, back when things were good. Which terrifies me. I shouldn't feel this excited at the prospect of seeing or talking to the hockey player I'm supposed to be working with.

Our text conversations are completely innocent. Ash hasn't sent any further 'accidental' pics, and he hasn't asked for any inappropriate ones from me. Our messages are devoid of flirtation, yet there's still something stimulating about them, as if the anticipation is there below the surface.

That's the way it feels for me, at least. I can't speak for Ash, and it's probably better that way, because if I get any inkling that he likes our conversations as much as I do, things could detour quickly.

We talk mostly about his game play and what he's thinking or feeling. Ash has started to recognize some of his triggers on the ice, but he's still unable to stop himself from reacting, so that's what we need to focus on moving forward. It's hard to do much over text, so we need to meet soon, but for now our message sessions are at least inching us forward in his treatment.

Alright, fine. Our text convos aren't entirely game-related.

There are occasional personal questions thrown in – What's your favorite ice cream flavor? Or where are you planning to take your next vacation? – but nothing too deep.

For my own part, I think I've latched onto Ash as a life raft because my online dating experiences have been abysmal. Worse than abysmal really, but I can't find a strong enough term to describe the clusterfuckery that is my romantic life.

I'm still on two dating apps at Celena's insistence, and she makes me go on a date at least once a week. Thankfully I haven't had much time for more, because the three dates I've been on recently have been duds.

To start, I finally had to break it to Barry that I didn't want a second date. I can't bring myself to ghost anyone, so I told him outright I didn't think we connected. He disagreed, but he ultimately accepted my decision and stopped messaging me. How he considered that date a success, I'll never know.

My next three dates weren't any better. The first was with an investment banker who spent half the date talking about banking and the other half talking about his car. Thankfully he never texted me again after.

The second guy started the date by being rude to our waitress, but I walked out when he began spouting homophobic comments about the two men together a couple booths down.

The third guy seemed promising for the first twenty minutes. He listened attentively to me as I explained my research, but things went downhill when he dismissed my statistical evidence and mansplained to me how the effectiveness of trash talk was in fact due to mental distraction for most athletes and not emotional disruption, as my study found.

I now text both Celena and Ash after each date to complain. Celena empathizes, then pushes me to get back on the dating apps and find someone else. Ash commiserates with me and assures me the men I go out with aren't worth my time.

He also convinced me I wasn't crazy for being disenchanted with the dating status quo. He's been single since he and Grace broke up, and he admitted he's not eager to put himself back out there again.

I didn't loop Ash into my dating drama on purpose. I told him one evening I had a date and would need to talk to him later, so he messaged me that night to see how it went. I told him the truth, and we spent the rest of the night texting back and forth about what happened.

After that, it became normal for him to check in with me after a date to see how it went, as Celena does. I figure it can't hurt to get the male perspective, so I tell him whatever he wants to know. Luckily the dates never get to the point of intimacy, so I don't have to worry about sharing such details.

My phone pings just as I get home and set my groceries on the kitchen island. At this time of evening, it's likely one of two people, and my heartbeat picks up a little as I swipe the phone open. It outright hiccups when I see it's Ash, and I chastise myself for the reaction.

He sends thumbs up and laughing emojis, and I smile.

Gray

How was practice?

Ash

Practice is always good. I just need to play that way in games.

My heart twists for him. I wish there's something more I can do to help, but the best I have right now is information and a few possible anger management strategies we've been working on.

Gray

We'll figure something out. I promise.

It's not a promise I can make, but I hope the lie is comforting at least.

Ash

What are you doing Saturday night?

I frown. That's a question people generally ask if they either want to invite you out or they need a favor, like help moving. With Ash, both seem equally unlikely, and now I'm wary.

Gray

Laundry? Why?

Gray

I'm not really good at lifting couches if you need help moving or something.

He LOLs the comment.

Ash

Nothing like that.

Ash

We have a free day Sunday, so the guys are going out to the club at the casino Saturday night. I've been told I'm not invited unless I convince you to come.

I huff a laugh.

Gray

Looks like you're doing laundry too then. 😉

He sends a crying emoji.

Ash

Pretty please? I want to go to the club! 🙏

I let the phone sit a good minute while I put groceries away. Going with Ash and the guys to hang out is entirely too tempting. It's been almost two years since I've been dancing at a club. Celena and I went out regularly in our early twenties, but then life took over, and somewhere along the way we became lame, responsible adults.

My phone pings twice more before I pick it up again to answer.

Ash

PLEASE?

Ash

Kelsier will never let me live it down if I don't get you to go.

I smile and type out my response.

Gray

Alright. But only so Kelsier can't hold it over you.

Ash sends a celebration GIF followed by details about the time and place, a private area the team uses in a club at one of the casinos.

Ash

You can invite Celena if you want.

Gray

She already has plans.

It's a little white lie. Celena has a problem with gambling, but luckily she knows it's a problem and tries to avoid temptation whenever possible, so I know she'd turn down the invitation. It would kill her, but she'd turn it down. Better that she doesn't know she was invited in the first place.

Part of me wishes Celena could come so I'm not alone with the guys and their puck bunnies, but another part – one I won't acknowledge – is excited at the idea of hanging out with Ash without having to split my attention with someone else.

I instantly feel guilty for the thought, but I also know Celena would understand and even approve of my selfishness in this case.

Ash

I'm still riding high from Gray's agreement to come out on Saturday night as I lie in bed texting her. It's only nine o'clock, but this week is kicking my ass, and I'm exhausted. I can't go to bed without checking in with her, though. These nightly text-fests have become as much a part of my daily routine as working out or brushing my teeth.

I've barely seen Gray the last few weeks. She did come to a few more practices, but she and I haven't had any real time to get together in a while. We've both been too busy to meet up at night, so we've worked on my trash talk issue either by talking on the phone or via text message.

Not seeing Gray has started to feel like withdrawal. It's the kind of itch I used to experience when Grace and I hadn't seen each other for too long because of our schedules, the kind of itch I get when I need to see a woman I'm dating…

I had a dream about Gray the other night. Yeah, that kind of dream. The kind where I had to change my underwear because I came in them after dreaming about Gray moaning beneath me while I pumped between her thighs. The kind where I pinned her hands above her head as she wrapped her legs around my hips, and I fucked her hard until we both came minutes later, panting with ecstasy.

I've given up denying I want her. I don't know when I decided it for sure, but the dream was – ironically – my awakening to the realization.

It's been difficult keeping our text conversations casual, because I'm dying to ask her what she likes in bed. I keep an eye out for any hint of flirtation in her messages so I have an excuse to move the conversation to something more intimate, but so far she's been all business. Or mostly business. The best I've gotten from her is that her favorite ice cream flavor is Amaretto, and she wants to go back to Croatia on her next vacation.

I never would have guessed either of those things, and it only makes her more intriguing to me.

My phone pings, and I see her friend Celena can't come out with us on Saturday. I tamp down a sense of relief. Part of me did want to meet her best friend, but the larger part is thrilled I won't have to share her attention with someone else.

I send a frowning emoji, then type out a quick follow-up.

Ash

Too bad. Maybe next time.

Gray is unlike other women I've dated or wanted to date. I've dated smart women before, but no one so…intellectual. I feel like I need to be on my toes with her.

But that's not the biggest difference. Most of the other women I've dated since joining the NHL have been those who fawned over me because I was a professional athlete. It was a status symbol for them to say they were with me. I didn't realize until Gray told me about her date with the investment banker that none of those women ever asked me much about myself. Who I was and what I liked wasn't as important to them as *what* I was.

Grace had her own fame, so she cared more about who I was as a person than anyone else before, and that's what first drew me to her. Ultimately our goals and personalities weren't compatible, though.

With Gray, I feel like she cares about me *and* we fit together well.

She doesn't seem interested, though. I swear I've caught her checking me out once or twice, but whatever I think I see is usually gone in a flash, and then she's back to being the prim professor.

It's occurred to me she might be keeping her distance on purpose. I'm sure dating your students is frowned upon at the university, and while I'm not her student per se, I'm close enough that I can see why she might not want to cross professional boundaries.

That will be a problem on Saturday because I'm going to be very tempted to touch her. The last couple times she came to practice, I had to stop myself from putting a hand on the small of her back or brushing stray locks of hair away from her face. Out at the club with alcohol involved, I doubt my resolve will be strong enough to keep my hands to myself. I only hope whatever walls Gray has up are made of paper.

My dick starts to go hard just thinking about Saturday. Not that it needs an excuse lately. Ever since my wet dream the other night, I've gotten myself off before bed to minimize any repeats of the incident.

My phone pings, and I note the way my heart leaps at the sound.

Gray

Is the whole team coming out?

Ash

Not everyone. Mostly the single guys with no wives or dates.

Then a horrifying thought strikes me. Kingston is single right now and might deign to grace us with his presence.

Gray hasn't met him yet. By sheer coincidence, he's always been at goalie practice or busy with something else the few times she's visited.

I'm fairly certain he knows she exists, but he hasn't said anything to me about her yet, and I hope that's a good sign. Regardless, I need to let him know one way or another that Gray isn't an option for him. Goalie privilege be damned.

Based on our recent text conversations, I know Gray has dated quite a few assholes, and putting her on Kingston's radar isn't going to help her track record. Honestly, I'm embarrassed to be a man, having heard about some of the jerks she's been out with.

She also told me about some guy she dated about a year ago who kept making plans and then canceling on her. Drew, I think his name was? Apparently things were great with him for a few months. They'd slept together several times, and he seemed really interested.

Then the cancelations started. They'd make plans only for him to cancel hours before. They messaged each other regularly, and the guy insisted he wanted to see her, but then he'd leave her high and dry a few times in a row.

According to Gray, they took a break for a while, and she tried to move on, but he began to message her again, telling her he missed her. They made plans but – you guessed it – he canceled a couple hours before the date. He always had some emergency or other problem to take care of, a medical issue or a project at work that he needed to stay late to finish.

Gray finally dumped him permanently, but I get the feeling she's gun-shy now about getting involved with someone.

Granted I only have her side of the story, but I can't imagine why the fucker would have done that to her. I wanted to beat the shit out of him when she was done telling me everything. She did admit to going stalker on him at the end, but honestly, I didn't blame her at that point.

Not that I haven't had my fair share of crazy women. I dated one bunny for about a week until I turned my phone back on after practice one day to find she'd left me a hundred and thirty-two texts messages and ten voicemails. She'd completely freaked when I didn't answer her first couple messages and spent the entire practice sending me increasingly unhinged texts. I'd ultimately had to get a restraining order against her.

So yeah, the crazy goes both ways, but I still feel like it's my duty to show Gray not all men are scum or hopeless assholes. Even if she and I aren't dating, she deserves to have someone of the male persuasion treat her right.

I pick up my phone and type out a message.

Ash

Are your midterm exams done yet?

The dots bounce right away, telling me her phone is close by.

Gray

I'm hoping to have everything graded and handed back on Friday so I can enjoy the weekend for once.

Perfect. She'll be done with work, and I'm off on Sunday. We should both be stress-free and ready to let loose Saturday night.

I can't wait to see what the prim professor is like when she lets herself have some fun.

Chapter 12

Gray

"I'm going home to change," I text Celena after tugging my dress down for the third time in two minutes as I walk through the casino Saturday night.

The bouncing blue dots appear to indicate she's typing.

Celena

No, you're not. You're going to go in there and rock that dress in front of those professional hockey players like the smoking-hot goddess you are.

I roll my eyes. Celena is good for my self-confidence, even if she's full of shit.

Gray

What if one of my students sees me?

Celena

And what? Realizes you're an adult woman with a life beyond school?

I don't have time to reply before her next message comes through.

Celena

Putting my phone away now. Just go.

I sigh. I really wish Celena could've come tonight, but she never would've made it past the slot machines.

I pull out my ID and show the bouncer at the entrance to the club. He takes a quick glance at it, then at my outfit before he waves me inside.

I'm wearing a tight-fitting black dress that has half sleeves and dips low across my chest to show some cleavage. It comes down mid-thigh, and although I've already seen women wearing shorter skirts, I feel practically naked in it.

I do look good in the dress, but I'm not used to wearing something like this. I only own the thing because Celena made me buy it a year ago, and I'm only wearing it now because she made me promise to. It's the dress's inaugural outing.

I head toward the back of the club to where Ash said the VIP areas are, and I see the guys sitting on a set of couches in a far corner. I walk toward them, but another bouncer stops me before I get anywhere close.

"I'm with the Hydra," I shout to him over the music.

He looks me up and down slowly, his gaze lingering on my breasts. "No bunnies yet," he says.

My brows shoot up. "I'm a friend of Ash Gunnarsson."

The bouncer laughs. "So not just with the Hydra. You're with their star player?" he says. "You should've shot lower. I might've believed you were with one of the rookies."

I tamp down the urge to knee the man in the groin, and I pull out my phone instead. I show him Ash's name in my contacts, but he gives me a dubious look. I consider showing him our text chain, but at least parts of it are protected by the NDA.

I grit my teeth and send Ash a message to let him know I'm here but that the bouncer won't let me in. I watch Ash across the room, but he's busy talking and doesn't notice he has a message. None of the guys are looking this way, so I bite the bullet and call him. Again, he doesn't acknowledge his phone is ringing. He either doesn't have his phone on him, or the ringer is off.

I leave a quick message when his voicemail picks up as I glare at the bouncer, then I head back to the main bar. I'll have one drink, and if Ash hasn't messaged me back by the time I finish, I'm going home.

I manage to slip up to the packed bar just as someone else is leaving, but it's still another couple minutes before one of the bartenders comes over and I can order a Sauvignon Blanc. I've just gotten my drink when I hear a painfully familiar voice.

"Gray?"

I nearly spill the glass of wine as a lead ball forms in my stomach.

Please, no.

I turn to see Drew standing behind me at the bar. Drew, who I haven't seen or heard from in a year. Drew, who strung me along for weeks before I finally couldn't take it anymore. Drew, who still looks really good, despite that I want to feel repulsed by him.

Why? Why do I still carry a torch for this man? We weren't even together that long, and by the end he was treating me like absolute shit. How can my body still react this way when I see him?

Shame wells up, nearly drowning me. It's followed by the inevitable spike of anger. Anger at him for being such a jackass. Anger at myself for missing him despite it all.

"Drew," I manage to say. I give silent thanks my voice doesn't shake. "It's been a while."

"It has," he says. "You look good."

His eyes run up and down my body, and I fight back the shiver of pleasure I feel as I remember how he used to look at me that way. I refuse to let myself get sucked back in by him.

"How have you been?" he asks.

Really? We're doing the pleasantries thing? We're going to pretend I didn't leave a tearful breakup message on his voicemail, and he never called or texted me again?

"I'm fine. You?" I say, then sip my wine. I'm a big girl. I can do this.

He steps closer and leans in to be heard over the blaring club music, and I'm torn between jerking away and leaning toward him.

"Not bad," he says loud enough to be heard. "I got a promotion at work, and the car is looking good. I'm almost done with her, but it was touch-and-go for a while."

Drew has been restoring a classic Corvette Stingray, and he launches into a story about the trouble he had finding some part. I nod along, not really listening.

I'm wondering how rude it will be of me to turn and walk away when a large hand lands on my hip, making me jump. A masculine scent I half-recognize winds its way up my nose, and I turn to find Ash behind me. My stomach somersaults as he presses his body to mine, and I feel the warmth of his hand even through my dress.

"Everything okay?" Ash asks as he looks over my shoulder at Drew.

I'm nearly sandwiched between the two of them right now, and my body threatens to combust. Moreso when Ash tugs me gently back against him away from Drew. If I didn't know any better, I'd call the gesture …possessive.

Drew's eyes widen. "Oh my God. You…you're Ash Gunnarsson."

I had no idea Drew followed hockey, but he looks totally starstruck.

"I am," Ash says over the music. "And you are?"

"I'm Drew," Drew says. "I'm a huge fan of yours."

"Thanks," Ash says. "Do you and Gray know each other?"

"We dated briefly about a year ago," I jump in. I give Ash a meaningful look, hoping he gets the message that this is the guy I told him about.

"Ah, I see," Ash says, and I can tell he does.

"You and Gray know each other?" Drew asks, looking between us.

I start to explain but realize I'm again handcuffed by the NDA the university's lawyers couldn't get fully removed. I can only discuss parts of my work with Ash if and when Mr. Kaladin determines Ash is 'cured' of his trash talk issue.

"We just started dating," Ash says as his hand slips further around my waist, and I think I stop breathing. Butterflies explode in my stomach, and my mouth drops open as I look up at him, but he just smiles at me.

Drew must notice my shock because he asks, "Does…she know she's dating you?"

"Yes," I say before Ash can answer. "I just didn't think we were telling anyone about it yet." I look pointedly at him. "You being a public figure."

He shrugs. "I'm not announcing it to the media or anything, but the cat's pretty much out of the bag with you being here tonight, hanging with me and the guys."

Ash gestures to their private area in the corner, and Drew's eyes widen as he looks at the two couches of pro NHLers near the back of the club.

"Holy shit," Drew says. "Is that Kingston? And Petruck? Wow, that looks like a fun time."

As loud as it is in here, I still hear the longing in his voice. He's hoping for an invite to come hang out or at least meet the players.

"It is," Ash says. "Good to meet you, Drew. Come on, baby."

Ash turns us around and shepherds me through the crowd with his arm still around my waist. I can't help giving the bouncer who wouldn't let me through a snide look as we pass, then chide myself for acting like I'm twelve.

"Sorry," Ash says as he leads me toward the couch. "I couldn't hear my phone. I just got your messages."

"No problem," I say. "I was getting a drink."

"Found her," Ash says to the group as he rejoins them, and the guys all greet me warmly with shouts of "Hey!" and raised drinks.

I've gotten to know many of them over the last few weeks, and they're a good bunch.

Mack, Fig, Kelsier, The Don, and Bouchard are all sitting on the couches, plus two rookies and another big guy I haven't met before. The last has black hair, piercing blue eyes, and the most chiseled face I've ever seen on a man. My brain kicks in a second later, and I realize this must be Kingston, the Hydra's elusive goalie.

"Looking hot, teach," Mack says, his tone slightly surprised. "Glad you could join us."

I pull the hem of the dress down again. "Thanks for having me. It's been a while since I've been out to a club."

Ash sits down, and I dare a glance back to where Drew sits with a group of friends, including some women. He's still looking our way.

I put my wine down on the table and start to sit, but I yelp as Ash grabs my waist and tugs me down so I'm sitting across his lap. His hand lands on my thigh near the hem of the dress, and heat spreads through my body as he pulls me against his chest.

"Whoa, Gunny, what's up with you and the doc here?" Fig asks.

"Guys, we've got a Code Ex," Ash says as he trails his fingers down my arm, making me shiver involuntarily with pleasure.

A murmur of understanding passes through the group. The music isn't quite as loud back here, so it's easier to hear.

"Yours or hers?" Mack asks.

"Hers," Ash says.

"Code Ex?" I ask, although I can guess from context what it is.

"It's a warning there's an ex in the house," Ash says, his face entirely too close to mine. "It puts certain protocols into action."

"Protocols?" I say, unable to do anything but parrot back his words. Ninety-five percent of my attention is on the way Ash's hand strokes my thigh lightly, and the other five percent is on the feel of my nipples peaking against my bra.

"Number one," Kelsier says, "the ex is off-limits to everyone on the team. Doesn't matter if they're a super model, a porn star, or the God damn President of the United States. No one touches them. No one engages with them other than polite comments, and only if necessary."

"Number two," Fig says, "the person whose ex is here becomes the VIP for the night. We may like to razz each other, but when Code Ex is in effect, that person is immune from anything that makes them look bad. No pranks, and they need to look like the center of attention at all times."

"And number three," Mack says, smirking, "Operation Wingman kicks in. We do our best to make sure the person looks like the most desirable one in the whole place. For us, that means the guy gets the pick of any bunnies who are hanging around. If there are no bunnies, we see if we can get him some other romantic attention."

"It'll be trickier with you," Kelsier says, considering me. "We can't pass you around, or we may give your ex the wrong impression."

"Already handled," Ash says. He nuzzles his face into my neck, making a wave of goosebumps rise on my arms. "I told him me and the doc were dating."

I shift on Ash's lap, my skin hypersensitized, and he lets out a low murmur as his hand tightens on my thigh.

"Well, that's one way to do it," Bouchard says. "But if that gets out, then you'll have to do the whole fake breakup thing later."

"I'll deal with that if the time comes," Ash says. "Right now, we manage the current issue."

"So what are we dealing with?" Kelsier asks me. "Cheater? Did you dump him, or did he dump you?"

Ash's hand inches higher on my leg as it also drifts inward, and my mind empties of thought as his thumb strokes the inside of my thigh.

He lifts his lips so they're against the shell of my ear. "Is this okay?" he asks softly, his breath tickling me in a delightful kind of way.

I catch the faint whiff of beer on his breath. I was late getting out tonight, and I wonder how much he's had to drink already.

All I can do is nod a couple times. It's been a long time since I've been touched like this, and the feeling has short circuited whatever part of my brain controls speech. My nipples are almost painfully tight right now, and I'm getting wet.

With some effort, I pull my attention back to the group. "No cheating," I manage. "Or at least, none I know of."

"He break up with you?" Kelsier guesses hesitantly.

Normally I wouldn't want to tell these guys the sordid details of my time with Drew, but Ash's thumb is still slowly rubbing my thigh, and I need to focus on something besides it burning my skin.

"Who broke up with who sort of depends on your perspective," I say, forcing myself to focus. "I technically broke up with him, but only after he canceled plans with me four separate times. Maybe I just wasn't taking the hint."

The looks of shock and outrage on the guys' faces are more

humiliating than comforting, and I wonder once again how I could've held on for so long to someone who, in hindsight, made it that obvious he didn't want to spend time with me.

The fresh wave of shame is smothered by the tingling I feel down my entire body when Ash brushes my hair back from my shoulder. I'm wearing it down for a change, and his fingers against my neck cause goosebumps to bloom anew all over my arms.

"Your skin is so sensitive," Ash says into my ear as he trails his fingers down my forearm. "And smooth. Also, Drew hasn't taken his eyes off you since you sat down on my lap."

I resist the urge to look at Drew. I don't care anymore if he's watching.

"Teach, why would you let a guy do that to you?" Mack asks. His voice is pained. "When I'm dating someone, she gets one cancelation for extenuating circumstances. Twice in a row, and I'm done."

"Hey, don't blame her," Kelsier says. "He's the asshole who kept stringing her along instead of just letting her go."

"I'm not blaming her," Mack insists. "I'm just saying the teach shouldn't take that kind of crap from anyone."

They begin to argue about whether or not Mack was blaming me for letting the thing with Drew go on too long.

"Can you hand me my beer, please?" Ash asks, and I lean forward to take his beer off the table. I hand him the bottle, then pick up my own glass of wine and take a deep drink. I'm going to need more alcohol to get through this night.

I feel odd sitting on Ash's lap, but my back is stiff from trying to hold myself up, so I give in and lean against him. There's something hard digging against my backside, and I shift, thinking I'm pressed against a fold of fabric from the fly of Ash's jeans. He groans as his hand flexes on my thigh and inches higher.

I freeze, realizing the lump isn't fabric.

"I'm sorry," I whisper quickly. "I didn't..."

I trail off, not sure how to apologize for his erection.

Ash's thumb is under the hem of my dress now, and I can't help thinking how close it is to my clit. He must be able to feel the heat pouring from between my legs, because I certainly can.

Ash trails his lips along my neck, and another shiver works its way down my body. A noise that's part sigh, part moan escapes my throat, and I resist the urge to press into his touch.

"You can tell me to stop if you want," Ash whispers against my throat.

No, I really can't. Every nerve in my body is alive and acutely aware of Ash's hands and lips. I'm soaking wet between my thighs, and I just pray the black fabric will hide it.

"Which one is he anyway?" Bouchard asks as Mack and Kelsier wind down their argument.

"The idiot with the blue button-down shirt who thinks having his hair lick up like that in front is cool," Ash says. He kisses the bare spot of my shoulder near my neck, and I'm not entirely sure we're acting anymore.

Ash's thumb strokes between my legs, and my traitorous body pushes into the touch. My hips undulate of their own accord as if to encourage him, and I try to force myself to sit still.

I feel Ash smile against my shoulder before he plants a kiss there.

"Does that feel good?" he says so only I can hear.

My answer is a soft moan as he squeezes my thigh again, and I wonder once more how much he's had to drink already. His voice doesn't sound slurred, but he's clearly had enough to make him a little horny.

"Easy there, you two," Fig says, chuckling. "Maybe you should take this out onto the dance floor before you get the couch all wet."

My face heats as I realize how shameless I've been acting in front of Ash's teammates. I'm sure they must deal with this all the time from puck bunnies, but I hate the idea of being yet another woman just rubbing myself all over a hockey player.

"Good idea," Ash says, and I squeak in surprise as he stands, taking me with him. He grabs my hand and pulls me toward the dance floor. I barely manage to down another gulp of wine and set the glass down before we go.

It's mostly women dancing in groups out on the floor, but there are a few couples dancing as well. And by dancing, I mean the man sways from side to side while drinking his beer as his girlfriend gyrates on him. There's only one couple that's really into it, and they're practically fucking each other. If they didn't have clothes on, she'd be pregnant by now.

Ash swings me around and pulls me against him as he starts to move to the music. What we're doing is somewhere between the dry humping couple and the other couples, but at least we're still a few stages away from needing a pregnancy test.

"I thought you didn't dance," I say as he tightens his arm around me.

He shrugs. "I don't usually have a reason to."

The hand not holding my waist threads into my hair, and one of his knees presses between mine.

"You don't have to do this," I tell him. "I don't want to put you in the middle of my drama with Drew."

"It's no problem," he says. "You're doing me a favor, so I'm happy to help."

"I'm getting paid very well to do you that favor," I remind him.

He shrugs again. "Fine, then maybe you'll just owe me."

I don't get a chance to respond because he flips me around so my back is pressed to his chest. He takes one of my wrists and pulls it up to pin it against his shoulder. His other hand slides down my body to splay across my stomach and pull me back against him. He grinds his hips into me, and I can feel his erection against my backside.

"Drew can't take his eyes off you right now," Ash reports.

Drew? Drew who?

"Does he have a longing look on his face?" I ask.

"He's practically drooling."

"Then he's probably looking at *you*," I say. "I didn't realize he was such a hockey fan."

He chuckles. "Should I slip him my number?"

"Hey! What happened to Code Ex?" I ask, feigning offense. "I thought exes are off-limits."

"Fair enough." He runs his hand back up my body to my sternum. My nipples peak again instantly, then tighten even more as his thumb brushes the side of one breast.

I hope he doesn't hear the whimper that escapes me, but he must because he says, "God, your body is so damn responsive."

I'm about to apologize when I catch sight of someone else I recognize across the room. I gasp and spin around again to hide my face in Ash's chest. Shit, shit, Shit!

"What's wrong?" Ash asks. He grasps my upper arms and tries to pull me away, but I hold onto his shirt for dear life.

"One of my students is here," I say. "I have to get off this dance floor before someone sees me grinding against you."

The kid wasn't looking at me, but that doesn't mean he didn't see me.

Ash's hand moves to the small of my back as he steers me through the crowd toward the VIP area again. We're met with a chorus of cheers and whoops when we return to the couches.

"When's the wedding?" Mack asks. "That was hot."

Ash tries to pull me back onto his lap again as we sit, but I manage to detour my ass onto the couch next to him. He doesn't say anything, but his hand is on my thigh again the second I cross my legs. I'm trying to decide if he's really dedicated to this Code Ex thing, or if he's at that stage of drunkenness where some men get especially handsy.

To be sure, I enjoy the attention, and I'm trying to live in the moment. I just don't want to get used to it or make the mistake of thinking there's anything more to Ash's touches than alcohol, friction, and the desire to help a friend out.

A friend? Is that what I am to him? Regardless, it would be a mistake to think the way Ash touches me means more than that.

"You should've seen the look on the guy's face when the two of you started dancing," Bouchard says. "He's definitely jealous."

"He was totally eye-fucking you," Mack confirms.

"I just learned he's a hockey fan," I say. "I'm pretty sure it was Ash he was eye-fucking."

The guys all laugh and tease Ash. All except the guy with the black hair who now has a woman on his lap. He's making out with her, but he lifts his lips from hers long enough to speak for the first time.

"If you really wanted to make the guy jealous, you should've told him you were with me," he says.

I blink at the blatant egotism. Ash's fingers twitch on my thigh, and he scowls at the guy.

"And you are?" I ask.

I know who he is, but I won't give him the satisfaction of proving it.

If he's surprised by the question, he doesn't show it. The woman on his lap looks more outraged than he does.

The man smirks. "You can call me 'Your Highness.'" He nods to the woman in his lap. "That's what she'll be calling me later tonight."

Unoffended, the woman grins and lays a hand on his chest.

"This is Kingston, our starting goalie," Ash tells me.

Kingston starts to speak, but all the other guys chime in to say his full name along with him. "Beckham Kingston III."

The guys laugh, and Kingston looks annoyed for the first time. The woman on his lap just glares at me.

"Don't get us wrong," Kelsier says. "Kingston is definitely a big deal."

"He's just also a big prima donna," Fig says.

Kingston rolls his eyes and goes back to making out with the woman.

"It's a wonder his head still fits in his helmet," Mack says to me.

"Honestly, he's a great goalie," Ash says close to my ear, and it sounds like the words almost pain him to admit. "He had nine shutout games last season. Kaladin paid a lot of money to get him here."

Mack nods, having heard. "Yeah," he says, just loud enough to be heard over the music. "It's too bad he's such a flaming dickbag."

Chapter 13

Gray

The next couple hours pass uneventfully. Drew leaves about half an hour after my dance with Ash, then it's just me and the guys. Well, me, the guys, and the woman fastened to Kingston's lap. I never do get her name before the goalie gets up and leaves with her after not too long, barely saying goodbye to his teammates.

I have another glass of wine, and the guys tell me crazy stories about things that have happened on the ice and in the locker room. They share some of the trash talk they've heard and used, and I pull out my phone to take some notes. As Celena said, I want to write a book eventually, and some of this is gold.

The bouncer lets a few women through later on, and the guys welcome them to join us. Whether they're actual bunnies or just a group of girls out for some fun who thought they'd try their luck with the hot men having a private party in the corner, I'm not sure, but their arrival is my cue to leave. The guys have been more than gracious, and I don't want to get in Ash's way if he wants to find a friend for the night.

He's clearly a bit horny. His arm found its way around my shoulders early on, and his other hand spent the evening keeping my leg warm, even after Drew left.

Truthfully, it's nice to be touched again. Ash noted earlier how responsive my body was, and it always has been, but it's even more so now after a year of celibacy.

I stand up, and Ash's hand falls from my leg for the first time since we sat down. His finger has been tracing patterns on my thigh for at least twenty minutes, while his other hand has been playing with my hair. I've barely been able to focus on anything else, and I desperately need to get home to have some quality time with my toys.

"Thank you for a great night," I say to the guys as I grab my clutch. "That was fun."

"Leaving already?" Kelsier asks. "It's not even a school night."

"It's been a long week," I say.

Ash stands. "I'll walk you to your car."

"That's not necessary," I say. "Stay and have fun."

I survey the group of women with us who seem less-than-happy he's leaving. The woman sitting on his other side who's been trying to get his attention away from me since she arrived looks especially put out.

"Don't be ridiculous," Ash says, oblivious to their disappointment. "I'm not letting you trek all the way back to the garage alone. You can get lost in this place."

True. These casinos are built like mazes to keep people in. I only had two glasses of wine before I switched to cran and seltzer, so I'm entirely sober, but finding my way back to the right garage will still be iffy. The company might be nice.

I shrug and head for the door with Ash on my heels. The bouncers wish him a good evening by name, and we head down an escalator to the main floor. My breath hitches as Ash slips an arm around me, and we walk in silence for a few seconds before he speaks.

"You really let that asshole cancel on you four times?" he asks as we pass a giant sculpture of hand-blown glass by Dale Chihuly.

"There are a lot of things I'm confident about," I say. "Relationships aren't one of them. I convinced myself he was just afraid to get close, that he'd come around eventually. By the fourth time, I was expecting the cancellation. I waited for it all day. I was so anxious I could barely eat. When the text finally came in, I was both devastated and relieved."

I don't know why I'm telling him this.

He's quiet, and I find him scowling when I look over.

"I'd have kicked the shit out of him if I knew that earlier," he says.

I smile. "Probably not a good idea to get into fights off the ice too."

"You didn't deserve to be treated like that."

I shrug. I want to make some comment about how women often endure much worse, but I remain silent. Rape, abuse, gaslighting, being fucked then dumped are common. In the grand scheme, what Drew did was crappy, but not nearly as bad as what many women go through.

I once had to sleep with a guy just to get him to leave my place. I didn't want to have sex with him, but he pushed until I finally agreed, just to get him to go. I lay there counting the minutes until he finished while he grunted above me. He called the next day and chatted on while I gave one-word responses. I declined to see him that day and finally broke things off the next when I realized I couldn't stomach seeing him again.

I couldn't claim it was rape. I'd consented to everything he did, but it was under duress, and I felt assaulted the next day nonetheless.

"I'm really glad you came out tonight," Ash says as we head down the hallway toward the parking garage. "The guys think you're great."

I smile again. "They're a fun group. Thank you for inviting me out."

We head into the garage, and I try to remember where the hell I parked my car. I press the unlock button on my fob and see the taillights flash down toward the right.

"I'm right there," I say. "I should be fine from here."

Ash just puts a hand on my back and steers me toward the car. When we get there, I turn to say goodbye to him, but he's closer than I expect, and I step back so I bump against the car.

"Thanks for walking me to my car," I say. Every nerve in my neck and scalp are alive at how close he is. God, he really is nice to look at.

"You're welcome," Ash murmurs.

Even in the dim light of the parking garage, I see he's not looking me in the eyes. His gaze is fixed lower...on my lips.

"Ash?" I ask hesitantly. "Are you okay?"

"I just need one taste," he says, and it feels like he's talking more to himself than me.

"Taste of what?" I ask. I don't dare to believe he's talking about what I think – what I wish – he's talking about.

His eyes move up to mine, and the connection locks into place like a deadbolt.

"Of you," he says.

My stomach does a backflip as Ash's hands land on either side of me on the roof of the car, caging me in.

"Tell me to stop now if you don't want this," he says, leaning closer.

I'm completely frozen as my breathing shallows. My body screams at Ash to touch me, and he obliges. He presses closer, pinning me gently against the car as one of his hands slides over my cheek then behind my head to secure my neck.

I have to suppress a whimper when his lips touch mine, gently at first, then more urgently. His tongue coaxes my mouth open and slips inside. I faintly taste the beer he's been drinking as he deepens the kiss, and this time I can't hold back the moan that climbs up my throat. I need more of him, and my hands anchor on his waist to hold him against me.

"Fuck, baby. Your lips are so soft," Ash whispers against them before he kisses me again.

Everything tightens between my legs to hear him call me "baby." He said it once for Drew's benefit, but there's something about the way he says it now that drenches me. I'm only wearing a thong, so I might need to put something on the seat of the car when he's done.

Ash's tongue pushes in further to explore my mouth, and the muscles between my legs begin to throb. I want to drag him into the back seat and ride the shit out of him, but I can't because I'm sort of his teacher-slash-therapist, and the ethics of the situation are…questionable.

I push on Ash's shoulders, and he pulls back reluctantly.

"You should go back to the club," I say softly. "The guys will be wondering where you are."

"Do you want me to go?" he asks.

Sweet Jesus, no. But that's not a good answer.

"You *should* go," I say, trying to deflect. "If someone sees-"

"What if I don't want to go?" he interrupts.

I have no idea what to say, and then words are impossible because Ash's mouth is on mine again, and I don't have the will to push him away. My nipples are painfully tight against his chest, and if he hiked up my dress and fucked me here in the middle of the parking garage, I'd let him.

It seems like minutes before Ash comes up for air, and I gasp as he pulls back just enough so our panting breaths mingle with each other. He has me sandwiched between him and my car, and I feel his erection dig into my stomach.

He's drunk. It's the only explanation I can come up with for his behavior and for the rock-hard dick I can't ignore. I have to leave now because I can't handle his look of regret later if this goes any further.

I open my mouth, fully intending to make him go back inside the casino, but I can't force the words out.

"You look fucking amazing in this dress," Ash says, and I blink at the pivot in topic. "Just one more new side of you."

I frown, not entirely sure what he's talking about. I'm ready to ask when he speaks again.

"What else are you hiding from me?"

My frown deepens. "Hiding? What are you talking about? I'm not hiding anything."

He brushes his lips against my temple as his hand plays with the hair at the nape of my neck, and it takes everything I have to keep my eyes from rolling back in my head.

"Don't hide from me," he says softly. "I see you, Gray. All of you."

My heart hiccups at his use of my name. It's the first time he's said it where it doesn't feel like he's uncomfortable with it. It feels almost reverent, and I close my eyes. What the hell is this man doing to me?

My stomach bottoms out. Drew made me feel this way our first few weeks together as well. He made me feel special, like I was someone he couldn't get enough of. It's why I didn't understand when he pulled back and started to cancel on me without reason. It's why I held on so much longer than I should have. I kept hoping things would go back to the way they were, the way that made me feel like this.

Somewhere I find the strength to push Ash away. He resists for only a moment before he lets me put some space between us. I force a smile onto my face so I don't offend him. I'm sure he's not used to women pushing him away, and I have to do this carefully so I don't risk our working relationship, such as it is.

It was a mistake for me to come tonight, to create a situation where Ash and I might cross a boundary.

"I need to get home," I say. "You should go back in and have fun with the guys. I appreciate you letting me tag along."

He looks like he wants to argue, like it's taking everything in him not to glue his mouth to mine again, but he finally pulls back. I saw an entire war waged behind his eyes in those few seconds, and I'm grateful that his sense of reason won the fight.

"I know what you're thinking," he says.

He can't possibly. *I* don't even know what I'm thinking.

"You're thinking I only kissed you because I'm drunk."

Oh, that. Well, yes.

"Maybe I am a little drunk," he says, "But I know what I'm doing."

I force a smile onto my face. "And it was nice, but it's time for you to go back inside."

His lips purse together, and I assume it's to keep him from arguing. Finally, he nods and steps back. I open my door and get inside.

Ash doesn't turn and leave until I'm safely in my car with the engine started. Only then does he give me another nod and head back toward the entrance to the casino.

I breathe a heavy sigh as I watch him go and put the car in gear, but I stop when I see there's something on my windshield. I put the car back in park, get out, and grab the piece of paper from under my wiper blade.

I hate when people leave advertising flyers on my car.

I catch what looks like handwriting on the paper, but that's the new thing nowadays, mass-printed postcards and flyers that look like they're handwritten. I crumple the paper up and throw it in the little bin I leave in the footwell of my back seat for garbage. I'm not in the mood tonight.

There's only one person trying to sell me something I really want to buy, and that's Ash.

Chapter 14

Gray

The undergrad sitting across from me Monday morning scrunches his face in confusion. I've been explaining statistical p-values and confidence intervals to him for the last five minutes, and he's still not getting it.

The Communication program at this university is a quantitative one, which means stats are part of the curriculum. Unfortunately, not all the students know that coming in, and the realization they'll have to work with numbers in order to graduate is a rude awakening for some.

I look up when I hear the knock at my door, and Melinda, my department chair, pokes her head inside.

"Can I see you when you're done?" she asks.

"Sure," I say. "It should just be another couple minutes."

That's an underestimate. It's another fifteen minutes before my student grasps the concepts well enough that he'll be able to answer the question about them on the next exam.

"Hey," I stop the guy before he heads out the door. "Did you get your last in-class quiz back from me?"

He frowns. "I think so. Why?"

"This isn't yours then?" I ask. I hold up a paper with no name on it, my finger covering the failing grade.

The guy steps closer, looks at the paper, and shakes his head. "Nope. Not my writing."

"Okay, thanks," I say as he heads out the door.

Every now and then I give an old-school quiz where I pass out a sheet with questions that only need relatively quick responses. The problem is that sometimes, like now, a student forgets to put their name on the paper, and in a class of three hundred students, finding the owner can be difficult. There are about eighteen students who don't have grades for that quiz, and I haven't been able to track them all down.

It's probably a moot point. The owner of the quiz barely scraped together thirty points out of a hundred. They spent half the time waxing poetic about the importance of communication in making connections and building relationships, rather than answering the questions on the quiz directly. I cobbled together what points I could give the student, but it wasn't much. Hell, I couldn't even give them points for remembering to put their name on the paper.

I close up my office, and head down the hall to see Melinda. I knock, and she tells me to come in.

"What's up?" I ask.

She gestures for me to have a seat, and I do.

"How's everything going with the hockey player?" she asks.

I shrug. "Well enough, given that I don't have a validated intervention I can use on him. It's mostly trial and error, but we've made progress."

She nods. "And how are the two of you getting along?"

I frown at the question. "Fine. Why?"

"Is there anything I should know about you two?" she presses.

My frown deepens. "Like what?"

"Look," Melinda says, leaning forward in her chair to put her elbows on the desk. "Normally this would be none of my business, but given the amount of funding at stake, I have to ask. Is there anything going on between you and the hockey player that could come back to bite us?"

My mouth falls open. "What? No. Why would you ask that?" But there's a sudden chill tickling up my spine.

Melinda clicks her mouse, and a picture pops up on her computer screen. She turns it toward me so I can see it better, and I feel the color drain from my face. It's a grainy cell phone pic of me and Ash on the dance floor of the club Saturday night. My ass is pushed back against his groin while his hands splay across my stomach and chest. My eyes are closed, and I look enraptured as he leans his face down close to my neck.

I knew we'd gotten too close on the dance floor, but this picture makes it look like we're one step away from heading up to a hotel room for the night. I'm mortified as color rushes back to my face.

"Oh my god. Where did you get that?" I ask.

"It's making the rounds on the celebrity gossip sites," Melinda says. "They haven't identified you yet, but my wife sent it to me. She remembered meeting you last year at David's retirement party."

Fuck, fuck, fuck. The media may not have identified me yet, but I have a COMM class full of three hundred students who've probably all seen the photo by now. Hell, the student I saw at the club that night might have taken it. I hope TMZ at least gave him a good price for it.

"It's not what it looks like," I say quickly.

"No?" Melinda says. "Because it looks like you put yourself in a very questionable position with a man whose boss is paying you and this university a shitload of money to have you help him. I know he's not technically your student, and you're not his psychologist, but you're close enough to both those things that this is concerning."

"I know," I say quickly, "and I shouldn't have let it happen, but I swear there's nothing going on between us." Except a lot of kissing and caressing I haven't been able to get out of my mind. "Ash invited me to come hang out that night with the players, and I figured it was a good research opportunity."

Melinda raises a dubious brow, but I hurry on.

"My ex-boyfriend was there that night, and apparently the guys have this thing they do when someone's ex is there that involves making the person the center of attention, and things like that. Ash was trying to help me make Drew jealous. It was all for show."

Melinda eyes the picture again, and I know she's not buying it.

I go cold again as I wonder if Ash has seen the picture and what he thinks of it. I pull my phone out of my pocket and swipe it open. I have fifteen notifications. There are three texts from Ash and two calls.

Yup. He's seen the pic.

Of course he has. The Hydra have a public relations manager whose job it is to know when these things happen. The guy probably knew about the picture minutes after it hit the media.

I look at the rest of the notifications. Most are from Celena – four texts and five calls, plus one call from my mother. As a rule, my mother doesn't do celebrity gossip, but one of her friends probably called her and told her about the picture.

I open the texts from Ash. The first one starts with, "Don't panic."

Never have the words 'don't panic' kept anyone from panicking, and now is no different.

"Gray?" Melinda says, calling my attention back to her.

"I'm sorry," I say. "I have texts and calls from Ash. I'm sure the Hydra's people are on this, but I should call him back and find out what the game plan is for…managing this."

The picture is humiliating, but I'm more worried for Ash. He wanted to keep my work with him quiet, and that won't be possible once they identify me.

Melinda waves a hand. "Fine, go. Just keep me in the loop on everything. I need to call the university's communications office so they're prepared in case they get inquiries about this, which they will."

"Yes, of course," I say. I'm already halfway out her door and dialing Ash. The phone rings twice, then goes to voicemail, and I frown as I pull it away from my ear.

No need to jump to conclusions. He's probably in a meeting with the PR manager right now. I look at the other two texts he sent.

Ash

Someone took a pic of us the other night. It's all over the media.

Ash

God damn you look hot in that dress.

My stomach cartwheels at the compliment. I'd almost smile if I wasn't so horrified by the whole situation.

This is the first I've heard from Ash since Saturday night. I spent all yesterday with a knot in my chest, wondering if he regretted kissing me. If he was mad at me for making him stop. If he felt like I rejected him. If I would come to work this morning to find an email from Mr. Kaladin saying he was terminating his contract with me.

I look quickly at the texts from Celena.

Celena

Call me!

Celena

Call me now!

Celena

Why aren't you calling me??

Celena

Why aren't you answering your phone?????

I don't bother listening to the messages. I just lock myself back in my office and call Celena.

"It's about fucking time!" she says upon answering the phone.

"I was in office hours with students," I say. "I only just found out about the picture. Melinda called me into her office to ask me if anything was going on with me and Ash."

There's a pause. "Can she do that?"

"If there's enough funding involved, apparently yes."

"So is it true?"

"Is what true?"

"Is it true you're dating Ash Gunnarsson? Did you spend the night in his hotel room? Are you pregnant with his love child?" Celena fires off. "Jesus, Gray! Take your pick of the rumors. Are any of them true?"

She can't see me roll my eyes, but I do it anyway. "You know I would've called you if any of them were true," I say.

"I assumed you would've called me if you ended up grinding on the dance floor with a hot-as-fuck hockey player too, but here we are," she shoots back.

Fair enough.

"I'm sorry. It's just been a busy couple days, and it didn't seem like a big deal at the time."

Lies. Blatant, boldfaced lies. It was a huge deal, but for some reason I didn't tell Celena about it when she texted yesterday. I told her the outing went fine and that I'd fill her in later.

The truth is I couldn't bring myself to tell her. It was too raw, too close to what I'd experienced with Drew, and I just couldn't revisit it yesterday. I planned to call her tonight, but I needed a day to process.

"Spill it," she says. "All of it."

I sigh and fill her in. When I'm done, there's a long pause.

"He called you 'baby?'" Celena asks finally.

"Twice. The first time was for Drew's benefit. The second time I think he was just drunk."

"But he put his hand up your dress after you saw Drew, gyrated against you on the dance floor, spent the night feeling you up, then walked you to your car and kissed the shit out of you?"

I consider, wanting to correct her summary, but I can't find any real flaws with it. "Yes," I confirm.

"Gray," she says, and there's light reproach in her voice.

"What?" I say defensively.

"The guy wants you."

I scoff. "No, he doesn't. He just-"

"Occam's Razor," she interrupts.

"Excuse me?"

"Before you twist yourself in knots to give me a convoluted explanation that dismisses everything Ash did Saturday night, I just want to remind you of Occam's Razor, which says…" She trails off, inviting me to fill in the blank.

"The simplest explanation of something is the most likely," I supply.

"And the simplest explanation in this case is what?" she presses.

"That Ash wants me," I say with resignation.

"And why don't you want to believe that?" she asks in frustration.

I wrack my brain for whatever explanation she's looking for.

"Because you're afraid of being hurt again," she says a few seconds later when I come up short.

"Right," I say doubtfully. Occam's Razor aside, I'm not convinced the simplest explanation is that Ash wants me.

"Gray, I can hear you overthinking this," Celena accuses.

"I should call Ash," I say as an excuse to end the conversation. "He left me two messages."

"You haven't called him back yet? Yes, call him, find out what's going on, then call me back right away."

"I will," I lie, then hang up.

I pull up the two voicemails from Ash and listen to the first. Hearing his voice helps calm me. He doesn't sound upset, and I dare to hope things haven't gone to complete shit.

"Hey there," he says in the first message. "Thanks for coming out the other night. I hope you had a good time. I wasn't sure if I should bother you yesterday or not, so I didn't call or text. Anyway, not sure if you saw the news but, uh…someone apparently took a video of us dancing."

God dammit. There's a fucking video? The pic Melinda showed me must have been a still from it.

"Anyway," the message continues, "it's nothing to worry about. Just give me a call when you get a chance."

Nothing to worry about. Right.

I click on the second voicemail. It's shorter but more concerning.

"Hey, it's Ash again. I just got called in to see Kaladin. I'm on my way there now. I'll let you know what he says after we meet."

That's why he wasn't picking up. He's already in with Mr. Kaladin.

I put my phone down and rest my head in my hands with my elbows on the desk. Patience is not one of my virtues, nor is trusting my future in someone else's hands. It will be absolute agony until I hear from Ash.

I'm not a religious person, but I start praying I haven't completely screwed everything up.

Chapter 15

Ash

I send the call from Gray to voicemail as I sit across the desk from Max Kaladin. I wanted to talk to her before I saw him, but now it will have to wait until after this meeting. One doesn't keep the billionaire who pays your salary waiting while you take a call.

"So," Kaladin says, tenting his fingers, "care to explain why you and Dr. Mackey are splashed across every tabloid in the country?"

Cedric sits in the chair next to me. I'm not sure what time the video of me and Gray hit the media, but Cedric looks like he's running on coffee, sugar, and sheer willpower right now. I don't envy the man his job, and I'm only mildly sorry I'm adding to his stress. Secretly, I'm thrilled the world thinks I'm dating Gray.

"Code Ex," I tell Kaladin.

He raises a confused brow. "Excuse me?"

"I invited Gray to come out and hang with me and some of the guys Saturday night at the club, but we had a Code Ex," I explain.

Kaladin cocks his head at something, but whether it's the Code Ex thing or the fact I called Gray by her first name, I'm not sure.

Thinking of her as Gray rather than Doc Mackey is easier now than it was before. I suppose having my hand between her legs and my tongue down her throat helped.

"Gray's ex was there," I elaborate, ignoring the look, "and the code says we had to make the guy jealous so he'd realize what he'd lost."

"Ah, Code Ex," Kaladin says, humoring me like he knows exactly what I'm talking about. "And feeling the good doctor up on the dance floor was part of the code?"

I shrug. "I was improvising."

Kaladin sighs and turns to Cedric. "What's the situation? Do we need damage control?"

Cedric looks up from his phone where he's been furiously typing.

"They identified Dr. Mackey about fifteen minutes ago," Cedric says, "and the news of her work with trash talk just hit the wires. There's already conjecture about her working with Ash, so we need to make a statement sooner rather than later to control the narrative as much as possible."

"What *is* our narrative?" Kaladin asks.

"We confirm what they already assume," I say. "I'm dating Gray."

Kaladin narrows his eyes. "*Are* you dating her?"

"No, but they don't know that," I say, "and it's better for us if they think I am, right? It confirms what the photo suggests, and it deflects attention away from her working with me while still giving us a reason to be seen together."

Kaladin's brows shoot up. "You want to…fake date Dr. Mackey."

It's not quite a question, and I tamp down the voice that says I want to date her for real. Instead, I just nod.

"How do we say you met?" Cedric asks.

"She reached out to me because she wanted to question me for some research she's been doing, and we hit it off."

Cedric and Kaladin look at each other, and Cedric gives a quick tilt of his head to indicate it's not a bad plan.

"We'd have to get the university to back the story," Cedric says, "but more importantly, we need Dr. Mackey on board."

I open my mouth to answer, then close it. I was about to assure him it wouldn't be a problem, but suddenly I'm not so sure Gray will go for it. It's her professional reputation on the line, and I don't know what kind of blowback she might get from being tied to me. As it is, that picture alone may have done irreparable damage to her image, and I can't even conceive of what she's telling her students. The need to return her call now is overwhelming.

"Gray tried to call a little while ago," I say. "Let me call her back and see if she'll agree to the fake dating plan, at least for a little while."

Kaladin nods. "Call her."

I stand and head to the end of the huge office that's farthest from the desk. It puts me well out of earshot of Kaladin and Cedric.

Gray picks up on the third ring. "Ash? What the hell is going on? What are we going to do?" she asks, and I feel a twinge of guilt at the obvious panic in her voice. The dance at the club was my doing, and it backfired spectacularly.

"It's going to be alright," I assure her. "Are you okay? Have the reporters started calling?"

"I had one follow me to my car," Gray says. "I'm currently hiding out in one of the parking garages on campus. I don't even want to know what I'll find when I get home."

I close my eyes. I need to fix this.

I open them again. "I'm in with Mr. Kaladin and our PR director now. We have a possible plan, but you'd need to agree to it."

A pause. "What's the plan?"

I explain the fake dating scenario, then wait for Gray to respond. There's a long silence on the other end of the line.

"Gray?" I ask when she still hasn't answered. I look at my cell to be sure we're still connected.

"Look, I know this isn't ideal," I go on when I see we are, "and if you're not down with it, we'll think of something else, but pretending to date, at least for a little while is the easiest way to handle this. There will be some interest from the media for the next few days, but they'll get bored soon enough. We can finish our work and…fake break up."

The words taste sour in my mouth already, and there's more silence on the other end.

"Gray?" I ask again. "Are you still there?"

I hear her huff a small laugh. "I just convinced my department head we weren't dating. Now I have to go back and tell her we're fake dating."

She laughs again, but there's little humor in it.

"We don't have to do it if you don't want to," I repeat.

Another pause. "No, you're right. It's the easiest way to explain the picture, and it's the only story that doesn't out me as a fraud to Drew or make me look like a puck bunny."

I breathe a sigh of relief, and excitement tingles in my chest at the idea that Gray and I will get to play the happy couple for a few weeks.

"Thank you," I say. "I appreciate this. We'll have to get the university on board with the story, but I assume they'll back us given the money Kaladin is promising."

I hear Gray's own sigh on the other end of the line. "What do I do until then?" she asks. "There are probably reporters at my house by now."

"Hold on," I say. I put the phone on speaker and head back to Kaladin's desk. "Gray is on board with the plan," I tell Kaladin and Cedric, "but the reporters have found her already. They're probably at her house. What should she do?"

"Dr. Mackey," Cedric says into the phone, "my name is Cedric Winston, and I'm the Hydra's PR director. If anyone approaches you, just tell them you're not answering any questions and refer them to me."

He gives her his phone number, and she confirms it with him.

"I can get a handle on the story today, but you should probably be seen in public together tonight," Cedric suggests. "It will sell the story and get the reporters off your back quicker. If you try to hide, they'll only think you have a reason to, and they'll hound you more. Throw them a bone."

The other end of the line is silent.

"Are you free tonight, Gray?" I ask. "I can take you to dinner."

More silence before she finally says, "Just tell me where and when."

"It would be better if you pick her up," Cedric says.

"I'll pick you up at your place at six thirty," I tell Gray. "Until then, just lay low. Cedric will get the reporters off your back."

Cedric gives me a look that says I shouldn't have promised her that, but I ignore him.

"I'll see you tonight," I tell Gray. She confirms, and we both hang up.

"See. No problem," I say.

Cedric rolls his eyes and looks at Kaladin. "I should get going on this."

"Go," Kaladin says, waving him off, and Cedric hurries out of the office to work his PR magic.

"Sorry," I say to Kaladin. "I was just trying to help the doc out."

I turn to go, but Kaladin calls me back. He stands with his arms crossed, the biceps straining against his Armani suit jacket confirming he must work out.

"Yes, sir?" I ask.

He picks up the picture of me and Gray from his desk, looks at it, then turns it to show me. "Are you sure this will be 'fake' dating?" he asks.

Something flips in my stomach, and I look at the picture.

I was definitely buzzed at the time it was taken, but I remember exactly how Gray smelled when I had my face buried in her hair. I remember the feel of her body pressed against mine and how hard my cock was as she rubbed against it on the dancefloor. I ached to slip my fingers between her thighs to see if she was as wet for me as I hoped.

If the entranced expression on Gray's face in that picture is any indication, she wanted me as much as I wanted her.

"We both had a little too much to drink," I tell Kaladin. "I'm sure you know what alcohol does to inhibitions."

He nods slowly, then turns to run the picture through the shredder behind his desk. "Fair enough," he says before turning back to me. "Just be sure to make it look real tonight."

"Yes, sir," I say and head for the door.

Make no mistake, for the next few weeks, I intend to convince everyone – including Gray herself – that we're a happily dating couple.

Chapter 16

Gray

"Can you put the other dress back on?" Celena asks as I twirl around in front of the laptop sitting on my bed.

I look down at the red dress I'm modeling for her through our Zoom call. "Not feeling this one?" I ask. "Too...red?"

"Too red," she says. "That's more for a third date when the paparazzi have lost interest, but you need to tell him you're ready to be fucked."

I roll my eyes hard at the camera. "There's not going to be a third date," I tell her. "This one's only for show to save both our careers, and then we'll quietly 'break up.'"

"Gray," she says, her tone dripping disappointment. "You have to fake date one of the hottest pro hockey players – no, hottest pro *athletes* – in the world right now. You need to milk this situation for all it's worth, if only so I can live vicariously through you."

I shake my head. "Not a good idea. You know my track record with men. Today we're only fake dating, but by next week I'll be checking my phone every few minutes, wondering why he hasn't texted, or checking his social media to see if he's posted anything lately. I'll drive by his office to see if his car is really still there when he says he has to work late-"

"We're not talking about Ash anymore, are we," she interrupts.

I don't answer, and my face burns with shame as I think how I went full stalker with Drew toward the end. I consider myself a relatively stable person, but I still cringe at how I acted.

It wasn't even that I wanted to be with him by that time. It just enraged me that he'd make plans with me, then come up with some lie to get out of them. I resented that he thought I'd believe the lies, and I was determined to catch him each time, just to show him I wasn't stupid.

I could've let him go if he'd just let *me* go.

"Put the other dress back on," Celena says gently.

I look at the pile of clothes sitting next to the laptop on my bed.

"Which other one?" I ask. "I tried on half my closet."

"The navy blue one," she says. "You look amazing in navy."

I fish in the pile and pull out the navy sheath dress she's talking about. The dress covers me up to the neck, has long sleeves, and goes just past my knees, so on the surface it seems conservative, but like the dress I wore to the club, it fits me like a second skin and shows off my figure.

My body isn't perfect. I have a few soft spots, and there are parts that are 'too this' or 'not enough that,' but overall I have a decent figure. Enough that, even with my confidence issues, I can wear a dress like this.

I slip off the red dress, toss it onto the pile, then shimmy the sheath dress up my body. I hear Celena whistle, and I look at her questioningly as I contort myself to pull up the zipper.

"You move like that for him, and the two of you won't make it to dessert," she says.

"You're not helping," I say.

"I'm your best friend. It's not my job to help. It's my job to talk you into buying fun stuff for yourself, urge you to do slightly crazy but not wholly dangerous things, and to be here to pick you up when the men you date inevitably let you down."

I give her a frustrated look. "How comforting."

She shrugs. "I don't make the rules."

I spin around in the dress. "Does this work?"

"Perfect!"

"Alright, I have to finish getting ready. I'll text you when I get home."

"You'll text me halfway through dinner from the restroom."

I sigh. "Fine."

"Have fun!" she says and hangs up the call.

I close the laptop, then work on finishing my look. I add a gold chain around my neck and slip into a pair of gold heels, then get to work on my hair and makeup. I took too long figuring out what to wear, and Ash will be here in twenty minutes.

I shouldn't be nervous – this isn't a real date – but there's a steady tremor in my chest that borders on giddiness.

Actually, fuck that. I have every right to be nervous. Every shade in my house is drawn right now because reporters have been camped out on my front lawn all day. Thankfully I was able to pull right into the garage and close the door on them when I got home.

I'm just barely done getting ready when my phone pings with a text from Ash telling me he just pulled up and is on his way to the front door.

My stomach drops, and I wonder if I have time for a shot of vodka.

No such luck. The doorbell rings, and I grab my clutch and shove my cell phone inside it before opening the front door.

Cameras flash, backlighting the tall figure filling the doorway and making me blink. When I can see again, I find Ash's eyes traveling back up my body.

"You look incredible," he breathes, and he sounds sincere.

I let my eyes run over him quickly. He wears a black suit with a royal blue shirt, and I decide the color was made for him. I hope I don't look too matchy in my navy dress, and it only occurs to me now that I'm wearing one of the Hydra's colors. I'm not sure if that's good or bad.

I'm about to return his compliment when he leans down, cups my face with one hand and kisses me. His lips move against mine tenderly, and the tip of his tongue flicks into my mouth before he pulls back. My body tingles, and I stop myself from falling forward to chase the kiss.

"Ready?" he asks, and I know he's not asking if I'm ready to go. He's asking if I'm ready to face the firing squad.

It takes me a moment to get my bearings, but I nod, and we turn to the group of reporters standing at the edge of my lawn. There's a steel-colored sports car in my driveway, but I know next to nothing about cars, so if it's not a Lamborghini or a Corvette, I'm clueless.

"I'll take three questions, and then you all need to leave my girlfriend alone from here on out," Ash says to the reporters as we head toward them. He slips an arm around my waist so his hand rests on my hip, and for several seconds my world narrows to that hand.

I highly doubt the reporters will honor his request, but they start shouting questions all at once.

"Is Gray working with you on your trash talk problem?" one shouts.

"*Dr.* Mackey," Ash says, emphasizing my title, "isn't a sports psychologist. And my problem isn't with trash talk. It's with no-talent jerks who need to chirp at others to make up for their inadequacies."

The reporters murmur at that, and I try not to react. He didn't directly answer the question about me, but the reporters seem more focused on Ash's own attempt at trash talk.

"How long have you and Gr-, uh, Dr. Mackey been dating?" another reporter asks.

"Six weeks, five hours, and…," Ash checks his watch, "forty-seven minutes. Not that I've been counting."

I give him an incredulous look, but he just grins at me and kisses my forehead. I do some quick math in my head, and while I'm not sure about the hours and minutes, six weeks ago sounds about the time Ash showed up at my office.

"Last question," Ash says, "then you all get lost."

"How do you feel about dating an older woman?" one of them shouts before anyone else can voice a question.

Both Ash and I go rigid. My stomach drops into my shoes, although I have no idea why I should care. It doesn't matter if I'm older than him because we're not actually dating.

I look up at Ash and pull back unconsciously at the expression on his face. I've seen it before. He's pissed, and he tightens his arm around me.

"That's a stupid question," Ash snaps. "She's barely three years older than me, and you're making her out to be some kind of cougar. But for the record, she could be twenty years older, and I'd still think she was one of the most amazing women I've ever met." He steers me toward his car, then calls back to the reporters, "Now clear out."

Ash opens the passenger side, and I slip into the seat as he shuts the door after me. The interior of the car is just as beautiful as the exterior, and I lean over to look at the logo on the steering wheel. It's a pair of wings with the words "Aston Martin" on them. Holy shit.

I sit up again as Ash opens the door and gets in. The car is already running, and he throws it in gear before backing down the driveway. I expect him to peel out faster than he should, but he backs out carefully and accelerates down the street like a normal human being.

"I'm sorry about that," he says.

I shrug. "Just reporters being reporters." I'm not entirely sure which part he's apologizing for.

"Yeah, well, fuck them. We're going to have fun tonight."

"Where are we going?" I ask.

"Chef Avery's new restaurant just got a Michelin Star," he says, "so we're going to go see if it was earned."

Sweet Jesus.

"You know you can take me to Outback Steakhouse and call it a day, right?" I tell him.

He side-eyes me. "No, I can't."

My phone dings with an incoming text, and I give him a small smile as I pull it out of my clutch.

"Sorry, it's probably my friend Celena checking in already," I say.

I swipe open the phone and pull up the message app, but my stomach bottoms out when I see who the text is from.

Drew

Hey.

Before I can react, another text comes through.

Drew

I've been thinking about you since the other night. I miss you.

My mouth hangs open, and I'm not sure I'm breathing. Months ago, texts like this from Drew would've sent me into a tailspin. I would've responded immediately, telling him I missed him too, and a dozen texts later I'd be asking to see him again.

Now, I can barely hold the phone, and the sight of the texts makes me queasy.

"Gray? You okay?"

Ash's voice jolts me back to reality, and I turn off the screen and shove the phone back into my clutch.

"Fine. It's just my mother. She drives me a little nuts sometimes."

"Who else do you have for family?" he asks. "Any siblings?"

"Just me," I say. "Only child. My dad is still around too."

"Did they see the news?"

"My mother's friend saw it and told her, and I got a call wondering how I could be such a neglectful daughter and not tell her about my famous new boyfriend."

"And you said?"

I shrug. "I was busy with classes and just didn't have time to tell her."

"And that worked?"

"Of course not. I owe her dinner and a full accounting of our relationship thus far."

He chuckles. "I haven't heard from my parents and sisters yet, but they're used to me forgetting to tell them things like who I'm dating. It's not the first time they'll learn about my love life online."

"Or your fake love life?" I offer with a half-smile.

He doesn't speak right away. "Right," he says finally, but his smile seems strangely forced.

The rest of the ride is comfortable enough. I learn that one of Ash's sisters is older and the other is younger. The older one works in corporate law, while the younger is finishing up an MBA, and according to Ash, they taught him everything he knows about feminism.

Someone had. People sometimes think I'm being pretentious when they call me "Miss" and I correct them with "Dr.," but women faculty members are far more likely to be misaddressed than our male counterparts. None of my male colleagues get called "Mr." They all get addressed as "Dr." or at least "Professor," but my female colleagues are frequently addressed as "Miss," "Ms.," or "Mrs.," even if they aren't married. It's just disheartening when you've gone through the same schooling as everyone else and published a dissertation to not have that achievement acknowledged based on gender.

It meant a lot that Ash insisted the reporters refer to me by my title, and I add yet another item to the pile of reasons it would be entirely too easy for me to fall in love with him.

They're starting to overshadow the myriad reasons I can't.

Chapter 17

Gray

We pull up to the restaurant twenty minutes later, and valets hurry to open the doors of the car for me and Ash. He slips both of them some money before he threads his fingers through mine and leads me inside to the maître d'.

I feel like royalty as we enter the lavish restaurant. Celena is right. Fake or not, I need to enjoy the hell out of this while it lasts.

Ash's hand rests on the small of my back as the maître d' leads us to an upper level with floor-to-ceiling windows that overlook the water. The upper half of the windows and parts of the sides are made of stained glass in abstract designs of blue, green, and purple that are lit from outside and must look absolutely incredible when the sun is still out.

We get to our table, and Ash pulls out my chair for me. I can't help remembering how I'd dreaded the thought of Barry doing this weeks ago, but all thoughts of Barry vanish as Ash's hand skims along my shoulder before he takes his own chair.

The second we're seated, waitstaff descend on the table. They pour water for us, hand us steaming towelettes that we use to wash our hands, and set down bread and a shot glass of what appears to be some kind of cold fruit puree.

"Would you like to see the wine list?" one of them asks.

Ash looks at me, and I nod at the waiter. "Yes, please."

Something tells me I won't find anything here in my price range, but I need to look out of morbid curiosity. Ash said he was 'taking me out to dinner' tonight, and I have a feeling he'll insist on paying, but I still plan to order as if I'm covering my half of the bill.

The waiter hands me a tablet, and I start clicking on options to see what they have for wine. As anticipated, most of the prices are out of my comfort zone, but I'm determined to find something I can drink.

"I take it you like wine," Ash says.

I give him an apologetic smile. "I love wine. I never developed a taste for beer. Do you like it?"

"I've never had good wine," he says. "Maybe you can teach me a thing or two about it."

"I've never had wine like this," I admit, gesturing to the menu. "This is all a bit out of my normal fare."

"Get whatever you want," he says. "Don't look at price. It's my treat."

I huff a small laugh as I continue to scan the options. "That's very generous, but…Oh my God. Scarecrow."

"What?" Ash asks.

I look up at him. "They have Scarecrow Wine. It's a vineyard that was owned by J.J. Cohn, who was an executive producer on *The Wizard of Oz*. His land was right next to Inglenook, and the winemaker there convinced Cohn in the 1940s to plant grapes he could buy. Now it's basically a boutique winery that sells almost exclusively to members. I didn't even know restaurants could carry it."

"Maybe Chef Avery is a member," Ash suggests.

I shrug. "Maybe."

"Have we found something we like?" a waiter asks, appearing tableside as if conjured from thin air.

"We'll take a bottle of the Scarecrow," Ash says.

I look up at him in alarm. I could buy a used car for the price of the bottle. I mean, not a good used car, a clunker maybe, but still.

"Ash, the bottle is-," I try to warn him, but he cuts me off.

"Scarecrow," he assures the waiter, who takes the hint and scurries off before I can protest any more.

I stare at him, but he just shrugs.

"I like spoiling my woman," he says.

I lean toward him. "I'm not actually your woman. We're pretending, remember?" I say in a low voice.

His jaw clenches, and I lean back, aware I've upset him somehow.

"Until we officially fake break up," Ash says, "you *are* my woman, and I plan to treat you like I'd treat someone I was dating."

There's a slight bite to his voice, and I nod slowly. Experience tells me I've wounded his masculine pride, but that doesn't fit with the Ash I've gotten to know the last few weeks.

"Okay," I say. "I'm sorry if I offended you."

His face softens, and he shakes his head. "You didn't offend me. I just get the feeling the men you've dated haven't treated you very well, so the men you fake date will just have to make up for it."

I can't help the smile that creeps up my face. "You're insane," I say, too moved by the sentiment to adequately express my gratitude. Saying thank you seems too trite or maybe too intimate at the moment, so I opt for a mild insult to mask my discomposure.

In truth, I'm terrified by how Ash is treating me. I can't fall for him. This situation is only temporary, and I'm heading for a world of hurt if I let myself make it real.

The waiter returns with the bottle and presents it to us. Ash looks at me for guidance, and I nod. The waiter opens the bottle and hands the cork to Ash, who looks confused. I try to mime smelling it, but he doesn't understand and just hands it to me. I bring it to my nose and inhale.

Some people think you smell the cork to see if you like the scent and thus will like the wine, but what you're really smelling for is cork taint. Sometimes bottles, especially older ones, can go bad, and a good whiff of the cork can usually tell you if there might be a problem.

On this cork, I only smell hints of cranberry, red currant, and maybe some baking spices. My mouth begins to water.

I nod to the waiter, and – having caught on – he pours an ounce of the wine into my glass. I swirl it and sniff, smelling the same things I got from the cork, plus maybe a hint of cocoa.

I take a small sip, letting it hang in my mouth before I swallow it down. I can't help but calculate how much money that one sip just cost Ash, but sweet God, it was worth it.

I take another sip, and the wine feels like velvet on my tongue. The acidity of the berry flavors hits me, followed by more savory notes of cedar and tobacco on the finish, which linger.

People who don't drink wine are often perplexed by how flavors like tobacco, fresh cut grass, wet stone, or graphite can be good, but for some reason, it just works in wine, and this wine works very well. Maybe not price-of-a-cheap-car well, but it's damn good wine.

"Excellent," I tell the waiter and set my glass down for him to fill it.

"Sir?" the waiter asks Ash after he's poured my wine.

"Yes, please," Ash says.

I watch Ash carefully as he sniffs the wine in his glass then takes a sip when the waiter leaves.

"What do you think?" I ask.

"I think I need red meat now," he says.

I laugh. "A good bottle of red wine will do that."

Gray

Forty-five minutes later, we're both on our second glass of wine, and Ash is enjoying his with a medium-rare steak. He let me try a bite, and it paired fantastically with the Scarecrow. I almost regret ordering seafood, but my dish is so orgasm-inducingly good that I can't bring myself to wish I'd ordered steak. I wouldn't normally drink red with seafood, but the lobster and scallop dish called to me, and we'd already bought the Scarecrow, so it is what it is.

The conversation is easy. Ash tells me more about his family and how he got into hockey, and I share the numerous ways my mother gets under my skin on a weekly basis. We covered some personal things during our recent text exchanges, but they weren't conducive to deep conversation, so this is our first time discussing a lot of these topics.

I also tell Ash more about Celena, who's the only person on my end that knows we're fake dating. Well, Celena and now Melinda.

"All the guys on the team know the relationship is fake, right?" I ask.

"Yeah, but they won't say anything. It's a PR issue, so they'll tow the line," Ash says.

He takes another sip of the Scarecrow. He's taken to wine quickly, but I hope he doesn't expect all wine to taste this good.

"Kelsier's the only one who doesn't believe it's fake," Ash adds.

"What? Why not?"

He shrugs. "He's convinced there's something between you and me."

I look at him carefully. There's a certain tone to his voice, almost as though he's probing for my reaction to this news.

"What makes him think that?" I ask. I drop my eyes to my food, pretending I'm more interested in that than the answer to the question.

"I don't know," he says. "Just little things he thinks he sees about the way we act around each other." He pauses. "Let's say this was a real date. What would you do to show me you were interested?"

My fork stops halfway to my mouth as I look at him. His eyes are bright with interest, and I feel the challenge in the question. Maybe it's the two glasses of wine, but he wants to push the date into flirtation, and it doesn't take more than his nudge for me to willingly follow.

"Let me think," I say as I bring the bite to my mouth. I close my lips around the fork, then slide it slowly back out as sensually as I can as I pretend to consider.

My hair is down tonight, so I reach up and push a stray lock behind my ear as I chew, then pull the rest back slowly over my shoulder to expose my neck. The dress doesn't allow me to show much skin, but this is the one place I can entice his gaze. I arch my head to the side to display the column of my neck and gently run my fingers down the side as I pretend to think some more.

"I don't know," I say. "I suppose I'd try to draw your eyes somewhere you might want to put your mouth."

I glance at Ash to see him sitting very still, his mouth parted, his eyes fixed on my neck.

"What about you?" I ask. "What would you do on a date to let a woman know you were interested?"

Ash drags his eyes away from my neck and smiles, realizing what I did. He puts his fork down and leans back in his chair. He crosses his arms over his chest, and his biceps bulge against the fabric of his jacket as he thinks.

"Me personally?" he says after a few seconds. "I'd find ways to touch her whenever possible. Like, I'd put my hand at the small of her back when we walk. Graze her shoulder when I pass by. 'Accidentally' grab the bottle of wine at the same time she does so our fingers touch."

I stare at him, and I swear my heart trips over itself. He's done all those things tonight, and now my mind reels with the question of whether all that was just for show as I'd assumed, or whether Ash really is trying to tell me he's interested.

No, don't be ridiculous, I chide myself. Fake dating needs to look convincing or it doesn't work. I can't let myself think the charade is real.

"So let's say the thing with your neck got the guy's attention," Ash says, spearing a piece of steak with his fork. "What's your next move?"

I shake myself back to reality and consider a moment. Honestly, I'm not much of a flirt, so my arsenal isn't big. I might find a way to draw a man's attention to my cleavage if I were wearing a different dress, but this one has too high a neckline. It doesn't matter, though. Ash and I are playing a game, so my next move can be something out-of-character. If he can pretend, then so can I.

I slip off my shoe on the side of the table facing the windows. The tablecloth is long enough so no one should be able to see what I'm doing unless they're looking for it, and I find Ash's ankle under the table with my toes. His legs are long, so he's easy to reach, and I run the top of my foot up the inside of his calf outside his pants.

Ash's knife screeches across his plate loudly, and my foot stops as he looks around and mumbles an apology to diners nearby. Thankfully, the tables are spaced relatively far apart in this area of the restaurant.

When the attention is off us again, I move my foot higher. I reach his knee, then push my luck and start to slide my toes along the inside of his thigh. His eyes flare, and I'm about to smile and withdraw my foot when he reaches under the table and grabs my ankle. I jolt in surprise, and my gaze locks with his.

"I'm not sure doing something like that is a good idea," he says, his voice taking on a huskiness that makes my stomach flutter.

"Why not?" I ask, barely above a whisper.

Ash's thumb caresses back and forth against the inside of my ankle, and it's all I can do not to whimper audibly.

"Well, if a woman ran her foot up my leg like that for real," he says in a low voice, still gripping my ankle, "I might just snap and haul her into my lap, hike up her dress, and finger fuck her pussy until she screamed her orgasm in the middle of a Michelin Star restaurant."

My jaw drops open, and Ash grins enough that his dimples appear.

"That seems like an extreme reaction to some teasing," I say hoarsely, but, God help me, I can't help picturing Ash doing it.

Ash shrugs. "I suppose it depends. If it was a woman I already spend half the daydreaming about fucking, maybe a little teasing like that would send me over the edge."

My mouth works, trying to form words, but I have no idea what to say. My brain tries to convince me he's still speaking in hypotheticals, but I know he's not. The realization Ash Gunnarsson might actually want me has caused a complete system shutdown.

"I…," I start to say but can't get any farther.

"Are you ticklish?" Ash asks suddenly, and his other hand moves under the table to tickle the underside of my foot.

It takes all my self-control not to scream, but I jerk my foot so violently that my knee hits the underside of the table with a loud thud, and everything on it jumps. Mercifully, the wine glasses stay standing.

Once again, the eyes of a few diners swing our way, but Ash stops tickling me, and we both sit perfectly still until they look away again.

Finally, Ash lets go of my ankle, and I slip it back into my shoe.

"I…hate being tickled," I say quietly.

"Sorry," he murmurs, and I feel bad for saying anything.

God dammit. I need help here.

"I'll be right back. I need to run to the ladies' room," I say as I rise from my seat and grab my clutch.

Ash looks alarmed.

"I'm not dining and dashing," I assure him with a smile. "I swear. You're my ride, and I'm too cheap to Uber."

He looks at me as if gauging whether or not to believe me, then nods.

I hurry to the restroom and duck inside a stall. I was hoping to call Celena, but there are a couple women in the restroom with me, so I have to settle for texting instead.

Gray

> Help. Ash bought me a bottle of wine that costs as much as my first car, and he just threatened to finger fuck me in the middle of the restaurant when I ran my foot up his leg.

I hit send on the text and pee while I'm waiting for a response. I've left out a lot of context, but I hit the important points.

My phone starts to ring, but I send it to voicemail and text Celena.

Gray

> Can't talk. Restroom is not secure.

The bouncing dots indicate Celena is typing, and her message comes through seconds later.

Celena

> WTF Gray! You can't send a message like that then tell me we can't talk!

Gray

Sorry, can't be helped. Wine isn't the important part. We were teasing each other with hypotheticals, and I ran my foot up his leg. He said "hypothetically" if a woman did that to him on a real date, he'd pull her onto his lap and finger fuck her.

I hit send but then add another nugget.

Gray

Then he implied he thought about fucking me half the day.

A string of exploding-head emojis pop up on the screen.

Gray

What do I do?

I wait as the dots start bouncing again.

Celena

…Let him fuck you?

I push out a long breath and roll my eyes.

Gray

Not helpful.

Celena

I refer you to our earlier conversation about this.

Gray

I can't have sex with him.

Celena

Why not?

My fingers hover above the screen, ready to type out my reply, but words elude me. The usual arguments about ethics don't seem relevant anymore. We've told the world we're dating, and nothing has collapsed. I haven't been given a scarlet letter to wear. Everyone assumes we're having sex anyway, so…Why not?

Gray

Celena

I roll my eyes again but send a thumbs up emoji and shove the phone back in my clutch. I let myself glance at the message app just close enough to see that there are no additional texts from Drew other than the first two, and I already promised myself I won't answer them.

The world thinks I'm dating Ash, so I can't even consider dating Drew, which is a good thing. Even responding to Drew's texts to remind him I'm dating Ash is just playing with fire.

It hits me that we told Drew at the club we were dating, and he still texted to say he missed me. Even if he hasn't seen the news, he's choosing to ignore I'm dating Ash, or he doesn't believe it, and now I'm pissed.

I leave the stall, wash my hands, and head back to Ash, suddenly feeling reckless.

Chapter 18

I glance at Gray in the passenger seat of my car as I drive her home, and I can't tell if I completely fucked up or if I'm getting laid tonight.

I clearly freaked her out when I threatened to finger fuck her in the restaurant, then I only made it worse by tickling her foot and nearly causing her to upset the table. She assured me she was coming back from the restroom, but part of me doubted it until she sat down again.

I'm completely out of my league with Gray. She's unlike any other woman I've ever dated…or fake dated. I haven't dated a lot of women, but most have been bunnies who fawned over me and wanted to show me off. Only two were different – the VP of a big insurance company and Grace – but even they imposed expectations on me, and it was one of the things that eventually drove a wedge between us.

Gray has seemed hell-bent on keeping her distance, and it was driving me crazy, but something changed about her since she got back from the bathroom. When we left after dessert, she pressed herself up against me as we waited for the valet, and I had to will my dick into submission so I wasn't tempted to throw her on the hood and fuck her right there when my car pulled up.

She seems back to normal now as we head to her place, but I'm wary of saying anything.

I checked my phone while she was in the bathroom, and I had twenty-seven messages. Two were from Kelsier on our private chat, asking me how the non-date date was going. The rest were on the Hydra's team chat and ranged from the benign – "Hope it's going well!" – to the suggestive

– "Should we tell coach you won't be at practice tomorrow?" – to the outright lewd – "Did you fuck her yet? Send pics."

God damn rookies. I'll have to have a little conversation with some of them about text chain etiquette.

"You okay?" I ask Gray finally. It's been several minutes since either of us has spoken, and I take a chance and lay my hand gently on her thigh just above her knee. She jumps, but I'm not sure if it's because of my hand, my voice breaking the silence, or both.

Her eyes linger on my hand, and I almost pull it back when she finally looks at me and smiles.

"I'm fine. Just thinking," she says. A pause, then, "I had a really nice time tonight. Thank you for dinner. That was amazing."

"I'm glad you enjoyed it," I say. Three seconds roll under my tires before I add, "Look, I'm sorry if I freaked you out earlier. I just-"

"No!" she assures me quickly. "No freaking out. You took me by surprise, especially since this isn't real, but I'm fine."

My jaw clenches on instinct the way it does now every time she reminds me this isn't a real relationship. If it's so God damn fake, then why does it feel like the most real thing I've had in my life?

And it's not just desire. Yes, I want to be inside her, to have her beneath me so badly it hurts right now, but it's not just my dick that aches. I feel it in my stomach too. In my chest. In my fucking toes.

This isn't a fake relationship, even if only one of us knows that right now.

I need to relax, though. Despite what Gray says, I definitely freaked her out, and if I don't ease her into this, she'll run for it. For one, I'm a little kinky in bed, and I don't want to scare her off.

I take my hand off her leg as I pull into her driveway and scowl at the news van parked across the street. There's only one, and I'm not sure if the reporters just didn't listen to me when I warned them off earlier, or if this station wasn't here before and didn't get the memo.

I turn off the car and hurry to open Gray's door. I help her out, then thread my fingers through hers as we walk to her front door. She fishes in her clutch for her keys and unlocks the door before turning to me.

"Thank you again for everything," she says, and I feel the sudden uncertainty between us.

If the news van wasn't here, I'd see if she invited me in, but I won't go in with it there. The world probably already assumes I'm fucking her, but I have no intention of giving them footage for the late news.

"You're welcome," I say. "I had fun. I like to see you happy."

I'm trying to play this cool, but I sound like an idiot. Still, it's better than what I really want to say, which is that I want to drag her into her house, tie her to her own bed, and fuck her raw until she's hoarse from screaming my name.

Maybe I'll save that revelation for date two.

Gray glances at her door, then back at me. "Do…you want to come in?" she asks, and my dick tries to answer for me by going rock hard.

I swallow down the string of curses that gather in my throat and step closer to her. I need to say goodnight, but I'll be damned if I'm not at least going to kiss her.

"Not with the news crew here," I say. "They don't need to think we're sleeping together yet."

"News crew?" Gray looks at me, confused, then spots the van. "Shit. I didn't even see them."

"I'm going to kiss you goodnight, then I'm going to go," I say.

Laying out the plan is more for my benefit than hers. Step one, kiss her. Step two, leave. Simple enough.

Gray nods slowly. "Okay."

I know what I need to do, I have her permission to do it, but I can't move. I'm afraid if I touch her, I'll end up mauling her. I can't remember the last time I wanted a woman this badly.

Gray waits patiently, and I finally reach out. I slip one hand around her waist and gently pull her toward me. My other hand glides up her neck to wrap around her nape, and I feel her shiver. Either I tickled her again, or she wants this as much as I do.

I lean in close and let my lips graze hers. Her head tips up, requesting more, and I have my answer. I press my lips down on hers and deepen the kiss. She parts her mouth, allowing my tongue in, and I will myself not to spontaneously combust.

I try to tether my mind in place, to remember I'm on the porch in front of Gray's house with a news van parked a few dozen feet away. Otherwise, I'll completely surrender to this moment. As it is, I'm fighting not to push her up against the house and let raw need take over.

Control. That's what Gray and I have been practicing, and that's what I need now. If it can keep me from beating the shit out of Lapointe the next time I see him, it can keep me from giving the neighbors a scene they might see on PornHub.

I step away from Gray, but my hand on her waist hasn't gotten the message that it's time to go, and I have to force myself to pull it back.

"Are you coming to practice tomorrow?" I ask.

I try not to let her hear the hope in my voice. I feel like I play better when she's there, and, according to the guys, I do.

"Um, yeah. I may be a little late, but I can be there," she says, and it seems like she's trying to get her own bearings.

I nod. "Sounds good." I try to sound casual, but the inflection in my voice is too high to pull it off. "Have a good night."

She smiles. "Good night. And thanks again."

I give her a quick nod, then wait for her to open her door and get inside before I head to my car. I dial Kelsier as I back down the driveway, and he picks up right away.

"How'd it go?" he asks eagerly.

"You alone?"

"Yeah, I'm home watching TV."

"None of this ends up on the team chat," I warn him.

"Dude, seriously," he says, offended. Then he perks up. "Wait, did something happen? What happened?"

"What happened is I bought her a ridiculously expensive bottle of wine then threatened to finger fuck her in the middle of the restaurant."

There's a long pause, then the background TV noise goes silent.

"I'm sorry. Can you repeat that?"

I tell him everything that happened from the moment I picked her up to when I dropped her off a few minutes ago.

"Holy shit," he says when I'm done. "You shelled out that much for wine and didn't even get laid?"

I make a noise of disgust as he starts to laugh.

"You're an asshole," I tell him. "Do you have anything useful to say?"

"I do, but I'm not sure you want to hear it."

"Try me."

"Well, it kind of sounds like you're in love with her."

There's silence while I digest that. "You're full of shit," I say finally.

"Yeah, told you you didn't want to hear it."

"I mean, I like her a lot, and I want her so bad my dick feels like it's about to fall off, but don't you think it's a little premature to throw around the L word? What if I fuck her and the sex is awful?"

"Are you planning to fuck her?" he asks.

I pause. "I want to. But she thinks this is all fake. I'm not sure how I convince her we need to have real sex to sell fake dating."

It's his turn to pause. "You said she thinks this is all fake. It sounds like *you* don't think it is."

I didn't expect him to catch that.

"I mean…there's no harm in her thinking it's just fake dating even if I know it's real dating, right?" I ask hopefully. "Do both parties have to agree it's dating for it to be dating?"

"No, as long as one party says it's dating, it's legit. Stalkers do it all the time," he says sarcastically. "What the fuck is wrong with you? Of course both parties have to agree it's dating!"

I consider potential loopholes, then ask, "Is there a standard timeline for both parties to agree it's dating before it can be official?"

Kelsier sighs. "Why don't you just tell her you like her and ask her if she wants to date for real?" he suggests.

I scoff. "Now who's being ridiculous?"

He sighs again. "Fine, do it your way. What could possibly go wrong?"

"That's the spirit."

"So are you going out again?"

"We didn't discuss it, but she's coming to the training center tomorrow," I offer. "I can ask her about a second date then."

"You're a regular Casanova," he says.

"I always thought I was more of a Romeo."

"Romeo dies in that play, you know."

"Really? Fuck. I should've paid more attention in English class."

"On second thought," he says, "you *are* pretty tragic. Let's stick with Romeo."

"Fuck you."

He chuckles. "So what are you going to tell the rest of the guys about the date? You need to respond to the team text chain eventually."

"I'll tell them the truth. We had a nice dinner, then I dropped her off at home and kissed her goodnight."

He groans. "Boring. At the very least you need to tell them about the wine. I bet you paid more for it than that piece of junk Fig drives."

I think a moment. "Any suggestions on what I should say? I need just enough to appease them without telling them too much." I pause before adding, "And I need to have a little conversation with the rookies."

"I'll help you with that conversation," he says. "Please tell me we were never that bad when we were that age."

I sigh. "I'm not sure about you, but I was probably worse."

I hear his sigh as well. "Yeah. Me too. Thank God we're older and wiser now."

I chuckle. "By the way, is all still quiet on the Kingston front?"

"Yeah, it doesn't look like he's interested in Gray," he says. "I brought her up casually around him earlier today, and he more-or-less ignored me.

If he was interested, he would've made a move at the club."

"He was focused on that puck bunny," I say, playing devil's advocate.

"And you don't think he would've taken them both back to his place?" Kelsier asks.

"Touché."

A small part of me is almost angry Kingston doesn't consider Gray worthy of his attention, but the larger, saner part is relieved he doesn't want her. Because fuck keeping the goalie happy. I'm not giving her up, even if Kingson implodes and it costs us the rest of the season.

Chapter 19

Ash

I feel like I'm flying rather than skating the next day at practice. Gray is in the stands watching, and I can do no wrong. Every shot I take finds the back of the net, and I weave in and out of players like I'm on the highway in the middle of a high-speed chase.

Kelsier and I have also checked the shit out of the two rookies who were the rudest on the team text chain, and I think they got the message.

If only I could play this way during games. Somewhere along the way I let the chirping get to me, and I need to find a way back to that Zen I used to have whenever I stepped onto the ice.

Oddly enough, this fake dating thing with Gray has given me a sort of peace. To be sure, I'm sexually frustrated as hell, but the idea that she and I have to spend time together to sell the dating story makes me stupidly happy. I'd almost consider Kelsier's suggestion we date for real, except that I'm not sure how Kaladin would take it. He's paying Gray to help me play, not date me.

Gray is waiting by the door to the locker room when I exit after practice, freshly showered, and I swear I see her run her eyes up and down my body.

I know now she's attracted to me. The way she reacted at the club and her flirting at dinner last night confirmed it. She's holding back for some reason, but I can work with that.

"Hey," I say, smiling at her. I pull her gently against me and press a soft kiss on her lips.

All the guys know about the fake dating ploy, so we're not fooling anyone here, but I don't care. Call me a method actor. I just think staying in character is the safest bet.

Plus it conveniently lets me touch and kiss Gray whenever I want.

Gray let's out a soft "Oh" when I pull back.

"You never know who could be watching," I say. "Best to be safe."

"Right," she says, although she sounds unconvinced.

I just smile and kiss her temple.

"Get a room, you two," Fig says as he comes out of the locker room.

"Hi, Fig," Gray says, smiling at him.

"Doc," he says smiling back and giving her a salute before he heads down the hall.

A few other guys exit the locker room and say hi as they head toward the garage. Kingston is with them, but he doesn't spare us a glance, and I let out a sigh of relief. Even if he was interested in Gray, our fake dating story keeps him from being able to take her from me. Still, it's comforting to know he doesn't want her, since I don't know enough about Gray's taste in men to determine if she'd be attracted to him or not.

She didn't seem impressed with him at the club, which made me entirely too pleased. On the other hand, he's an asshole, and that seems to be exactly her type. I'm not sure what it says that she's attracted to me but won't let herself act on it.

"Hey, love birds," Kelsier says as he comes out of the locker room, and we both roll our eyes at him.

"Mirroring each other's mannerisms already," he says, laughing. "The next step is finishing each other's sentences."

"Fuck off, Kels," I tell him, but there's no bite, and he just chuckles.

"I heard the date went well last night," he says to Gray, and her cheeks pinken prettily.

Oh, the things I want to do to this woman that would make her blush.

"Exactly what did you hear about the date?" she asks suspiciously.

Kelsier shrugs. "I heard something about a private jet to Italy, dinner at a Tuscan vineyard, and an orgy, but Gunny does tend to exaggerate."

I glare at him, but he grins back unapologetically.

Gray laughs. "Definitely an exaggeration. Only the orgy is true."

Both my mouth and Kelsier's drop open at that. Well fuck me. The prim little professor doesn't mind joking about sex.

"Doc! You kinky minx!" Kelsier says, feigning shock. He punches my arm. "And you didn't invite me, you asshole?"

"You said you were busy washing your hair last night," I shoot back.

He runs a hand through his dark blonde locks. "Yeah, well, it takes a lot of work to look this good." He points a finger at me. "But next time I'm in."

"I'll make a note," I deadpan.

My phone rings, and I pull it out of my pocket. The screen says it's my father, who almost never calls unless he needs something important.

"Would you excuse me?" I tell Gray and Kelsier. "It's my dad. I have to take this."

Both of them tell me to go, and I step away to answer the phone.

"Dad, hey," I say. "What's up. Is everything okay?"

The voice that answers, however, is not my father's.

"No, everything is not okay," my older sister Inga says on the other end. "I've been trying to reach my baby brother for weeks now, but he's been dodging my texts and calls."

I close my eyes. Fuck.

"Inga, why are you using Dad's phone?" I ask, although I know why.

"Because you won't answer when I use mine," she shoots back. "I knew you wouldn't ignore him, though."

I sigh. "What do you need?"

"For one, I need to know who this woman you're dating is," she says. "Where did you meet her? How long has this been going on? When are you bringing her up to meet the family? Is she coming to the wedding? And why are your sisters and parents finding out about her on the news rather than directly from you?"

I groan inwardly. I knew this phone call was coming, but I've been too distracted to worry about it.

"Sorry," I say. "I've been a bit busy lately."

"Too busy to let your family know you met someone, and a university professor at that?" she counters.

I had a feeling Gray's job would score some points with Inga. She always looked down on Grace and the other women I dated because they didn't fit her definition of a strong, successful woman. The only woman she liked was the VP I dated for a while. If she knew what that woman let me do to her in the bedroom, though, she might have changed her tune.

"I was going to call this week," I lie.

"Bullshit," she says. "You finally meet a woman with brains, and I have to find out about it on the internet." She pauses. "Although if she's dating you, maybe I have to rethink how smart she is."

"Fuck you," I tell her. Inga and I have always had an antagonistic relationship, but I know she's just teasing me.

"When are you bringing her up to meet everyone?" Inga presses.

"I don't know. We're in the middle of the season. I'd have to find a stretch where we don't have a game and then see if I can work around practices. I'm not sure I can swing it anytime-"

"Ash?" My mother's voice comes on the phone, and I squeeze my eyes shut. Inga called in the nuclear option.

"Hi, Mom. How are you?" I say, softening my voice. "I miss you."

"I miss you too," she says. "We'd love to see you if you can find a little time to come up."

I open my mouth to answer, but she goes on before I can.

"Make sure you bring your pretty new girlfriend," she says. "What's her name?"

"Gray, Mom," I say. "Her name is Gray."

"Oh, that's fun," she says. "Ash is a shade of gray."

That stops me, and I huff a laugh. The color connection between our names never occurred to me.

"Listen, Mom," I try again, but Inga knew what she was doing putting my mother on.

"I know you're busy, *elskan mín*," my mother says, using her Icelandic endearment for me, "but it's been a while since you've been home, and your father could really use some help with a few things if you have time to come up."

I sigh heavily, realizing I've lost the battle.

"I'll see what I can do," I say. "Gray may not be able to get the time off, though. She has to teach class."

"Oh. But, isn't the American Thanksgiving coming up in a few weeks?" she asks. "She'll get a break then, won't she?"

My mother may pretend to be sweet and innocent, but she's as sharp as a tack.

I make one final attempt to get out of a drive up to Canada.

"Yeah, but she may want to spend the holiday with her own family. I'll have to see."

"I know you'll do your best," my mother says, and I will, because disappointing my mother is never an option.

"I…I'll find a way to make it happen," I say. "I have to go now. I'll be in touch soon."

"Oh good," she says. "But I think Inga still-"

"Bye, Mom. I love you!" I hang up the phone before she can put my sister back on and head to where Gray and Kelsier are waiting.

"Everything okay?" Kelsier asks.

"Yeah, Inga just used my dad's phone to ambush me."

"Inga? Your older sister?" Gray asks, fishing the name from our conversation last night.

"She's been trying to talk to me for weeks, and I've been avoiding her," I say. "The news about us dating threw her over the edge, though."

"Let me guess," Kelsier says. "She's not happy she found out about it secondhand."

"She got my mother involved," I say.

"Oof," he says. "What's your penance?"

"That's the tricky part," I say. "And I'll need help with it."

"What kind of help?" Gray asks.

I catch her gaze and smile apologetically. "How would you feel about driving up to Canada the week of Thanksgiving to meet my family?"

Chapter 20

My heart pounds in my ears as we pull up to Ash's parents' house for dinner a few weeks later. What the hell was I thinking to agree to this?

This isn't just any dinner. This is a meet-the-family dinner we had to drive seven hours up to Canada on Thanksgiving Day to have. Luckily, Ash's parents live just over the border in Niagra-on-the-Lake. His sisters live much closer, one in Buffalo, New York, the other in Hamilton, Ontario. We'll spend the night so we don't have to do fourteen hours of driving in a day.

"I can't do this," I blurt out as Ash turns off his Aston Martin in front of the sage-colored ranch-style house. There's already two other cars in the driveway, which means his sisters likely beat us here.

Ash raises a brow. "It's a little late for that, don't you think?"

"I'll wait in the car," I say.

"I'm not driving back to Connecticut tonight."

"Just bring me out a blanket and pillow after dessert," I insist.

Ash gives me an indulgent look and gets out of the car. He comes around to my door and tries to open it, but I lock it quickly. Ash gives me a look through the window that says '*Really?*' and unlocks the door with his fob. He yanks it open before I can hit the button again.

"Let's go," he says. "My family doesn't bite, and my mother is an amazing cook."

I sigh and get out of the car. I'm wearing a knee-length teal dress and flats. Nice but not overly fancy.

Ash closes the door, then goes around to the trunk and slings both my overnight bag and his own over his shoulder. He comes back and offers me his arm. I take it, because what else am I going to do?

The front door flies open as we ascend the porch stairs and a woman in her fifties rushes out with a huge smile on her face. Ash drops the bags on the porch just in time to catch her as she flings herself into his arms.

"You made it. Right on time," the woman says as she pulls back and cups his face in her hands. "Did you have a good trip? No problems at the border?"

"The guards hassled me about not playing for a Canadian team," Ash tells her with a smile, "but otherwise everything was fine."

The woman's blue eyes swing to me, and I freeze like a rabbit spotted by coyote. Her smile widens as she surges toward me, and I force myself not to scurry back from her. She pulls me into a hug, and my eyes widen as I hug her back awkwardly.

"And you must be Gray," the woman says. Her face goes serious for a moment as she pulls back. "Or do you prefer Dr. Mackey?"

I nearly choke. I'd never make my fake boyfriend's family call me by my title. "Gray is more than fine," I tell her.

"I'm Ash's mother, Sigga," the woman says as she steps back.

I manage a smile of my own. "It's wonderful to meet you."

"Mom, at least let them get inside first," a younger woman with golden brown hair says from the doorway.

Sigga waves a dismissive hand. "Right, right. Come on in."

She heads into the house, and Ash and I follow her into the living room where we're greeted by another woman and an older man who is unmistakably Ash's father.

Ash hugs his father and sisters, and they all turn as one to look at me.

"Gray," Ash says, coming to stand next to me, "this is my father Gunnar, and my sisters Inga and Petra."

I can't help my blink. Somewhere in the back of my mind, I knew that with the last name Gunnarsson, Ash's father would be named Gunnar, but it still takes me by surprise. Working with hundreds of students a year, you'd think I'd be used to different international naming conventions, but this one slipped by me.

Ash turns to his family as he puts an arm around my waist. "This is my girlfriend, Gray Mackey."

His father and sisters step up to shake my hand and greet me warmly.

I look at Ash. "Is…Ash an Icelandic name?" I ask him softly. It never occurred to me to question it, but the rest of his family all have names that sound distinctly Icelandic.

"No, it's not," his sister Inga answers before he can. "In fact, the word for 'ash' in Icelandic, *aska*, is feminine." She wears a half smirk, and I'm suddenly sorry I asked.

I look at Ash with apology, but he must be used to this because his look is resigned.

"Ash was our first child born in the US when we moved there from Iceland," Sigga explains. "We wanted to give him an American name, and one of our neighbors at the time suggested Ash because one of the volcanos had just erupted back home in Iceland."

"I think he was joking," Gunnar cuts in.

Sigga shrugs. "We checked, and it was a common enough name for boys over here, so we decided to go with it."

"We gave him a good Icelandic middle name, though," Gunnar adds, making me think the name Ash was mostly his wife's idea. "So he can use that when he visits Iceland."

"Which I do," Ash says to me softly.

I think back to my search on Ash and try to recall his middle name. Dagur, I think?

"The council never would've approved the name Ash," Inga notes.

"Council?" I ask.

"Iceland has a council of three people who approve names for children," Petra explains. "They reject anything that isn't Icelandic enough. They would've had a problem with the word being feminine."

Inga shakes her head. "There have been gender exceptions before," she says. "A family went to court to let their daughter keep the name Blær, even though it's a masculine word. They won the case, but probably because the name at least has some basis in Icelandic. They likely would've rejected Ash for being too American."

I recall Inga is a lawyer, so her familiarity with the case isn't surprising.

"I'll bring those to the spare room," Gunnar says, taking our bags from Ash. He's clearly trying to change the subject or just get out of the room. "Sit down and relax."

We all sit down in the living room and Sigga brings out a charcuterie platter. She goes back into the kitchen and returns with two bottles of wine and two glasses. There are already wine glasses on the coffee table that must belong to the other family members, and Inga and Petra both pick up half-full glasses when they sit down.

Ash and I sit next to each other on the loveseat, and he slings his arm over the back of it, almost on my shoulders but not quite. I wish he'd just touch me already because I can practically feel his arm there. My skin tingles with its nearness, like there's some kind of magnetic field trying to draw me toward it. It's more distracting than if he was just touching me.

"Ash said you like wine," Petra says, smiling warmly at me. "These bottles are from local wineries. Did you know the Niagra-on-the-Lake wine region has close to seventy wineries?"

"No, I didn't," I say, surprised.

"Including Wayne Gretsky's winery," Inga says, although the comment is contemptuous.

I look at Ash. "Wayne Gretsky has a winery?"

"Yeah, it's not far from here," he says. "If you want, we can visit some of the wineries tomorrow before we leave."

I must be crazy, because his eyes seem soft as he looks at me.

"I'd like that," I say.

"Riesling or Merlot?" Petra asks me as she holds up the bottles Sigga brought in.

"Merlot, please," I say. I hold up my glass, and she fills it. I swirl the wine and take a sip. It's dry but smooth, and I get those familiar notes of cocoa and clove that Merlot is often known for. It's well-made wine.

"Tell us about yourself, Gray," Petra says. "Ash has been short on details."

I give Ash a panicked look. He told me more about his family on the way up, but he didn't mention what he told them about me. I'm also not sure what they know about how we met, and I'm afraid of unraveling whatever he might have said to them.

He seems to read my thoughts because he says, "They know how we met and why you're working with me."

"Is it really true you study trash talk?" Petra asks.

"More broadly, I study Sport Communication," I say. "Trash talk is my focus area."

"And why did you choose that?" she asks.

"I grew up in a family of trash talkers," I say. "We all play competitive volleyball, so family picnics can be a bit hardcore. I've always been fascinated by how aggressive language and verbal sparring can affect people during competition. It's a surprisingly understudied area."

"Why is that?" she asks.

"Based on my experience, people like to dismiss trash talk as unethical. They think that if you ignore its existence, it will go away. But that's not the case, and the consequence of that thinking is that when someone is having trouble dealing with it in the game," I give Ash a quick glance, "there's no strategy for dealing with it."

"Do you think using trash talk is unethical?" Inga asks me, and it feels like a challenge. She's not the first person to ask me this question, though.

I take a careful sip of my wine before I answer. "I think there are lines competitors shouldn't cross, but trash talk is far more complex than people give it credit for. For instance, teammates will often trash talk to hype each other up."

I look at Ash to see if he'll confirm or deny this, and he gives a conceding head tilt.

"Yeah, that's true," he says. "Nilsen and Fig have this really weird dynamic where they shit talk each other non-stop, but it does seem to make them both play harder."

"Trash talk has also been around for a long time," I say. "People like to make David in the Bible out to be this innocent young man up against an evil giant, but if you actually read that story, David trash talks Goliath before their fight."

Surprise crosses Inga's face, and I dare to think I've silenced her for the moment.

"It sounds fascinating," Petra says.

Gunnar returns from taking our bags and sits down next to his wife.

"So what made a smart woman like you decide to date a lunk like my brother?" Inga asks. She's smiling and her tone is teasing, but I feel like she's throwing shade at Ash.

I'm tempted to point out the irony to her. She was ready to challenge me on the ethics of trash talk, but her own interactions with Ash are playfully aggressive in the same way trash talk often is.

Then her question hits me, and I come up blank. What am I supposed to tell her about why I'm dating Ash? Because he accidentally sent me a pic of his dick the day I met him? Because we got cornered into fake dating when he tried to help me out with an ex? Because he's hot as hell and part of me is entirely too proud of being able to say I'm dating a man who looks like a Greek god?

Then the answer hits me, and I look at Ash.

"He's sweet," I say. "I always thought of hockey players as aggressive idiots who just liked to fight, but Ash isn't like that, and neither are most of his teammates. He's also really smart, which I'll admit I also wasn't expecting based on my own unfair biases."

Ash's face splits into a genuine smile, and I'm rewarded with the appearance of his dimples. Damn those things.

"Aww," Sigga coos. "Aren't they an adorable couple?"

"So you'll be coming to the wedding with Ash then?" Inga asks.

Ash's face goes serious, and I feel myself flush at her words.

"Wedding?" I ask, my panic rising again.

"I didn't have a chance to ask her about that yet," Ash says to Inga, his tone clipped.

I meet Ash's eyes again, and he explains, "Inga is getting married, and she needs to know if I'm bringing a plus one. I figured I'd ask you if you wanted to go with me after we saw how dinner went, but I should've known my sister would jump the gun."

"Sorry," Inga says, although she doesn't sound it.

"Where is Justin tonight anyway?" Ash asks.

"Still traveling," Inga says. "He comes home tomorrow night. He was sorry not to be here to meet Gray."

Her fiancé I assume.

"I know it's early to say this," Petra says, "but I really hope you decide to come to the wedding, Gray. We won't have nearly enough time to get to know you in one dinner."

Petra is refreshingly friendly compared to Inga, who clearly has harder edges, and I feel like I'm being hit with a good cop-bad cop routine from them. Petra's kindness is disarming, and I resist the urge to tell her I'll check my calendar to see if I'm available.

I flinch when Ash's arm slips forward on the back of the loveseat to rest on my shoulders. His thumb grazes back and forth over my upper arm, and I stop breathing for a few seconds.

Only Inga seems to notice my reaction, and she cocks her head at me. I give her a quick smile and force myself to relax. If we're going to make Ash's family believe we're dating, I can't freak out every time he touches me. Touching each other needs to seem natural. Comfortable.

I lean forward to take a sip of my wine, and when I sit back, I purposely settle closer into Ash's body. He gives a long exhale before his arm tightens around me, drawing me in even closer. He turns his head to plant a light kiss on my temple, and my heart does a backflip.

I take deep, calming breaths to steady myself as the family moves on to other topics of conversation. It didn't occur to me just how much acting we'd need to do this trip to fool Ash's family into thinking we're dating, and I'm suddenly terrified.

That kiss on my temple felt all too real, and I have to remind myself Ash and I are pretending. Just as I put on a façade when I step into the classroom and turn myself from an introvert into a performer, I need to turn myself here from a single woman who recently struggled her way through online dating into the girlfriend of an NHL hockey star.

How hard can it possibly be?

Chapter 21

The rest of dinner with Ash's family goes well enough. The wine helps. I'm careful not to drink so much that I'm tipsy, but two glasses later, I'm relaxed enough that I don't jump every time Ash touches me.

His touch doesn't bother me. Far from it. It sends a thrill through my body every time he puts his hands on my shoulders or brushes his fingers down my cheek before pressing a kiss to my forehead. Hell, his touches are so tender he almost has me believing they're real. It's just been a while since I've been touched like this, and it still surprises me to find Ash's hands on me.

I touch him back as well, but nothing overly bold. I place a hand on his forearm a few times, and once I go so far as to brush a lock of hair out of his eyes. He smiles as I let my fingers trail down the side of his face.

During dessert, Ash's hand lands on my leg under the table and I nearly drop my fork. His thumb strokes my thigh, and my face flushes as I remember his hand creeping between my legs that night at the club.

Our other touches have been for show, a display for his family, but they can't see his hand under the table.

He wants you. Celena's declaration comes back to me, but I ignore it.

Ash slides his hand slowly up and down my thigh, and my body goes warm. God damn him. I put my own hand on his to stop it as I feel wetness gather at my apex. A smile crooks up the corner of his lips, and he squeezes my leg before his thumb begins to stroke again.

Mercifully, dinner ends shortly after that. We clear the table and clean the dishes, then sit down to play Setback. The teams are Sigga and

Gunnar, me and Ash, and Petra and Inga, so Ash and I can no longer sit next to each other. I get some relief for a couple hours as we play, and as a bonus, Ash and I wipe the floor with his family at cards.

I'm relaxed as we head down the hall to our room, until it occurs to me for the first time that we have to share a bed.

There's a queen in the spare room, and that's fine for just me, or if I had to share a bed with someone like Celena, but the bed looks laughably small as I try to imagine myself fitting into it with Ash's muscled 6'4" frame. I look around the room for another sleeping option, but there isn't one, and sleeping out on the living room couch would raise questions.

"Shit."

"Something wrong?" Ash asks as he rummages through his overnight bag for whatever he packed to sleep in.

"It didn't occur to me we'd be sharing a bed. And a small one at that."

Ash looks at the bed and shrugs. "We'll fit."

Of course we'll fit. But how well? Are we going to end up ass to ass? Will I wake up with my leg slung over him?

I'm already aroused from having him stroke my thigh at dinner. This will be torture.

"I'm going to shower," Ash says as he heads out down the hall to the guest bathroom.

I go to my overnight bag and contemplate my options. I brought my sleep shorts and a cami. I normally take my bra off to sleep, but I decide to leave it on this time.

I want to shower as well, since seven hours of driving made me feel grimy, so I wait for Ash to return. He comes back wearing a loose pair of black sleep pants and a plain white undershirt.

I'm grateful he has the shirt on. I can see a few inches of some kind of tattoo down his left upper arm, but his shirt covers most of it. His chest and shoulder look darker under the left side of the white shirt, which makes me think the tattoo covers that whole side.

Ash is already in bed when I return from showering. I wear my bra, cami, sleep shorts, and – unusually – underwear. As I suspected, the bed looks so much smaller with him in it, but I stuff my dirty clothes into a plastic bag and head over resignedly.

Ash is on his back with his hands under his head, elbows out over his pillow. I climb in under the covers and lay on my back as close to the edge as possible before I turn out the lamp.

"How was dinner?" Ash asks me in the dark.

"It was nice," I say. "A bit nerve-wracking, but your family is very welcoming."

"Think we convinced them we're dating?"

"You tell me. You know them better." I pause. "I think Inga gave me a strange look at one point, but we may have saved things by the end."

Ash turns over in bed toward me, and I jump as his hand slides over my stomach under the sheets.

"Does it bother you when I touch you?" he asks. "You seem to flinch when I do. I'll stop if you don't like it."

The heat of Ash's hand burns right through my cami, and I force myself to breathe before swallowing hard.

"I like being touched," I say. "It just feels strange to have you do it. I know we're supposed to be dating, but my mind knows we're not, so I can't help reacting."

Ash skooches closer on the bed, and his damn thumb starts to stroke near my navel. His hand feels huge against me, and I'm acutely, achingly aware of how close it is to the waist of my sleep shorts.

"Maybe we just need to practice," he says. "To let your body get used to me touching you."

His breath ghosts across my ear as his shin presses into my calf under the sheets. My mouth goes bone dry, and my stomach feels like I suddenly swallowed soda and Pop Rocks, but the warmth of his body next to mine makes me want to snuggle into him.

Ash gently tugs the hem of my cami up so he's touching bare flesh as he continues to stroke his thumb over my stomach, and I remind myself to breathe. I should stop him, if only because this feels entirely too good, but I can't move.

Ash moves even closer when I don't stop him, and his hand slides higher so his thumb brushes the underside of my breast through my bra. His body is flush against mine, and I smell the musky scent of his bodywash. Air punches from my lungs as I let out a ragged breath.

"That's it," he whispers against my ear. "Just breathe."

Ash props himself up on an elbow so his face hovers above mine. "We should probably practice kissing as well."

The line is so cheesy and so obvious I want to laugh, but I can't bring myself to call him on it. Or to stop him for that matter. I'm paralyzed as he lowers his head, and his lips brush mine. I lift my own head the barest amount to meet him, and Ash rewards me by pressing his lips down more firmly. Every nerve in my body comes alive as his hand cups my breast under my cami, and I grab his forearm to anchor myself. I feel the steely muscles and snaking veins under my fingertips.

Ash's tongue parts my lips to slip into my mouth, and I taste the mint of his toothpaste. He deepens the kiss as his hand kneads my breast, and I can't stop the needy moan that escapes my throat.

Ash breaks off the kiss and rests his forehead on mine. "Fuck, Gray. Don't make noises like that, or I'll lose what little self-control I have left."

We're both breathing hard.

"I'm sorry," I murmur as I slide my hand up to his bicep.

"It's okay," he says. "We just have to remember why we're doing this."

I swallow. "Why is that again?"

Ash pulls his hand out of my cami to grip my hip instead. He moves his mouth to my neck, and I arch my head back to give him access as he begins to kiss and lick down my throat. Each spot he touches sends off fireworks in another part of my body.

"We're just letting you get used to my touch, so we can sell the fake dating thing," he says between kisses. "We don't want to get too intense. I mean, you don't really want me to fuck you in my parents' house, right?"

Both my nipples and my pussy tighten at the suggestion. I must be hearing things because his tone sounds hopeful, like it wouldn't take much to talk him into fucking me.

"It wouldn't be right to pull open your thighs and climb between your legs," he goes on hoarsely, his restraint seeming to fray. "To press my cock into your hot, wet little pussy. I know you'd feel amazing wrapped around my dick as I fucked you, baby, but I shouldn't do that, right? Not here? Not now?"

His words send blood screaming through my body as I imagine him doing exactly as he says. His body moves gently against me, and I'm soaking wet as I finally find my voice.

"That would probably be…inappropriate," I whisper. I'm trying to stay still, trying not to writhe in response to his own movement, but it's nearly impossible.

"Completely inappropriate," he agrees before nipping my neck, and I manage to stifle the moan that threatens.

Ash moves back up to my mouth and begins to kiss me again, but far from being gentle and teasing, his kisses are deep and intense.

He pulls back suddenly, and I force myself not to chase his mouth.

"Do you feel more comfortable with me touching you now?" he asks.

It takes a moment for me to recognize the sounds I hear as words, and once I do, I just want to tell him to shut up and keep kissing me. But I force myself to answer.

"Yes."

"Maybe *you* should practice touching *me* now," he says. His voice is full of gravel and a bit unsteady.

Ash takes my hand off his arm to guide it toward his stomach, and I shift so I'm on my side.

He presses my hand over his shirt, and I feel the firm washboard of his abs beneath. He lifts the hem so I touch bare skin, and I'm shocked at how smooth it is. I feel a patch of hair below his navel and a little above, and I move my hand up slowly, letting my fingers surf the swells of his abdominal muscles. They feel especially taught, like he's clenching them, and I move my hand higher until I reach his pecs.

My thumb brushes over one of his nipples, and he releases a long breath. The nipple is peaked, and I shift my hand toward his other pec, getting bolder in my exploration of his body.

I startle as Ash catches my hand, but he only moves it slowly back down his torso.

"You're going the wrong way," he whispers.

My fingers bounce over his abs again, but Ash doesn't stop there. He pulls my hand past his navel until it rests over his groin through his pants.

My breath hitches to feel how big he is. How thick. How hard.

He doesn't move again, his hand resting over mine over his cock, and I slowly wrap my fingers around his shaft, making him swear under his breath. I start to move my hand up and down his length through his pants, and he groans.

"Fuck, Gray," he says, thrusting lightly against my palm. "No practice needed, baby. That feels so good."

I swallow again. My mouth now has an abundance of saliva.

"Do you…want me to…?" I leave the offer open.

Ash groans again, but he goes still a second later and exhales. "Fuck."

"What's wrong?" I ask.

"Nothing. I just…I'll be right back," he says as he gets out of bed and heads out the door, I assume toward the bathroom.

I sit up and wrap my arms around my knees as I wait for him to return. It's a few minutes before he comes back, and it's not hard to guess what he's been doing. If I knew how much time I had, I would've taken care of a few things myself, and now I'm envious of the relief I'm sure Ash feels.

He climbs back into bed. "I'm sorry about that."

"Is everything okay?" I ask, my arms still wrapped around my knees. "Did I do…or not do something?"

"No, no, everything's fine," he insists.

I nod and lay back down. Ash leans over me again.

"I...I took things too far. I'm sorry," he says. "Are you okay?"

I try to decide if he means emotionally or if he's asking if I need the same kind of relief he did.

"I'm good," I assure him. It's a lie on both counts.

He nods. "You sure, baby?" Again, he almost sounds...hopeful?

I nod. "I'm sure."

"Good night then." He kisses me lightly on the forehead before he lays back down and settles in.

I don't close my eyes.

He keeps calling me "baby." He doesn't need to keep up the act when we're alone, but I reason that maybe it's just easier to stay in character all the time so he doesn't have to think about it.

The more I consider it, the more it seems like calling me "baby" is just a matter of convenience.

I'm not his baby, after all, and I don't want to be.

Really.

Chapter 22

Ash

The sound of my name on Gray's lips sets off a deep longing I feel in my bones. Her eyes are soft as she lies beneath me, and I recognize the desire in them. She wants me as much as I want her, and I groan as I savor how perfectly her body fits against mine.

"Ash," she says, her voice a purr.

"I'm here," I tell her, and my cock hardens even more as she wiggles beneath me. "Do you want me to fuck you? Just tell me what you want, and I'll do it."

I lift myself off her enough to part her legs, then settle myself between them. I notch my cock at her entrance and press forward.

"Ash," she breathes.

I'm about to bury myself inside her when her face fades, and my vision goes a bright white.

"Ash."

My eyes flutter, and it takes me a moment to realize I was dreaming. Well, mostly dreaming. The voice calling my name is real, and I force my eyes open against the sunlight streaming through the window. The sheer curtains were drawn last night, but I forgot to pull the shade, so the room is painfully bright.

"Ash, are you awake?" Gray asks.

I groan. I don't usually drink wine, and the feeling in my head says I should never do so again. I had a headache the day after that first dinner with Gray as well, and now I wonder if there's something in wine that doesn't agree with me.

"Yeah, I'm awake. You okay, baby?" I ask softly.

"I…need to go to the bathroom," she says.

I blink, wondering why she woke me to tell me that. Then I feel something shift against me and realize the issue. My body is wrapped around Gray's. She's spooned up against me, and my arm is banded around her torso to tuck her into my chest like I'm a wide receiver and she's a football.

She can't move until I let her go.

"Shit, sorry," I say, pulling my arm back and rolling away from her.

"Thanks," she says. She throws off the covers and heads for the door.

My eyes follow her the whole way. Her blonde hair spills down her back, hiding the wing tattoos I know are there, but the camisole and sleep shorts she wears do nothing to hide the curves of her body. I nearly groan again as I watch the sway of her hips and imagine holding onto them as I pound into her from behind. I'd guess her breasts are at least a C cup, if not a D, and her waist tapers in to give her a lush, hour-glass figure.

Gray leaves the room, and my trance breaks enough that I remember I was having a wet dream about her before she woke me.

I swear and quickly lift the elastic waist of my sleep pants and boxers to look down at my dick. Mercifully, I haven't come in my pants like last time. The dream hadn't progressed far enough before Gray woke me, but I still have a raging hardon. When Gray gets back, it'll be my turn to hit the bathroom.

I lie there patiently until Gray returns a couple minutes later, and I'm once again mesmerized by the way her breasts bounce gently when she walks. Rather than coming back to the bed, she goes to the dresser where my dad dropped her overnight bag and begins rummaging in it.

"I should hit the bathroom too," I murmur as I get out of bed carefully and make my way to the door. Gray is still busy in her bag and doesn't notice anything as I head out and hurry down the hall.

I hear my parents clanking pots in the kitchen and smell the coffee as

I slip quickly into the bathroom, close the door, and turn on the shower.

I showered last night, but the sound of the water will help mask what I really need to do, which is fucking come. I jerked off last night too, but my parents were asleep then.

I undress, step into the shower, soap up my hand, and wrap it around my cock. I close my eyes and remember what it felt like to touch and kiss Gray last night. Her skin was so soft, and the way her body surrendered made me hard as all fuck.

When I suggested I shouldn't fuck her last night, part of me wanted her to say she didn't care, that she wanted me to take her then and there, my parents' house or not.

Another part was glad she didn't give me the go-ahead. We would've needed to be quiet, and if I fuck her, I want to be sure we're free to make noise, because I want to hear her cry out my name.

Yeah, forget *if*. *When* I fuck Gray, she'll cry my name.

I want her so bad. It's become increasingly difficult to control myself, and last night was the straw that broke the camel's back. Now that I've touched her and kissed her and woken up with her wrapped in my arms, I can't go back.

I grip my cock and picture what might have happened last night. I picture myself nestling into the cradle of her heat. I press a hand over her mouth to keep her quiet as I push into her, and I watch her eyes widen as my cock fills her up, stretching her tight little pussy wide. Her body tenses and she makes that whimpering sound I love, but I hush her and tell her how well she's taking me as I begin to thrust. Her body relaxes, and I pull my hand off her mouth as she moans my name.

In the shower, I pump my hand over my cock. I'm already close, so this won't take long. It only takes a few seconds more of picturing Gray coming apart beneath me before I climax. Milky jets of cum shoot onto the tile, and I splash water to wipe them away. Then I lay a forearm on the wall and press my head against it as my body sags in relief.

I nearly jump out of my skin as a loud knock sounds at the door.

"Ash? Is that you?" My mother's voice carries over the running water.

"Yeah," I call, praying she didn't hear any of what I just did.

"Do you want eggs?" she asks.

"Sure. That sounds great," I say, and my heart slows again.

"Do you know if Gray wants eggs?"

"I don't know," I call back. "She's awake if you want to ask her."

"Okay."

I wait a few seconds, but I don't hear anything more. I check the shower stall to be sure I haven't left any evidence of jerking off, then I shut off the water and towel dry.

I forgot to bring in clean clothes, so I toss on what I slept in and go back to the room. Gray isn't there, so my mother must have coaxed her into the kitchen for breakfast.

I can't help looking at the rumpled bed as I dress. All things considered, my restraint last night was admirable. Gray would've given in to me if I'd tried to seduce her. I know that. As it is, she started to offer me either a hand job or a blowjob, but I shouldn't have put her in a situation where she felt like she needed to offer either.

I run a brush through my hair. I thought the idea of fake dating Gray was genius when Kaladin first confronted me with the video of us. It seemed like the perfect way to get closer to her, since she has to be near me to keep up the ruse. We have to touch and kiss occasionally back home, but not nearly as much as I'd hoped. As Cedric predicted, the media lost interest quickly, so we didn't need to be seen in public together.

The problem is that I need more now, and the terms of fake dating don't require the kind of intimacy I want. Gray may need to be near me, may even need to kiss me occasionally, but she doesn't have to fuck me.

More importantly, I want her interactions with me to be real, not just an act. I want her to want me. I want the relationship to be real.

It's not an impossible task, but I can't force it like I tried to do last night. I have to take things slow. It's possible I can convince Gray to date me for real, but it's going to take time and patience.

Gray

Ash is quiet on the ride back to Connecticut, and I get the impression he's lost in thought.

All in all, the trip to meet his family was a success. Ash seemed genuinely happy to see his parents and sisters, even if he did butt heads occasionally with Inga. He also managed to avoid giving her a definite answer about whether or not he was bringing me to the wedding, although he told me he thought it might be fun to go together.

After we left his parents' house, he took me to several wineries in the area. He didn't do much sampling himself, and when I asked him about it, he admitted to having a headache from drinking the night before.

People think it's the sulfites in wine that give them headaches, but sulfites are just a preservative found in lots of foods. For most wine drinkers, it's actually a flavonoid in red wine that affects them because of its abundance in the grape skins. Or sometimes it's the tannins and histamines. Either way, Ash likely has a sensitivity.

I'm lost in thought myself most of the drive. Something about the discussion with Ash's family nags at me, but I can't put my finger on what.

"You okay?"

I snap to attention at Ash's voice. He glances over at me as he drives, and I smile back at him.

"I was going to ask you the same," I tell him. "You've been quiet."

"Just thinking," he says.

"About what?" I ask, then add, "If you feel like telling me."

He's quiet a moment before he answers. "I'm thinking about this whole fake dating thing."

My face falls. Is he regretting the plan already?

"What about it?" I ask casually.

He shrugs. "Just thinking how complicated it is. Some people know it's fake, like the team, but others think it's real, like my parents."

Guilt grips me. "I'm sorry about your family. Do you really have to lie to them? Can't you tell them the truth?"

He chuckles. "Honestly, I don't really want to. As long as they think I'm dating someone, Inga won't try to set me up with one of her friends at the wedding."

I raise a brow. "Ah. Well…you're welcome?"

He chuckles again. "Yeah. Sorry you had to get off your dating apps." His tone turns sarcastic. "I mean, it seemed like you were having so much fun going out with those guys."

I roll my eyes and huff a laugh. "Right. It's sad that my fake dates have gone so much better than my real ones."

"You're welcome?" he says, mimicking me from a moment ago.

I smile. "I'm just too old and jaded for this bullshit."

He scoffs. "Thirty is hardly old."

"Just too jaded then."

A few moments of silence slide by before Ash speaks again.

"If you think about it, we're still getting most of the benefits of real dating," he says.

I look at him. "Like?"

"Like someone to talk to and spend time with. And the occasional kissing and touching isn't bad, right?" he says.

"No, I suppose not," I say, side-eyeing him.

"And as a bonus, my family doesn't try to set me up, and you have an excuse to give Celena as to why you can't be on those dating apps."

"True," I admit.

"It's a win-win," he says. "I mean, the only thing we're really missing is sex." He pauses. "And we don't need to have sex, right?"

There it is. The topic we've been skirting around since this started.

I'm not some inexperienced teenager that I don't catch the subtext of his question. He wants to know if I want to have sex.

The big question is why he wants to have it.

Occam's Razor. The simplest explanation is that, since he's fake dating me, he can't date anyone else. If he can't date anyone else, he can't have sex with anyone else, so if he wants to have sex, it has to be with me.

Almost immediately I hear Celena's voice in the back of my mind. *That's not the simplest explanation, you idiot. The simplest explanation is that he wants you.*

I tamp down the voice. Nope. I still won't let myself believe that.

A sound of disgust that sounds like Celena echoes in my mind.

"We don't *need* to," I say, emphasizing the need part. "But we're consenting adults, so we could if we wanted to." I pause to look at Ash. I think he's stopped breathing as he stares straight ahead at the road. "The question is whether or not that would be a good idea."

His lips part enough to release the breath he's been holding.

"For the sake of argument," he says, "what's the worst that could happen if we have sex?"

The worst? The condom could break, my IUD could fail, and I could get both pregnant and a venereal disease, for one. Not that I think Ash has an STD. He seems responsible enough to practice safe sex, but with my luck...

I don't say any of that, of course, and Celena would slap me for living under my usual cloud of doom, but Ash asked for the worst. I opt for something a bit less dire when I speak, though.

I shrug. "If we're...incompatible, it could make things uncomfortable for the next couple months," I say. "And what would Mr. Kaladin do if he found out? He's not paying me to sleep with you."

Ash nods slowly. "And what's the best that could happen?" he asks.

The best? My brain isn't wired to think that way, but I try anyway.

Great sex.

A relationship.

Love.

Happily ever after...

Yeah, right. Keep dreaming, Gray.

Chapter 23

It's the Monday after Thanksgiving, and Gray warned me this week is always crazy at the university. There are only a few weeks left in the semester, and everyone is rushing to write final papers or cram for exams, so Gray's office hours are in high demand. She's answering emails at all hours of the night, and one of her grad students is also defending her dissertation, so she's helping with that as well.

I've just gotten to the arena and dropped my stuff at my locker for our game today when my phone rings. It's the guard station at the administrative entrance.

I frown. I wasn't expecting Gray today, but the guards have approval to let her in whenever she comes, so I'm not sure why they'd be calling me. Unless it's a new guy who doesn't know her yet?

"Hello?" I answer.

"Hello, Mr. Gunnarsson. It's Ben down at the guard station," Ben says. So not a newbie.

"Hi, Ben. Is there a problem?"

"There's someone here asking to see you. Says his name is Raymond Mackey. Do you want me to have someone escort him up?"

My stomach turns over. Raymond Mackey. Gray never told me her father's name, but I'm a hundred percent sure this is him.

"Yeah," I hear myself say. "Um…bring him up to the press room."

"Everything okay?" Kelsier asks as I hang up the phone. He pulls up his hockey pants and sits down to put on his skates.

"I think Gray's dad is here."

His head snaps up again. "What? Are you sure?"

"Ben says Raymond Mackey is here to see me."

Kelsier is quiet a moment. "And you're sure he's not just some guy here to talk to you about a sponsorship or something?" His eyes widen. "Wait, are you sure she's not married? What if he's her husband?"

I give him a '*Don't be ridiculous*' look, although now there's a small doubt in my mind.

"What did you do to warrant a visit from her father then?" he asks.

I shake my head defensively. "Nothing."

Well, mostly nothing. Yet…

"You want me to go with you?" he asks.

"No, I'll be fine," I say. "I'm sure he just wants to meet."

"Good luck."

I head out the door and take the stairs up a floor before I head into the press room. It's still empty, so I sit down in the front row of seats to wait. It's a few minutes before a guard named Pedro leads an older man into the room, and I stand.

"Thanks, Pedro," I say, and he gives me a "No problem" as he leaves.

I turn to the other man. He looks to be in his mid-to-late fifties, about six feet tall, a little round around the middle, but still relatively fit for a man his age. The resemblance to Gray is subtle, but I see it now that I'm looking for it. He wears a baseball cap that has, "Grumpy Old Veteran" embroidered on the front.

I hold out a hand. "Mr. Mackey," I say. "I take it you're Gray's father? It's great to meet you."

Raymond takes my hand and shakes it. If his grip was any harder I'd think he was trying to intimidate me, but it's only firm and sure.

"Mr. Gunnarsson," he says. "It's good to meet you as well. I'm not sure when my daughter plans to introduce us, so I wanted to stop by briefly to meet you myself. I won't keep you long."

"Does…Gray know you're here?"

He smiles as he lets go of my hand. "No, and let's keep it that way if you don't mind."

I raise a brow. "You want me to lie to your daughter?" I ask. "This feels like a test that I'm screwed on either way."

He chuckles. "No, not lie. Just…keep a secret for now."

"That still feels like it's going to bite me in the ass," I insist.

He shrugs. "Fair enough. I'll tell Gray I came to talk to you. How about you just don't mention it for a few days until I have a chance to come clean?"

I give him a quick nod. "That I can do."

"Great. Do you have a minute to talk then?"

"Yeah, sure." I gesture to the press chairs. "Let's sit down."

He and I both sit, and I wait for him to speak. It's several seconds before he does.

"So," he says at last, "what's going on between you and my daughter?"

I blink at him. "We're, um, dating?" Somehow this feels like a trick question too, so I stick to the basics.

He pulls out his phone, touches the pad a few times, then turns it to show me the pic of me and Gray on the dance floor at the club. My hand is nearly on her breast, and her face looks painted in the throes of ecstasy. The way my body presses into hers makes it look like I'm thrusting my cock into her, and I feel my face heat. I didn't pay much attention to the pic before, but it looks so much dirtier on the phone of the man whose daughter I felt up.

"This your idea of dating?" Raymond asks.

"Um…no, sir. But in fairness, we both had a little too much to drink," I say sheepishly.

He raises a brow as if to say, '*Not* my *little girl.*'

Fine. *I* had a little too much to drink.

When he remains silent, I attempt a defense. "Don't tell me you never drank too much and let things get a little too intense with a woman."

He puts the phone away. "Of course I have," he says. "Hell, I didn't need to drink too much to let things get more intense than they should've, but I'm not a famous athlete. My fuck ups don't make the tabloids."

I wince. Score one to dad.

"Fair point," I say, "and I'm sorry for any problems I caused Gray or your family. But let me just assure you-"

I cut myself off, suddenly not sure what I intend to tell the man. It's one thing to lie to the press. It's quite another to outright lie to the father of the woman I've dragged into the clusterfuck of fake dating a pro athlete. I need to tell him something true.

"Let me assure you," I start again, "that the last thing I want to do is hurt Gray, and I will do everything in my power to make sure this thing between us doesn't come back to bite her."

I do a quick mental check and confirm everything I said is accurate.

He nods absently as he takes me in, and I have the disturbing feeling he's either searching my face for subtle ticks, or he's mentally counting the pulse beats in my neck to see if my heartbeat is elevated, like he's a God damn human polygraph.

"This thing between you serious?" he asks.

Again, I give myself a second to decide how to answer, and I hope he doesn't see that as a sign of evasion.

"I can only speak for myself," I say, "but I'm pretty invested right now. Things are still new, and – drunken night at the club aside – we're taking things slow. I don't want to call things serious-serious, but neither of us is seeing anyone else."

He nods again, and I pray to God he's not forward enough to ask me if we've had sex yet.

"It must be decently serious if you took her up to meet your parents," he says. "She skipped Thanksgiving with her own family for that."

My mouth drops open. His words are more an observation than an accusation, but I still feel like an asshole now.

"I'm really sorry about that, sir," I say. The address just slips out again, and I wonder if it's the veteran hat that makes me say it. I've never called anyone else's dad 'sir' before.

"It's hard for me to get up to see my parents during the season," I go on, "so I have to plan visits around holidays. I'm sorry I had to steal Gray for that last one. But yeah, I guess it's semi-serious between us. I feel like I might want more than she does right now, but she's been willing to go along with things."

I don't mention that the 'more' I want is sex. After sharing a bed with her, I want to fuck Gray so bad it's almost all I can think about.

We left the option of sleeping together up in the air after our ride home from Canada. I don't think she's opposed to it, but she's hedging. If she ever gave me the go-ahead, my pants would be around my ankles before she finished getting the words out.

Raymond nods, as if my response passed some kind of litmus test.

"I'm sure Gray can arrange a day for us to all get together and-," I start to suggest, but Raymond waves a dismissive hand to stop me.

"Gray and her mother have a complicated relationship," Raymond says. "Gray will introduce you when she's ready, which – if the past is any indication – could be months from now. I just wanted to meet you sooner rather than later given your…unique circumstances."

"You a hockey fan?" I ask, then immediately regret it. It sounds like I'm accusing him of using Gray's relationship to meet me.

He smiles. "Football and golf. Never really took to hockey, but if this thing lasts between you and Gray…" He shrugs. "I might have to start watching. You any good?"

That last is definitely a test. He wants to know the size of my ego.

I shrug. "I do alright. I learned the hard way the last couple years that I'm not as bullet-proof as I thought, but I'm working to get back to where I was. Being with Gray has helped."

He cocks his head. "So she *is* working with you on your trash talk issue?" he asks, although the question sounds more like a confirmation.

"Her research helps, but honestly, just being with her has been good for me."

I don't realize until the words are out of my mouth how true they are.

Gray hasn't necessarily helped my hockey game – yet – but being with her *has* been good for me. I feel more grounded around her.

Raymond stands, and I stand with him.

"I've taken up enough of your time," he says. "Thanks for seeing me."

"Of course," I say. "I hope we get to hang out more soon. Once Gray decides she's comfortable enough to officially introduce us, I mean."

"Do you golf?" he asks.

I shake my head. "No, sir."

"Well, as far as I can see, that's your only flaw," he says, "but you've got a few months to learn how to swing a club."

"I'll work on that," I promise.

We shake hands again.

"I like the hat, by the way," I say. "Which branch did you serve in?"

"Air Force," he says. "The hat was a gift from Gray. Did you serve?"

"No, sir," I say. "But thank you for your service."

He nods. "I was part of a special unit that got marksman training. My eyesight isn't what it once was, but with the right rifle, I can still hit my target from about five hundred meters out."

He smiles at me, and I understand it's a lighthearted threat.

"So you can easily hit me on the ice from the nosebleeds," I observe with a smile. "Got it."

He laughs and claps me on the shoulder. "I'm glad we understand each other."

"Loud and clear."

I walk Raymond back down to the guard station, say goodbye, then head for the locker room. Gray and I have now both met each other's parents, sort of, and that pushes this thing between us closer to being real.

Far from freaking me out, this feels right.

Chapter 24

Ash

I push off onto the ice and take an easy circuit of the rink before I do a few sprints back and forth to wake up my legs.

Gray is supposed to be here today watching practice, and that's both exciting and terrifying, more so than in the past.

She called me late last night to congratulate me on our win against Boston and to apologize profusely for her dad coming to see me yesterday. She was horrified by his overstep – her words – but I assured her it was fine and that I was glad to meet him. She grilled me on the details of the conversation, but I was vague with my answers, and I left out his veiled threat to snipe me.

I scan the area for Gray as I do some skating maneuvers to loosen my joints up a little.

Some people perform better with an audience. Being watched fires them up, but I'm usually indifferent to it. I go out and play because I love the game, not because I need people to see me. All that goes out the window when it's the thought of Gray watching me, though. I've never wanted to play better than I do with her here.

She is here, right?

I stop and look around before I finally spot her in the bench box. Kelsier stands on the ice next to her as she leans in and says something close to his ear. Her hand rests on his arm as he listens and nods.

Instantly, my blood boils, and I clench my stick so hard I'm surprised it doesn't break as I watch a smile quirk Kelsier's lips. Best friend or no, he needs to step the fuck away from my woman.

And she *is* my woman. I decided that even before her father's visit. She's the first person I think of when I get up in the morning, and the last person I think about at night before bed. Usually while I have my cock in my hand.

I skate toward Gray and Kelsier, and Gray's eyes dart to me. She says one more thing to him and they step away from each other. Kelsier pushes off and starts his own laps around the ice as I stop in front of Gray.

"What was that about?" I ask her.

She frowns. "What was what about?"

"You and Kelsier. What were you saying to him?"

She cocks her head at me. "That's between me and him."

I start to say something but think better of it and clamp my trap shut again. "I'll just get it out of Kelsier," I say instead.

She gives me a half smile. "Good luck with that."

"You underestimate how persuasive I can be," I shoot back as I turn and skate out onto the ice before she can respond.

This fire in my gut is completely irrational. I know that, but I can't help it. The thought that something might be going on between Gray and Kelsier makes my stomach churn. He's my friend, and I should trust him, but a monster has suddenly taken control of my brain.

I head straight for Kelsier and stop in front of him, getting in his face. "What were you and Gray talking about?" I ask without preamble.

He looks at me in confusion. "What?"

"Just now, what did Gray say to you?"

He frowns. "Nothing. We were just talking."

"About what?" I press.

"About nothing. We were shooting the shit. You know, 'Hi, how have you been?' 'Fine. You?'"

I glare at him, and he glares right back. I don't believe him for a second, but he's not going to tell me anything, so I skate away. I'll beat it out of him later.

Coach starts practice a couple minutes later, and I try to focus. We get through our drills, but I can't get my head on straight, and Kelsier doesn't help things. I mishit a shot that tips off the end of my stick and only goes a few feet. He chuckles as he comes up behind me.

"Did you hit that with your purse, Ethel?" he asks before skating away, laughing.

Kelsier tried to chirp at me in the preseason to help me build up an immunity, but I just found him funny. Not so anymore. My anger spikes at the comment, and everything I've been doing with Gray to control my emotions goes straight out the window.

On the next play, I slam into Kelsier so he's thrown back against the boards, but he only laughs.

"You hit like a girl, Gunny," he says before he skates off.

He gets his revenge a few minutes later when he checks me so hard I lose my footing and fall. I look up at him from on my ass as he leans over.

"You've been on your back more than a puck bunny today," he says. "Too bad you're not my type."

I blink as Kelsier skates away. He's not usually this chirpy, and he's definitely not this much of an asshole. I don't know what the fuck's gotten into him today, unless…

He must be trying to make me look bad in front of Gray. Was I right? Does he want her, and this is his play to get her?

The thought sends fresh fire through my gut, and I surge to my feet.

The rest of practice is a travesty. I'm too preoccupied by what Kelsier's intentions may or may not be toward Gray to be effective, and I see the frustration in Cote and Bouchard's faces as we head to the locker room. Under my ire, I at least have the decency to feel bad I'm fucking things up for them. They need to be able to count on me, and I'm nothing but a headcase right now.

Even worse is that Gray's involvement is supposed to be helping me, but now it's exacerbating the situation, and it's only a matter of time before Kaladin figures that out. If he does, he'll fire Gray, and I'll have no excuse to see her anymore. Somewhere along the way, I fell for her, and the thought of not seeing her anymore sends ice through my veins.

That's what rattles around in my head as I let the hot water run over me in the shower after practice. I have to talk to Kelsier, but he's not in the locker room when I get out of the shower.

I text him to see where he is, but he hasn't answered by the time I dress, so I head out to find him. I find Gray first.

She's waiting down the hall from the locker room, and she comes toward me as I head her way.

"What's going on between you and Kelsier?" I snap as we stop in front of each other. The words are out of my mouth before I realize it, and she blinks at me in surprise.

"What?" she asks.

I loom over her, something primal driving me to display dominance at the threat of a potential rival for her attention.

"You were having a very cozy conversation before practice," I say, "and I want to know what it was about."

Gray

I stare at Ash as he hovers over me. I have to crane my neck back to see his face, and the look in his eyes sends a shiver through me, although not necessarily an unpleasant one. I know Ash enough to be confident he won't hurt me, yet there's something dangerous about him right now that tightens everything below my waist.

A high-pitched squeak hits my ear as movement in my periphery draws my attention, and I see a guy with a cleaning cart coming down the hall. Ash and I freeze in place, glaring at each other as the squeal of the cart wheel grows steadily, jaw-clenchingly louder until the man is on us.

We don't move or say anything other than to step apart so the guy with the cart can pass. It takes the man forever to move between us, and he glances at us as if he knows what he's interrupting. Finally, he disappears around the corner, the squeak of the cart's wheel receding down the other hall before it stops altogether.

"Are you actually jealous?" I ask when the guy is finally out of sight.

"Do I have reason to be?" he counters. "You were touching Kelsier."

I blink. Was I? Maybe I put a hand on his arm, but I can't be sure. I continue to stare at Ash, not believing we're having this conversation. Finally, I cross my arms and cock my head.

"Sure," I say with a grin. "I'm fake cheating on you with Kelsier. What do you plan to do about it?"

His face darkens, and for a second I think I'm playing with fire, but then his expression eases.

"Well, later I'm going to beat the shit out of Kelsier," he says, "but right now I'm going to remind you why you're dating me."

"Fake dating," I correct him.

"Whatever," he says.

I jump as he reaches past me to open a door I didn't realize was there. He grabs my elbow and spins me around to usher me inside a dark room.

"Hey, what are you-," I start to protest.

Ash flicks on a light switch just before he closes the door after us.

We're in one of the equipment rooms. Hockey sticks line one wall while shelves in the middle are stuffed with skates, pads, pucks, and everything else the team needs.

"Ash, what are we-," I try again, but he pushes me up against the wall next to the door and plants his hands next to my head.

"What were you talking to Kelsier about?" he asks.

I narrow my eyes as understanding dawns. "You really are upset, aren't you," I say. "You're jeal-"

Ash crushes his mouth down on mine before I can get the words out, and I'm stunned into silence. I can't move for a few seconds as he kisses me hard, his tongue pushing past my lips and stealing my breath. I've never been kissed like this before, not just passionately, but aggressively. He isn't just kissing me. He's claiming me.

I'm panting when he finally pulls back enough for me to inhale.

"What were you talking to Kelsier about?" he asks again. Huskier.

"Nothing, I just…" I'm too lightheaded to form a coherent thought.

"Tell me," Ash says as his lips move to my ear, and his warm breath tickles my skin in a delicious way.

"I told him to trash talk you," I say, finally managing to get a handle on myself. "I was testing a theory."

He lifts his head. "That's why he was chirping at me all practice?"

I nod, and he huffs a laugh.

"I thought he was…" He trails off. "Never mind. You said you were testing a theory. What theory?"

I shake my head. "Not here. I can call you later to discuss it."

He frowns, then nods. "Fine. Call me when you get home."

His words sound like an end to our conversation, but he still has me caged in his arms against the wall, and damn me, but I don't have any urge to make him move.

"Did you really think there was something going on between me and Kelsier?" I ask when he continues to stand there.

His eyes refocus, and he meets my gaze.

"You're sure there isn't anything going on between you?" he asks.

I throw an annoyed look at him for meeting my question with a question, but he only presses closer, pinning me against the wall. My breathing labors, but the issue isn't physical.

Ash brushes his fingers along my cheek before he slides them down my body all the way to the fly of my jeans. My eyes flare as he pops open the button and grins at me. I only swallow as I look up at him.

"Just in case, maybe I need to remind you who you belong to," he says as he pulls my zipper down.

I consider myself a feminist, but I go wet as a water park at his words.

"I only fake belong to you," I whisper, unable to help myself.

I yelp as he flips me around so I'm facing the wall.

"We'll see about that," he rasps in my ear.

Ash grabs my hands and places them against the wall near my head.

"Don't move those," he orders. One of his hands snakes up to wrap around my opposite shoulder, and I inhale sharply as his other hand moves slowly down into my panties toward the apex of my thighs.

Am I really going to let him do this? The question flashes in my mind, but I have no will to stop him.

"Is…this a good idea?" I ask. It's all I can muster by way of protest.

Ash buries his face in my hair over my shoulder. "Probably not," he says softly. "But I really want to do it. Are you going to stop me?"

I try to say yes. I really, really try, but after five long seconds get sucked out through the air vents, I shake my head.

He pushes out a deep breath, and his fingers find my clit to massage it slowly. Any further thoughts of protest vanish as I moan and let my head fall back against his shoulder. Ash only slips his hand further into my jeans and pushes a finger inside me, making me whimper.

"Shit, Gray. You're so fucking wet," he says against my ear. "Open your legs wider for me, baby."

I obey automatically, then moan again as he pushes a second finger into me. My body shudders, and Ash pulls me back tighter against him.

"Good girl," he purrs, and my pussy clenches around his fingers.

He must feel it because he groans. "Oh fuck, baby. Do you have a praise kink?" he asks, and there's an eagerness in his voice.

I shake my head.

"Don't lie to me," he says. "Your pussy just clamped me like a finger trap. Now tell me the truth. Do you like to be praised?"

"I…I don't know," I say honestly. I can't remember ever being called a "good girl" before, and while I feel like I should find it demeaning, I can't deny my body's reaction to the words.

He chuckles softly. "Oh, we're going to find out then, baby girl."

Ash pushes his fingers deeper inside me and curls them as he rubs my clit with his thumb. I let out a cry and thrust my ass back against him on instinct. The hard ridge of his cock presses against my tailbone.

"Mmm, is that the spot, baby?" he says in my ear. "Are you going to come for me?"

I bite my lip instead of answering, but Ash only moves his hand faster as his thumb rounds my clit. It's been too long since a man touched me like this, and my body is a live wire. Every thrust of Ash's fingers sends electricity through me that I feel from the roots of my hair to my toenails.

"Fuck!" I yell as he presses down on my clit and my body jolts.

Ash's other hand moves up to cover my mouth, and he shushes softly into my ear. "Quiet now. We don't want anyone to interrupt us, do we?"

He thrusts his fingers harder as his thumb continues to work my clit, and it's all I can do to stay on my feet. I whimper against his hand, but he doesn't let up.

"That's my good girl," he says, and we both feel my pussy clench around his fingers. He chuckles again. "Oh yeah. You've got a praise kink. I'm going to fucking enjoy this. Now come all over my fingers. I want you dripping down them when I'm done."

My eyes roll back in my head as Ash works his hand between my legs, and I can't stay still to save my life. I buck against him, and he tightens his hold on me again as he pins my head to his chest with his hand still over my mouth. I can't keep my hands on the wall any longer. Instead, I grab Ash's forearms and hold on as hard as I can. His muscles are like steel, and the hardness of his body against mine only drives me wilder.

"Come for me, Gray," Ash says, his voice graveled. "Be a good girl and come all over my fingers."

The last "good girl" does the trick, and I scream into Ash's palm as my climax rocks through me. It's an entire-body experience that sends shivers across my skin, and my reaction is so extreme I'm embarrassed. Ash must think I'm starved for sex by how hard I come on just his fingers.

Well, I *am* starved for it, but he doesn't need to know that.

"Fuck, baby," he says. "I felt that orgasm in my balls."

He pulls his fingers out of me, and I force myself not to whimper at the feeling of emptiness. He holds his hand up in front of my face, and his first two fingers glisten with my slickness.

"Look what you did to my hand, you dirty girl," he says.

Ash slowly pulls his other hand away from my mouth, even as he lifts the slick hand to his own. I sense rather than see him suck on the digits as I continue to pant wildly against him.

"You taste so good," he says against my hair. "I can't wait to get my tongue into that sweet pussy."

"What?" I manage to ask.

Ash doesn't answer. Instead, he turns me around so my back is to the wall again. He presses his body against me, and his cock pushes into my stomach. It occurs to me that I should offer to reciprocate, but before I can get the words out, the door swings open.

"You think you need a bigger size?" Jack, the equipment manager, asks as he walks in, followed by Fig.

Ash and I break apart, and Jack and Fig stop short as they catch sight of us. Ash shunts me behind him as he steps in front of me, and I remember my pants are still undone. I hurry to rezip and button them as Jack and Fig stare at us.

"Hey Gunny, whatcha doing in here with the doc?" Fig asks, grinning.

"Showing her the equipment room," Ash answers. "What does it look like I'm doing?"

"Yeah?" Fig says as his eyes dip to Ash's groin. "Exactly what equipment were you showing her?"

Behind Ash, my face burns as I imagine this story raging through the training center like wildfire.

"Don't be an asshole, Fig," Ash says as he reaches behind him and searches for my hand. I slip it into his, and his fingers close around mine. "Let's go, Gray. We can finish this later."

He tugs me past Fig and Jack, and I don't just hear the promise behind those words. I feel it.

Chapter 25

Gray

Half an hour later, I still feel Ash's hands on me, inside me, as I walk in my front door. I barely remember driving, but I must've stopped in the right places and hit the gas when I needed to, because I'm home, I'm alive, and I don't recall being honked at.

Still, it takes me several seconds with my hand poised above the keypad to my alarm to realize what's wrong. I don't need to punch in the code because the alarm didn't go off when I walked in.

I frown and try to remember if I set it when I left this morning. I was in a hurry, so it's possible I walked out without doing so. I'm always so worried I'll forget one thing that often I neglect others.

I look at the alarm again. I'm sure I just forgot to set it…

I head into the kitchen to see what I have for dinner. I'm only just realizing how hungry I am.

My phone pings, and I swipe it open. I'm mad at myself for hoping it's Ash, but I'm disappointed to see it's Drew. Months ago I would've been thrilled to see a text from him, but I've found someone else to hyper-fixate on, and the sight of Drew's name just makes my body sag.

I open the text out of sheer morbid curiosity.

Drew

> Is this still your phone, Gray? Just wondering if you got my last texts. It's Drew.

He's texted one other time since the night Ash took me to dinner, but I didn't answer that time either.

Maybe his interest has nothing to do with me, and he's just hoping to become friendly again so I'll invite him to hang out with me and Ash.

Now that I think about it, that's probably the case. He doesn't want me. He wants Ash.

I'm about to put the phone down when I remember I need to call Ash. I dial, and he picks up on the second ring.

"Hey, baby," he says, and my stomach hiccups at the smooth, deep timbre of his voice.

I have no idea why it affects me so much when he calls me that. I know some women consider it infantilizing, but I can't get enough of it.

It sounds like he has me on speaker. I put him on speaker too as I rummage in the freezer for a frozen meal since I'm too lazy to cook.

"Bad time?" I ask. "It sounds like you're out."

"I'm driving, but I can talk. What's this breakthrough you had that made you rope Kelsier into chirping at me the whole practice?"

"You didn't really hit him, did you?" I ask.

"Not yet," he says, but I hear the smile in his voice.

I find a frozen Indian meal and put the phone down to unbox it.

"I didn't just have Kelsier trash talking you today," I say carefully as I put the meal in the microwave. "I had him use very specific trash talk."

I'm wary of telling Ash what I suspect, but he needs to know this if we're going to address it.

"Okay," he says. "What kind?"

I pick the phone back up. "Gender-based trash talk," I say, deciding not to ease into it. "I had him make comments that challenged your masculinity, that…suggested you were womanish."

There's silence on the other end of the line for several long moments.

"Ash?"

"Yeah," he says.

"Did Kelsier do what I asked?"

"Yeah. He told me I checked like a girl and asked me if I hit one of my shots with my purse. Shit like that."

I smile as I turn the microwave on. That last is objectively funny.

"I'm sorry," I say. "I had the idea when I found out your name is feminine in Icelandic. It's clearly something you think about, so it made me wonder if you were more susceptible to misogynistic trash talk."

More silence on the other end as I head over to the dining room table to find the academic text I was reading earlier. The book is where I left it, but I frown to see it's closed. I swear I left it open to a particular page I wanted to read more carefully. Shit. I'll have to find the page again later.

"Ash?" I ask again when he remains quiet.

"I'm here."

"Are you okay?"

"Yeah, I just…I guess I always considered myself, you know, a male feminist or something," he says. "My sisters made sure I knew the kind of shit they went through with men and with their jobs, so it's a little jarring to think maybe I'm not as enlightened as I thought I was."

Something in his tone breaks my heart. Ash is a good guy. I don't doubt he's more cognizant of women's issues and experiences because of his sisters, but what's more enlightened, in my opinion, is that he *wants* to be cognizant of them.

A light bulb goes off in my head.

"Ash, maybe I'm wrong about how we're looking at this," I say.

"No, you-"

"Shut up and listen," I tell him.

A brief pause, then, "Yes, ma'am."

"Let's think about this in terms of your ideal image," I say. "Your ideal image isn't that of a macho man. It's that of a man who views women as equals, one who cares about their struggles and wants to view them as strong. To use your own word, you're a feminist."

"Okay."

"But you've also got this thing in the back of your mind that, in your culture, your name is feminine, and that bothers you. But worse, it bothers you that that bothers you."

More silence, then another, "Okay."

"The image being threatened isn't your masculinity," I tell him. "It's your image as this enlightened 'male feminist.' You don't want the gendered trash talk to affect you, but it does, and *that* makes you ashamed."

A longer pause this time. "Okay, I think I followed all that. So…what do I do about it?"

I pull my dinner out of the microwave and set it on the small kitchen table because my large dining room table is covered in books. "I haven't gotten that far yet," I say as I open the refrigerator. "I'll have to-"

I freeze as I catch sight of the bottle of wine on the top shelf. It's not mine, and I have no idea where it came from.

"Gray?" Ash asks. "You'll have to what? I think I lost you there."

I stare at the wine, and suddenly the fact that my alarm wasn't armed when I came home is much more salient.

No, don't panic yet. Maybe the wine is mine. Maybe I brought it up from the cellar and just don't remember. Maybe…

That's when the open shade catches my eye. There's a low window off the kitchen that I always keep the shade drawn down on because it looks into the neighbor's house, and I've seen my seventy-eight-year-old neighbor walk around in his underwear too many times to keep it up.

But it's up now.

"Gray?" Ash's voice comes through the phone louder now.

I walk over to the window and push it up. It's unlocked. I can't remember if I keep this window locked or not, but I know I keep this shade down. I haven't opened it in months.

"Oh God," I whisper.

"Gray?" Ash's voice has a touch of urgency. "Gray, are you alright?"

"Oh my fucking God," I say again as adrenaline-fueled panic races through me, and I start to shake.

"Gray!" Ash's voice is sharp now. "What's going on?"

"I think someone was in my house," I say.

Then an even more terrifying thought hits me, and I drop my voice to a whisper. "Or they're still here."

"What? Did you just say someone broke into your house?" Ash asks.

"I don't know," I say, fear making my voice quiver. I hurry to the counter and pull the largest knife I can find out of the knife rack. "My alarm was disarmed when I came in, someone closed the book on my table, there's a bottle of wine in the refrigerator I didn't buy, and the shade I always, always keep closed is open," I say in a terrified whisper.

"Gray, get out of the house now," Ash says. "I'm only a few minutes away. Stay on with me and text 911 as soon as you get outside."

I look at the front door. It looks a million miles away. I have a back door that's closer, but what if the intruder is waiting out there? At least I know there's no one out front, and my neighbors will be able to see me if I'm attacked.

But I have to make it all the way to the front door first.

"Gray? Are you out yet?" Ash asks.

"I…I can't," I say. "The door is too far away. I'm still in my kitchen."

"Baby," Ash's voice is softer, still urgent, but coaxing. "Listen to me. You need to get out of that house now. Do you have a weapon?"

I nod, then say yes when I realize he can't see me.

"Then go now. Just run for the door," he says.

My legs feel like jelly as I try to work up the courage to go for the door, but I can't move. Finally, Ash's voice spurs me to action.

"Gray, go now!" he shouts through the phone.

I bolt for the door, somehow having the wherewithal to grab my purse as I streak by the kitchen table. The entire way to the door I swear I see the shadows in my periphery move, ready to grab for me, but nothing touches me. I wrench open the door and fly through it, still expecting someone to grab me from behind as I dash down the stairs of the porch into the front yard and all the way to the sidewalk. When I stop, I'm breathing like I sprinted the 100-meter dash against Usain Bolt.

"Gray?"

"I'm out," I say at the phone. It's clutched in my left hand with my purse strap while I hold the ten-inch carving knife in my right.

"Good girl," Ash says. There's no sexual overtone to it this time, and I'm too scared to be aroused by it anyhow. "Text 911. I'm almost there."

I toggle screens to my text messages and type 911 into the "To" field. I type out a quick message to say I think someone broke into my house, and I give my name and address.

I get a message back almost immediately asking if I'm in a safe place and if I'm hurt. I type back that I'm outside my house and unharmed.

"Did you text 911?" Ash asks over the speaker.

"Yes, I'm texting with the dispatcher now. They're sending police."

"Alright. Stay on with me. I'm only a couple minutes away."

I nod again, but I don't have the words to spare right now. I'm shaking like a leaf, mostly from fear, but it also hits me that I left my jacket inside and it's cold out. Every little sound or movement makes me jump, though, so I'm not really focused on the temperature.

"Baby, keep talking to me," Ash says. "I need to know you're okay."

"You…you don't have to call me that when we're alone," I say.

Why I decide to bring that up now of all times, I'll never know.

"Call you what? Baby?" Ash asks, confused.

"Yeah. I mean, if it's easier just to keep it up so you don't forget, it's fine," I say. "I just don't want you to feel like you have to call me 'baby.'"

My heart beats five times before he asks, "And what if I *want* to call you that?'"

My stomach somersaults.

"Do you dislike it?" he asks.

"No," I assure him quickly. "No, it's not that. I just…I don't…I mean…" I fumble for how to explain things in a way that won't offend him or make me sound like a headcase.

I'm saved from deciding on something when I hear a car screech to a halt at the curb. I turn around, and relief floods me at the sight of Ash's Aston Martin. He's already half out the door before the car is in park and turned off, and I rush toward him without thinking.

He pulls up a few feet from me and holds out his hands. I stop, confused for a moment until he looks at my hand.

"Hand me the knife," he says, reaching out carefully.

I look down and see I'm still clutching the blade, and it's thrust out like I'm ready to stab something. I would've cut him.

Ash extends his hand, and I shift the knife to give it to him, handle first. He takes it from me and lays it on the ground. Then he straightens, takes my still out-stretched hand, and pulls me to him. I throw myself into his arms and try not to hyperventilate against his chest. I was afraid I might burst into tears when he got here, but my eyes stay dry. I'm probably in too much shock to cry.

"Are you okay?" Ash asks. I feel his chin rest on top of my head.

"Yes," I say, then rethink my answer. "No."

"You're safe now." He holds me for another few seconds before gently setting me away from him. "Where's your coat?"

My teeth chatter as I point to the house. "Inside."

Ash takes his jacket off and helps me put it on. It's warm from his body, and it smells like a mix of his bodywash, his deodorant, plus some general man-scents I can't distinguish right now. It soothes me instantly.

Ash picks the knife back up from the ground.

"What are you doing?" I ask.

"I'm going inside to check things out."

"Don't," I say, shaking my head. "The police will be here soon."

"Did they say how long?" he asks.

I look at my phone. The dispatcher texted a few seconds ago. "They're six minutes out," I say.

"I'm not waiting that long," Ash says. "Stay here."

I want to argue with him, but he heads toward the house before I can, his long legs eating up my front yard. My stomach sinks when I see him disappear inside. I look down at my phone, but his call has disconnected.

Chapter 26

Gray

It seems like forever that I wait alone on my front yard, but I finally hear a siren. Seconds later a police car comes around the corner and pulls up behind Ash's car.

An officer gets out and comes toward me.

"Are you the homeowner?" the officer asks. "Gray Mackey?"

"Yes," I say. "My friend…my boyfriend went inside to look around."

"Do you have some ID?" the officer asks.

I'm surprised for a moment until I realize he has no way of knowing who I am. I fumble in my purse and manage to pull out my driver's license. He takes it, looks carefully, then nods and hands it back to me.

"How long ago did your boyfriend go in?" the officer asks just as another police car pulls up in front of the house.

"Five or six minutes?" I say.

"Can you call him and have him come out?"

I nod, but before I can dial, Ash appears at the front door and heads down the steps toward us. Wisely, he seems to have left the knife inside.

The second officer comes up next to me. "Holy shit, is that Ash Gunnarsson?"

Of course the man is a hockey fan.

"Who?" the first officer asks.

"He's on the Hartford Hydra," the second officer says.

"Oh. I don't follow hockey," the first guy says.

The second officer gives him a baleful look but doesn't say anything.

"Good evening, officers," Ash says as he joins us. "I just did a check of the house, but I didn't find anyone inside."

"Hi, Mr. Gunnarsson," the second officer says with a half-grin. "I'm a big fan. You, uh, probably shouldn't have gone inside, though."

Ash gives him an apologetic, dimple-rich smile. "Sorry. I just didn't want anyone to get away if they were still here."

The first officer turns to me. "Can you tell us why you think someone was in your house, ma'am? Did you see someone?"

I launch into the story of all the oddities I found when I got home and how the last straw was the window with the shade pulled up.

The officer just looks at me when I'm done, as if expecting more. Like he wants me to say, "Oh right! And there was also the guy in the mask who chased me out onto my front lawn."

"And no one else could have put the wine in your refrigerator or turned off your alarm?" he asks finally.

Ash's hand lands gently on my hip in a gesture of support as he moves behind me. I start to shake my head until something occurs to me.

"My parents have a key to the house," I say.

The officer looks at me expectantly, and I dial my mother's number.

"Gray? Is everything okay?" my mother asks when she answers. This is later than I usually call her, and she's rightfully worried.

I put the phone on speaker so I don't have to repeat everything she says. "Hi, Mom. Did you come to the house today and drop off a bottle of wine by chance?"

"Oh, yes. I almost forgot. I meant to text you to let you know, but your father called right as I was leaving, and I got sidetracked."

I close my eyes and feel my face heat. I panicked, then panicked everyone else for nothing.

"And did you remember to reset the alarm when you left?" I ask.

A pause. "No, I'm sorry. I think I forgot. Your father drives me crazy. He couldn't find the peanut butter, even though it's in the same cabinet it's been in for the last-"

"Did you touch anything else while you were here?" I cut her off.

"Any of the books on the dining table or any of the windows?"

Another pause. "No, I don't think so. I know better than to touch your books."

"You're sure?" I ask. My mother's visit explains at least two of the anomalies, and at this point, I'm hoping I can blame the other two on her as well, even if it makes me seem like a crazy lady who overreacted to a bottle of wine in her fridge.

"I'm pretty sure I didn't," she says. "I was only there to drop off the wine, then I left. I found it at the store and thought it was that kind you like, so I picked it up and figured I'd drop it off on my way home."

I manage some sincerity as I answer her. "Thanks, Mom. I appreciate you thinking of me. Just…let me know you stopped by next time."

"Sure. Is everything alright?"

"Fine. I'll talk to you later. Love you. Good night."

I don't wait for her to say 'good night' back before I hang up the phone and look at the officer.

"It might have been a false alarm," I say. "Sorry about that."

"Better safe than sorry," the second officer says before the first can answer, and I'm grateful to him for not making me feel like an idiot.

The first officer takes my information while the second goes inside to double-check that no one is there, but he comes back out several minutes later and gives the all-clear.

The first officer leaves, but the second stays to get an autograph from Ash. I take their picture together as well. Finally, he leaves, and Ash puts an arm around my waist to lead me back up to the house. Once inside, he sits me down at the kitchen table and gets me a glass of water.

He picks up the plastic tray of food on the table. "Indian?" he says. "Looks good, but it's cold now. How about I order something?"

"I'm not really hungry," I say.

"You have to eat," he says. "I can order real Indian food?"

I sigh and shrug. "Sure."

I agree only because Ash will stay longer if there's food, and I don't want him to leave yet.

Ash orders the Indian and throws out my microwave dinner while I sit in a daze. Normally I'd protest – I don't like to waste food – but the thought of eating doesn't appeal to me in the least right now.

Ash takes a seat across from me. "Are you okay?"

"I just feel so stupid," I say. "I nearly gave myself a heart attack and had the police here because my mother brought me a bottle of wine and forgot to tell me."

"Hey, don't do that to yourself," he says. "Like the officer said, better safe than sorry. You still don't know why your shade was up."

I shake my head. "I must've put it up at some point."

"Maybe, but I still want you to be careful for the next few days. Keep an eye on your surroundings and take note of anything that seems off."

I eye him, trying to decide if there's a tone to his voice.

"It freaked me out when you were scared tonight," he says. "I nearly caused three accidents trying to get to you. I just want to be sure everything is safe. I don't want you to have to go through that again."

"I'm sorry," I say. "I didn't mean to worry you."

He shakes his head. "I'm just glad you're safe. Like I said, just be careful the next few days."

"I'll be in Orlando for a conference after tomorrow anyway," I say. "I've been meaning to tell you."

"Oh." He looks a little shellshocked at the news.

We fall silent, and I start thinking about what it will be like to stay here alone when he leaves. There was apparently no real danger, but I'll be on edge the whole night. Sleep won't be in the cards.

Ash seems to read my mind.

"Do you want to spend the night at my place?" he asks.

It's on the tip of my tongue to tell him yes, but I don't like the idea of imposing on him, and going to his place would only put off the real problem until tomorrow. I need to feel safe in my own house.

"No, it's fine. I'll just-"

"Then I'm staying here tonight," he interrupts.

I look at him in surprise. "What? No, I can't-"

"Look, either you're coming to my place, or I'm staying here, but you're not going to be alone tonight," Ash says with finality.

"Alright," I agree before I realize what I'm saying.

The Indian food arrives a little while later, and we eat it with the bottle of wine my mother left. After that, we sit on the couch and watch a movie, but I'm too distracted by both the night's events and the man sitting next to me to take in much of the film.

"Just let me know where you keep your spare blankets," Ash says as we get up from the couch after the movie. "I'll make myself at home."

I look at him strangely until it hits me that he plans to sleep on the couch. I just assumed he'd sleep in the bed with me.

"I have a king bed," I blurt out. "We can share…if you'd be more comfortable."

A smile turns up Ash's lips. "Sure. I'll always take a bed over a couch."

I smile back and head upstairs, Ash behind me.

"I'll be right back," I say as I grab some clothing out of a drawer in my room and head into the ensuite bathroom.

I brush my teeth and hair, then change into my sleep shorts and cami as quickly as possible. I should shower, but I don't want to keep Ash waiting too long. I can't believe he agreed to stay over and sleep in my bed with me, and I don't want to give him a chance to change his mind.

Do I want a repeat of what happened at his parents' house?

If I'm honest with myself, yes. But maybe not tonight? It's a toss-up whether I'm too upset to enjoy anything that might happen between us or if it would be a welcome distraction.

I open the bathroom to find Ash still fully clothed and sitting on the edge of the bed.

"You don't have anything to sleep in," I say, realizing the problem.

"Yeah, I wanted to talk to you about that," he says. "I'd have to sleep in my boxer briefs. I figured I'd give you a chance to reconsider the sleeping arrangements if you wanted."

"No," I say quickly. "It's fine. I'll get in bed and turn the lights out, and you can get undressed."

He nods as he stands up. "Sure."

I head to my side of the bed and climb in under the covers before turning out the light on the nightstand. The room goes dark, and I turn over in bed so I'm facing away from Ash.

The room is so silent I can hear the rustle of fabric as he takes off his shirt, then the rasp of his zipper as he removes his jeans. A few seconds later, the bed dips as he climbs in.

There's a pause before he moves closer, and his hand touches my hip gently. I hold my breath, not daring to move. My bed is bigger than the one in his parents' house with plenty of room for us to sleep without touching each other, but...

But maybe I want him to touch me.

Ash

Gray doesn't flinch or pull away when I carefully nestle up behind her. In fact, I hear her let out a deep breath, and she snuggles in tighter to my body. My cock takes that as an invitation to harden, but I will it into submission.

Down boy, I scold it. *Not tonight.*

Gray's had a stressful night, and I'm not going to add more stress to it by trying to seduce her. She seems willing, but I want to be sure she's not just riding the extreme emotions of the last few hours.

The truth is that I'm too distracted myself to really fuck Gray properly, even if she did let me. It's enough for now to be here in her bed with my body wrapped around hers.

I grimace in the dark as I remember the scene I found in this room just a couple hours ago when I searched Gray's house for intruders. I didn't find anyone in the house, but I did find a dozen roses-worth of petals strewn across her bed. This bed.

There was also a note in the center. *"You belong with me, not with him."*

It was proof someone had in fact been in Gray's home today, and my blood had gone cold at the realization.

My next thought had been how Gray might react to seeing her bed covered in flower petals put there by an unknown intruder, and the horror and terror I knew I'd see on her face had made up my mind. After taking a picture for evidence, just in case, I quickly collected the petals and shoved them down the garbage disposal in the kitchen sink, letting the water run until I was sure every vestige of the flowers was gone.

The note is still in my wallet, and I'm not sure yet whether to keep it or burn it. I only know Gray will never, ever see it.

The other thing I know is that tomorrow I'm hiring private security to watch Gray's house and discreetly follow her wherever she goes. Her conference in Orlando is a complication I didn't anticipate, but it's not a problem. I'll just send a secret bodyguard to Florida with her. She'll be protected, and she'll never have to know the truth about what happened.

I lift a hand to pull a few locks of Gray's hair back behind her ear.

"You're safe, baby," I whisper. "I won't let anything happen to you."

"Mmm," she murmurs and wiggles her ass back against me.

God fucking dammit. Any other day, that would be enough for me to yank her shorts down, throw her ankles over my shoulders, and plunge my cock into her tight little cunt to fuck her until she can't walk.

But not today. Today isn't the right time to take Gray for the first time. She doesn't know why it's not the right time, but it's better that way.

Instead, I tighten my arm around her chest. "Sleep now," I say into her hair. "Tonight's not the night for that, but soon."

I hear her breath catch, and I smile. Yeah, I'm certain she wants this as much as I do, because that note is bullshit. Gray most certainly belongs with me. She *is* mine.

And I protect what's mine.

Chapter 27

Gray

Two days later, I sit with three other panelists in a meeting room of the convention center in Orlando. We just finished our presentation session, and it's time for the Q&A portion.

"This question is for Dr. Mackey," a man says as he stands, and I cringe inwardly.

When I was younger, I used to hope people asked me questions at these conferences because it felt like their interest validated my work. I've learned better since. Chances are, this man's question will either be an excuse to argue with me, or it will be preceded by a five-minute summary of his own research. Or both.

I go cold as I realize people may also ask me about my relationship with Ash. God, I hope not. Is it too much to hope I'll be spared the scrutiny of my love life at an academic conference?

"So I recently published a paper that suggests," the man starts, and I breathe a sigh of relief. I've never been so happy to get a monologuer in my life, and I settle back in my chair to listen to his theory and the tenuous way he thinks it might inform my research.

Fifteen minutes later, the session is finally over, and I make it out unscathed. No one asked me about Ash, and my faith has been restored in my fellow scholars.

"Dr. Mackey?"

I turn to find two young women and a young man standing there, and I know I've relaxed too soon. I smile politely. "Yes?"

"Sorry to bother you, but…is it true you're dating Ash Gunnarsson?"

one of the girls asks, and I'm careful to keep my expression neutral even as I clench my teeth.

"That's what the media seems to think," I say coolly.

"And are you working with him on trash talk?" the guy asks. "Because the news says you aren't, but that seems like a missed opportunity."

I raise a brow at the kid, and he tries to backtrack.

"I mean, no offense, but you have access to a professional athlete-," he hurries to explain.

"I'm sorry to cut this short," I say in the most apologetic voice I can muster, "but I have a meeting with a colleague."

I turn and walk away without another word. Normally I'm happy to talk to grad students, which I assume these three are, but my relationship with Ash, or whatever it is, is off-limits.

I pull out my phone to check my messages. As if mentioning his name summoned him, I see a text from Ash. I pull up the message but stop dead in the middle of the hallway when the picture text comes through.

"Excuse me," someone says as they knock into my shoulder. The man veers to the side to get around me, and I apologize as he hurries past.

I cut to the side so I'm near the wall out of traffic, and I look down at my phone again…at the new dick pic Ash has sent me.

I was too shocked the first time he sent me a pic to take a good look, but I study it now like I'm a detective examining a crime scene photo. Christ Jesus. Is *that* what was grinding against me the other day?

I stare at the pic for a good minute before deciding how to reply. Finally, I type out a message and send it.

Gray

> You did it again. This is GRAY's phone, not GRACE's.

I stare at the screen, watching for the three dots, but they don't come. I can't stand in the hall all day, so I'm about to put my phone away when a laughing emoji pops up and the dots appear.

Ash

Oh shit! Not again!

Ash

Well, since you've already seen it, what do you think?

There's a couple different ways to take that, and I purposely choose the wrong one.

Gray

The lighting is good, but I'm not sure about the angle of the picture. Remember that photography is all about framing.

A pause before the dots appear again.

Ash

I never took art in school. What's wrong with the angle?

Gray

The camera position makes it look foreshortened. It's hard to tell how big it is. Try a different angle. Also, do you have something you can put next to it for scale?

Another pause before the dots bounce.

Ash

Hmm. I see your point. Hold on.

I wait, but there's nothing for another minute. When a second pic finally comes through, I clamp a hand over my mouth to hold in a snort of laughter. The pic is taken from an angle that better showcases Ash's ample length, and he's holding a cucumber against his erect cock.

I stand there for several seconds trying to hold in my laughter before I'm able to start typing again.

Gray

Much better angle, but cucumbers can vary by type. I mean, is that a pickling cucumber? An English cucumber? A Kirby?

The dots bounce.

Ash

There's more than one type of cucumber???

Ash

Hold on.

I smile. The hall around me is almost clear as the next presentation sessions begin, but I no longer have any desire to listen to a lecture.

I look around to be sure there's no one close by. There's a guy that looks more like a bouncer than a professor typing on his phone a little ways down, but he glances at me and goes back to his own conversation a second later.

A pic comes in. This time Ash has taken all the guesswork out of things. There's a tape measure rolled out against his dick that reads seven and a half inches.

Holy shit. The man is nearly eight inches long.

Another pic comes through, this time with the tape measure held lengthwise across his cock. Just over two inches. He's thick as well.

We never measured Drew, but I'd guess he was five inches, and I try to imagine where my body would fit nearly three more inches of Ash.

I lean back against the wall and push out a deep breath as I contemplate my response for a long while before starting to type.

Gray

Impressive. But why are you sending me pics of your dick?

Ash

Do you want the snarky answer or the real one?

I want the real one, but...

Gray

The snarky one.

The dots bounce for a while.

Ash

It's fun to think of you sitting in your conference

listening to some stuffy old academic drone on while you look at a pic of my cock. Are you blushing? Please tell me there are tons of people around you.

I chuckle.

Gray

Asshole. 😉

Gray

Actually, I'm standing in the hall alone. You caught me between sessions.

And I won't go to the next one now. I need to go back to my hotel room and relieve some tension.

My phone pings with the next text.

Ash

Now do you want to know the real reason I sent the pics?

More than anything in the world, but I shouldn't say yes. To let him tell me is dangerous. Dangerous to my emotions. Dangerous to my mental equilibrium. Just...dangerous.

Gray

Yes.

The dots bounce for a long time as I hold my breath. There's a tempest in my chest that makes me wonder if I should see a cardiologist.

Ash

I'm showing you my cock because you should get used to the idea of having it inside you. To want it inside you. I want you to spend the rest of your trip imagining what I plan to do to you when you get back, because I'm done waiting, and I'm done pretending. I want you, and I plan to have you.

I brace myself against the wall as my legs almost give out. Forget trying to make it back to my hotel room. I'm not sure I can walk anymore.

Scratch that. I have to get out of this hall before I start moaning.

I marshal my strength and force myself to move unsteadily back toward my room. I should leave the conversation at that…but of course I can't. Or I won't.

I type out a new message, hesitate, then send it.

Gray

And what exactly do you plan to do to me?

Ash

Gray

And what exactly do you plan to do to me?

Her text comes in, and I nearly blow my load right there. I was fairly certain she wanted me too, but there was always a chance I misread her cues, and she'd be horrified by that text I just sent.

She's not. She wants to know what I have planned, and I'm more than happy to tell her. After I tease her a bit.

Ash

That depends. Do you want me to make love to you, or do you want me to fuck you?

That's a hazardous question, but her answer will tell me how to proceed. After all, she doesn't know about my particular appetites yet, and I don't want to scare her off.

I wait.

And wait.

My phone doesn't indicate she's typing, and I start to panic. If the question alone scared her, that's not a good sign.

Finally the dots bounce, and I hold my breath until her reply pops onto the screen.

Gray

I want you to fuck me.

I sag in relief into the couch. I'm not opposed to being gentle once in a while or going slow, but it's the emotional landmines of 'making love' that worry me. I want Gray, but I'm not looking to plan a future with her just yet, and I hope she understands that.

I freeze as something occurs to me. What if Gray does know that, and she's only giving me the answer she thinks I want to hear? What if she doesn't really want me to fuck her but she suspects making love would be a non-starter for me?

I'm paralyzed with indecision as my fingers hover over the phone's keyboard. Can I take her answer at face value and tell her all the dirty, filthy things I want to do to her, or should I play it safe for now?

I need to do some more testing.

Ash

Can you take all of me?

I'm only half hard, so the pic with the tape measure probably undersells me, but let's see how she reacts.

The dots bounce.

Gray

I don't know. I've never had a cock that big.

Ash

So I'll be stretching that tight little pussy of yours?

The thought of how snug she'll be makes me harder. I gather from our conversations she hasn't had sex in a while, although I don't know what her self-pleasuring habits might be. Still, I'm confident she's going to squeeze me pretty hard.

Gray

Yes.

Ash

Are you afraid it will hurt?

Gray

It's alright if it does. I can handle it.

I push out another breath of relief as I stiffen even more. She's not afraid of a little pain, which means I can be rough with her.

I'm not a sadist. I don't enjoy hurting women – the opposite, in fact – but I also don't hold back when my passions are driving me, and I don't want to worry about handling Gray with kid gloves. I need a woman who can take what I give her, however hard and fast that may be.

Time to see how far I can push things.

Ash

> What would you do if I wanted to put you on your knees and fuck your mouth?

The seconds tick by as I wait for the dots to appear, and I'm again afraid she's trying to think of the answer I want to hear rather than giving me her honest response.

Finally, the dots start up.

Gray

> I'd take you as deep as I could and swallow you down when you came.

My cock twitches, and I run my hand up the shaft. I've been trying not to touch myself because I'm ready to explode now, but I can't help the surge of lust that pulses straight to my balls at that answer. I can already imagine her kneeling before me, her hands tied behind her back as I grip her hair and pump in and out of her mouth. I'd come down her throat, just to take the edge off, then I'd put her on the bed and do what I do best.

Ash

> Good girl.

I pause, and I'm deciding where to take this, when Gray's next text comes in.

Gray

> Then what would you do to me?

Oh fuck. She wants more.

My cock pulses again. I won't last much longer, so I type fast.

Ash

> You'll need to be good and wet to take me, so I'd lay you down, spread your legs wide, and lick your cunt until you were dripping for me. I'd make you

come at least twice before I drove my cock inside you and fucked you until your legs were shaking from the pleasure.

I pause before hitting the 'Send' button, then throw caution to the wind and cast the message on its way.

Seconds pass, and I decide to send a follow-up message.

Ash

Would you like that?

I don't have to wait long for her response.

Gray

Yes.

I will my dick to calm down. We're starting to get somewhere, and I need a little more information before I can give in to this overwhelming urge to come.

Ash

Do you like to be edged?

The dots don't appear right away, and I wonder if she had to look up the term. Finally, she answers.

Gray

I don't know.

Fair enough. She didn't say no, and I feel like she'd be up for some exploration, but I get the sense she's never done anything kinky.

Actually, that's a good question.

Ash

What's the kinkiest thing you've ever done?

Gray

It's lame. No judgement…

Ash

Never.

I'm dying to know her answer, and excitement flares in my chest as I watch the dots.

Gray

When I was in college, two friends and I, along with our boyfriends, rented a house for Spring Break. The house had a hot tub, and one night when we were drunk, the six of us all had sex in the hot tub at the same time.

Gray

With our own partners. Not an orgy.

I smile. She's right. It's not extremely kinky – I had a similar experience myself in college – but at least she's not shy.

My mind drifts to the idea of letting someone else watch me fuck Gray. I imagine Kelsier walking in on us in the shower at the training center, then him standing there as I pound into her. Part of me is painfully turned on by the idea. Another part is too possessive and needs to have her all to myself. I can't decide which inclination is stronger.

My phone pings, and I realize I've been staring into space for the last minute.

Gray

Are you disappointed?

I grin. She suspects I'm kinky, and she sounds willing to go further.

Ash

Not at all. It means I get to introduce you to lots of new fun.

Gray

Like what?

Whatever the hell she wants. I have my preferences, but there's very little I won't try at least once.

I google an article in a magazine that lists about fifty different kinds of kinks, and I text it to her.

Ash

Look at this list and tell me which ones you'd be willing to try. I need to know more about what you like.

A couple minutes go by as I assume she scrolls the list on the website. Finally, my phone pings, but it's not her list.

Gray

Tell me one of your kinks first.

Fair enough. She doesn't want to put herself out there until she knows more about what I'm into. My thumbs fly over the keyboard.

Ash

When I'm fucking your mouth, your hands will be tied behind your back.

I wait, but the dots don't appear. I send a follow-up when I can't stand it anymore.

Ash

Would you let me do that?

Several more seconds dance away before her response comes in.

Gray

Yes.

Excitement churns in my chest until I realize I've asked the wrong question. I type the more relevant question and hit send.

Ash

Would you LIKE that?

Her answer is quicker this time.

Gray

Yes.

I nearly pump my fist in the air but refrain.

Ash

Now tell me what you want to do.

I watch the screen as the dots bounce every few seconds while I presume she goes down the list of kinks I sent and adds the ones she likes. I count at least eight or nine possible items, and my dick throbs with anticipation. The little professor is more adventurous than I thought.

Gray's list finally pops up, and I read it eagerly.

Gray

> Bondage/Ropes, Submission, Role Play, Exhibitionism, CNC, Mirrors, Hunter/Prey, Tentacles, Voyeurism, Somnophilia.

My brows shoot up at Tentacles. I didn't see that coming, but I'm all-in if that's what she wants. I went through my own Hentai phase growing up, and I have a healthy appreciation for tentacle sex.

I also see a theme in Gray's list. She may be a strong, independent woman in her public and professional life, but in the bedroom, she wants to be dominated.

I can't help the grin that spreads across my face. Perfect.

My phone pings.

Gray

> What do you think?

I smile again.

Ash

> I think we're going to have a lot of fun, baby.

Chapter 28

Ash and I have barely seen each other the last few weeks, and it's been excruciating. It's like every force on the planet has conspired against us since that text conversation. First, Ash had a string of away games just after I came back from my conference. Then I came down with a cold, and after that I was underwater with end-of-semester finals and grading. Next, we had a freak December snowstorm, then the Christmas holiday hit, and Ash went back up to Canada while I stayed here with my family.

I was surprised when he presented me with a Christmas gift just before he left. I felt bad, since I hadn't thought to get him anything, but I was shocked when I opened the package to see it was a bottle of 2017 Pétrus Pomerol.

Actually, I nearly dropped the bottle, since, as I confirmed later, it cost more than the Scarecrow he'd gotten me at the restaurant. I tried to get him to take it back, but he refused, so it now sits in a place of honor in my wine cellar. I'm not sure I can bring myself to ever drink it.

I feel guilty that Ash and I have done very little the last few weeks to fix his chirping issue. Our conversations start out on-topic, but they always seem to evolve – or perhaps devolve – from trash talk to dirty talk.

To be clear, I don't feel guilty for taking Kaladin's money, although I expect to get a call or email from him any day now asking for a progress report. Ash has been playing a little better, so perhaps it's been enough to keep Kaladin satisfied for the moment.

It's more that I feel guilty for not helping Ash because I know how much hockey means to him. On the other hand, he's usually the one that sends our conversations spiraling off into debauchery, so at least I'm not completely at fault for our lack of progress.

I just don't try very hard to help keep us focused.

In any case, we made plans earlier in the week to spend a quiet New Year's Eve at his place. This is the first time we've both been free in way too long, and I'm eager to spend some time with him that doesn't involve navigating around the rest of the team and the coaching staff.

I usually spend New Year's Eve with Celena, but she gave me her blessing to stand her up this time. Supposedly Ash and I are just going to watch movies until the ball drops, but I'm pretty sure both of us expect the night to end in sex.

Or at least I desperately hope it will. Other than a make out session in a stairwell at the training center on one of my visits before Christmas, Ash and I haven't been able to do anything more than text-tease each other, and I'm ready to combust. He's made big promises, but we'll see if he follows through. Drew was big on talk as well, so I'm not counting my orgasms before they're…whatever.

When Ash opens his door that evening, I'm struck dumb by how good he looks. This is the first time I've seen him out of a hockey uniform in a while, and the man wears the hell out of a henley and jeans.

The smile Ash gives me is lopsided and shy, just big enough for his dimples to make an appearance. His eyes scan my body, and I'd give anything to know what he's thinking.

I had no idea what to wear tonight. I wanted to dress up, but watching movies is a casual event, so I opted for a pair of jeans that make my ass look great and a nice sweater.

"Hey, come on in," Ash says as he steps out of the way to let me pass.

I feel the awkwardness as we head into his living room. I'm sure we're both wondering if we should actually try to watch a movie or just strip naked and fuck. At least that's what *I'm* wondering.

"Any preference on movie?" he asks as he heads into the kitchen. "Comedy? Action? Drama?"

"Surprise me," I say as he puts a bag of popcorn in the microwave, then pulls two wine glasses out of a cabinet. I walk over to the counter and set down a bottle of rosé I brought from home.

"Popcorn and wine," Ash says, looking at the bottle. "Nice."

I pour the wine as the popcorn begins to pop. When it's done, Ash puts it in a bowl, and we settle onto the couch as he scrolls through one of the streaming services to see what's new. He sits close, one arm across the back of the couch but not touching me, and we decide on an action movie that was just released. He offered to watch a romcom, but truthfully, I prefer action.

About an hour into the movie, my phone dings with an incoming text, and I pull it out of my purse. I push a breath out through my nose when I see who it's from.

Drew

Happy New Year.

Ash leans over to look at the screen.

"Drew?" he questions. "Why is he texting you?"

I look at him in alarm. I don't want him to think I'm back with Drew.

"Sorry, I didn't mean to be nosey," he says.

"It's fine," I assure him. "He's been texting me since we saw him at the club, but I haven't responded." I swipe open the screen and show him the string of texts from Drew I've left unanswered.

Ash huffs a laugh as he looks through the messages. "He wants you back now that he thinks you're taken," he says.

I grunt in agreement as I put the phone down on the coffee table. "Why do men do that? Is it something in your DNA that only makes you see something as valuable when someone else has it?"

Ash chuckles as he pauses the movie. "I think we need a refill on wine and popcorn."

I agree and get up. My wine glass has been empty for ten minutes, but I didn't want to move.

I refill our glasses as Ash puts more popcorn in the microwave.

"Hey, can you look in the cabinet in front of you?" he says. "I think there's some popcorn seasoning I forgot I had."

I open the upper cabinet and look around. I do see the seasoning, but it's on the top shelf. I stand on tiptoe, and my fingers graze the container, but I only push it further back into the cabinet. I swear under my breath and try again, but it's out of reach now.

"Sorry," Ash says coming up behind me. "I forget not everyone is as tall as me."

I turn to face him as he presses forward against the counter and reaches up to pluck the container of seasoning off the shelf. It jumps out of his hand, and we both grab for it on instinct. The container ends up between us, my hand wrapped around the seasoning, his hand wrapped around mine…our bodies pressed together.

We both freeze, and I can't tell if my heart is beating fast from the momentary excitement of trying to catch the container or…

Who am I kidding? My heart is pounding because I'm pressed between the counter and Ash's body, and the look in his eyes says he's hungry for more than popcorn.

I let out a breathy laugh. "Close call."

Ash looks down at the seasoning wedged between us and pulls it gently out of my hand to set it on the counter.

"I can't wait any longer," he says softly.

"Any longer for what?" I ask. I'm sure I know, but I need to hear him say it to believe it.

Ash doesn't answer. He snakes one hand up my neck and threads it through my hair as his other arm wraps around me. Then his lips are on mine, and my mind empties of conscious thought as every nerve in my body sparks to life, making it possible only to feel, not to think.

A second later my feet leave the ground, and I find myself sitting on the counter with Ash standing between my legs. He's kissing me like he'll die if our lips part, and I have to suck in a deep breath through my nose because I've ceded complete control of my mouth to him.

Ash's lips leave mine only to fasten on my neck, and pleasure shoots all the way down my body. I know I've already soaked my panties.

"I've been thinking about this for weeks," Ash says against my throat. "The thought of fucking you has been driving me crazy. Tell me you knew that's what was going to happen tonight and that you want it as bad as I do, because I'm going to God damn explode if I'm not inside you soon."

Butterflies are an inadequate description for the chaos that erupts in my chest, and I can only nod before I'm able to push out a breathy, "Yes."

"Thank fuck," he says as he bands an arm around my waist, and his other hand grips me under my thigh. I wrap my legs around his hips, and he lifts me off the counter like I'm a pizza box he's bringing to the couch.

I revel in the feeling of being weightless. Oh, to be a professional athlete and feel the laws of gravity less than everyone else.

He sets a knee on the couch and lays me down before easing on top of me. Then his lips are on mine again, his tongue exploring deep in my mouth as I catch breaths that seem optional right now. I could live on this man's kisses.

Ash leans back to pull his shirt off, and I'm mesmerized by his sculpted chest and abs. I knew they were under there, but they still take me by surprise.

My three days a week at the gym now seem completely inadequate, and I decide to add three more days, an extra hour per workout, and a personal trainer. I'm relatively fit, but I'm not lean and muscular like an athlete. I have some soft spots, and my hips and thighs are generous.

I take in the ink that covers Ash's left pec, shoulder, and part of his upper arm. It's a black and gray realistic tattoo of ornate plated armor, and the detail is astounding. At quick glance, it actually looks like Ash is wearing part of a chest plate and jointed shoulder plate.

Ash smiles as he watches me take in his body. "Like what you see?"

My eyes meet his, and it's on the tip of my tongue to meet his pride with a snarky remark about being unimpressed or only being able to see five of the abs in his six-pack – not even remotely true – but I can't give in to the sarcasm. Not when literal perfection is staring me in the face.

"You can touch if you want," he says as he takes my hand and places it on his stomach.

I run my hand over the ridges of muscle, and I'm almost certain I feel my ovaries twitch. I didn't think I wanted kids, but Ash's abs are making me rethink every God damn one of my life choices, and I suddenly wonder if it's possible to remove an IUD at home. I'll google it later.

Ash lets me explore for a few seconds, but he groans when my hand trails lower toward the obvious bulge in his pants. Before I can get there, he grabs the hem of my sweater and pulls it up. I lift off the couch so he can get the garment out from under me, but just as it gets past my elbows, he stops. My hands and forearms are still caught in the sleeves, and I start to pull, trying to free them.

His large hand clamps down over the bunch of sweater at my wrists to stop me, and I meet his eyes again. There's an excited gleam there, and he bends to kiss me long and hard.

I'm breathless and dazed when he's done, which is why I barely notice him slip a hand behind me and pop open my bra. The feel of my breasts springing free brings me back, and I look at him in confusion as he pulls the bra up my arms until it catches on my sweater.

Ash leans back to take me in, his hand still pinning my wrists. I want to throw his words back at him, to ask if he likes what he sees, but I'm just not that confident.

"What are you doing?" I ask instead. "Help me get my hands free."

He shakes his head. "You said you didn't mind a little restraint."

He cups a hand over one breast and teases the already taut nipple with his thumb. I'm unsuccessful at stifling a whimper as pleasure shoots straight to my core before working its way down to curl my toes.

"Fuck, these breasts are gorgeous. I've been dying to touch them," he says. He grins down at me. "Did I see your nipples harden when I mentioned restraint?"

"They're cold," I lie, but the words come out strained.

He smiles wider, seeing through my bullshit.

"I guess I'll just have to warm them up then," he says, and he lowers his head to close his hot mouth over one stiff peak.

I bow off the couch and make a noise I'm sure is half moan, half wildebeest mating call. Ash holds my hands firmly above my head, but the rest of me writhes beneath him, completely unable to hold still as he sucks and licks and teases one nipple and then the other.

"I fucking love how your body responds," he says as he lifts his head. "It's perfect."

Ash unbuttons and unzips my jeans, then slides his hand into my pants. His fingers find the folds of my pussy as I try to keep from panting, and he runs his middle finger over my clit before pushing it inside me. I buck beneath him, amazed how easily he can make me react with the simplest touch. And he hasn't even taken his pants off yet.

"Fuck, Gray," he says, sliding his finger in and out. "You're drenched for me."

My instinct is to deny it, despite the obvious evidence to the contrary, but I don't get the chance. Ash lifts himself off me, and for a few horrifying seconds I'm afraid my excessive arousal turned him off, but he hooks his hands over the waist of my pants and yanks them down my legs. He looks down at me, and I take a moment to thank the lingerie gods I wore a lacey pair of black panties. They only last a couple seconds more before Ash strips them off as well.

He fishes in the pocket of his jeans and pulls out his wallet. He opens it, pulls out a condom, and tosses both the condom and the wallet on the coffee table.

"If you don't want this, Gray, say so now," Ash says as he unzips his jeans and pulls them down his legs.

I'm still laid out on the couch naked, hands tangled in my sweater above my head as I watch him shed his boxer briefs, and his cock springs free, hard and ready. It looks just as I remember it from the dick pics he sent, thick and veiny with a slight upward curve. It's big. Bigger than any other guy I've been with, and I kick myself mentally for not using my larger dildo this week to prepare.

Ash kneels on the couch, pushes my thighs open, and reaches for the condom.

"I'm sorry," he says as he opens the package and rolls the rubber down his length as I watch. "Normally I'd spend some time worshipping your sweet little cunt with my tongue, but I'm about to blow my load, and I want to be inside you when I do. I'll make it up to you next time."

Next time.

I'm not sure if he's just saying that to trick me into thinking this won't be a one-night stand or if he really believes we'll do this again. God, he hasn't even entered me yet, and I'm already hoping for more.

His use of the word "cunt" doesn't phase me. Many countries outside the US don't find the word as offensive as we often do, and I've learned that his filthy mouth only arouses me. I can barely stand it right now, in fact. I'll scream if he doesn't fuck me soon.

Ash pulls the back pillows off the couch to make more room, and my legs fall open wider as he settles between them.

"You want this, right?" he asks. "You consent to letting me fuck you like you've never been fucked before?"

I blink. He's asking for consent, and it hits me that I'm about to have sex with a professional athlete. This is his reality, perhaps more so than other men, and now I'm surprised he hasn't whipped out an electronic form for me to sign.

How many women has he slept with anyway?

I shake myself mentally. This is not the time to think about his other women. I couldn't back out now if I tried, so thinking about the women who came before and those who'll come after isn't doing me any favors.

Ash waits for my answer, and I nod. "Yes," I add, realizing he probably wants verbal consent, and now I'm wondering if he's recording this so he has me on record.

"Good girl," Ash says as he lowers himself onto me, and I feel my pussy clench. He reaches between us to line himself up, then presses forward. I have half a second to realize this is really happening before his tip parts me. I press my head back against the couch as I feel his cock stretch me open, and my hips jerk as he gives one tentative thrust.

"God dammit, baby. You're so fucking tight," Ash says as he pushes forward again, withdraws, then buries himself inside me.

I cry out and Ash stops immediately. His hand comes up to cradle the back of my neck. "Gray? Are you alright? Did I hurt you?"

There's a bit of a sting since it's been more than a year since I've had an actual cock inside me, and never one this thick, but my scream was about ninety-five percent pleasure and five percent pain. My response is to wrap a leg around his hip to keep him from going anywhere.

"I'm fine. Keep going," I say.

I try to wrap my arms around his neck, but I forget I'm still tangled in my sweater, and Ash has to pin my hands back down on the couch to keep from getting a face-full of it.

He pulls out slowly before pushing back in, and I swear I can count every inch of him as he enters.

"Fuck, baby, I'm not going to last," Ash says as he starts to move. "I should've jerked off before you came over so I could go longer. I've been thinking about fucking you ever since I kissed you in the parking lot. No, scratch that. I've been wanting to fuck you since I saw those tattoos on your back. We're doing it doggy next so I can see them."

I have the urge to ask him why he wanted to fuck me so bad. I'm pretty enough when I try, but this man has dated actresses and probably models. This doesn't seem like the right time for a conversation about my feelings of inadequacy, though.

Ash picks up speed as his thrusting grows more intense. My own climax builds as he grinds into me, and I push my hips up to meet him, chasing my release. I almost never come this way, but if Ash holds out long enough, it might actually happen.

I jolt as the chorus of the song *Hello* by Adelle swells on my phone.

The phone buzzes around on Ash's coffee table, and I'm horrified to realize Drew is calling me. He's never called me. Ever.

Also, I need to change that ring tone, like, yesterday.

"Sorry, I should've silenced that," I say as I struggle to get one of my hands free from my sweater, but Ash tightens his hold on my wrists.

He slows his thrusting to look over at my phone, and damn me if the slower pace isn't even better.

"This guy is persistent," Ash says as he pushes in, making me take all of him. "Maybe you should answer it."

I blink. "What?"

I see the evil glint in his eye too late as he reaches over and swipes to answer the phone.

My eyes flare wide. Oh God.

"Hello?" Ash says, still moving inside me.

Now I'm trying in earnest to free my hands, but he holds me firm.

"Uh…hi," Drew says. "I'm looking for Gray. Is she there?"

"She's here, but she's busy right now," Ash says.

"And who's this?" Drew asks.

"It's Ash. This is Drew, right? We met a while back at the club."

Silence on the other end of the line, then, "Yeah, this is Drew. This is …Ash Gunnarsson from the Hydra?"

Ash thrusts into me hard without warning, and I can't help the mewl that escapes my throat. An actual God damn mewl.

"Gray?" Drew questions. "Is that you? Are you alright?"

"Go ahead, baby," Ash whispers in my ear. "Tell him how you are."

"What the hell are you doing?" I whisper back, but his next thrust has me biting back a moan.

"Gray?" Drew's voice sounds again.

"I'm fine," I croak out. "Can't talk right now."

"Yeah, sorry," Ash says toward the phone. "I'm balls deep inside her right now and about to give her the first of several orgasms."

My eyes bulge as I let out a choking noise. Ash just grins down at me and keeps thrusting.

"You haven't been fucked right in a long time, have you, baby," he says as I give him my best glare under the circumstances. "But we're gonna fix that tonight. You're not leaving until that sweet, needy little pussy of yours is fully satisfied."

I want to be annoyed, but his words swirl deliciously in my stomach, then travel south to my clit. I didn't realize how much I liked dirty talk.

"If you want to hold on, Drew, Gray can talk in a minute or two," Ash says toward the phone. "She's so fucking wet that she should be coming any second now." He looks at me. "You're gonna be a good girl and scream for me, right, baby?" he purrs loud enough for Drew to hear.

I bite my lip to stay quiet, but Ash takes long, hard strokes as he pounds into me, and soon I can't hold in the moans of pleasure.

I start invoking the Lord's name in vain, and there's a few seconds of silence before my phone bloops to indicate the call disconnected.

Finally, I find my voice. "What the fuck were you thinking?" I hiss.

Ash closes a hand over my breast and flicks the nipple with his thumb, which makes my eyes roll back in my head. He keeps moving, and now I'm starting to see stars.

"I was thinking," Ash says, "that you're mine now, and I want that motherfucker to know it."

A flutter works its way all the way down my spine and into my toes.

Ash looks down at me and something in his gaze turns feral. "And now I want *you* to know it too."

He picks up his pace again as he drives into me, and if I thought I saw stars before, I see whole galaxies now. Ash still holds my hands over my head, and I buck beneath him as I can't contain my ecstasy anymore.

"Fuck, Gray," he breathes into my ear. "You're gonna make me come, but I need you to come first."

He moves the hand not holding my wrists down between us to find my clit, and I cry out as he begins to rub it in time with his thrusting. It's like hitting the accelerator, and several seconds later, I pull a Thelma and

Louise over the cliff of my orgasm. I scream, and Ash's mouth covers mine as if he's trying to consume my pleasure.

My body jerks and shudders as he continues to massage my clit, and aftershocks rack me as my pussy clamps around him. Ash grunts loudly, driving into me several more times until he seats himself fully, and I feel the pulse of his cock as he comes.

"Fuck, Gray!" he says against my lips as his own body shudders, and he eases down on top of me. "Just…holy fuck."

I'm pinned to the couch, his solid weight holding me in place so there's no hope of moving.

I don't give a damn. I don't ever want to move again, and I'm honestly not sure I can, so really the safest thing to do is lie here.

I'm settling in for a long winter of keeping this man's cock warm when Ash pulls out and lifts himself off me. My body sighs in disappointment.

Ash stands and walks naked across the living room and into the kitchen. He pulls off the condom and drops it in the trash before he strolls back to me, cock bobbing.

I sit up and finally pull my hands free from my sweater. I turn it right-side out again and start to put my bra back on since I assume we're done with the movie and it's time to go.

Ash snatches the bra out of my hand.

"What are you doing?" he asks.

I stare at him. "Getting dressed?"

"Why? So I have to undress you again when the movie is over?"

He has his own boxer briefs in his hand, and he pulls them back on before flopping down next to me on the couch.

I continue to stare at him. "I just thought…"

"You thought I was going to fuck you and kick you out?" he supplies.

"I…didn't want to overstay my welcome," I say weakly. "I didn't know if…um, I mean…Am I supposed to sign something?"

Ash blinks at me. "Sign something? Like what?"

"I don't know. Like a consent form or an NDA?"

"Consent forms and NDAs are for one-night stands. You're my girlfriend."

"Fake girlfriend," I correct.

His face darkens, and I yelp as he grabs me by the waist and hauls me across him so I'm straddling his lap, still naked. His hand wraps around the back of my neck so I have to look at him.

"There was nothing fake about what we just did, Gray," he says, "and there won't be anything fake about what I'm going to do to you when this movie is over." He grimaces. "Christ, I normally need a good twenty to thirty minutes to recover, but I'm almost ready to go again."

Ash reaches forward and grabs his shirt off the table where he tossed it. He gathers it up and slips it over my head, then helps me thread my hands through the sleeves. I'm swimming in it, but the henley smells like whatever cologne or deodorant he wears, and I vow to never take it off.

"I want you to listen to me carefully," he says as he takes my face in his hands. "This may have started out as a fake relationship, but it's real now. Look at me and tell me it's not real for you."

His eyes lock with mine, and all I can do is work my mouth open and closed as words elude me.

"I told you that you were mine, and I meant it," Ash says, his gaze piercing through every chink in my carefully constructed emotional armor. "Look me in the eye and deny you belong to me."

The feminist in me wants to lecture him about claiming gender-based ownership, but my inner hussy has the feminist hogtied and gagged.

Ash grips the back of my neck again. "Say it."

His hold is firm but not painful, and something deep inside me is compelled to obey his command.

"I belong to you," I whisper.

"Again," he orders, and I feel myself get wet again.

"I belong to you," I say with more surety.

He smiles. "Good girl."

Chapter 29

Gray

We watch the rest of the movie, but I couldn't tell you what happened if my life depended on it. I spend the time tucked up against Ash, wearing his shirt, and watching his cock slowly harden in his underwear until the credits roll. When they do, Ash turns off the TV and begins to kiss me.

"Longest fucking movie ever," he says as he pulls his shirt off me.

I gasp as his mouth fastens on my breast, and I thread my fingers through his hair to hold him in place against my chest. He starts to tug at my panties, which he let me put back on for the movie, but the position is awkward, and he's having trouble getting them off.

"Shouldn't we…maybe…go into your bedroom?" I suggest as he continues to work at the panties while suckling my breast.

Ash stills, and I immediately know I've said something wrong. He doesn't want me in his bedroom.

He lifts his head to look at me.

"Forget I said anything. Here is fine." I try to play it off, but the fact he doesn't want me in his room stings a little.

Ash shakes his head. "You don't understand," he says as he stands up and starts to pace.

I want to take back the words and apologize, but pride won't let me. There was nothing wrong with suggesting we go to his room.

"It's fine," I say again because it's all I can manage.

"No, it's not," he says. "Come with me."

Ash grabs my hand and pulls me up from the couch. We're both only wearing our underwear as we head across his living room and down the hall to his bedroom.

"Ash-," I try again, but he cuts me off.

"There's a reason I don't want to go into the bedroom tonight," he says, "but it's not what you're thinking."

"And what am I thinking?" I ask.

"Probably that I don't want you in my bedroom because I don't want you to stay, or some bullshit like that."

"And that's not it?"

Ash stops at the threshold to his room and looks down at me.

"Definitely not," he says. He lets out a deep sigh. "I have…particular tastes I indulge every so often, but I don't want to get into them tonight, and if we go in the bedroom, I'll be too tempted."

My eyes narrow. "Tastes?"

"Nothing too extreme," he says, "but they aren't for everyone, and I don't want to scare you off."

My eyes widen. "Scare me off?"

"I'll show you my room," he says quickly, "and you can decide before I see you next if it's something you can handle. We've got more road games this week, so you'll have a few days to think about it."

My heart drops as I remember he's going to be gone for a while. He says I'm his now, but I've had too many guys disappear on me after sleeping with them, and my abandonment issues flare like hemorrhoids.

"Does that work?" Ash asks when I don't say anything, and I force myself to nod.

Ash turns on the light in his bedroom and tugs me inside. At first glance, nothing looks out of the ordinary. I was expecting the red room of pain or something, but this looks like a regular bedroom with a large king bed against one wall, a trunk at the foot of it, and an armchair near a small side table. There's a dresser between two doors on the wall opposite the bed. I assume one door goes to a closet and the other to a bathroom.

Ash leads me to the bed, and I raise a brow at him.

"Absolutely terrifying," I deadpan as I survey it. "That duvet is clearly dry clean only."

I yelp as he slaps my ass for the remark. Then he goes to the foot of the bed, bends, and reaches under it to pull something out that he tosses onto the covers.

I stare at the black strap that snakes across the top of the bed before it ends in…a buckle cuff.

Holy shit. It *is* the red room of pain.

I glance at the walls. The light blue room of pain.

Ash goes around to the other corners and pulls three more straps out of hiding to toss them on the bed before he comes back to stand behind me. His hands land gently on my shoulders, and something akin to excitement twined with alarm skirts up my spine.

"What do you think?" he asks.

I stare at the cuffs and imagine myself strapped spread-eagle to Ash's bed while he fucks me. The thought turns me on more than I care to admit, but then something occurs to me.

"Who are those for?" I ask. I shouldn't assume anything. Maybe he's the one who likes to be tied down.

Ash chuckles. "That depends how you look at it, but technically they're for you," he says softly. He leans in so his breath ghosts over my ear. "How do you feel about being strapped to my bed while I do dirty, unspeakable things to you, Gray?"

I feel the husky purr of his voice between my legs as I swallow audibly.

"What kinds of dirty, unspeakable things?" I ask.

Ash let's go of my shoulders and kneels down next to the bed. He pulls a large case out from under it, hefts it onto the bed, and opens it.

I step forward to look inside. There are several lengths of rope, a pair of handcuffs, a riding crop, a leather flogger, a feather tickler, a blindfold, and a ball gag in the case.

I turn to Ash. He watches me carefully, but when I don't react, he bends down and pulls another smaller case out from under the bed and opens it. I peer into that one to see an assortment of dildos, vibrators, anal plugs, and what I take to be nipple clamps.

Sweet Jesus. The man has more toys than I do.

"That is quite a collection," I say. My mouth has gone a bit dry, but not from fear or revulsion. On the contrary. My mouth may be dry, but other parts of me are very, very wet.

"And what do you think of my collection?" he asks. "If I strapped you to my bed, would you let me use some of these things on you?"

I swallow again. "You'd want to hurt me?"

"No, not at all," he says forcefully. "I'm a pleasure dom. I use these things to control your pleasure."

I blink at him. "There are different kinds of doms?"

He smiles. "Yeah, several kinds. Doms that punish or use pain are what everyone thinks of first, but that's only one kind of BDSM. I'd use the things in these cases to tease you and test your body."

His voice drops to a husky purr as he moves behind me again and trails a couple fingers lightly down my neck, drawing goosebumps. "I'd sensitize your skin so I could make you come with the slightest touch. I'd explore you for hours so I knew exactly where your most erogenous spots were, and then I'd work those spots until you were so mad with desire you couldn't remember your own name."

He runs his fingers across my shoulders, and I shiver under the touch before he moves in closer so his body presses against me from behind.

"Is that something you'd let me do, Gray?" he asks, his voice barely a whisper. "Would you give me control and trust me with your pleasure?"

My first instinct is to say, "Fuck yeah," but it sounds too good to be true. There has to be a catch.

"What about *your* pleasure?" I ask.

Ash's hand curls up gently around my neck under my chin and pulls my head against his chest. His other hand dips into my panties to massage my clit and I moan as I start to writhe against him.

"What some men don't understand," he says, "is that a woman's pleasure can enhance their own. Some men will just fuck you until they come, and they don't care if you come too. But when I've got you coming so hard your eyes roll back in your head, your pussy is going to squeeze me like a vise, and that's going to make me come all the harder. Your pleasure *is* my pleasure."

I barely take in what he's saying because his finger working my clit does indeed have my eyes rolling back in my head.

"Do you understand?" Ash asks, and I have to force myself to focus.

"What? Um, yeah. Right, like a vise," I say against his hand still holding me just under my jaw.

He chuckles. "I think it's time for me to make good on all this talk."

I exhale as he pulls his hand out of my panties, but I squeak as he swings me up into his arms and heads back out toward the living room. He stops in the guest bathroom to pull a towel off one of the racks, then heads into the kitchen. He sets me down near the island and lays the towel on top of it.

"Ash, what-"

I cry out as he wraps his hands around my waist and lifts me onto the island. He presses me back onto it and pulls my panties off before he grabs my ankles and lifts them up so they're resting on his shoulders.

He smiles down at me. "I've been waiting to taste you for weeks now," he says as he runs his hands down my thighs. Goosebumps follow in their wake, and he chuckles again.

"If you agree to let me be your Dom," he says, "the next time we do this you'll have nipple clamps on, a plug in your ass, and your hands will be tied to my headboard."

My mouth falls open. I feel like I should say something, but how exactly does one respond to that? Was that a threat? A promise?

Then the opportunity to say anything is lost as Ash pushes my knees open, lowers his head, and begins to feast on me.

I cry out as he suctions his mouth around my clit before flicking his tongue against it.

"Fuck! Ash!"

I grind my hips against his mouth, and he makes a humming sound as he moves lower so he can spear his tongue into me.

My fingers find his hair, and I thread them through his semi-long locks, desperate to have something to hold onto as my pleasure starts to crescendo already. Ash fastens his mouth on my clit again, sucking hard, and it's only a minute or so before I scream as my orgasm crashes over me. I've never come that fast in my life.

My body tries to buck off the island, but Ash presses a hand to the center of my chest and holds me down as his mouth continues to work me, coaxing the last throes of my climax from me as I moan and pant.

Finally, he lifts his head and looks down at me. I can't speak as I take deep gulping breaths of air.

"My turn," Ash says, and my eyes flare to realize there's more to come.

I'm not sure my body can handle it.

Ash helps me off the island and turns me around so my back is to him. I sense him removing his boxers, and I let him press me down on the towel so I'm bent over the island.

"Are you alright?" he asks. "Can I fuck you again?"

Despite my concerns, I nod. Maybe I can't take any more, but I'm going to try. "Yes. Fuck me again."

"Don't move," he says, and I watch him head down the hall toward his bedroom. He comes back a few seconds later with a strip of about five condoms, and my eyes widen.

"Just how many times are you planning to fuck me?" I ask, leaning up off the island.

He rips one condom off the strip and tosses the rest onto the counter.

"As many times as I want," he says as he rips the wrapper open, and I feel the muscles between my legs clench.

Ash puts the condom on, then pushes me back down. He hooks a hand under my knee and lifts my leg so it rests on the island as his hand grips my thigh to hold it up. He swipes the head of his cock through my folds, then lines himself up at my entrance and pushes forward.

I let out a moan as he stretches me open again. As thick as his shaft is, his head is even thicker, and my body strains to accommodate him.

"Try to relax so you can take me easier, baby," he whispers.

I manage to stop straining my muscles, and he slides in to the hilt.

"Good girl," he says on a groan. "See how perfectly you take me when you let go of all that tension?"

Right on cue, my pussy clamps down at the words 'good girl,' and he grunts. "God damn. That is one hell of a praise kink you have," he says, chuckling. "I'm going to have to be careful not to abuse it."

Ash leans over me and braces his other hand on the island as he begins to thrust. My fingers curl around the corners of the towel he laid down, and I try to convince myself again this is really happening.

"You're doing so well, sweetheart," he praises as he takes long, hard strokes. "You should see how amazing your wet little cunt looks when it's sucking my huge cock inside you."

My inner walls convulse around him, maybe not as hard as when he calls me a good girl, but still hard enough that he groans.

"Reach down and work your clit for me," Ash says.

He pushes my hair to one side, and I feel him trace the outline of the wings on my back with one finger. I twitch as he gets to my mid-back where I'm more ticklish.

"I think I just unlocked a new kink," he says. "We're going to roleplay the evil demon corrupting the innocent little angel one of these days. Would you like that?"

I nod. I have no idea why that turns me on, but it does.

He pulls me back against his chest and fastens his mouth on my neck before he kisses and nips his way down to my shoulder. More goosebumps spring up all along my arms as pleasure shimmies its way down my body. Ash bites down gently in the crook of my neck as he thrusts, and I cry out in bliss.

"Your clit, Gray. Now," Ash orders as he moves. "I'm going to come any second now, and you need to come with me."

I get a shaking hand between my legs and swirl it around my clit, but I stop a second later. I'm almost too sensitive, and the potential power of the orgasm frightens me. I pull my hand back.

"Baby, you need to-"

"I can't," I say. "It's too much."

Fear courses through me as Ash pulls out. An apology jumps to the tip of my tongue, but it dies as he spins me around, lifts me into the air, and impales me down on his cock where he's standing.

I gasp and wrap my arms around his neck as he bounces me up and down along his length. The new position rubs him against my clit, but it's not as intense as before, and I sigh in relief as a much smaller orgasm than I feared shudders through me.

Ash pumps me up and down faster against his body, and a few seconds later, he roars into the silence of the room as he pulses inside me.

When he recovers a few seconds later, he meets my eyes. I smile, but his face is serious. He turns and strides with me still impaled on his cock to the couch. He eases us down onto it and braces himself above me, but he doesn't withdraw.

"We're going to need a safe word," he says as he looks down at me. "Or we can use the color system if you want, but we need some guidelines sooner rather than later."

I blink at him. "Color system?"

"Green, yellow, red," he says. "Like a stoplight."

I nod hesitantly. "Okay."

"If you don't want to do something, or you don't want *me* to do something, use those colors. Otherwise, I'll expect you to obey me when I tell you to do something."

I blink at him again. "What?"

"Obey me," he repeats. "If you let me dom for you, then you do what I say." He narrows his eyes. "You're not a brat, are you?"

"Excuse me?" I ask indignantly.

"It's a type of sub," he explains. "Sort of. Brats get off on disobeying so that they have to be punished. Are you going to be a brat?"

My eyes widen, and I shake my head. "I…don't think so?"

His face eases. "Good. I'm not really into brat taming. You said in your text you'd be into hunter-prey play, so I don't mind if you fight me when we're doing that, but I can't handle brats."

I stare at him. Clearly BDSM is a lot more complex than I knew.

"Is there a rule book about all this you can point me to?" I ask. "I feel like I need to do some research."

He smiles. "I'll teach you as we go. Just ask questions when you're not sure, and there are no dumb questions."

I want to laugh. That's more or less the speech I give my students at the beginning of each semester, and the irony isn't lost on me.

"I want you to feel comfortable, so just ask," Ash goes on. "I'll go easy on you until you get the hang of things."

"You'll go easy on me?"

"That sounded more threatening than I intended," he says. "I just meant we'll go slow."

I nod.

"I'll try, anyway," Ash qualifies. "You drive me fucking mad, so it's going to be an effort to control myself around you. I'll be patient with you if you can be patient with me."

I nod again.

"BDSM is all about control, so we'll have to work on that together."

"And you're in control," I say. I think I understand, but he shakes his head.

"No, you are," he says.

I frown. "Me? But you said-"

"A dom is only in control on the surface, but in true BDSM, it's the sub who has ultimate control. If you don't like something and use the safe word, things stop immediately. It doesn't matter how into it I am, things stop," he repeats more forcefully. "You obey me until it's time for me to obey you."

I exhale deeply. That eases my mind.

Ash finally lifts himself and slips out of me. He's no longer hard, but he's not much smaller when he's slack, so I feel every inch of him withdraw.

"I'm starving," he says as he disposes of the condom. "Want to order a pizza? I could use some fuel before I fuck you again."

It takes a moment for my brain to kick in, and I lean up on my elbows. "Again?"

He stops with his cell phone in his hand. "Do you not want me to fuck you again?" he asks, and I hear the disappointment in his voice.

"No, that's not what I meant," I assure him quickly as I sit up. "I've just never been with a guy who had so much stamina…or this intense a sex drive for that matter."

He grins at me. "Oh, baby. You ain't seen nothing yet."

Chapter 30

Ash

I'm like a zombie the next morning as I walk down the aisle of the team plane to where Kelsier already has seats staked out for us. I kept Gray at my place way too late last night before I finally let her go home, and then it was another hour before my body wound down enough to fall asleep. We missed the ball drop, but we rang in the new year in a much more satisfying way.

Between the lack of sleep and the memories of being inside her sweet-as-hell body that are playing on repeat in my head, I'm not all here. For that matter, I'm already planning the twelve new ways I'm going to fuck her when we're done with this road trip.

I jerk to a stop in the middle of the aisle and look down to find Kingston's hand wrapped around my forearm. My eyes meet his where he sits in his seat. His expression is hard, and I return it with a look of annoyance.

"I'm not sure what you and that professor have been doing," he says, "but I hope you have your shit together for these games."

I scowl at him. "You just worry about doing your own job and let me worry about mine," I say before pulling my arm out of his grip and continuing on.

I throw my bag in the overhead compartment and thump down into the seat next to Kelsier, the sex-high I've been riding now spoiled.

"Problem?" he asks, noticing my mood.

"Fucking Kingston," I say. "He needs to get off my case."

Kelsier chuckles. "Good luck with that."

"Whatever," I mumble as I swipe open my phone. I'm hoping for a message from Gray, but there's nothing.

I decide to text her myself. It seems like she's been used by a lot of men, and I get the feeling she doesn't expect to hear from me again now that we've slept together. Nothing could be further from the truth. If I could've packed her in my luggage and brought her with us to Winnipeg, I would've. I'm starting to get hard just thinking about her, and I have to get that shit under control before Kelsier notices.

But first, I send her a couple texts.

Ash

Good morning, baby.

Ash

How do you feel today?

It's a few seconds before her response comes in.

Gray

Like I was thoroughly railed almost half a dozen times last night.

I smile and type back.

Ash

I hope that's a good thing.

There's a few seconds before her answer.

Gray

Yes. Very good.

There's a pause, and then the dots bounce again.

Gray

I like that I'm sore. I can still feel you inside me.

That does it. My dick goes full mast, and I barely manage to force back the groan that tries to pry its way up my throat.

I go to respond, but Kelsier's voice stops me.

"Dude! Do you have an erection?" he whisper-hisses.

"Sshh! Keep your voice down," I warn him.

"I'm trying," he whispers, "but you're about to pop your pants here, and I'm not sitting with you if you're gonna sport a stiffy the entire flight." He glances at my phone and his eyes widen. "Wait, did you fuck the doc last night?"

I shut the screen down and put a finger to my lips to shush him. I look between the seats to see who's behind us. Mack is already passed out in the window seat. He hates flying, so he usually hits the melatonin hard and goes to sleep when he gets on the plane. Samsonov sits next to him with his noise-canceling headphones on.

Only Fig is in the row in front of us, and he listens to audiobooks the entire flight.

"Not one word to the rest of the team," I warn Kelsier. "Especially not on the team chat, or I swear to Christ-"

"Yeah, you'll beat the shit out of me," Kelsier interrupts. "Just fucking tell me."

I exhale deeply and sink back into my seat. "Yeah, we had sex last night. A lot."

Kelsier raises a brow. "A lot?"

"Like four times before she went home."

His eyes widen. "Jesus Christ!"

I give him a warning look, and he lowers his voice again. "I take it that it was good sex?"

I groan. "You have no idea. It was like I no longer needed a recovery period. I was almost ready to go again by the time I got the condom off."

"That good?" he asks in surprise.

I look around to be sure no one is listening. "She has a praise kink," I tell him. "One of these days she'll squeeze my dick off if I call her a good girl too many times."

He claps a hand over his mouth to stifle whatever reaction he was about to make. "Fuck, man," he says when he pulls his hand back. "You hit the fake dating jackpot."

I jerk my head to him. Everything with Gray was so real last night that I forgot the rest of the team thinks I'm only fake dating her. Before last night, they were the only ones who knew the truth about us. Now, they're the only ones who don't. The rest of the world thinks I'm *actually* dating Gray…and they're right.

I have the urge to bolt out of my seat and announce to the whole plane I'm dating her and that they all need to keep their eyes and hands off, but one thing stops me. If she and I date for real, will she still be allowed to work with me? Maybe Kaladin will think we've gotten too close and call it off. Are there ethical issues with him paying her if we're dating? It's not a problem right now because he thinks we're only fake dating, but if he knows the truth…

No, I can't tell anyone yet.

Well, almost anyone.

"I need to tell you something, Kels, and it will seriously fuck things up if you say anything to anyone," I say. I'm wary of divulging this to him, but he's been my best friend since I got here. Granted that hasn't been long, but I trust him.

He looks at me seriously. "Okay. What? Everything alright?"

"Swear you won't say a word."

He frowns. "I swear. What is it?"

I inhale deeply and let it out. "I'm not fake dating Gray. I'm actually dating her. I told her last night she's mine for real."

He stares at me for what seems like minutes as I wait for him to say something.

"Holy shit, Gunny," he says finally. He grins. "Congrats. It sounds like you've got it bad for her."

I sigh again. "I can't stop thinking about her. I want her so much."

He cocks his head. "Do you want to be with her, or is this just lust?"

I take a moment to consider, but I already know the answer. I got angry with the reporters who suggested I was dating an older woman, mainly because I'd felt her stiffen next to me when they said it. The thought of the way Drew and other men have hurt or used her makes me want to throw furniture across the room. And, yes, I couldn't wait to get between her legs while we were watching the movie, but I also loved the feel of her tucked up against my body. I want to protect her. Make her feel safe and desired.

I'm not yet sure if it's love like Kelsier suggested a while back, but it's a whole lot more than just lust.

"Not just lust," I say, and he nods slowly.

"You'll have to tell the team and Kaladin eventually," he says.

"I know," I say, "but not yet."

"Why not?"

I give him the reasons about not being able to work with her and possibly having Kaladin pull her funding.

He waggles his head in a *'Yeah, that's possible'* way.

"So what are you going to do?" he asks.

I pull out my phone again. The flight attendants are going through their preflight spiel, and I realize I never responded to Gray's last text. I suspect she has abandonment issues, and I don't want to leave her hanging, so I quickly text back.

Ash

Getting ready to take off. Gotta shut down now. Miss you already. Will text when I land.

The dots bounce almost immediately, and I suspect I was right, that she was freaking out after not hearing back after that last intimate text.

Gray

Miss you too. Safe flight.

I shut down my phone and turn back to Kelsier. "For now, I'm just going to stay under the radar as much as possible. Hopefully everyone will just think we're great actors."

Kelsier huffs a laugh. "Don't bet on it. Fig is already on to you. He told half the team he caught you and Gray in the equipment room. He didn't see anything, but he could guess what you were doing in there."

I grimace. "Fuck."

Kelsier cocks his head again. "What *were* you doing in there?"

I sigh. "I finger fucked her. It's where I learned about her praise kink."

Kelsier nearly chokes. "You finger fucked the doc in the equipment room?" he hisses under his breath.

I nod.

"And you didn't tell me?" he asks indignantly.

It's my turn to laugh. "We were in there because of you."

"What?"

"I saw her talking to you before practice that day she had you chirp at me, and I got jealous," I explain. "I told her I was going to prove to her who she belonged to."

He stares at me before he cracks a grin. "You possessive asshole."

I shrug just before the plane begins to taxi.

"You guys do any roleplaying last night?" Kelsier asks.

I frown at him. Kelsier and I have never gotten into the details of each other's sex lives, so I'm not sure what makes him suspect I'm into roleplaying.

"Like what?" I ask.

He looks at me disbelievingly. "Like naughty professor and bad student," he says, as if this answer is obvious.

And now that he says it, it is.

"Oh shit," I say. "No, we haven't done that yet, but we are absolutely going to when I get back."

He grins. "You know what you need to do to make it realistic, right?"

My brows shoot up. "Are you suggesting what I think you are?"

He grins even wider. "Probably."

I sink back in my seat again. Gray and I did get a chance to talk last night about what it will be like when she lets me dom for her, and we went over what her hard and soft limits are. For instance, she wasn't opposed to light slaps, but she nixed any serious impact play, which was fine by me. I'm not into that either. She also didn't mind something around her neck, including my hands, but more serious breath play was off the table.

More importantly, Gray agreed to let me use her body whenever and wherever I want. Unless she red lights, of course. I was shocked she agreed to that request, but, then again, she strikes me as eager to please when it comes to sex. I'll have to be careful with that and watch for signs that she wants out but is afraid to safe word me.

For now, at least, I have her permission to start a scene anywhere, anytime, which makes Kelsier's idea completely doable. I'm not sure Gray realized what she was getting in to when she agreed to that, but she'll find out soon enough.

The thought doesn't help the situation in my pants. When we hit cruising altitude, I'll have to take a little trip to the bathroom for both my sake and Kelsier's.

Gray has no idea what she's in for when I get back.

Chapter 31

Ash

The next night in Winnipeg, Kelsier, Fig, Mack, and I clink beer bottles to toast our win after the game. It wasn't my most brilliant performance, but I scored one of our two goals and managed not to implode when the Jets started chirping at me.

I used some of the techniques Gray's been teaching me to defuse my temper. Weeks back she advised me to collect a cache of happy memories I could draw on to help manage my anger, and I did just that. When players started getting on me, I remembered what it felt like to finally be inside her, and the thought did wonders to lighten my mood. Granted I was half-hard the entire third period, but whatever it takes at this point.

My phone chimes with an incoming text, and I immediately swipe it open. As hoped, it's Gray.

Gray

Congrats on the win and your goal tonight.

I smile and type.

Ash

You were watching?

Gray

Of course. Gotta keep an eye on my star student.

My dick twitches at the reference. Ever since Kelsier mentioned roleplaying the student-teacher thing, I've been running through possible scenarios in my mind, and it's driving me crazy. I never had a hot-for-teacher experience like he did in college, but that doesn't mean I can't imagine the fantasy very vividly.

It helps that Gray is a little older than me. It emphasizes her authority, which is the crux of the student-teacher fantasy. I've always been a dom in the bedroom, but part of me is ready to hand the keys to the handcuffs over to Gray and see what she'd do with the power.

Fig's voice pulls me back from the daydream.

"You were like a new man out there tonight, Gunny," he says. "You get laid recently or something?"

I nearly choke on my beer, but I keep it down without spitting it across the table at him. I meet Fig's eyes, and there's a wicked gleam in them as his mouth turns up in a knowing smirk. He's remembering the equipment room.

"Yeah," I say. "Your mom almost made me late to catch the plane because she wouldn't let me get dressed."

Mack and Kelsier roar with laughter at the comment as Fig glares at me. I met his mother once and liked her a lot, so part of me feels bad for dragging her into this, but he started it.

"Fuck that. Out with it, Gunny," Fig says. "I know what I saw that day. Don't tell me you haven't fucked the doc yet."

"Keep your voice down," I hiss. "First of all, as far as anyone knows, I *am* fucking her since we're supposed to be dating. You questioning it in public doesn't help."

Fig presses his lips together, conceding the point. "Fine," he says, his voice lower. "But something tells me the two of you have taken the ruse farther than you need to."

I wave my bottle dismissively at him. "You have no idea what you're talking about," I say before I take a sip.

"Bullshit," he counters. He turns his attention to Kelsier, who's a little too late hiding the faint smile turning up his lips. "Spill it, Kels. What do you know?"

Kelsier holds up his hands. "Don't look at me. Gunny and I don't kiss and tell. I have no idea where his dick's been, and I prefer it that way."

Fig throws up a frustrated hand. "You're both full of shit. Mack, what do you think?"

Mack rests his chin on his hand and strokes it like he's contemplating me. His eyes narrow as I raise a brow at him.

"Oh yeah, he's definitely fucked her," Mack says, leaning back. "We just need to find out when so we know who won the pool."

I growl at him. "Both of you need to get laid yourselves and stop worrying about my love life…or lack thereof," I add when Fig looks like he's about to 'Gotcha' me.

"Ask and the universe provides," Mack says, and I look toward the door of the bar where his attention is now.

Several women, all dressed in tight clothes and done up like Barbies, just walked in. They take in the tables of hockey players sitting around the place and whisper to each other.

I groan inwardly. Bunnies.

Don't get me wrong. In my rookie season, plus a few after that, the arrival of bunnies always got me going. As I look around the bar, in fact, our current crop of new bloods seems to sit up straighter and look toward the women.

The last few years, though, the allure of taking a random stranger to bed has lost its luster. I'm not sure when the hell I became an adult and started wanting a relationship instead, but that shit snuck up on me.

I pull out my phone, wanting nothing more than to text chat with Gray. Well, really I want to see her, but this is the best I can have for now.

Ash

You going to sleep soon?

I don't want to keep her up if she's tired, but I just need a little more of her before I let go for the night.

Gray

Just finishing up my syllabus for next week. Almost done.

The woman really doesn't stop working. In exchange for not teaching her large lecture class this spring, her department head roped her into teaching a short winter session class, so instead of having most of January off like usual, Gray starts teaching again next week.

Gray

How about you?

I feel guilty for being out while she's home working, but I type out a response.

Ash

At a bar with the guys celebrating the win. Not staying long.

Gray

Have a beer for me.

I smile and type out a reply.

Ash

You don't drink beer.

Gray

Then have a glass of 2019 Château Lafite Rothschild for me.

I chuckle to myself.

Ash

Beer it is.

Her laughing emoji comes in just before Fig pulls the phone from me.

"Sexting with the doc?" he asks. He tries to look at the screen as I grab for the phone.

"What the fuck, Fig!" I yell as I reach for it while he holds it away. "Give it back."

"What the hell is a Chat-o La-fight Rothschild?" Fig asks, butchering the pronunciation.

Kelsier grabs the phone out of his hand and passes it back to me. I give him a nod of thanks.

"The two of you talking nerd to each other or something?" Fig asks.

"Satisfied that we're not sleeping together now?" I say.

Fig scoffs. "Nope. More convinced of it than ever. You're just not being obvious about it."

My retort is cut off by the appearance of two bunnies at our table.

"Hi guys," the blonde one says. "Mind if we join you?"

She drapes an arm over my shoulder, and her perfume shoves itself up my nose. Jesus Christ. Did she bathe in it?

I try not to gag on the overpowering aroma as I push my phone back in my pocket.

The other bunny, a taller woman with light brown hair sidles up between Kelsier and Mack. A year or two ago, she would've been just my type, but she looks way too done up now, too…artificial.

Blondes were never my type until Gray. Technically they still aren't. The blonde hanging on me doesn't appeal to me at all, and maybe that's because I can't help comparing her to Gray and finding her lacking by just about every measure I can think of.

I meet Kelsier's eyes, and I can tell he's ready to leave. He's single, but I don't think I've seen him take a bunny home yet. I know enough about him that he's not above a one-night stand, but he doesn't seem to care much for low-hanging fruit.

Mack, on the other hand, has his arm around the brunette's waist.

"Buy me a drink," the blonde says, and her forwardness annoys me. I've gotten too used to Gray resisting me. Like Kelsier, I think I enjoy the chase a little too much.

I point to Fig. "He'll buy you a drink," I say. "I don't think my girlfriend would appreciate me buying you one."

The blonde frowns and runs her hand down the side of my cheek. This close, I can see every imperfection in her makeup, like her lashes clumped together by mascara and the small smudge of dark pink lipstick on her teeth.

"I heard you were dating someone," she says, "but I thought that was bullshit. At least, that's the word in my circles."

I blink at that bit of news before hot anger rises in my gut. Her circles. The bunnies don't believe I'm dating Gray. It also doesn't escape my notice that she knows exactly who I am.

"It's not bullshit," I snap at her. "I have a girlfriend."

My pique doesn't phase her. She only pushes closer so her breasts press against my arm. I take another sip of my beer and set the bottle down harder than I intended. The loud clunk makes her jump.

"But isn't that woman, like…old, or something?" the blonde asks. I'd guess she's maybe twenty-two herself.

The swear that jumps to the edge of my lips teeters back before it can plummet off. Why the fuck is everyone so obsessed with Gray's age? She's a whole three God-damn years older than me. If she were three years younger, it would be a complete non-issue.

I audition a number of responses to her absurd observation but dismiss every one.

'*She's mature, not old.*'

'*She's only older by three years.*'

'*Fuck off, bitch.*'

They all sound defensive, and, ultimately, I don't owe this woman an explanation. Instead, I pull out my phone and text Gray. I don't bother hiding the screen from the blonde as she reads over my shoulder.

Ash

> Heading back to the hotel now, baby. I need you to send me a pic of that beautiful body of yours so I have something to give me sweet dreams tonight.

I catch the soft whimper of the blonde as I put my phone away. Two birds, one stone. I've shut her up, and – if I'm lucky – I'll have a pic of Gray to jerk off to when I get back.

I stand, and the blonde's arm slides off me. "I'm heading out."

Kelsier stands too. "I'll walk you back. Don't want you to get lost."

"Nice to meet you ladies," I say politely.

The brunette barely acknowledges me, since Mack has his arms around her and is whispering in her ear. The blonde looks extremely put out, but Fig takes her wrist and pulls her gently toward him.

"There now," he tells her. "Let me buy you that drink and explain why

Gunny is an idiot for passing you up."

He gives me a quick wink.

Fig rarely takes bunnies home either, but he'll likely make out with her, then go back to his hotel room and get reacquainted with his hand like I plan to do. Of the four of us, only Mack is getting laid tonight.

The blonde reluctantly lets Fig pull her over as Kelsier and I head for the door. She still doesn't look happy, but Fig will keep her distracted.

The cold blasts me in the face when we step outside, and I pull my hat out of my pocket to tug it down low over my head. I know I play a sport on ice, but I got too used to living in Florida and haven't acclimated to really cold weather just yet. I'm grateful I was only traded as far north as New England. Dealing with Canadian winters would kill me.

"I assume that was Gray you were texting," Kelsier says. "The blonde didn't seem happy about it."

I grunt an all-purpose affirmation to both questions.

"And you're really not going to tell the rest of the team about you and her yet?" he asks.

"If it was just about them, I would," I say. "I wanted to stand up on that plane yesterday and announce to everyone that she's mine, but it's Kaladin I'm worried about."

He nods. "Right."

My phone chimes with an incoming text, and my blood pumps faster.

Kelsier glances at me. "You need to look at that?"

I shake my head. "If it's what I hope it is, it's not something I should open in public."

He chuckles. "Forget I asked. Are you always this way with women you date?"

I shake my head again. "Nope. It took me a little while to realize I wanted Gray, but now that I have, something about her completely short circuits my brain and automatically reroutes blood flow to my dick."

"Yeah, well, you know my theory on that," he says.

I pull my coat tighter around me at the shiver I'm not entirely sure has anything to do with the cold. "You think I'm in love with her."

"It doesn't matter what I think," he says. "What do *you* think?"

I don't answer right away. I let the idea rattle around in my head for a few seconds before I turn to him. Whatever I was going to say flies out of my head when I realize he's not wearing a hat.

"Dude, it's like below zero out here," I say. "How can you stand not wearing a hat?"

He shrugs. "I grew up in Alaska."

I fall silent, letting his question about how I feel for Gray go unanswered. We've got two more games before we head home, so I have some time to consider just how deep my feelings for her go. I know I like her a lot. *A lot*. But am I ready to use the other L word yet?

I haven't known her that long, but does that matter? If you know, you know, right? But do I know?

The only thing I know right now is that my phone is burning a hole in my pocket as I walk. I want to see what Gray sent me.

My steps feel lighter as we head toward the hotel. I want Gray, and it's fine if lust is the driving force behind our relationship at the moment. I'm not going to put pressure on myself or her to make it more. There's no reason to heap expectations and questions on top of what we have. It's okay to just…enjoy each other.

There will be time to worry about the bigger stuff later.

Much, much later.

Chapter 32

Despite my resolution to be more punctual, I'm late to meet my mother for dinner after the gym. I had a surge of energy toward the end of my workout when I thought about sex with Ash a week and a half ago on New Year's Eve, and I stayed on the treadmill an extra twenty minutes to harness it.

Unfortunately, my larger plan to add an extra ten hours of exercise a week to my routine has already fallen by the wayside. I just don't have the time, but I vowed to at least take advantage of these pockets of energy when they arise.

At first, I felt guilty for not becoming a gym rat. Ash is so fit, and I wanted to give him a girlfriend worthy of his physique, but I didn't make it two days before I gave up on that.

I was reprimanding myself for being lazy until it occurred to me Ash gets paid to work out. It's literally his job to stay that ripped, and I decided that until someone was willing to pay me to develop muscle tone, gently rounded would have to do.

Ash seems to like my body the way it is, in any case. He was kissing me all over the night we had sex, and I got self-conscious when he reached the bit of pudge at my stomach. I tried to push him away from it, but he grabbed my hands and pinned them to the couch so he could kiss me there freely. Then he flipped me over, dragged my ass into the air, and speared into me with one thrust before fucking me so hard that there was a second or two I considered yellow-lighting him before he eased up.

When we were done, he pulled me back against him and wrapped a hand gently around my throat. "Don't try to stop me from touching you again," he rasped into my ear. "Your body belongs to me now, and I'll worship it any way I want. Do you understand?"

All I could do was nod.

"Good girl," he said, and I was once again a puddle.

The academic in me desperately wants to understand the psychology of why I let him talk to me like that when we're naked. In any other context, I'd tell him to shove that attitude up his ass, but I can't deny that, when it comes to sex, I'm his to command.

My cheeks are probably extra pink from the memory when I sit down across from my mother at the restaurant, but I can blame it on the biting cold outside if she asks.

"Sorry I'm late," I say as I pull off my coat. "I lost track of time."

"No problem," my mother says. "I learned a long time ago you operate on GST."

I frown at her across the table. "GST?"

She looks up from her menu. "Gray Standard Time."

I want to be annoyed, but honestly, she's right. I want to tell her how I was half an hour early to meet Ash that one time after my date with Barry, but I don't want to explain why, so I keep my mouth shut.

"One of these days I'll be early, and then you'll be sorry," I say casually, opening my own menu.

"Just don't do it when your father is with me," she says. "I think another heart attack would kill him."

I clamp my mouth shut to bite back a comment about how her cooking will most likely do him in first.

Is it really a surprise I study trash talk?

"When do I get to meet this handsome man of yours?" my mother asks. "His family got to meet you. I was hoping he might be with you tonight, but apparently he's too busy to meet your mother?"

"The team is traveling this week, Mom."

Plus I plan to keep my mother away from Ash as long as possible.

Guilt creeps into my chest. All things considered, my mother isn't a bad person. She does have sporadic bouts of passive aggressiveness and an annoying habit of asking a question and then launching into a ten-minute story before the person can answer. She also has a lead foot when driving that I'm shocked hasn't turned my hair the same color as my name, but all that is minor in the grand scheme. Her major flaw is her tendency to pick up fads or interests, learn about them superficially, practice them intensely, even obsessively for a short time, then discard them.

For instance, when everyone was wrapped up in the Marie Kondo method of cleaning, my mother went through the whole house and purged just about anything she could lift by herself. Except she didn't completely discard it all. She packed everything in boxes and stored it in the garage for a few months so my dad had to park his truck outside until she finally gave up and brought everything back in.

Feng shui, juice cleanses, salsa dancing, the gluten-free diet. You name it, my mother has tried it. She even turned wiccan for a period when I was in college, but she gave it up when none of the spells she tried worked.

Once my mother finds a fixation, my father and I have learned to ride it out to its inevitable end, but it can be rough until then. As far as I know, she's between crazes right now, but it's only a matter of time before the next one hits.

"Have you two slept together yet?" my mother asks.

Did I mention she also has no sense of personal boundaries?

"I'm not at liberty to answer that," I say, flipping to the wine list.

Telling her yes will only lead to more questions. Telling her no will lead to unwanted advice. Uncertainty is the closest thing to a safe answer I can give.

"He's a good-looking boy," she says. "I'd have jumped his bones on week one."

I slap down my menu. "Mom!"

My mother is *never* meeting Ash. Ever.

She gives me an innocent look. "What? You know I speak my mind about these things."

And how could I forget the summer my mother got into tantric sex. That's some PTSD no amount of therapy will ever cure.

"Can I get you ladies something to start?" the waiter asks as he appears at our table.

"A glass of the Fumé Blanc and the crab cakes," I tell him. I was planning on a salad, but fuck it.

My mother looks up at me, and I wait for the comment about watching my figure now that I have a boyfriend, but in an uncharacteristic show of restraint, she looks back down at her menu.

"I'll have an Old Fashioned and a cup of clam chowder," she tells the waiter.

I furrow my brows at her when he leaves. "Since when do you drink hard liquor?"

"Joyce got me into bourbon," my mother says.

And there it is. Her latest craze. I'll have to text my father later to find out how many new bottles of craft bourbon are in the liquor cabinet.

I have an addictive personality myself, and I'm sure I get it from my mother. That's undoubtedly why her tendency to fixate on things drives me nuts, because I see myself slowly turning into her. Unlike my mother, though, I fixate on things for longer periods. My love affair with wine has been going on for several years now.

My newest obsession with hockey, and with one player in particular, is still in its infancy, but I'm already into the stats-tracking phase. For example, I know Ash's goal-scoring is behind where it was last year at this time, although he seems to be doing better lately.

"I just hope you're practicing safe sex," my mother says. "Those professional athletes sleep with a lot of women."

I close my eyes, take a deep breath, then open them. I'm not having this conversation with her, and I glance over at the bar to see if the hockey game pre-show is on yet. Tonight is Ash's last road game for a while, and I can't wait to see him again.

Alright fine. I can't wait for him to fuck me again. It was cruel to finally sleep together and then have him leave for almost two weeks. He called me last night, and we actually had phone sex, which I've never done.

I don't see anything hockey-related on the TVs over the bar, but I do a double-take as I catch sight of a middle-aged man seated there. I swear I remember him from the gym. I think he was walking on a treadmill about five or six machines down from me. He's got a beer and the bartender is just setting down a plate of sliders in front of him. Looks like I'm not the only one undoing all the exercise I just did.

I look back at my mother to find her watching me carefully.

"What?" I ask.

"Are you embarrassed by me?" she asks. "Is that why you won't let me meet this man?"

I sigh deeply. "It's not you, Mom."

And if I'm being honest, it really isn't her that's the problem.

She frowns. "Your father?"

"No, not him either."

I don't think my dad told her he came to see Ash yet.

"Then who?"

It's me, I want to say, but my mother will never buy the '*It's not you, it's me*' argument.

But it is me.

Meeting Ash's parents was one thing. If something happens, and things don't work out between us, I'll never have to see those people again. But if things don't work out between him and me, and he's met *my* parents, I'll have to live with their pitying looks for weeks. My mother will inevitably love Ash – Because what's not to love about him? – and then I'll have to deal with the disappointment in her face when I explain why we broke up.

My mother's disappointment will be there no matter what, but at this point, I'd rather not build the memories that will make it that much more a stab to my heart if I lose Ash.

I hear Celena tsk at me in my head for imagining my breakup with him before we've even had a chance to enjoy our relationship.

Yeah, yeah, I know, I tell my inner Celena.

My mother is still looking at me, waiting for me to tell her why she can't meet Ash.

Because I'm terrified of letting him into my life, I want to say. Because every thread that ties him closer to me is one more potential frayed edge when we inevitably rip apart.

Because I already think I'm in love with him, and I just…can't be.

"I'll see what I can do, Mom," I say.

It's a vague promise to buy me time until I can figure out how to un-fall in love with Ash Gunnarsson.

Chapter 33

A knock sounds on my office door the next day, and I look up to find Ash in the threshold. My heart does its usual stutter step to see him.

"You're back," I say, surprised. "I didn't realize your plane was in already." I look at my phone, but there are no messages from him. "Why didn't you text when you landed?"

Part of me wants to get up and go to him, to literally jump into his arms and kiss him, but a couple things stop me. First and foremost is that I'm at work, and I need to stay professional. Next, but secondarily, is that I'm extremely busy right now. One of my grad students needs me to review her study proposal, and my winter session class just turned in outlines for their research papers, so I have to give feedback.

Ash's road trip went well – two wins in three games – so I assume he's not here out of frustration. I'm not sure whether to take him seriously when he says he's been using sex with me as his happy memory for stress inoculation, but I'll let myself think it's true for now.

I'm nervous about why he didn't message me before coming to my office, though, and I eye him warily as he enters and closes the door behind him. I swear I hear the lock click, and he turns to face me with the hint of a grin on his face.

"Ash?" I ask. "What's going on?"

"You don't have class until 1:15, right?" he says.

"Right," I confirm, narrowing my eyes. "Why?"

He sits down in the chair on the other side of my desk and leans in.

"I need to talk to you, Professor Mackey," he says.

I frown. This doesn't sound good.

"Why are you back to calling me Professor Mackey? Maybe we should talk tonight when you've-"

"I know I'm failing your class," he interrupts, his expression serious, "but I need to pass, or they won't let me play hockey."

My frown deepens. "Who won't let you play hockey? Mr. Kaladin? He knows our meetings aren't really a class, right?"

He stands and puts his large hands on the desk to lean toward me.

"Maybe I can do some…extra credit," he says huskily. "I'll do *anything* to bring my grade up. Just tell me what I need to do."

I'm about to ask him what the fuck he's talking about when it finally hits me that he's roleplaying.

My eyes widen. "Oh no," I say, holding up a hand. "We're not doing this. Not here."

He begins to walk around the desk toward me.

"Ash, please," I say as sternly as I can muster given the hungry look in his eye.

He kneels in front of me, and I give him a pleading look. He's been gone for almost two weeks on a three-game away stretch, and I've spent every one of those days imagining what it will be like to have him fuck me again. I figured I might see him tomorrow after he rested, but…

The conversation we had before he left about what I will and won't allow him to do as my Dom comes back to me. He asked that I let him have complete control of my body, which also gives him permission to fuck me whenever and wherever he wants.

At the time I said yes. The thought excited me. It never occurred to me he'd show up at my office and want to play desperate student/naughty teacher, and I feel every bit of my resolve to stay professional wash away like a sandcastle in the tide.

"Please, Professor Mackey. I'll do anything."

I jump as Ash clamps his hands down on my knees. He runs them up, pushing my skirt higher as his thumbs trace the insides of my thighs, and

I try not to start panting.

He looks at my laptop sitting on the desk.

"That document looks important," he says. "You should save it."

"Ash, Please…," I try once more, begging him not to shatter my resolve. Not to shatter *me*.

He only looks at me like he's been on a diet and I'm a double cheeseburger. I reach over quickly and click save on the document. I barely hit the button when he shuts the laptop with a snap. He stands, picks it up, and places it on the chair he was sitting in before he comes back around the desk.

Ash takes my hand and pulls me to my feet. Then he's back on one knee as his hands slither up my legs. My nipples pebble into hard peaks as he hooks his hands over my panties and pulls them slowly down my legs. I step out of them automatically, and he shoves them in his pocket.

"I know I'm failing class right now," he says before I can protest about the panties. "What can I do to make you reconsider my grade?"

His hands snake up my legs again to grip my hips. He pushes my skirt up to bare me to him and plants a kiss just under my navel. The breath wooshes out of me, and I have to grab his shoulders to steady myself. He continues to plant kisses, working his way lower.

"Oh fuck, baby," he says. "You waxed."

I'd never done that before, and it hurt so much I'll never do it again.

Ash kisses the bare skin at the apex of my legs and flicks my clit with his tongue, and I know immediately I'll do it again. I'll keep it as smooth as silk down there as long as he keeps doing that.

I look down at him for a long moment. He's so beautiful, and he wants to play this little game. I've never considered doing anything with a student before. The undergraduates are all way too young, and even if I did find the occasional grad student attractive, the ethics always kept me well away from crossing any lines.

But this…this is roleplay with a man who isn't really my student. Not in the traditional sense anyway. I don't hold his grade in my hand, although he clearly wants to pretend I do.

And he's my boyfriend now, I remind myself. He assured me we were no longer fake dating but real dating. There's nothing unethical about this.

"I…I'm not sure there's anything you can do to bring your grade up at this point, Mr. Gunnarsson," I find myself saying. "You've been slacking off all semester, and saving your grade now would require a lot of *hard* work." I emphasize the word "hard" breathily.

Ash's mouth curls into a grin as he looks up at me.

"I can work hard," he insists. "Give me a chance to prove it."

I sit on the desk and slide back, and his eyes flare with desire.

"Fine. I'll give you a chance," I say. "Shall we start with an oral exam?"

His eyes flare again, and he growls as he surges forward to hike my skirt up. He drags my hips to the edge of the desk, and I barely have time to throw a hand back and brace myself before he dives into my pussy. His lips close around my clit, and I cry out, then clamp a hand over my own mouth as I remember where we are.

I grab his head as his tongue plunges inside me, and I thrust my hips up. I don't mean to, and I worry I'm suffocating him, but he only groans and presses his face into me so deep I seriously wonder if he can breathe. He wraps his muscled arms around my legs and pulls me even closer to him, and I stifle a scream as he sucks hard on my clit again.

I can't stay still as he licks and sucks and teases between my legs for the next few minutes. I writhe on the desk, trying desperately to remain quiet, but I'm falling apart quickly under Ash's tongue as he works me.

One hand is still on his head, gripping a fistful of his hair. My other hand searches desperately for the edge of the desk to give me something to hold onto. I find it just in time and grip down hard as he pistons two fingers into me and I spasm around him as my orgasm rocks through me. I fall back, whimpering as I press my lips together to keep quiet.

"Fucking delicious," I hear him murmur against my pussy.

I'm panting like I just escaped a masked killer when my body finally goes limp. I lift my head, and Ash looks up at me from between my legs.

"Did I pass, teach?" he asks.

I have to take several more breaths before I can answer him.

"I said you'd need to work hard," I manage. "Do you feel like you worked hard enough yet?"

"I'd say that deserves an A, don't you?" he says as he stands.

I give him a coy smile. "You've brought your grade up to a C," I say. "The question is whether you're satisfied with that."

"Just a C!" he chokes out. "That's all?"

I rise on my elbows to look up at him. "Did you think this would be easy, Mr. Gunnarsson?" I say sternly. "You've only finished one assignment. If you want an A, you need to finish the rest."

He looks down at me and grins. "And what are the rest?" he asks as he leans over me, bracing his hands on either side of my hips.

"Well, you've learned all the theory. The real test is the practical application. Can you take what you know and apply it?"

He considers me before his face goes serious, and he pulls his wallet out of his back pocket to fish a condom out. He slaps the wallet down on the desk and lays the condom next to it.

Does he carry any money in that wallet, or is it only for prophylactics?

Ash yanks his hoodie and t-shirt up over his head, and I'm treated to that luscious expanse of his muscled chest and the tattoo over his left shoulder and down his arm. I instantly go wet again.

He undoes his belt next and whips it out of his jeans. I give a little yelp of surprise as he loops it around my neck and pulls it tight, not enough to cut off my air, but just enough that I feel the pressure on my throat. The muscles tighten between my legs.

"So you want to know what I've learned so far," he says, his voice a deep gravel. "I'll show you what I've learned."

Keeping hold of the belt, he undoes the fly of his jeans with one hand. He pushes the jeans and his boxer briefs down just low enough to let his cock spring free, and I bite my lip.

"I've learned you're a strong, capable woman who – outside of sex –

exudes confidence and doesn't take crap," he says. "I'm sure you've needed that to succeed as a woman in academia, particularly in a field like sport communication, and I respect the hell out of you for that."

I swallow against the belt and try to pretend he didn't just turn me on even more with his feminist awareness. There's a knot in my throat that has nothing to do with the belt, and I mentally repeat my new mantra that I cannot fall in love with this man.

"I find your-take-no-shit demeanor incredibly sexy, by the way," he says as he rips the condom open with his teeth and rolls it onto his cock with one hand, the other still holding the belt tight to my throat.

I'm convinced I've somehow fallen into an alternate dimension.

Ash steps between my legs and presses his crown to my entrance. I arch toward him, and he lifts one of my legs, urging me to wrap them around him. He presses in just enough to be sure he's lined up.

"During sex, however," he says as he braces one hand next to my chest and tugs on the belt with the other, "I've learned you like to be dominated."

Ash shoves into me to the hilt in one hard thrust. The cry that erupts up my throat is mercifully stifled as his hand on the desk moves to clamp down on my mouth just in time. Then he's over me, driving into me hard and fast, and all I can do is grip his steely biceps and hold on tight.

"You like being used," he says close to my ear. "You like being fucked. It turns you on when I throw you down and take charge of your body."

Images of our first night together flash through my mind, and my eyes roll back in my head. True to his word, Ash didn't push me too hard that night, but he was dominant, even aggressive at times, and he hadn't been shy about giving me orders.

I'd loved every second of it.

I can't say anything with his hand over my mouth, but I also can't deny the truth of his words, even if I could speak. The upward curve of his cock hits just the right spot inside me in this position, and my vision goes fuzzy from both the pleasure and from his utter domination of me.

He grunts above me, and I feel the desk rock with each of his thrusts. I tighten my legs around his waist, and he groans. His hand is still on the belt around my neck, and he holds it like a leash, not pulling it, but just reminding me it's there, reminding me he owns me, body and mind.

"Do you like the way I fuck you, baby?" he rasps near my ear, and the only answer I manage is a whimper of pleasure.

There's a knock at the door, and both of us freeze.

"Gray? Are you there?" a voice calls.

It's Melinda, my department head.

My brain races to decide if it's better to call out and tell her I'm busy or to just stay silent. No, silence is best. There are few excuses you can give a department head for not opening the door to them.

Ash looks down at me in question, his hand still over my mouth, but I shake my head. He grins and starts moving again, taking long, slow strokes. My eyes widen at his audacity, but he only lets out a low, unrepentant groan and begins to fuck me faster.

Melinda hasn't said anything else, but I'm not sure she's gone. I'm convinced she's listening at the door, and if so, she must hear my heart hammering in my chest, because I'm sure it's audible across campus.

Ash takes his hands off my mouth and the belt just long enough to pull my legs up so my ankles rest on his bare shoulders, then he covers my mouth and grabs the belt again. He presses me forward so I'm nearly sandwiched in half, trapped beneath his body. I whimper against his hand as the new position hits a spot inside me that's even more sensitive than the last.

"Have I earned my A yet?" he whispers in a sultry voice.

I shake my head.

He chuckles softly. "You're a tough grader, teach," he says. "I'll have to put that in my review for you on ratemyprofessors.com."

I let out a sound of protest, and he chuckles again.

"You want to know the last thing I've learned?" he asks, and I nod.

"I've learned my pretty little professor likes to be praised," he says, "so be a good girl now and fucking come all over my cock."

He drives in, then grunts as my pussy dutifully clamps around him. I close my eyes, but he stops when I do.

"Open your eyes, Gray," he orders, giving the belt a quick jerk. "You keep your eyes on me when I fuck you. Do you understand?"

My eyes pop open as the belt tightens around my neck. He starts to move faster again, and I'm held captive by the intensity of his gaze as he pistons into me.

"That's it, baby. That beautiful little cunt of yours takes my cock so well. One of these days I'm going to rip this condom off and fucking fill you up so I'm dripping out of you. I want to sit in the back of your class and watch you teach while my cum runs down your thighs as you talk about nonverbal communication and multimodal messaging."

I nearly choke at that. It makes my eyes water, and tears trail down the side of my head. He's been doing his homework on Communication.

Ash doesn't stop moving, and I think I'll die if he does now. I have one hand wrapped around the back of his neck, and the other still digs into his bicep as he thrusts into me. I'm vaguely aware I should be getting ready for class, but I can't worry about that now. I just need to come.

I cry out into Ash's hand as my second orgasm explodes through me. He swears softly and lets go of both my mouth and the belt so he can brace his hands on the desk. He thrusts into me three more times before he comes as well, tensing above me as his face contorts in pleasure before his body relaxes.

We're both covered in a fine sheen of sweat, and I'll have to make a trip to the restroom to wipe myself off before class, but I can't bring myself to care. Hopefully I still have my emergency deodorant in one of my desk drawers.

Ash takes my ankles down from his shoulders, but I don't get a chance to say anything before his lips are on mine. He kisses me deeply, and I'm very aware of his cock still inside me.

He finally pulls back and loops some strands of sweaty hair behind my ear. "Mmm. I missed you while I was gone," he says.

My heart flipflops, and the urge to immediately say I missed him too overwhelms me. The words race up my throat, but I clamp my mouth shut before they can escape.

"I...I have to get to class," I whisper instead, still half afraid Melinda is outside the door. Please God, don't let her still be outside the door.

"Do I get an A?" Ash asks, not moving.

I groan. "Yes, you get an A," I whisper. "Now let me up."

He kisses me soundly again, and I nearly forget about my class. Finally, he pulls out of me and unloops the belt from around my neck. I slide off the desk to fix my clothes.

"Are you okay?" he asks as he runs a hand down my arm and kisses the top of my head.

"I need my panties," I say by way of answer and hold out my hand.

He grins. "Sorry, I'm holding onto these."

I make an indignant noise. "I can't go to class without panties on!"

"You're going to have to," he says shoving them further into his pocket. He pulls the condom off, ties it closed, and tosses it in my trash.

I close my eyes. I need to get some paper towels to wrap that in so I can take it with me and drop it in a dumpster far, far away from the scene of my crime. That's all I need is for a colleague, or worse, a student to find a used condom in my trashcan. That would be fun to explain to the university ethics board.

"Fine," I say, realizing the futility of arguing with him. "But you need to go now. I have to clean up before I go to class."

He tucks his cock back into his pants and zips them up, then re-loops and fastens his belt. He grabs me by the waist and pulls me to him.

"We'll be playing a different game when you come over later," he says with a grin. "You're going to be the nerdy student who has to tutor the star athlete."

I raise a brow.

"I'll put you on your knees, and we'll see how much of my cock you can swallow," he says.

Just the thought has my pussy clenching again.

"I'll be a good student after you let me come down your throat," he promises.

I'm trying to think of a response to that when it occurs to me I can't see him tonight.

"I can't come over. I have a stack of outlines and a study proposal to read."

He sighs with disappointment. "That's probably for the best. I really should rest tonight anyway. If you came over, I'd just spend all night fucking you, and then I'd be useless at practice tomorrow."

"You had a good road trip, at least," I say. "Two out of three wins."

He shrugs. "Not bad. I had two goals, but I can still be better."

I nod. "It's progress. One step at a time."

I pull out of his arms, and I'm about to push him toward the door when I realize he's still bare-chested. I retrieve the t-shirt and hoodie off the chair he tossed them on and wait for him to pull them over his head. I open the door and peek out. By some miracle, the hall is empty.

"What are you doing Saturday night?" he asks. "The team is attending a fundraiser gala for the aquarium, and I want you to come. It's black tie. I can get a ticket for Celena too. It's about time I meet her."

"I can go," I say. "I think Celena is free as well. I'll ask her and text you. You're right. It's past time for the two of you to meet."

He smiles and leans in to try to kiss me again, but I urge him out the door. Ash plants himself in the threshold and grins down at me.

"I'll see you again soon," he says. "Until then, try not to think about the way I just fucked you on your desk while you're standing in front of all your students without your panties on."

He flips his hood up and saunters down the hall as I stare after him, my mouth hanging open.

It's going to be a long fucking class.

Chapter 34

Gray

Ash looks incredible in his crisp black tux as we enter the ballroom for the fundraiser gala on Saturday night. The tux is tailored perfectly so it accommodates his broad shoulders while also showing off his trim waist, and I'm already having impure thoughts about him.

I'm wearing a strapless black gown with Swarovski crystal accents that Ash insisted on buying me for the occasion. I doubt I'll ever have another place to wear it, so it seems like a waste of money, but I have to admit I feel red carpet-worthy in it.

The gown is accented with some faux diamond costume jewelry. I refused to let Ash buy me a real diamond necklace, although I have a feeling I'll lose that argument eventually if whatever this is between us continues.

Celena isn't here yet, but she texted to say she was only a few minutes away. The one-shoulder red and gold gown she found isn't nearly as pricey as the gown Ash bought for me, but she looks stunning in it, and only the biggest fashion snob would be able to tell the difference.

I scan the room and see several of the players mingling with the guests. Some look more comfortable in their penguin suits than others. Mack and Fig, for example, look like they'd pay any amount of money to take theirs off, while Kingston looks surprisingly at-ease in his. Who knew a man who wears a mask half the day could wear a tux that well?

I continue scanning the room but do a double-take when I see…actual penguins. Some of the aquarium staff are here with two penguins, and there's a small crowd gathered around them.

I can't help the squeal of delight that jumps out of me at the sight of the birds, and Ash looks at me in alarm.

"Penguins!" I say, pointing.

His face eases, and he smiles. "I suppose you want to go see them?"

"Let's put it this way," I say. "You can either lead me over there in a very calm and dignified manner, or I can leave you here and run across the room in heels squealing like a three-year-old."

Ash contemplates this. "I'd like to see you run in heels."

I give him a look that says, *'Try again.'*

He chuckles and holds his arm out for me. When we get over to the penguins, we learn that, for a fee, you can get your picture taken with them. I only half-heartedly protest as Ash whips out his credit card to pay the fee, and we get a picture of ourselves with the penguins.

I see Celena enter the ballroom just as we're finishing up, so Ash and I head over to her. I let go of Ash as we approach, and Celena and I throw ourselves into a hug.

"I'm so glad you could come," I tell her as we part. Then I turn to Ash, who's standing behind me. "Celena Bernacki, this is Ash Gunnarsson. Ash, this is my best friend Celena."

Celena steps forward and shakes Ash's hand. "It's great to finally meet you," she says. "Thank you for the invite and for covering my ticket."

"No problem. You're welcome," Ash says. "I just figured it was long overdue to meet my girlfriend's best friend."

Ash stops short and looks at me questioningly. I give him a small nod to indicate Celena knows we're actually dating. He nods back as he slips an arm around my waist.

Celena gives Ash a too-wide smile. "And what better place to meet for the first time than a very public, very lavish gala where I can't threaten you with bodily harm if you do anything to hurt my girl."

He chuckles. "From what Gray has told me about you, I didn't really expect that to stop you from threatening to cut off my balls if I do anything to hurt her." He winks at Celena.

She smiles back genuinely and looks at me. "I like him." Then she gives Ash a wicked grin. "But make no mistake, you make Gray cry and forget your balls. They'll never find your body."

Ash nods. "Duly noted. Rest assured, making her cry is not on my 'to do' list."

"Alright," I interrupt, putting a hand on his chest. "Now that you're both done posturing for each other, can we get a drink and some food?"

"Sounds great," Celena says as we all grab glasses of champagne off a passing tray. "What's this a fundraiser for again?"

"The aquarium," Ash says, pointing to the penguins. "I think they need to upgrade the beluga whale tank, and they want to put on a new addition to the main building."

"New addition for what?" she asks.

Ash shrugs. "I don't know. I just show up for these things when Cedric tells me to." He turns to me and puts a hand on my bare shoulder. "Do you want something else to drink?"

"Sauvignon Blanc if they have it," I say.

He nods and looks at Celena in question.

"I'm good with champagne. Thanks," she says.

Ash kisses my temple, then brushes my arm as he heads off.

"Does he ever stop touching you?" Celena asks with a smile.

I smile back. "Not if he can help it."

She shakes her head. "God damn, woman. You have got to be the luckiest bitch on the planet. I'm happy for you, but God damn."

"There's plenty of other single players here tonight," I say. "I can introduce you."

And Celena can probably have any one of them she wants. She's petite with beautiful auburn hair, full lips, and deep brown eyes. She's also wearing the hell out of that gown. Her hair is down tonight, unlike the French twist at the back of my head, and at least a few of the guys have already noticed her and are casting appreciative glances this way.

"Are you alright?" Celena asks me. "You keep shifting like you're uncomfortable or something."

I blush, not realizing my fidgeting was so noticeable.

I sigh. "Do not react to what I tell you."

She frowns. "React to what?"

I lean closer to her. "I have a butt plug in."

Her eyes widen. "What!" she almost shouts.

I shush her quickly. "Way to not react."

"I'm sorry, but you can't just casually drop that you have a plug up your ass and expect me to play it cool," she whispers back. "Why the hell are you here with a butt plug in?"

"Ash put it in before we left," I say. "He wants to start preparing me for anal sex."

I flush even hotter as I remember him making me kneel on my bed on all fours before we came so he could ease the plug into me. He told me we'd need to keep increasing the size of it until I'm stretched enough to take him. This one is small, but I'm well aware it's there.

Celena opens her mouth to speak when we suddenly experience an eclipse. Or what feels like one.

I turn to find Kingston standing behind me. His huge body blocks out some of the light from the ballroom, casting me and Celena in shadow. He's eyeing Celena like she's a medium rare steak.

"Good evening, Professor Mackey," he says, not looking at me. He's the only player who doesn't call me either Gray, doc, or teach.

"It looks like you brought me a little present," he continues. "How thoughtful of you." He boldly looks Celena over. "I like her."

Both me and Celena's mouths drop open at the comment. I know Kingston is an ass from the brief encounters I've had with him, but his boldness surprises even me.

Kingston reaches into his pocket, pulls something out, and hands it to Celena. She looks down at the small white plastic card in her hand before her head snaps back up.

"This better not be what I fucking think it is," she says.

Kingston's expression doesn't waiver from its cool cockiness. "And what do you think it is?"

Celena holds the card up between her pointer and middle fingers. "A hotel room key?" she guesses.

Kingston smiles at her. "Room 532. I'll see you there later," he says before he turns and strides away.

Celena and I are both standing in stunned silence when Ash returns with Kelsier in tow.

"What the hell did Kingston want?" Ash asks as he hands me my wine, and I discard the champagne on a table.

"Celena," I answer. "He had the audacity to give her his hotel key."

"Well shit," Kelsier says. "So much for that idea."

I frown. "What idea?"

"I figured I'd introduce Celena to Kelsier," Ash says. "I thought they might hit it off, but if Kingston has already staked a claim-"

"Staked a claim?" Celena cuts in indignantly. "Don't I get a say? I'm not a plot of land. He can't just stick a flag up my ass and say, 'Mine!'"

Ash and Kelsier exchange a look that says that's exactly what they believe Kingston just did, and they intend to honor that flag.

"I mean, in principle, no," Kelsier says. "But if the guys on the team think he wants you, they'll all steer clear."

"Including you?" I ask him incredulously.

"Especially me," Kelsier says. "I pissed Kingston off once last year, and he talked the coach into benching me a game."

"Seriously?" Ash asks him, and Kelsier nods.

"Holy shit," Ash says before he turns back to Celena. "Well, not that it matters anymore, but this is my best friend, Zane Kelsier. You can call him Kels. Kels, this is Gray's best friend Celena."

Celena shakes Kelsier's hand, then steps closer to him and puts her hand on his chest as she leans in.

"It's nice to meet you, Kels," she says in a sultry purr as she runs her hand up his chest. "And it still does matter, because I'm not spoken for."

Celena glances to the side, and we all follow her gaze to see Kingston glaring daggers from where he stands near the bar.

Kelsier throws up his hands and steps away from Celena like he's been zapped by a heart defibrillator. "Whoa! Are you trying to get me benched for a week?" he asks Celena.

She rolls her eyes. "Really? This guy can't actually have that much power over the coaches."

"I don't know for sure if he does," Kelsier says, "but just in case, I can't be anything more than friends until you two get this figured out."

Celena's brows shoot up. "Get what figured out? I think I made my feelings about his bullshit claim pretty clear."

"Sorry, Kels," Ash tells him. "It should have been obvious as soon as I saw her that Kingston would be interested."

Kelsier nods. "Yup. Should've seen that coming."

"Should have seen what coming?" I ask.

"Celena is just Kingston's type," Ash says. "We usually see him with really short, pretty women." He looks at Celena. "What are you? Like 5'0" maybe?"

"I'm 5'1", and I repeat, I'm not interested in that arrogant prick."

"So none of the guys can have a woman if Kingston wants her?" I ask incredulously.

Ash shakes his head. "Nope. Not until Kingston gives up on her, which has never happened from what I hear."

"Gunny was afraid Kingston might be interested in you when he first brought you around," Kelsier tells me, "but luckily he wasn't. We think you might be a little too tall for his tastes."

I look at Ash in surprise and catch him throwing a '*Why did you tell her that?*' glare at Kelsier.

"So you would have backed off if Kingston had staked a claim on me?" I ask Ash, a little hurt.

His face goes serious. "No. Absolutely not," he says. "I didn't want to have to fight Kingston for you, but I was prepared to do it if I had to.

You've been mine for longer than you know."

I blink at the earnestness in his expression, and it feels like Cirque du Soleil is doing a tumbling routine in my stomach.

"Awww," Celena says, looking at us with a sappy expression on her face. "You two are adorable." She looks at Ash. "I guess I don't have to kill you and bury your body in a remote location after all."

He smiles at her. "Thanks?"

"If you'll excuse me," Celena says, "I'm going to go work the room a little. One of these players has got to be willing to defy that asshole to take me on a date."

Ash and Kelsier exchange a glance but then shrug.

"Best of luck," Ash says. "Cote and Samsonov are married, FYI." He points them out to her. "And Nilsen doesn't play for your team."

Ash points to one of the Norwegians across the room that I thought was Anders Aasgaard. They really do look alike.

"Did Novich and his girlfriend break up?" Ash asks Kelsier.

"Not that I know of," he answers.

"Then avoid him too," Ash says, pointing out the defenseman.

"You may also want to avoid the rookies," Kelsier suggests. "They're still a bit immature."

Celena waves a dismissive hand. "No, they're perfect. I don't mind having to teach a man a few things, and maybe they're dumb enough to defy this Kingston guy."

She squares her shoulders and heads off with her champagne.

Ash looks at Kelsier. "I'm not sure you could've handled her anyway," he says. "She would've eaten you alive."

"I would've enjoyed it, but yeah," Kelsier says.

They both look at me, and I raise a brow at them.

"And I say that with the utmost respect for Celena," Kelsier tells me.

I roll my eyes at him, but shrug. "You're not wrong," I concede. "Celena is small, but she packs a punch."

"I'm going to go mingle some more before I get myself in trouble,"

Kelsier says. "You two behave yourselves."

Ash gives him a look of feigned innocence. "What trouble could we possibly get into at a fundraiser gala?"

Kelsier shoots Ash a look that says he knows exactly what he means before he heads off.

As soon as he's gone, Ash slips his arm around my waist and pulls me against him.

"How's the plug feel?" he asks against my temple before kissing it.

I feel myself blush, and I turn my head away from the ballroom to hide it. "It feels fine," I say. "You're sure this thing won't get lost up there? I can't be one of those people who goes to the ER and has to explain that something I shoved up my ass got stuck."

Ash chuckles. "It'll be fine," he says. "They're designed to catch, but I plan to check it later anyway."

I look up at him. "What?"

"You didn't think I planned to go the whole evening without fucking you, did you?" he asks. "A little later when people are drunker and not as watchful, we'll find an empty bathroom or closet, and I'm going to pull that gown up over your hips and fuck you silly."

My mouth drops open, but I catch the objection before it tumbles out. None of the other men I dated were ever this adventurous – or this insatiable, for that matter – and I've decided to just enjoy it while it lasts.

There's something about Ash that makes me feel safe, and maybe a little reckless, and I don't intend to fight the latter. It's time for me to let go of the 'fear of life' Celena always accuses me of having. So bathroom sex with a butt plug at a five thousand dollar-a-plate fundraiser gala it is.

"Enjoying the evening so far?" a voice says from behind us, making Ash and I step apart.

We turn to find Mr. Kaladin standing there with his hands in his pockets. He looks immaculate in what I'm sure is a custom-made tux.

This is the first time I've seen him in person. He's in his mid-thirties, fit and handsome, but the images I've seen of him online fail to capture the 'presence' he has in person. He's stupidly rich and powerful, and everything about his bearing says he knows it.

Ash's hand hasn't moved from around my waist despite us stepping apart, and I feel his fingers close tighter around me. I recognize it for the possessive gesture it is. He feels Kaladin's magnetism as I do, and he's enforcing his claim on me in the face of a potential rival. As if I could somehow attract both a hockey star and a billionaire mogul in one lifetime, let alone have them compete for me.

"Dr. Mackey," Kaladin says, reaching out a hand by way of greeting. "It's good to finally meet you."

I step forward a little to take Kaladin's hand. Ash's grip loosens just enough to let me, but his hand remains lightly on my waist.

"Mr. Kaladin," I say, shaking his hand. "It's great to meet you as well. I haven't had a chance to thank you for this opportunity."

Kaladin smiles as we let go. "I take it things are going well?"

He looks between me and Ash before his eyes dip to the hand Ash still has on my waist, and I have the distinct feeling he's not asking about our work on trash talk.

"Great," Ash responds before I can say anything. "The doc and I made some progress on pinpointing my triggers, and now we're working on…" He trails off, searching for the word.

"Interventions," I supply.

"Interventions," Ash confirms. "Which I was happy to learn are different from the kind of interventions that require hugging."

Kaladin nods as he takes us in. "And the fake dating? Are people buying that you're together?" He looks again at Ash's hand, which has drifted to my hip. "You do make a convincing couple."

There's definitely a tone to his words.

Ash drags me closer and envelopes me exaggeratedly in his arms. "Gotta sell the story," he says to Kaladin.

"You've been playing better recently," Kaladin says. "I'm glad to see the good doctor is having a positive influence on you."

Both Ash and I stiffen. On the surface, the words are complimentary, but I'm sure we both sense something more in them. A threat?

"You should find your seats," Kaladin says. "Dinner will start in a little bit. It was good to see you both."

He turns and saunters off toward a group of people I'm certain are politicians.

Ash's hand finds mine, and he threads our fingers together. "Come with me," he says as he pulls me after him.

"Where are we going?" I ask.

"We're going to drop our drinks at our table," he says, "and then we're going to find somewhere private for me to fuck you."

Chapter 35

Gray

I'm flushed and self-conscious when me and Ash sit down at our table twenty minutes later. We found a supply closet and slipped inside for some privacy, but the door to the closet didn't lock. We were far enough away from the ballroom that we didn't think we'd be disturbed, though.

Ash crushed his mouth onto mine as soon as he closed the door and started to pull my dress up, but I stopped him. I could see he was agitated by the encounter with Kaladin, and I wanted to reassure him. His look was anxious when I pushed him against the shelves, but he swore under his breath as I went to my knees in front of him, unzipped his pants, and took him into my mouth. He tried to put his hands in my hair, but I pulled them away to keep him from messing it up, and he gripped the storage shelves instead.

He only let me work him a minute or so before he pulled me to my feet, though. "I'm coming in your pussy, not your mouth," he'd said.

Then he turned me around and, as promised, hiked my dress up over my hips. Seconds later, he had a condom on and was fucking me hard against the wall of the supply closet.

"Do you feel the plug?" he asked breathlessly. "Because I do."

It had taken everything in me to stay quiet. I could indeed feel his cock rubbing against the plug in my ass through the thin wall between them, and it drove me wild. I came in record time, pressing my lips together to hold in my moans.

When we were done, Ash opened the door a crack and checked to be sure the coast was clear. It was, and we slipped back into the ballroom, hoping no one noticed us missing.

Back in our seats for dinner now, Celena thumps down next to me.

"I can't believe none of the players will take a chance with me as long as that asshole has staked his claim," she says.

"None of them?" I ask, a little surprised. Celena is beautiful. Like, drop-dead gorgeous. I can't imagine anyone turning her down.

"None of them," she confirms. "I nearly had one of the rookies on the hook, but his friend pointed out that Kingston wants me, and I've never seen a man backpedal that fast."

She looks across the way, and I follow her gaze to where Kingston sits a couple tables over. The corners of his mouth turn up ever-so-slightly as he looks at her.

"I'll be right back," Celena says as she rises and heads toward him.

I try to grab for her hand but miss, and I can only watch as she beelines for his table. She stops in front of him, and he looks up at her. She says something to him I don't catch, then she drops the hotel key card he gave her into the glass of amber-brown liquid he's drinking.

The people at Kingston's table look scandalized, and I hear one of the other players, possibly Fig, say, "Oh shit," from somewhere off to my left. For his own part, the expression on Kingston's face doesn't change as Celena turns on her heel and stalks back to our table to sit down.

"Um…everything alright?" Ash asks her.

"Perfectly fine," she says, taking a sip of what looks like a new glass of champagne. "Just wanted to return his key card, since I won't need it."

The three of us look over at Kingston, who pulls the card out of his drink, raises the glass toward Celena, and takes a sip.

Celena just turns to me. "So where have you been?"

I shrug. "Just…mingling."

She narrows her eyes. "You're flushed. What are you…" Her eyes widen again as she looks at me. "The two of you were off fucking somewhere, weren't you," she says in a low voice, just so I can hear.

"What? No. Why would you think that?" I sputter, but even I can hear the lie in my denial.

Celena gives me a '*Don't bullshit me*' look, and I relent.

"Fine, yes. We talked to Mr. Kaladin, and Ash was wound up after that, so we found an empty supply closet, and…"

I let her fill in the blank.

She smirks knowingly at me. "You little slut. How was it?"

I glance around to be sure no one else is listening. "Why has no one told me about the joys of anal plugs before now?" I whisper.

Celena barks out a laugh, drawing Ash's attention as well as that of a few other people at our table. There are one or two Hydra per table so other guests get a chance to hobnob with the players. Ash is the only player at our table.

He looks at me and Celena questioningly, and Celena waggles her eyebrows at him.

"Shit," he says.

I give him an apologetic look. "She saw that I was flushed and guessed," I say softly. "It's your fault for making me come that hard."

He shrugs, conceding the point.

The rest of dinner is fairly uneventful. I end up getting drawn into a conversation with one of the men at our table, a state congressman I think, about my research. As usual, it starts with me having to justify the importance of the topic, but once I'm done, he seems convinced I'm doing the Lord's work.

Celena has since wandered off again, possibly to retry her luck with some of the Hydra after her public rejection of Kingston's advances, so Kelsier takes her seat when he comes by. The music has turned from ballads to dance songs, and people wander onto the dance floor.

"How long are we expected to stay at these things?" Ash asks him.

Kelsier looks at his watch. "I'd give it another half hour before you try to slip out," he says. "The rookies have to stay until the major VIPs leave."

"Have you seen Celena?" I ask Kelsier. "I'm just wondering if she's had any more luck with the players since her little display with Kingston."

Kelsier gives me a doubtful look. "Yeah, she may have rejected him, but that look on his face said he hasn't given up yet, and until he does, no one will go near her."

I look around. "Where is she anyway?"

"I think I saw her wander into the poker room," Kelsier says.

I jerk my eyes back to him from scanning the room.

"Poker room? What poker room?" I ask urgently.

Kelsier points to a door off the ballroom where a few people move in and out. "The games are an additional fundraising activity," he says.

I look at Ash in panic. "You didn't tell me there'd be gambling."

He frowns. "I didn't think it mattered. They announced the games would be starting while you were arguing with the congressman about trash talk. Did you want to play or something?"

I shake my head. "No, Celena has a gambling problem," I say. "That's why she couldn't come to the club with me that time. She tries to stay away from it, but – shit!"

I shoot out of my chair, and Ash and Kelsier are half a second behind me as I head for the door to the poker room.

"I'm sure she'll be fine," Ash tries to reassure me, his long strides helping him keep pace with my short, quick ones.

I don't answer as I step into the poker room and look around for Celena. I find her at a table with three other people in the back right and head straight for her. I slow my pace for just a moment as I recognize the large form of Kingston sitting across from her, then I double-time it.

"Celena!" I call as I come around to stand next to her. Everyone at the table looks at me like I've gone mad, and I try to calm myself. "Ash and I are leaving soon," I say as calmly as I can muster. "You should come with us. We can give you a ride home if you're not good to drive."

Celena doesn't take her attention from Kingston, whose eyes also seem locked with hers across the table.

"I'm not going anywhere until I finish taking this asshole for all he's worth," she says, her eyes still fixed on the goalie.

I look down at the table. Celena has a decent pile of chips in front of her, while Kingston's pile appears to be dwindling. Still…

I bend down next to Celena and turn my head away from the other players so I can whisper to her.

"Are you sure this is a good idea?" I ask her. "Maybe you should-"

Celena turns to look at me. "I'm not leaving."

I sigh and stand up. Celena is a grown woman and can make her own decisions. I won't force her to leave, but I have a feeling this isn't going to end well.

I step back to watch the end of the hand.

"Call," Kingston says, pushing part of his last few chips into the pot.

"Show your hands," the dealer says.

I look at the row of five cards on the table. There's a pair of deuces showing, and the rest is a whole lot of nothing.

Kingston turns his cards over. He has a Jack and a seven. The Jack does nothing for him, but his seven, along with the other seven already showing, gives him two pairs.

Celena smiles as she turns over her cards. A three and a deuce. She has three of a kind, which wins the hand.

I let out a small breath. Maybe things will be okay this time. Celena's almost done finishing Kingston off, and then we can get her out of here.

The dealer collects the cards and sends them through the shuffler.

"They need to leave," Kingston tells the dealer as he points to me, Ash, and Kelsier. "We can't have them giving her signals."

I let out an indignant noise. "I would never-"

"Even unconscious ones," Kingston cuts in.

"Sorry, ma'am," the dealer says. "He's right. If you're not playing, you need to go back out into the ballroom."

I look desperately at Celena.

"Go," she says. "I'll be fine. This won't take long."

I don't move, but Ash slips an arm around my waist to steer me away.

"Come on," he says softly. "There's nothing you can do."

Ash and Kelsier escort me back into the ballroom, and I head straight to our table to chug the remaining wine in my glass. Ash slips his arms around me and pulls me close when I set the glass back down.

"You okay?" he asks.

I nod. "If you want to go, I can catch an Uber home," I tell him. "I just don't want to leave until I'm sure Celena won't do anything stupid."

"I'm not going anywhere until you do," he says. "Why don't we dance?" He grins. "We can recreate that night at the club."

I smile despite myself. "That night got us in trouble, if you recall."

He shrugs. "Oh, I don't know. Things didn't work out too bad." He leans down and kisses me lightly on the lips. "Come on. Let's dance. You need to take your mind off the poker game, or it'll drive you crazy."

"I'm going to go mingle some more," Kelsier says. "You two are so sweet it's making my teeth hurt."

Kelsier turns and heads off, and Ash takes my hand to pull me onto the dance floor. Reluctantly, I let him lead me out, but it takes me a while to get into it. Ash dances around unapologetically, twirling me and being a goofball until I finally relent and start dancing with him in earnest.

I keep an eye on the poker room, but it's a long time before I finally see Celena stalk out. Nearly an hour according to the clock on the wall.

I stop mid-dance and head straight for her, Ash right behind me.

"Celena, are you okay?" I ask, throwing myself in front of her. Ash is there a second later.

Celena pulls up short, and she looks furious. Not good.

Instead of answering me, she looks at Ash. "Your goalie is a giant fucking asshole," she tells him, just short of shouting.

Ash chuckles. "Yeah, we're aware."

"Celena, do you-," I start to ask, but she cuts me off.

"Don't worry," she says, "I didn't overdo it. Not too much, anyway. I'm fine. I'm just pissed. I'll talk to you tomorrow."

I look at her for a long moment, trying to decide if she's too angry to drive, but her outburst at Ash seems to have vented some of her rage.

I nod, and we hug before Celena stalks off toward the exit.

"Ready to go?" Ash asks me.

"More than ready," I say.

He slips his fingers through mine, and we head toward the door.

"More than ready is what I like to hear," he says.

"What?" I look up at him, and he's grinning. "Oh!" I say, finally getting the innuendo. I wasn't thinking about sex, but I am now.

"Maybe my girlfriend will invite me in for a nightcap," he muses.

I roll my eyes. "A nightcap? Does anyone say that anymore?"

He shrugs. "I don't know, but it sounds more polite than saying, 'Maybe my girlfriend will invite me in to fuck the hell out of her.'"

"Touché," I say. "Seriously, though. I'm not complaining, but have you always been this horny?"

He chuckles. "*This* horny? No. I mean, yeah, I've always had a pretty healthy sex drive, but I've never been as horny as I am with you."

I stare at him as we walk. "Is that true?"

His face goes serious. "I wouldn't say it if it wasn't. For Christ's sake, Gray, my subconscious sent you a dick pic the night after I met you."

I laugh. "Your subconscious was trying to send your ex a dick pic."

"My subconscious knew exactly what it was doing," he insists. "It was trying to tell me something that I was too dense to get at the time."

I stop walking, and he does too.

"You're really that attracted to me?" I ask. Celena would chastise me for even questioning this, but I can't help it.

Ash stares at me for several seconds, then narrows his eyes. "Why are you questioning this?"

I shrug, trying to play it off. "I don't know…I just…," I say, trying to search for a way to explain that doesn't sound completely neurotic. "The jock and the nerd only end up together in movies," I say finally. "It doesn't happen in real life. We just have so little in common…"

He stares at me another few seconds. "That's really what you're worried about?" he asks.

I give him a half-hearted, one-shoulder shrug.

"First of all," Ash says, grabbing my shoulders, "I told you in your office, I love that you're smart. It gets me hard to watch you argue circles around people who try to challenge you."

My mouth falls open, but I'm not sure what to say to that.

"Also," he says, giving me a small shake to emphasize his point, "you are a beautiful fucking woman, and when your intelligence isn't getting me hard, then the way your breasts bounce is. Or the way your hips sway when you walk. Or when you part your lips and run your tongue along the bottom one." He runs a hand through his hair. "Jesus, Gray. You have a thousand things you do that turn me on so much it hurts."

It's my turn to stare. "You really want me that much?" I ask.

Ash takes my chin between his thumb and forefinger and tilts my head up so I have to look into his eyes. "Yes, baby," he says with conviction. "And I need you to start believing that."

Chapter 36

Gray

"How much did you lose that night at poker anyway?" I ask Celena as I head down the aisle of the grocery store just under a week later with my Bluetooth earbuds in. I've been craving peanut butter since my mother mentioned it weeks ago, but I keep forgetting to buy it.

Celena and I have texted as usual, but this is the first time we've talked since the gala. I think she's been avoiding me, and she was dodging my questions over text about what happened in the poker game with Kingston. She can't put me off any longer, though.

"I only lost twelve hundred," she says, "but money isn't the issue."

Only twelve hundred. I would've been having heart palpitations if I'd lost that much, but gamblers measure money differently.

"The more important thing I lost was my dignity," Celena goes on.

I stop walking. "What the hell happened in that game?"

"I'll tell you soon. Just not today," she says. "I still need some time to recover from my humiliation. He played me, Gray. He card-sharked me."

I think back to how Celena had been winning by a lot against Kingston when the dealer asked us to leave. Something had obviously changed after that.

"He started playing better when we left," I guess as I push my cart up to the peanut butter and grab a jar of the store's generic brand.

"The next hand, he took me for three hundred dollars," she says. "He was watching me the whole time, losing on purpose, learning my tells."

"Oh, Celena. And you didn't stop when you figured that out?"

"What part of 'gambling problem' is unclear to you?" she snaps.

She makes a noise of disgust that I know is self-directed.

"He tried to give me his room key again after the game," she goes on. "Told me I could come up and collect back what I lost."

"I hope you shoved it up his ass," I say. I haven't moved on down the aisle yet, and now I'm contemplating marshmallow fluff to go with my peanut butter.

No, no fluff. I start walking again. Seeing Ash's incredible body all the time has made me more health conscious as I consider the things he has to do to keep fit. He may like my body the way it is, but sleeping with him has inspired me to get more in shape. Not necessarily thinner, but stronger. I need to ask him to help me with some strength training, since I feel so weak next to him. Maybe I'll also get back into cardio kickboxing. I did that a couple years ago, and it was both fun and therapeutic.

Celena's voice brings me back from mentally planning my new health and exercise routine.

"No, I took the card," she says, "and I gave it to some puck bunnies on my way out."

I stop dead again. It's going to take me forever to finish my shopping this way.

"You what?" I ask.

"There were some women hanging around outside the ballroom," she says. "I assumed they were those puck bunnies, right? So I asked them if they were interested in spending a night with the Hydra's goalie. They were, so I gave them the card and told them to go wait up in his room."

My mouth hangs open. "You didn't."

"I most certainly fucking did," she says. "Not all of them went, but two of them were more than eager to go. I hope he had fun with them."

She spits the last part out with more than a little venom.

I'm about to say something else when I catch sight of a familiar face. There's a man at the end of the aisle I just turned down, and I can't place him at first. He glances my way, and our eyes meet. He puts the can he's examining down and leaves the aisle, and that's when it hits me.

"What the fuck?" I say unconsciously.

"Gray? You okay? What's up?" Celena asks in my ear.

"I just saw a guy who was at my conference in Florida," I tell her.

Specifically, I remember seeing him in the hall after my presentation when I was texting Ash about the new dick pic he sent me. The man was texting on his phone as well.

"I saw him a few times at the convention center. I figured he was just interested in the same panels and presentations I was, but now he's here."

"Could he be from Connecticut, and it's just a coincidence he shops where you shop?" she asks unconvincingly.

I consider this until something else hits me. "He didn't have a shopping basket or a cart," I say. "He either only came in to get one item, or he's not actually shopping."

"What the fuck?" Celena says.

I wheel my cart around and head in the direction I saw the man go. I hurry across the back of the store, looking down each aisle as I pass it.

"Gray, what are you doing?" Celena asks.

"Looking for the man. I'm going to introduce myself."

"Gray, honey, I don't think that's a good idea," she says. "There are a lot of crazies out there. I'm not sure you should confront one of them."

"I want him to know I'm on to him if he really is following me."

"No, absolutely not," Celena says. "Gray, stand down, girl. Abort!"

I ignore her and continue to head past the aisles until I get to the end of the store. The guy isn't there, so I head down the last aisle toward the front and start my search over. I also check the register lines, but the man didn't have any groceries in his hands, so there would be no reason for him to check out.

Celena is in my ear the whole time, trying to talk me out of facing him.

I get to the other end of the store, but there's no sign of the man.

"He's gone," I say, cutting off her monologue about stranger danger. "He must have slipped out when I made him."

"When you *made* him?" she says. "Sweety, this is not some buddy-cop show. It's time to take it down a notch. If you think he's following you, call the real police."

"No, not yet," I say. "Like you suggested, maybe he just lives in Connecticut and happens to shop at the same store I do. I need proof I'm being followed. I already overreacted once, and it was humiliating."

Celena stays on with me while I do the rest of my grocery shopping and check out. When I leave, I scan the parking lot to see if I spot the guy sitting in a car waiting for me, but he's nowhere to be seen.

"Can you look up 'How to spot a tail while driving'?" I ask Celena as I put my groceries in the car.

"Excuse me?" she asks.

"I don't see the guy in the parking lot, but I want to be sure no one's following me home," I tell her. "Just look it up, please."

"You're probably going to get some BS that Google pulled from half a dozen Hollywood movies," she says.

"Yeah, but they have police consultants on those movies, right?"

I hear her sigh, and there's a pause as she looks up the info.

"It's what you'd expect," she says. "Just keep an eye out for a vehicle that stays behind you, although not necessarily directly behind you. Watch a few cars back and look for someone who turns every time you do."

I knew most of that already.

"Ooo, here's a useful trick," she says. "If you're on a highway, you should exit, then immediately get back on in the opposite direction."

"I'm not on the highway. I'm at the grocery store."

I finish putting my bags in the car, then wait in the driver's seat with the car on. The car's Bluetooth picks up the call, so I pull my earbuds out.

"So get on the highway, go up one exit, get off, then immediately get back on," she says. "Isn't there an entrance ramp to the highway right near the store?"

"There is. Good idea."

"Shit, wait," she says. "Why am I encouraging this?"

"Because you're a good friend, and you want me to be prepared in case I'm actually being stalked," I say as I put the car in gear and back up.

Celena sighs heavily on the other end. "Fine. Just keep talking to me until you get home so I know you're safe."

"Wait, should I even go home?" I ask. "If I am being followed, I don't want to lead the stalker to where I live, right?"

Celena sighs again. "Honey, I hate to break it to you, but if you do have a stalker, he probably already knows where you live. Chances are the guy left the store and just went straight to your house to wait for you."

My stomach bottoms out. "Holy shit. What do I do?"

"Do you want me to meet you at your house?" she asks. "I can go in with you to be sure it's safe."

"So we can both be killed?" I say, trying to quell my hysteria.

"Gray, you have groceries getting warm in your car. You have to go home eventually. Last time it was a false alarm, and I'm sure it is this time too. I'll meet you there, and we'll check together."

"Do you have time?" I ask as I pull out of the parking lot and head for the highway. I'm going to do the off-then-on-again thing anyway, even if it's pointless.

"I can take a break," she says.

Celena owns a ceramics studio downtown that offers both paint-your-own pottery for the general public who want a taste of art, as well as classes and memberships for the more serious crowd who want to throw their own pottery on a wheel. She herself has a home studio where she does her work, which sells pretty well in certain circles. I have a number of her pieces that she's given me or that I've insisted on buying from her over the years. She's incredibly talented.

"I don't want to interrupt you if you're working on something important," I say.

"Just go home, and I'll meet you there," she says.

I pull into my driveway ten minutes later, and it doesn't look like anyone followed me home. In any case, I didn't see anyone get off the highway with me and then get right back on when I did.

I wait in my car in the garage for Celena. She doesn't live too far away, so she should be here soon. We hung up with each other so I could concentrate on watching for tails.

I want to text Ash, but he's at practice, then he needs to rest to prepare for a quick trip to Florida tomorrow. He wanted me to come over tonight, but we always stay up way too late when we're together, and as much as I want to have sex, I can't be selfish. Kaladin is already suspicious of us, and if he finds out I'm keeping one of his star players from getting his rest, there will be consequences.

We still haven't done anything in Ash's bedroom. He either comes to my place, or if we go to his, we've had sex pretty much everywhere but the bedroom. He seems to have this fear that if he takes me in there, I'll run screaming.

We need to break through this barrier, so I'll have to come up with a strategy for when he gets back.

Celena's car pulls into the driveway, and we both get out.

"Thanks for – Jesus Christ, Celena!" I say to her as I see the small pistol in her hand. "Why did you bring that?"

She looks at me incredulously. "What do you mean why did I bring it? We're about to search your house for stalkers, right?"

Celena and I have never seen eye to eye on guns. I hate them, but a small part of me understands why she has one. Celena is a beautiful but tiny woman who lives alone. I get her desire to have protection, even if I think she's just going to end up accidentally shooting her housekeeper one of these days.

"Isn't it illegal to drive with that?" I ask.

"I had it in the lock box," she says.

I sigh and head toward the front door. I'll leave the groceries in the car until I know the coast is clear. I did a quick scan of the neighborhood earlier, but I didn't see any unusual cars parked anywhere.

"You go first, John Wick," I say, opening the door.

Celena goes to the firing range, but I still don't trust her behind me with a gun.

Celena and I enter the house. I feel like I should call out to see if my mother is there delivering another bottle of wine, but I don't. Instead, I grab a knife from the kitchen, the same one as before, and Celena and I go room by room to check the house.

We find no one there, and my body relaxes once we've cleared everything, including the basement and attic.

I need to get myself under control. I'm not sure why I'm convinced I'm being stalked, but I can't live like this.

"All clear," Celena says. "Are you going to be okay here alone?"

I let out a breath and head for the car to get my groceries. She follows.

"I'll be fine," I say. "Apparently I'm just paranoid."

Celena grabs a couple bags and helps me schlep them into the house.

"It's completely understandable," she says. "Warranted or not, you had a scare a little while ago, and it's going to take some time to get past that." She pauses. "Maybe you should consider-"

"I'm not getting a gun," I say, cutting her off.

She shrugs. "Fine. How about a dog?"

"I don't want a pet," I say. "I don't want to worry about coming home early to let a dog out or spending money to board one when I have to travel to an academic conference."

She nods. "Fair enough, but then you have to find a way to relax and not let your imagination run wild. You'll give yourself an ulcer."

I hug Celena and thank her for coming over before I head back inside to put away my groceries.

I put away the perishables first, then grab my peanut butter. I go to shelve it but jerk to a halt and drop the jar as I'm confronted with my seventy-eight-year-old neighbor walking around his living room in his underwear.

The shade to my kitchen window is up again.

Chapter 37

Ash

I'm distracted the next day when I get on the plane to Florida for so many reasons, not the least of which is that it will be my first time playing my old team. They know me, and more importantly, they know my weaknesses. To say I'm worried is an understatement.

More than that, I'm worried about Gray. I slept at her place last night after she called me, panicked, to say her shade was open again and that she thought she was being followed at the grocery store.

The grocery store was definitely my guy. He called to tell me Gray spotted him and that he'd needed to break off surveillance, so I had him switch places with the woman watching Drew.

I still have someone watching Gray's house when she isn't home as well, and that guy swore he didn't see anyone around her property, so the shade is still a mystery. I suggested to Gray, and half to myself, that maybe the shade was broken now and that it keeps creeping up on its own.

She seemed to buy that explanation about as much as I myself did, and I searched the house casually for more notes or 'gifts' while I was there. Whoever broke in before didn't leave any more rose petals anywhere, though.

Gray regaled me last night with the story of how she attempted to catch someone tailing her home from the grocery store by watching for cars behind her, then getting off and back on the highway. A small part of me was amused by her 007 efforts, but a larger part felt guilty at contributing to her anxiety and paranoia.

When I get back from this road trip, I need to tell her about the security team I have following her. It's not a conversation I'm looking forward to, since I expect her to be angry, and she'll inevitably want to know why I had the team following her in the first place.

The whole situation makes me mad. Mad there's some sicko out there stalking my woman and scaring her. Mad I have to get on this plane and travel halfway around the country when I should be taking care of her. Mad that having to worry about Gray is distracting me from a game I love so I can't play my best.

I work myself into a frenzy as I head down the aisle of the plane, all the tension I relieved by having morning sex with Gray now gone.

We went to bed last night without doing anything, but I woke this morning to her stroking my cock. She apologized when I asked what she was doing, and she said something about getting my consent first next time. I told her she always had my consent to grab my cock, and I let her stroke me a little longer until I couldn't stand it. Then I pulled her over and let her ride me until we both came hard.

The memory almost calms me until I jerk to a halt in the middle of the aisle and look down to find Kingston's hand once again wrapped around my forearm. He opens his mouth to say something, but I don't give him the chance.

"I'm not in the mood for your bullshit, Kingston," I say, yanking my arm out of his grip. "Keep your fucking comments to yourself."

I start to head down the aisle again but stop and look back at him. His mouth hangs open, and I'm sure no one has dared to talk to him like that in the recent past.

"And another thing," I say, "Celena isn't interested in you, so just back off and leave her the fuck alone."

I turn and stalk down the aisle, only vaguely aware the plane has gone dead-silent as everyone has stopped what they're doing. They're waiting to see what Kingston will do, but I don't give a shit. I shove my carryon into the overhead compartment and thump into the window seat.

Kelsier makes it to the row about half a minute later and waits for me to look up at him.

"You okay there, Gunny?" he asks, wary amusement on his face.

"Not one God damn word," I tell him.

He holds up his hands in surrender. "Not a word," he says. "I mean, Kingston will probably beat the shit out of you later, but at least for now you have him too shocked to do anything."

I look up over the seats and see the top of Kingston's head several rows ahead of me, the band for his headphones in place over his black hair. He won't confront me now, but Kelsier's right. I'm probably in for it after our game.

Kelsier stows his bag and sits down next to me. He starts to put his seatbelt on but then frowns and inhales deeply through his nose. "Do you smell like…lavender?"

I sniff my shoulder, and Gray's scent fills my head. Lavender is a soothing scent to begin with, but instinctively I know the sudden calming effect I feel has more to do with Gray herself than aromatherapy.

"It's Gray's bodywash," I say. "I spent last night at her place and forgot to bring my own stuff to shower, so I had to use hers."

He sighs. "I might have to find a new seatmate until this thing between the two of you blows over."

I resist the urge to glare at him. Just the suggestion that things with Gray might end someday has my bad mood returning.

"So what's got you all riled up today?" Kelsier asks. "Nervous about playing Tampa Bay?"

We were supposed to play them back in December, but a freak blizzard canceled the game, and the makeup day was tacked on to the end of the season. The delay only kicked up my anxiety, though. It was as if the universe was telling me I wasn't ready to face them yet.

I shrug. "A little," I lie. "I'm more worried about Gray."

"Uh oh," he says. "Things going south between you two already?"

I wave a dismissive hand. "Nothing like that. Some shit went down at her place a little while ago, and…I may have done something unwise to try and fix it."

He narrows his eyes. "How unwise?"

I'm not sure why I never told Kelsier any of this. I told Cedric about the break-in just in case it became a PR thing, but the press never got wind of the police presence at Gray's that night. As for Kelsier, I guess I knew he'd have something to say about my decision to have Gray secretly watched, so I kept it to myself for the time being.

I sigh and tell him everything now, how someone broke into Gray's house and left rose petals on her bed, and how she doesn't know that and still thinks her mother was the only one there that day. I confess to hiring the private security, and I explain about Gray seeing the guy yesterday, then coming home to find her shade open again.

When I'm done, Kelsier stares at me like I've lost my mind. He's not wrong, but…

"Someone was in her house?" he asks. "And you didn't tell her?"

"Kels, you should have seen how freaked out she was just by the window and the wine," I tell him. "She would've lost her shit if she'd seen her bed covered in rose petals. I nearly lost my own shit when I saw it."

"Yeah, that's creepy as fuck," he admits, "but you better hope she never finds out or you're in deep trouble. Women don't appreciate things being kept from them, even when you're trying to protect them."

"I hope the security guys catch this sick fuck soon," I say.

"And she doesn't know about the security either?"

I shake my head.

"You are so fucked if she finds out."

"I'm planning to tell her when I get back," I say. "About the security at least. I want to avoid telling her about the rose petals."

He shakes his head. "I hope the last sex you had was good, because I don't think you're getting any more for a while."

His words bring up the memory of Gray's full breasts bobbing up and down as she bounced on my cock this morning, and I groan. Once a night with her is never enough, and the nights I don't get to have her at all are hell. The thought of her denying me sex indefinitely or even breaking up with me over this sends a chill through me.

"Yeah, well, that's a problem for Future Me," I tell him.

He angles his head. "I'm really surprised Future You hasn't kicked the shit out of Past You yet."

I shrug. "Future Me is usually too busy cleaning up Past Me's fuck ups to have time for that. It's a careful balance. As long as Past Me doesn't do anything to get Future Me arrested or fuck up his hockey career, it's generally a live-and-let-live situation." Then I add, "Plus Past Me and Future Me are never in the same place at the same time."

Kelsier shakes his head. "As long as you know what the hell you're doing, carry on, man."

That's the problem. I knew exactly what I was doing until I met Gray. Now I don't know which way is up.

Ash

It's a funny thing about anger. It's not always a bad emotion.

I took a course on Human Emotion as an elective back in college when I was working on my Kinesiology degree, and I learned that when a person gets angry, the body releases adrenaline, which is part of its fight-or-flight response. The adrenaline helps prepare the body for physical action, to key it up – either to fight or to run. Certain systems kick into gear to increase heart rate, blood pressure, and breathing, as well as to tense muscles in preparation for movement.

In small doses, then, anger can be a good thing in sports. I learned that for some athletes, anger gives them hyper-focus, and they're able to channel their physical responses into a heightened ability to play.

The issue is that there's a threshold at which too much anger becomes a liability. Pushing your heart rate, blood pressure, or breathing too high can lead to shakiness or dizziness. If that happens, fine motor control and mental focus break down, and athletic performance can suffer.

When guys chirp at me, that's what happens. Apparently my shame-induced anger sends my body straight past the stage of useful anger and right into the *'Jesus Christ, does he even know how to play hockey?'* stage.

Interestingly, the anger I've been storing up for my old team and for Gray's stalker seems to be just the right amount to keep my adrenaline levels at *'can of whoop-ass'* stage.

My first goal in our game against the Lightning in the second period is a thing of beauty. Cote, Bouchard, and I pass the puck between us like there's no one else on the ice. The Lightning's goalie, a new guy, shifts back and forth as we pass it between us, and I send the puck to Cote, intending for him to take the shot. One of the defensemen reads the pass and moves to intercept, though. The only thing Cote can do is send it back to me at the last minute. I'm almost past the goal, but I take the shot without thinking.

The angle is nearly impossible. I have maybe three inches to play with between the post and the goalie's shoulder, and there are two other players between us. The puck flips in the air, and I see it, almost in slow motion, turning so its short side faces me. It slips between the post and the goalie like a coin feeding into a slot. How it made it past the elbow of the Lightning's defenseman and over Samsonov's knee, I'll never know.

I pump my fist in the air as my team swamps me against the boards in congratulations, and now my anger-fueled adrenaline is bolstered by elation. The period ends a few minutes later, but I'm still riding high.

As expected, my former teammates have tried chirping at me, but they're the least of my worries right now. I barely hear them as I play.

When the third period starts, I'm out on the ice for less than twenty seconds into my shift before I steal the puck away from one of my old friends on the Lightning and streak down toward the other end on a breakaway. There's no one near me, and I fake a shot right before flicking the puck left. The goalie falls for the fake, and I have the whole left side of the net to put my shot in for my second goal of the night.

I'm firing on all cylinders right now, and my old teammates have gone strangely quiet. I haven't been buzzing like this in a long time, and it feels incredible. Almost as good as sex with Gray.

With three minutes left in the last period, Kingston has been perfect, and we're riding a 2-0 lead as Tampa Bay pulls their goalie.

My anger still simmers below the surface, but it's not the anger of shame, not the anger that says my ideal image has been challenged. It's the anger that my old team didn't value me enough to try to save me. My contract was up, and rather than help me fix my issue, as Kaladin is doing, they let me go.

It didn't hit me until I was back here on the ice, in this stadium I know so well, just how much their vote of 'no confidence' hurt. That anger is what drives me now, and it's squarely in the *useful as fuck* category.

My last goal of the night is at once the most and the least exciting. I feel the desperation of the Lightning players as they try to get the puck close to Kingston, who looks like nothing short of a giant boulder in the middle of the net. He's big, and he's faster than any guy that size has a right to be. There's very little daylight for the Tampa Bay forwards to find.

One of the Lightning wings, another old friend, takes a wild shot at the goal, but Kingston gets his glove up just in time to deflect the puck into the air. It pops up back toward center ice…Right to me. I snatch it out of the air, drop it in front of me, and head toward the open goal before half the other players have realized what's happening.

My shot is dead center, and the few Hydra fans in the audience erupt in cheers. Only a few hats land on the ice as the Lightning fans head for the doors, and the stadium's staff quickly scoop them up before we play out the last two minutes of the game.

We win 3-0, all thanks to me, and I'm on cloud nine. Old friends on the Lightning come over to congratulate me on my hat trick, and my old coach claps me on the back to say, "Revenge is sweet, hey, Gun."

My skates barely touch the floor as I head back into the locker room with what I'm sure is a ridiculous smile on my face. I'm undressing when I notice everything has gone quiet.

I turn to find Kingston looming over me, his extra three inches feeling like extra feet right now as he stares me down. I straighten as much as I can and stand my ground. He can't really want to start something right after I scored a hat trick and he played a shut-out game, can he?

We glare at each other for what seems like forever before he finally says, "Good game, asshole."

My brows shoot up, and it's several seconds before a smile creeps onto my face. "Yeah, you too, dickhead."

The corners of his mouth twitch before he turns away, but he stops and turns back to me.

"You're wrong, though," he says.

I frown. "About what?"

"About your doc's little friend," he says. "You should have seen the way she was eye-fucking me across the table that whole poker game. She wants me alright."

My mouth falls open a little before I angle my head to concede the point. "I'll take your word for it," I say.

He grunts and tromps back to his locker as I sit on the bench to take off my skates.

"Word of advice, Gunny," Kelsier says softly as he leans in. "Buy a fucking Megamillions ticket before this streak of luck runs out."

Chapter 38

Ash

Gray is wrapped in my arms as we lay on the couch watching TV a couple days later. Well, she's watching TV. I'm absently letting my fingers trail through her hair and wondering how long is a suitable amount of time to just 'hang' before I pull off her pants and eat her out.

She makes the most amazing noises when my head is between her legs, and it's killing me not to take her into my bedroom, strap her to my bed, and bury my tongue in her sweet cunt.

My cock is painfully hard just thinking about it, but I don't move. I can't seem to take that final step to bring her into my bedroom. I feel like I have a good handle on what she will and won't allow, but I'm still too nervous to put theory into practice. If she ends up hating the experience, it will ruin what we have together, so we've had sex everywhere *but* the bedroom.

I remind myself she didn't balk at the scene I instigated in her office, but that was still tame compared to what I want to do to her. Her easy acceptance of the belt around her neck that time gives me hope, though.

The show ends, and Gray shifts on top of me so we're face to face. She's cradled between my legs like a reverse missionary, and she puts a hand on my chest as she looks up at me.

"So are we just going to watch TV all night, or are you planning to fuck me at some point?" she asks.

Well, shit. If I knew she was waiting on me…

"You were immersed in the show," I say. "I didn't want to interrupt."

"How was I supposed to concentrate on the show with your erection digging into my back?"

I laugh. "So we've both been lying here uncomfortably when we could have been having sex?"

She smiles. "Looks that way."

I start to get up off the couch, and she leans back to let me. I get to my feet, but before she can follow, I lean down, pull her forward, and toss her over my shoulder. She shrieks as I stand up.

"Ash! What are you doing?" she yells.

"I'm taking a chance," I say as I head toward the bedroom. It's time to get over this mental block I have about letting Gray sub for me. She said she wants this. It's time I let her prove it.

I just get to the hall when my phone pings, making the sound that says someone is at the door. A second later, my doorbell rings, and I stop dead.

"What the fuck?" I say as I head over to look at the door cam on my phone, Gray still slung over my shoulder. It's not terribly late, only a little before eight, but I can't imagine who could be here at this hour.

"Ash," Gray says. "All the blood is rushing to my head."

I ignore her, my hand clamped tight against the backs of her legs. I pull up the doorbell app to look at the live video and swear.

"Ash?"

I bend down and set Gray back on her feet, snaking an arm around her waist until she's steady.

"What is it?" she asks.

I sigh heavily. "My parents and Petra are here."

And I know exactly why.

"Your family? Did you know they were coming?" she asks.

I sigh again. "No, but I should have."

I slip my hand in hers and pull her toward the front door. I doubt my parents will realize what they interrupted, but maybe Petra will get the hint. Not that it matters. They obviously just drove down seven hours from Canada. It looks like I'll have house guests tonight.

I open the door, Gray at my side.

"Surprise!" my mom says when the door swings open, but the look on her face says she's the one surprised when she catches sight of Gray.

"I told you that was her car in the driveway," Petra says.

"Oh!" my mom says. "It didn't occur to me you'd have company." Obviously not.

"No worries," I say. "Gray and I were just watching TV."

Petra thrusts the white bakery box in her hands at me, and I take it from her. I'm a hundred percent sure it contains a cake.

"TV. Right," my sister says knowingly. "Looks like Inga owes me twenty dollars. She didn't think you two were really together."

My lips thin. Gray was right about Inga's suspicion.

"Happy early birthday!" my mother says, breaking the tension before I can respond to Petra. "Inga couldn't get away from work, but we wanted to come down to celebrate with you."

"It's your birthday?" Gray says. "Why didn't you tell me?"

"It's tomorrow," I say, stepping aside to let her and my parents in. Luckily, the situation in my pants eased when I realized they were here.

I lead the way back into the kitchen and living room as everyone follows. I hadn't bothered to turn off the TV when I scooped Gray off the couch, so it's still on. Hopefully that will deflect suspicion about what me and Gray were really up to.

"Do you have candles?" my mother asks as she sets her purse and another bag on the counter. "It's the one thing we forgot."

She and Petra both start opening kitchen drawers while my father sits down at the kitchen table.

"I don't need candles," I say as I give in to the inevitable and take out dishes and forks.

"Of course you do," my mother says as she opens the cabinet where I keep my canned goods.

"Found them!" Petra says as she pulls a small box from the back of the junk drawer. She shakes the box. "Well, I found one."

She opens the box and dumps one lonely candle into her palm. I'm actually surprised I have that one. When I moved up here from Florida, I dumped everything from my junk drawer into a box. The candle must have been left over from the last time my parents came for my birthday.

Petra takes the cake out of the bakery box, sticks the candle in it, and lights the wick. They all sing happy birthday to me, and I quickly blow the candle out before they can perform an encore.

"How have you been, Gray?" Petra asks as she pulls a knife from my knife block and cuts the cake. "How's my brother been treating you?"

Gray looks at me, and I feel like we're both thinking about how I threw her over my shoulder a few minutes ago. Or perhaps we're thinking about what I planned to do to her when I got her into the bedroom.

I raise a sly brow at her that seems to ask, '*Well?*'

She gives me back a '*Don't tempt me to tell them*' look.

"He's great," she says, smiling at Petra. "I've almost got him trained."

I snort. She'll pay for that remark when I get her strapped to my bed.

"Eat your cake," Petra says to me. She pushes a plate of cake thick with buttercream frosting toward me. "The ladies are talking."

I snort again but dive into the cake. That's a comment I'd expect Inga to make. She's starting to rub off on our little sister.

"Has Ash met your parents yet?" my mother asks Gray.

Gray seems to go a little pale at the question.

"I met her father," I say before she can answer. "He came to vet me, as any good father would." I add that last part for Gray's benefit, to assure her I don't blame her for her father coming to see me.

"And her mother?" my mom presses.

"We haven't had a chance to get together yet, but I'm sure we will when Gray can arrange it. We're both a little busy right now."

Gray's been dragging her feet about letting me meet her mother, but I won't push her. I know it's more about her relationship with her mother than anything having to do with me, so I can be patient.

I give Petra a look that begs her to change the subject, and she gives a quick nod. I've always been closer to Petra than Inga, and she's good at reading my nonverbal cues. I learned that term from Gray.

"Are you teaching right now?" Petra asks Gray.

"Just one class," Gray answers. "It's an intensive session that meets every day. The trade-off was that they gave my large lecture intro course to someone else this coming semester, so I'll have more time to work with Ash. I'm only teaching seminars, which will be really nice."

"That's great," Petra says before diving into her cake.

My father is half finished with his piece and has yet to speak.

"You're working on an MBA, right?" Gray asks my sister.

"Yes. In fact, I wanted to ask Ash a favor while I was here."

I raise a brow at Petra. "Oh?"

"I need to find an internship for my program," she says, "and since you work for one of the richest, most powerful men in the country, I thought you might be able to help your little sister out."

My other brow jumps up, joining the first. "You want me to ask Mr. Kaladin about an internship for you?"

She nods. "Yes, thank you! I knew I could count on you."

The thought of Petra working for Kaladin makes me uneasy for some reason, and I open my mouth to argue, but Petra only gives me a wink and turns back to Gray.

"He's the best, isn't he," she says to Gray.

Gray gives me a commiserating look that says she knows I've just been roped into something I don't want to do.

I sigh. "Right. I'll see what I can do."

It's another five minutes and a second piece of cake later before my father finally speaks, and then it's only to ask what I have for beer. After cake, he goes out to the car to bring in their overnight bags.

When he comes back in, Gray politely says her goodnights, even though Petra and my parents insist she should stay over.

I've stayed at Gray's house a few times, but she's never stayed here, mainly because we can't go into the bedroom without me worrying I'll turn into a sex-crazed monster and permanently tie her to my bed. My family doesn't know any of that, of course, so Gray heads home, leaving me with a case of blue balls that my hand will have to take care of later.

Mental note. Sex first, then TV next time.

Although in this case, it was probably better I hadn't started anything with Gray yet. If I'd had her strapped down when my family arrived, I might've been tempted to send them to a hotel, birthday cake and all.

"Here," my mother says, handing me a bag when Gray leaves. "I didn't want to give it to you when she was here because I wasn't sure if it was a surprise or not."

I look in the bag and pull out a recipe card and a package that contains dried parsnip, carrots, leeks, and soup seasoning. It's part of what I need to make a traditional Icelandic soup called Kjötsúpa. I don't do much cooking myself, but Gray was curious about Icelandic culture, so I planned to make the soup for her at some point. I asked my mother for the seasoning packet and recipe, and she said she'd give me both the next time she saw me.

I could've ordered the seasoning packet online myself, but my mother usually buys them by the dozen, and she insisted she had one she could spare, so I figured I'd wait.

"Remember," my mother says, "oats, not rice."

It's a point of contention among some Icelanders about whether rice or oats should be used to thicken the soup, and it usually comes down to family tradition. According to my mother, we're an oats family. My dad also has dibs on the bone marrow.

"Thanks," I say, but I stop short of promising her I'll use oats. Rice would be more familiar to Gray. I'm not sure how she'd handle oats in a soup, since that isn't typical in the US.

"It must be serious if you're making her Kjötsúpa," my mother says.

"I just wanted to do something to thank her for working with me."

It's a lie, but I can't get my mother's hopes up until Gray and I get past our first session in my bedroom.

My mother shrugs. "If you say so. Just know that your father proposed to me after I made this for him the first time."

I smile. "So I should expect Gray to propose to me?"

She winks and heads toward the spare bedroom.

My father comes up next to me on his way after her.

"For the record," he says, "the soup is good, but I really decided to propose after the first time she-"

"Dad, I beg you not to finish that sentence," I cut in.

He looks surprised for a second, then frowns. "What exactly did you think I was going to say?"

"I don't know, but I'm just fine believing it's the soup that sold you."

He clucks his tongue and heads after my mother.

Petra takes his place at my side.

"So how serious is it between you and Gray?" she asks.

I side-eye her. "Serious enough that I'm pissed you didn't give me a heads up you all were coming down. Fuck, Petra. Next time just shoot me a warning text when you're an hour out."

She chuckles. "So we *did* interrupt something. Should I start trying to get ideas from her about what she wants for a ring?"

I huff. "We're not anywhere close to that yet."

"Maybe you're not," she says. "But you should see the way she looks at you when you're not aware."

I can't move or speak. Petra is the more intuitive of my sisters, but I can't admit how much I want her observation to be true. I can read Gray's body better than her face, and her body tells me unequivocally she wants me. But could she really want more from me than just sex?

For that matter, do *I* want more from *her* than that?

Again, the answer is unequivocal.

Yes, I want more from Gray than just her body. I want her mind and soul as well.

Chapter 39

Ash

The next day, I stand at the stove stirring the soup I made when I hear the knock at the door, and my heart leaps into my chest.

The whole house smells like Kjötsúpa, a traditional Icelandic lamb soup. The soup isn't fancy by any means, and I made sure Gray liked lamb before I made it, but I think it came out good. I couldn't decide between rice or oats, so I used both, half and half. I'm not much of a cook, but my mother made sure I knew how to make this soup before I left home.

Gray offered to take me out for my birthday, but I insisted she come here instead. I plan to get her into my bedroom tonight, and I didn't want to try and make it through a whole dinner with blue balls.

I get to the door, already unable to contain the smile on my face at the thought of seeing her. Kelsier was right. I've got it bad, and after talking to Petra yesterday, I realize just how bad.

My parents considered staying another day, but Petra convinced them they needed to leave and give me and Gray some time alone. They came to the arena today, and I showed them around, but they left mid-afternoon to head back to Canada, and I went home after practice to cook soup.

I swing the door open wide.

"Hey, I hope you're hung-" I start to say, but the words choke off in my throat as I take in the figure before me.

Gray stands there wrapped in a trench coat with her hair pulled into pigtails on either side of her head. Her lips are painted a deep red, and I'm vaguely aware she seems taller than usual. I look down to see she's wearing black stilettos.

My mouth goes dry. Jesus Christ. Is she naked under that coat? If she is, I think I might come in my pants.

"Happy birthday," she says with a smile. She cocks her head when I don't answer. "Can I come in?"

I realize I've been standing in the door staring at her.

I promised myself I wouldn't maul her the second she walked through the door, but I have a feeling that promise will be dust in the wind the second I see what's under the coat.

I step aside, and Gray enters, her heels clicking on the hardwood of the entryway.

"Uh, what are you doing, baby?" I ask, my voice low and graveled.

She cocks her head in question. "What do you mean?"

I nod to the coat. "I mean, what are you wearing? Are you…are you naked under that?"

She frowns. "No, of course not. What if I got pulled over or got into an accident on the way here?"

I let out a deep exhale. Thank God for small favors.

But my relief is premature. Gray unties the belt of the trench coat and pulls it off, and I stop breathing. She wears a short plaid skirt that barely covers her ass and a tight white blouse that's unbuttoned far enough to see the fiery red bra she has on beneath it.

My cock goes rock hard, and I really hope she had something to eat before she came over because we won't get to the soup anytime soon.

My expression turns serious as my brows pinch almost angrily, and Gray's smile falters.

"Is…something wrong?" She looks down at herself, trying to figure out what I don't like.

"What the fuck were you thinking coming here dressed like that?" I ask, and she looks up, worried now.

"I just thought-"

I grab her arm and pull her against me before she can finish the thought. I told Gray I liked control, but God fucking damn it, I'm holding on by a thread right now.

"Ash," she gasps as I wrap one hand around the back of her neck and the other around her waist.

"It's taking all my willpower not to fuck you right here on the floor of the foyer," I snarl at her.

Despite my tone, I feel the tension leave her body, and she lets out a soft, "Oh."

"You don't get to walk in here looking like that and think I'm not going to fucking devour you."

"What if I want you to?" she whispers.

I take a moment to calm myself before I say, "Let's test that theory."

I pull her head to the side and bite down on her neck. It's not hard enough to hurt, but she gasps in surprise as I move my mouth urgently over her throat, pressing my teeth into the soft skin. Her hands grip my shoulders as she moans, and I suck harder, trying to burn off some of my desire before I explode.

"Oh God! Ash!" she cries, and I lift my mouth so it's against her ear.

"Do you have any idea what you just woke in me?" I ask her. "I'm not sure you're ready for what I plan to do to you."

"I'm ready," she insists. "Do whatever you want."

I groan against her ear as my dick reacts to her words by jumping against my pants.

Gray squeals as I bend down and toss her over my shoulder, picking up where we left off yesterday.

"Ash!" she cries out, but I pay her no mind as I carry her down the hall to my bedroom. The soup is already turned down to a simmer, so it should be fine.

When I get to my bedroom, I set Gray down and steady her as she adjusts to being right side up again. When I'm sure she won't fall over, I rip my shirt off over my head, pull her against me again, and crash my mouth down on hers for a fierce kiss.

Gray moans as she wraps her arms around my neck, and I take a moment just to enjoy the taste of her as my lips rove over hers. I break the kiss after about a minute, but I don't let her go.

I expect her lipstick to be smudged when I lift my lips from hers, but somehow it's still in place, and now I'm on a mission to see what it takes to smear it.

I take one of Gray's hands from around my neck and bring it down to my groin. "Do you feel how hard I am for you?" I ask, and she nods. "You'll need to take care of this first or I'm not going to be able to concentrate on what I'm doing to you."

She bites her lip and nods again.

I let go of her and head over to the bed to pull one of the boxes out from under it. I take out two items, and her eyes track me as I return. I hand her the first of the two items, a small foam ball, and she frowns.

"Squeeze it," I say.

She does, and the stress ball emits a high-pitched squeak, much like a dog toy. It makes her jump, and she looks at me in question.

"Your mouth is going to be full," I tell her, "so you'll use that instead. One squeeze for green, two for yellow, and three for red. Do you understand?"

Her eyes flare, but she nods. "Yes."

"Good, then turn around and put your hands behind your back."

Her eyes flare wider, but she does as I tell her, and my cock throbs at her compliance. I take the other item I brought from the box, a length of black satin fabric, and tie it around her wrists. I have several kinds of cuffs I can use, but there's something about tying her hands like this that drives me insane.

I turn her around again when I'm done and push her backward until she's almost up against the wall.

"Now get on your fucking knees," I tell her.

She bites her lip again but does as I say without a word. My eyes lock with hers as I undo my jeans and pull out my cock. Her eyes drop to it as I fist the base with one hand and wrap my other around one of her pigtails.

"Open," I order, and she parts her lips.

I push my cock into her mouth, watching her beautiful red lips widen around me, and I swear this is what paradise feels like. Her tongue works along the bottom of my shaft, and I push in further, drawing a noise of either surprise or protest from her.

"You good, baby?" I ask, and I hear the ball squeak once. I wait a beat for a second squeak, but when it doesn't come, I begin to move.

I start out slow, but I pick up my pace and push deeper as I start to fuck her mouth in earnest. Gray chokes around my cock and tries to cough, and I pull out to give her a breath.

She sucks in a lungful of air. "I'm fine," she says.

I smile. "Good job, baby girl. You like sucking my cock?"

She starts to say yes, but I don't let her finish the word before I plunge back into her mouth. I feel her jerk as I hit the back of her throat, but there's no squeak, so I keep going.

My balls are tightening already, and I know I only have a matter of seconds as I brace a hand against the wall and thrust into Gray's mouth. She gags again, but I don't pull out. She has the ball if she needs it.

"I'm almost there, baby," I groan. "You're doing such a good job."

She moans deep in her throat, and the vibrations nearly send me over the edge, but I manage to hold back a little longer.

"You still good, baby?" I ask. "Get ready to swallow me down. You're gonna take all my cum, right?"

The ball squeaks once, and I push deep, prompting a muffled cry from her. A second later, I explode in Gray's mouth with a roar. I feel her throat work to swallow me down, and it only makes me come harder.

"Fuck, Gray! God damn it, baby!" I yell as I push once more into her mouth as far as I can go. She moans, and I pull out slowly. I still lean against the wall because I'm not sure I can stand on my own yet.

When I have my equilibrium again, I look down. My cock rests against Gray's red lips as she tries to catch her breath, her lipstick still unsmudged. God damn that's some stable makeup. She must have some kind of fixative on it.

Gray's cheeks are wet with tears from when I pushed my cock in deep, but she never used the ball, and I need to reward her for taking all of me like that.

I bend down and pull Gray to her feet before pressing her back against the wall. I take her face in my hands and kiss her deeply, tasting some of my lingering saltiness in her mouth.

I lay my forehead on hers. "I think that's the best fucking blowjob I've ever had," I say softly.

It's true. I've never had a woman's mouth feel that good wrapped around my cock, and now I'm addicted.

"You took me so well," I praise as I wrap my hand lightly around her throat. "Are you ready to be rewarded?"

She makes a noise of affirmation and nods.

I turn her around so she's facing the wall, take the stress ball back, and untie her hands. I place her hands on the wall near her head, and she sucks in a breath as I run my own hands up the outsides of her thighs. I loop my fingers over the straps of her thong and pull it down her legs. She steps out of it and kicks it aside off the toe of her shoe.

I press myself against her back and reach around to start unbuttoning her shirt with one hand as my other splays against her stomach.

"Are you ready for this?" I breathe against her ear.

She nods, and I pop the last button on her shirt open. She gasps as I slip my hand inside her bra to knead her breast and pinch her nipple. My other hand slips down between her legs to massage her clit, and she lets out a moan.

"Are you sure?" I ask. "Because I'm about to do things to you I have a feeling you've never experienced."

She nods again.

"Don't move," I say as I let go of her and head back to my box. I return a moment later with a bottle of lube and a plug. It's bigger than the one I put in her for the fundraiser, but she's ready for it.

I show her the plug. "Can you take this?"

She nods, and I lube up the plug.

"Spread your legs wider and push your ass out," I tell her.

She does as I ask, and I press the plug to her hole. She tenses, but I reach around to massage her clit some more.

"Relax your muscles, baby. It will go in easier if you're not so tense."

Her body eases just a little, and I press the plug forward as my fingers continue to work her clit. She whimpers as the plug stretches her open, and I stop to give her a few seconds to adjust.

My cock is nearly erect again. I wish it was me pushing into her tight little ass, but she's definitely not ready to take me yet. I'll enjoy getting her ready, though.

I push the plug forward again, and it pops past the outer ring of muscle. Gray lets out a soft noise.

"Color?" I ask.

It's a couple seconds before she lets out a deep breath. "Green."

"Good girl," I say as I turn her around. "Now come with me."

I take her hand and lead her to the armchair next to the bed.

"Sit down," I tell her, "and scoot forward so your ass is near the end."

She does as I ask, and I move behind the chair.

"Put your arms up," I order, and she does. I grab her wrists and pull them over her head against the back of the chair. There are hidden cords attached there, and I tie her hands.

A surprising number of women enjoy restraint, and Gray appears to be one of them. She shifts in the chair as I come back around to face her. In my hand is an adjustable strap I keep under it.

Gray shifts again, but far from looking uncomfortable, the movement looks sensuous, like she's trying to entice me. Fucking hell.

"What is that?" she asks.

I only smile at her and start to wrap the nylon strap around her thigh just above her knee. Velcro isn't the sexiest thing, but it's fast and it holds well as I secure the strap around her leg. Then I feed the strap under the chair to the other side and pull on it. Her leg that's tied snaps open against the arm of the chair, and Gray lets out a soft, "Oh!"

I quickly loop the other end of the strap around to secure her second thigh, then pull the buckle clip that shortens the strap. Her other leg is yanked back against the arm of the chair so her thighs are spread wide for me while her hands are secured to the top of the chair.

She's completely spread open and at my mercy now.

"Ash, what are you-," she starts to ask, but I press a finger to her lips.

"Sshh now," I say. "I don't think you're ready for a gag yet, so I need you to be a good girl and stay quiet for me, alright?"

Her eyes widen at the mention of the gag, but she nods and watches me. I take a moment to look at her splayed out, ready for me to do whatever I want.

"Do you trust me?" I ask, and she nods again.

My cock is hard already, but it's her turn to come before I fuck her. I get on my knees between her legs and pull her breast out of her bra. Her nipples are relatively small for the size of her breasts, but they're the perfect shade of rosy pink. They're peaked already, but I intend to get them harder and more swollen.

Gray cries out as I close my mouth over the nipple and begin to suck hard. She's trying to be quiet as she squirms in the chair, but she can't manage it. Her stifled noises are even better than a gag, and I grow harder.

I switch to her other breast as I thumb her clit, and she starts falling apart at the seams already as she fights against the restraints that hold her fast. It's so God damn hot.

I'm not sure why her body is so responsive, but I intend to take full advantage and see how many orgasms I can give her.

I pull away from her breast and lower my head between her legs. She cries out and her hips thrust up as my mouth closes over her clit to suck on it. I put my tongue to work licking every part of her sweet, needy pussy, and she screams as I plunge my tongue into her cunt. I have to press her hips down to keep her from bowing off the chair, but her bucking only arouses me more.

"Ash! Please!" she yells, and I feel her pussy start to pulse. I double down as I push two fingers inside her and curl them up as my tongue flicks against her clit.

She comes a second later, and I can barely hold her in place as she throws her head back against the chair with a cry and tries to clamp her legs shut. The strap holds them open, and I continue to lap at her pussy as her body eases with the last throes of her climax.

"Good girl," I say as I look up at her from between her legs. "I bet you have another one in you, though."

Her eyes fly open wide. "What?"

"You're going to come for me again before I fuck you," I tell her.

She shakes her head frantically. "Ash, no! I can't," she says.

"You can and you will," I tell her. I dip my head down and run my tongue all the way up the length of her pussy. "Unless you have something specific to say about that?" I challenge.

I meet her eyes. She knows what I mean, but I see the defiance in her expression. She doesn't want to red light me our first time doing this. I don't plan to push her too much, but she's nowhere near her limit yet.

I dip my head between her legs again, and Gray groans as my mouth begins to work. She writhes and whimpers beneath me as I push her unrelentingly toward another orgasm, this time working the plug in her ass as well. It's only a few minutes more before her body shudders with the pleasure of a second release.

Her cry of satisfaction is long and languid this time. I always love the sound of a woman coming under my tongue, but with Gray, that sound is nothing short of Mozart.

I ease back to sit on my heels as Gray pants in the chair, and I take a moment to enjoy the sight of her rapture. Strands of hair stick to her temples, and her cheeks are flushed beautifully as her mouth hangs open, lips red and wet.

I stand and undo the straps from her legs before untying her hands.

Her arms fall limp at her sides, and I chuckle as she goes boneless.

"Oh, sweetheart," I say as I lift her in my arms and carry her to the bed. "We have to work on your stamina. I'm just getting started."

I lay her down on the bed before going around to take the box off it. There's so much I want to do to her, so far I want to push her body, but if I try to do too much too soon, I may put her off. I'm already pushing things farther than I should for a first experience, but her little schoolgirl schtick snapped something inside me. I need to fuck her, so she needs to hang on a little longer.

I work slowly as I pull the restraints up from the corners of the bed, giving her time to rest. She watches me as I go but remains quiet.

If there's one thing I've learned, it's that sometimes the women who enjoy bondage are the ones you'd least expect to like it.

Take that VP of the big insurance firm I dated once. She was the epitome of the poised corporate type, a 'barracuda in the boardroom,' from what her colleagues said of her. She was always in control, always one step ahead of everyone else in her job.

When I got her into the bedroom, though, she became the perfect submissive, obeying commands immediately and doing whatever I asked.

I learned eventually it was her way of relaxing. In real life, she always had to be 'on,' always had to be the one calling the shots, and it occurred to me one day she found it exhausting. When she stepped into the bedroom with me, she could let all of that go. She could hand over complete control to someone else and revel in the freedom of letting them make decisions for a while without it affecting her life or career.

With Gray, it's not quite the same thing, but I suspect it's similar. Gray is an academic, a scholar and a researcher, but I've learned she overthinks and over analyzes, and I see the stress it puts on her.

I suspect Gray is open to being a submissive because it means she doesn't have to think. By putting me in charge of her pleasure, she's free to simply feel.

I look down at the woman on the bed, her body half-curled on her side as she waits for me to tell her what to do. She still has her clothes on, and I try to decide if I want her to take them off or if I want to fuck her with the schoolgirl uniform on.

I decide on something in between.

"Take off your shirt and bra," I tell her, "and lay on your back."

My little professor wants to feel, so I'll make her feel.

Chapter 40

Gray

I sit up on the bed and start to pull my shirt off.

"Slowly," Ash says when I work at it too quickly.

I slow down, forcing myself to make it more of a strip tease. Ash watches me intently from the side of the bed as I finish pulling the shirt off and hold it up. With a flick of my wrist, I toss it toward his head so it covers his face. He pulls it off, and for a second I'm not sure if it's anger or passion I see in his eyes.

I yelp as he surges forward onto the bed, and I have to lean back as he hovers over me, his face serious.

"You told me you weren't a brat," Ash says as he continues to loom over me. "Did you lie?"

I search my memory for our conversation about brats, then shake my head. "I…I was just trying to be playful," I say. "I'm sorry."

Ash's face eases. "No, I'm sorry. I just had a bad experience with a brat once."

I nod my understanding. Or what little I can understand based on my limited knowledge of BDSM.

"Take off your bra," he says more gently.

He still looms over me, and I manage to reach a hand behind me to pop the clasp on my bra. Ash's eyes drop to my chest, and he watches as I pull the bra loose and toss it off the side of the bed.

He smiles. "Good girl."

I go wet again between my legs and reach for the zipper of the plaid skirt, but Ash grabs my wrist.

"Not the skirt," he says. "That stays on."

I nod again, and Ash eases himself back off the bed. He goes to the head of it and picks up one of the restraints. When he just stands there, I finally get the hint and lay back on the bed. I put my hand above my head, and he wraps the cuff around my wrist. He lets go when he's done, and I tug on the restraint to test it. It holds me firm, and I feel a jolt that's somewhere between thrill and fear.

Ash walks to the other corners of the bed, and each time I dutifully present him with a limb that he straps down.

I have no idea why I'm submitting. Almost every fiber of my being is screaming at me that this is not what strong, smart women let men do to them. *Almost* every fiber. A few remaining ones have locked the objectors in a basement and are assuring me it's not wrong to like this.

When Ash is done and I'm lying spreadeagle across his bed, he goes to his box and pulls something out. He turns and looks down at me, taking me in, before he holds up what's in his hand. A blindfold.

My heart skips, and I tug unconsciously at the restraints.

"You're going to blindfold me?" I ask warily.

"I want you to focus on what you feel," Ash says. "This will help."

Ash kneels on the bed and slips the blindfold, a fancy sleep mask, over my head.

I feel him get off the bed, and my ears instantly sharpen to listen for what he's doing. I can't hear anything for several seconds, and my imagination runs wild. Is he taking pictures of me strapped naked to his bed? Will he send them to his teammates? I would die of mortification if my students ever saw me like this.

I begin to thrash. "No pictures!" I yell. "Ash, what are you doing?"

I feel his weight dip the bed almost instantly, then his body is pressed against the side of mine. He's still wearing his jeans, and they're rough against my legs, but his naked chest pressed to mine is warm and soft.

"Gray, sshh," he whispers. His hand cups my cheek. "Easy, baby. I'd never take your picture like this without your permission."

The nervous patter in my heart is still giving a hummingbird's wings a run for their money, but I force myself to inhale deeply to calm down.

"Do you want me to take the blindfold off?" Ash asks. "Maybe you're not ready-"

I feel his hand move to the mask, but the denial leaps off my tongue before he can remove it. "No!"

His hand stops. "Are you sure? This is supposed to enhance your pleasure, not your anxiety. If you-"

"Promise me," I gasp out, cutting him off. "Promise me you're not taking pictures, and I'll believe you."

There are two very long seconds of silence before Ash says, "Gray, I promise, I'm not taking pictures of you like this. I would never, ever."

Something in his tone eases me instantly. Maybe I'm a fool for believing him, but the sincerity in his voice is almost palpable. As if he's hurt I'd even consider the possibility he was doing something devious.

I nod. "Then leave the blindfold on." I must be mad, but fuck it.

"You're sure?"

"Yes," I say. "Green light."

Another few seconds drift away before Ash shifts, and something grazes over my breast. I jump at the sudden sensation, but I realize on the next graze that Ash is running the leather flogger over my breasts.

I hear his murmur of appreciation as my nipples peak, and I exhale a slow breath as pleasure spreads through my body.

Ash shifts again, and it feels like he's sitting up next to me on the bed.

I let out a soft cry as the tails of the flogger slap against one breast, making the nipple harden. Before I can recover enough to react further, Ash snaps the flogger against the other breast, just hard enough to make it sting a little.

I shift against the restraints as my body comes alive. I'm suddenly aware of every place something touches my skin, and I swear I can even feel the warmth of Ash's body near mine, not touching, but close enough to sense his nearness.

There's a sharp sting against my outer thigh as Ash slaps it with the flogger, then he drags it over my inner thigh and up to my apex. The buzz of a vibrator catches my ear, and I lift my head.

"Ash?" I ask.

"Sshh," he hushes. "You're supposed to be trusting me."

I feel the vibrator on my nipple and bite my lip. Ash moves it to the second nipple, and my hands jerk against the restraints, fingers flexing.

Ash chuckles and trails the vibrator down my stomach. He pauses near my pubic bone – for effect, I'm sure – then touches it to my clit.

I let out the moan I've been holding back, and instinct makes me try to open my thighs wider.

"Mmm, that's a good girl," Ash praises. "Is your needy little pussy getting all wet for me? Let me check."

I moan again as Ash pushes a finger inside me, and I can't stop myself from trying to ride it.

"Fuck me," Ash breathes. "Baby, you're soaked again."

Ash removes his finger, but he props the vibrator against my clit before I feel him get up from the bed. The swish of heavy fabric tells me he's taking his jeans off. Then there's the crinkle and tear of a condom wrapper, and I barely hear the slick sound of him rolling the condom over his cock.

The bed dips again, and Ash climbs between my legs.

"Sorry, baby," he says. "I really wanted to draw this out longer, but I don't seem to have any self-control around you. I need to fuck you now."

"Yes," I say as he pulls the vibrator away and the buzzing stops.

I try to open my legs as wide as the restraints will allow, and Ash settles between them. He runs his cock up and down through my wetness before notching it at my opening.

"I don't know if you're on birth control or not," Ash says, "but I'm giving you fair warning that the next time we do this, I'm going in bare. I need to feel your hot, wet little cunt around me."

I whimper in need, then gasp as Ash pushes into me in one smooth thrust. He starts to fuck me, and I'm close already. I've never had this many orgasms so close to one another, and I'm stunned my body is so ready, even eager, for another one.

Ash's grunts aren't loud, but with the blindfold on, they seem magnified in my ears. I'm also so much more aware of how big he is, of how hard his body is, and of how good he smells. I smell myself on him too from when he had his mouth between my legs, but it doesn't detract from the smell of 'man' that is him.

I'm usually good at being able to pick out particular scents – I do it all the time when wine tasting – but with Ash I only smell indistinct things like 'virility' and 'dominance' and 'future father of my children.'

"You're so God damn beautiful, baby," Ash says against my cheek, and the words shoot straight between my legs.

I can barely hold myself together beneath him as he thrusts into me. I instinctively try to wrap my arms around his neck, but my hands jerk to a halt as they meet the limits of the restraints, and I let out a whimper.

Ash slows and lifts himself from me a little.

"Are you okay? What's wrong?" he asks.

I can't tell him. This is the way he wants me, and I'm still too uncertain of this thing between us to complain.

"Nothing," I say, the word sounding false even to my own ears.

Ash stops moving altogether, and I bite back the urge to apologize and beg him to keep going.

"Don't lie to me, Gray," he says. "Tell me what you want."

The words are an order, and I obey automatically. "I want to touch you," I gasp out. "Please."

The three-second pause that follows is the longest of my life because I can't see his face. I'm certain I've made him angry until I feel his hand on the cuff at my wrist, and there's the snick of metal as he releases the clasp from the strap to free my hand. He pulls my hand up to wrap it around his neck, and I let out a breath of relief as my fingers curl in the hair at his nape. My other hand is free and around his neck seconds after that, and I feel like the sun has just broken through the clouds.

"Thank you," I whisper.

"You have to talk to me, baby," he scolds gently. "If you want something, you have to tell me. That's the only way this works." He starts to thrust slowly again, and I wrap my arms tighter around his neck, resisting the urge to remind him that he kept shushing me.

Ash snakes his arms under me, and I let out a noise of surprise as he lifts me. The next thing I know, I'm sitting on his lap, fully speared on his cock. I feel it press deep inside me, and I suck in a long breath.

One of Ash's hands fumbles at my ankle, and there's the snick of the clasp as he frees the cuff from the strap holding it to the bed. Then he pulls my stiletto off too, and I hear it thunk on the floor next to the bed. He repeats this with the second ankle and shoe.

As soon as both my legs are free, I wrap them around his waist, and he chuckles.

"That's it, baby," he says. "Fucking perfect." Then his mouth is on mine, kissing me hungrily as he cups one hand under my ass and one around my back. He helps me move up and down his cock, and pleasure shoots through my body as I grind my clit against him.

Even without the cuffs attached to the restraints, there's something about the feel of them on my wrists and ankles that arouses the hell out of me. I'm already unraveling fast when Ash starts talking dirty to me.

"You better come soon, baby, because that greedy cunt of yours is swallowing me whole, and I'm about to blow my load right through this fucking condom." He bucks his hips into mine, making me moan. "I want to come inside you so bad. I want my fucking cum dripping down your legs when I'm done with you. Are you going to be a good girl and fucking come for me, or do I have to turn you over and drive my cock between those pretty thighs of yours until you're screaming my name?"

I open my mouth to tell him I'm close, but he reaches between us to roll my nipple between his fingers, and that's all I need to send me over the edge. My climax hits like a torrent, and Ash grunts as I spasm around him. Then I'm on my back again as he pounds into me. He buries himself inside, and I feel his cock pulse as he wraps himself around me, his hips giving two more shuddering thrusts before he collapses on top of me.

We lie like that for several minutes, panting hard, before I finally reach up and pull the blindfold off. My eyes find his in the semi-darkness. Strands of hair cling to the sides of his face as he looks down at me with the hint of a grin.

"How am I supposed to be the Dom when you're clearly the one calling the shots?" he asks with a laugh.

Chapter 41

Two hours later, Ash and I lie tangled together on his couch. We haven't moved for the last twenty minutes. The TV isn't even on.

He has on his boxer briefs, and I have my bra and thong back on as we cuddle under a blanket together. We've eaten some soup, had sex in his bedroom again, and talked about his declaration that he'll be going in bareback next time. Not today, but in the near future. He's been tested, but I have to go.

Every now and then, Ash kisses my temple, and I have to keep from pinching myself. If this is a dream, I don't want to wake up.

But because I can't help rocking the boat…

"What is this?" I ask. My voice breaks the silence like someone dropped a plate on the floor.

"Hmm?" Ash asks.

I think I pulled him out of his own daydream.

I turn my head where it rests on Ash's chest. "You said we're dating. Officially. Does that mean the rest of the team knows about us? Should we tell Kaladin?"

His body tenses beneath mine.

"Kelsier knows," he says. "And I should probably tell the rest of the team at this point, but Kaladin is a different story."

"You're afraid of what Kaladin will do if he finds out we're really dating," I say. I had the same concerns.

"I don't want him to pull your funding," he says. "Or worse, make us stop working together because of a conflict of interest."

I start to nod against his chest, but then something occurs to me, and I sit up to face Ash.

"Do you think Kaladin already suspects?"

He frowns. "Why do you think that?"

He's going to think I'm crazy, but…

"I thought I was just being paranoid since the whole thing at my house, but maybe I really am being followed."

The expression that crosses his face looks like panic. "Like the man you saw at the grocery store," he says, and there's something in his voice I can't place.

"Exactly," I say. "I swear I saw him at my conference in Florida. It can't be a coincidence he's up here now."

Ash sits up on the couch, and he looks…troubled?

Several seconds of silence congeal with the leftover soup before he says, "I have to tell you something, Gray."

It feels like that other shoe I've been waiting for has just dropped. My stomach goes queasy, and I pray the soup I ate doesn't come back up.

I try to stand, but Ash catches me around the waist and pulls me back.

"Wait," he says.

"You're married, aren't you," I say. "You're married and your wife hired a private investigator to see if you've been cheating on her and…" The words come out in a chaotic rush, as I tug at Ash's arms in an attempt to free myself. "Oh God. I'm the other woman, aren't I."

I knew my pessimism would prove right one of these days.

Ash frowns and tightens his arms to hold me in place. "What? No. Don't be ridiculous."

"Then what do you need to tell me?" I ask, trying and failing to keep the hysteria at bay. "What do you know about the man who's been following me?"

"Men," he says.

I go still and blink at him. "What?"

Ash sighs. "The *men* who've been following you. As in more than one.

They're a private security team I've had keeping an eye on you since your house was broken into."

I'm stunned into silence. I'm not sure which part of that I find more insane. That there hasn't just been one man following me, but several, or that Ash actually hired a security team to keep me safe.

I'm also not sure if that's the sweetest thing someone's ever done for me or if that's a giant red flag. I mean, do I break up with him for crossing a line, or do I suck his cock again to show my appreciation. Both?

"But my house wasn't broken into," I say. "It was just my mother."

It's the least of the issues on the table, but my brain apparently feels the need to start small and work up to the whole '*I hired a security team to secretly follow you 24/7*' thing.

"I…well, right. But we still can't fully explain the window or your book, so better safe than sorry," Ash says, seeming flustered.

I make another attempt to throw off the blanket and get up from the couch, and this time he lets me.

"I don't know whether I should be grateful to you or furious with you," I say as I start to pace.

"Baby, you need to put some clothes on while you decide," Ash says, not looking at me. "It's making my dick hard again to watch you walk around like that."

I stop pacing and raise a brow. He gives me a '*Sorry, but I can't help it*' look, and I resume pacing.

Ash gets up. "Look," he says, "I didn't tell you because I didn't want to worry you or make you self-conscious. I figured I'd just have the guys follow you for a little while and keep an eye on your house when you weren't there until we knew for sure there wasn't any danger."

My brows shoot up again. "They've been watching my house too?"

He grimaces. "Yeah."

I look away from him. I need to think about this, and that's nearly impossible to do with a tall, well-muscled hockey player standing a few feet away in his underwear. I'm about to get dressed to buy myself some time when I realize Ash is right next to me. He grabs my shoulders lightly and turns me to face him.

"Gray, I'm sorry I didn't tell you, but I really thought I was doing the right thing to protect you."

I let out a mirthless laugh. "You mean you really thought you were doing the right thing to protect your hockey career," I snap at him.

Okay, so my psyche is defaulting to anger for now.

Ash's eyes narrow, and his grip tightens on my shoulders. "Fuck hockey," he says. "I did it because I love you and want you to be safe."

And just like that my rage evaporates. It takes Ash a second longer to realize what he just said, but he steels his expression, refusing to backtrack or qualify the statement.

"What did you just say?" I whisper.

"You heard me," he says. "I love you. You're fucking mine, and I protect what's mine."

I stare at him for several long moments as I try to wrap my head around that.

"I…I…" The words are there on my tongue, but I can't seem to speak them. "I don't know what to say," I say instead.

If he's disappointed I didn't say 'I love you' back, he doesn't show it.

"Say you forgive me," Ash says, "and I'll eat your pussy for the rest of the night to show you how sorry I am."

I give him a *'Be serious'* look, but he shoots back an *'I am serious'* one. He steps up to me, and I put my hands on his chest to push him back, but he wraps me in his arms so my own are pinned between us. He starts to kiss a path down my neck, and the goosebumps that rise on my skin betray me.

"Forgive me yet?" he asks against my throat, and I curse my weakness where this man is concerned.

I groan as I feel his teeth graze my skin. "Fine. Just promise me you won't keep anything like this from me ever again," I tell him.

I'm letting him off the hook easy, but to my surprise, his mouth stills, and he pulls back.

"What is it?" I ask.

"There's…one more thing I should tell you," he says.

My stomach plummets again. I knew it was too good to be true.

"What?" I ask as I pull away from him.

"Come sit down," he says, his hand on my shoulder to steer me toward the couch.

I shake off the hand. "Just tell me."

Ash looks at me, presumably deciding if he should insist on having me sit. He lets out a long breath. "Don't freak out when I tell you this."

"Oh my God. I'm already freaking out! Just tell me," I snap.

Ash inhales deeply. "There…there *was* someone in your house that night besides your mother," he says finally. "I didn't just hire the security team to be on the safe side. I hired them because I knew for a fact someone broke into your house."

My blood goes cold. "How do you know?" I ask. The words are a puff of air, not even a whisper. They aspire to be a whisper.

Ash goes over to where he dropped his jeans when we came out of the bedroom earlier. He finds his wallet in the pocket and opens it to pull out a piece of paper that he hands me.

I open the paper with shaking hands and read it. "*You belong with me, not with him.*"

I jerk my head up. "What is this?"

"I found that on your bed that night when I went into your house. Along with red rose petals," he says.

It takes a second for his words to sink in and another three seconds for me to remember the dried rose petal I found on the floor under the kitchen sink the morning after the supposed break in. I couldn't conceive of where it came from unless one of the police officers tracked it inside that night, but the horrifying reality hits me like a sandbag to my stomach.

The entire world tilts sideways as my vision blurs and my legs give out. Strong arms catch me before I fall, and Ash scoops me up to carry me to the couch and lay me down.

"Oh my God," I whisper.

"Gray, stay with me, baby."

My eyes meet his. "Did you tell the police what you found?" I ask.

He looks at me apologetically. "No. I thought about it, but if I told the cops, they would've told you, and I was afraid it would fuck with your mind. I hoped the security team I hired would notice something and catch whoever broke in if they tried again."

He's right about one thing. Knowing the truth is completely fucking with my mind. Not only was someone in my house, but they went into my bedroom and put flower petals and a note on my bed.

The mental image of that alone sends me shooting off the couch toward the bathroom. I just barely make it to the toilet before I lose my battle with the soup, and it comes back up.

Ash is there a second later, and he pulls my hair away from my face as I retch into the toilet again. His hand rubs slow circles on my back.

"Easy now," he says softly. "Just breathe."

The toilet flushes, sending the contents of my stomach down the drain, and I pull back enough so I don't get a face full of toilet spray.

Part of me would give anything to unlearn what I just learned, and I rest my head on my forearm as I lean over Ash's toilet again.

"How are you doing?" he asks a few seconds later. His hand still makes slow circles over my back.

"Your toilet is clean at least," I say weakly.

Seriously, that's a blessing. I've been in the bathrooms of men who live alone, and they're not always pretty.

"The housekeeper came today," he says.

Of course he has a housekeeper. Apparently I'm the only one who doesn't.

"Are you done?" Ash asks. "Do you want to get up?"

I pull my head off my forearm and spit bile into the bowl. Ash gets up from the floor and pulls me to my feet. He helps me to the sink where

I swish my mouth with water.

"I wasted your soup," I say as I lean over the basin.

"I can make more."

I lift my head and look at him in the mirror. There's concern written all over his face and perhaps a bit of fear. I want to be angry with him for not telling me about the rose petals and the note, but the intensity of my reaction suggests his decision to keep it from me wasn't entirely bad.

I feel his hand rest on my hip, and I look down at it in the mirror. The touch isn't sexual. It's meant to be comforting, but I'm not sure I'll ever be comfortable again.

I consider pulling his hand off me and laying into him for keeping secrets, but ultimately he came clean. If I punish him now for telling me the truth, he'll be more reluctant to do it in the future.

I don't have the energy to be mad at him anyway. I'm too terrified. Instead of pushing him away, I turn around and throw myself against him. Ash wraps his arms around me as I take deep breaths, refusing to cry.

"What am I supposed to do?" I ask. "Is it too late to go to the police?"

"We can tell the police if you want," he says. "I took a picture of the bed so we'd have a record."

We. He says it like this is his problem too.

Then it hits me that he has a picture of the bed. The request to see it jumps to the tip of my tongue, but I bite it back. Part of me wants to see the picture, but a much larger part isn't prepared to see what some sick fuck did to my bed when I wasn't there.

I suck in a breath as the other implications hit me. "Oh God."

"What is it?" he asks.

I shake my head against his chest. "I just realized I need to count my underwear and my, um…toys when I get home."

When I get home…What the hell am I thinking? I'm not sure I'll ever be able to go home again after all this.

I pull back from Ash. "Can you come back to my place with me? I need to grab some clothes."

I let go and move past him into the hall. A few seconds ago, I wasn't sure my legs would hold me. Now I'm mobilized with urgent purpose.

"I need to call my mother to see if I can stay at her place for a few days," I say, more to myself than Ash. The words alone threaten to make me queasy again, but I swallow down the new feeling of dread at the thought of having to move back in with my parents. Maybe Celena can put me up for a little while.

I jerk to a stop in the hall as Ash catches my wrist and spins me back around to face him.

"You're not staying with your parents," Ash says. "We can go get some of your clothes, but you're coming back here to stay with me."

My mouth slowly falls open as I stare up at him. Then I shake my head. "No, I can't. It's-"

"It's non-negotiable," he interrupts.

"But-"

"Gray, don't make me tie you to the bed again," he says.

I snap my mouth shut, although as threats go, I'm not sure that's an effective one.

"Come on," Ash says as he pulls me toward the living room. "Let's get dressed and go pick up some things from your place. Looks like we're starting the cohabitation part of this relationship early."

Chapter 42

Ash

I zero in on the goal as I streak down the ice on a breakaway the next night as we play the Maple Leafs at home. I've done nothing all game, and I need to get my head on straight. I sense one of the defenders on my heels, but I put him out of my mind and try to focus. I'm one of the fastest skaters in the league, and it's just me and the goalie.

I shoot the puck high, hoping to put it in over his shoulder, but the fucker manages to get his glove up just in time to deflect the shot. The puck tips up over the top of the goal, and the home crowd groans.

I swear violently. A couple years ago, that's a shot I'd make ninety-nine times out of a hundred. Now I'm lucky to have a fifty-fifty chance at it. I thought my luck had changed after that last game in Tampa, but apparently not.

I swing around behind the goal, not looking at the faces of the disappointed fans. A Leafs defender says something to me as he skates by, but I'm oblivious.

The one thing I've got going for me tonight is that I can't hear the chirping. Several players have tried to get in my head, but their taunts go in one ear and out the other. I'd call it progress, except that the reason I haven't heard a word all night is because I can't think about anything but Gray right now.

I head to the bench for the end of my shift, and my eyes immediately seek her out in the stands. My stomach lurches when I find her seat empty, and I panic as I look around.

I relax when I see her come down the stairs with a plastic cup of wine in hand. Because of course my girl would drink wine at a hockey game. At least she wasn't here to see me miss an easy shot.

Having Gray spend the night at my place last night and waking up with her body curled against mine this morning was a special kind of heaven. I wish her first time sleeping there had been under different circumstances, but for the moment, I'll take what I can get.

I really wanted to fuck her this morning, but she had a long night, and I didn't push. She was jumpy as hell when we went to her place to get her things, and she only relaxed when an inventory of her underwear drawer and her box of dildos and vibrators yielded nothing obvious missing.

She blushed furiously when I saw all the toys she had, including a dildo shaped like a long tentacle, but I reminded her I had plenty of toys as well. I also made her pack the tentacle to bring to my place.

There hadn't been time to use it, though. We went to bed almost as soon as we got home, and it took Gray a long time to fall asleep. She tossed fitfully next to me for nearly half an hour before I pulled her into my arms and she finally quieted enough to drift off.

She had an early class this morning, and I came to the rink for game prep, so I haven't seen much of her.

For my own part, now that Gray knows about the intruder, I can't help dwelling on who it is and whether the creep will be back again. My money is still on it being Drew, but I've had a security guy watching him as well, and Gray's ex hasn't come anywhere near her house.

"You okay, man?" Cote asks next to me. "You seem spaced out."

I want to laugh. I've finally found a way to block out the trash talk, but it involves spending the whole game worrying about my girlfriend.

"Fine," I say. "Just got some things on my mind."

"Well fucking get them off your mind," Mack snaps at me from my other side. "We need you to get your shit together."

I purse my lips. He's right. I do need to get my shit together. This thing with Gray's stalker is a distraction I can't afford right now.

The buzzer sounds the end of the game. We won 2-1, but it was no thanks to me.

Ash

When I get out of the shower forty-five minutes later, Cedric is waiting for me in the locker room.

"Mr. Kaladin wants to see you in his office," he says.

I swear inwardly. This can't be good. I hurriedly towel off and get dressed.

"You going out?" Kelsier asks me as I grab my stuff.

Tomorrow's an off day, so some of the team are going out tonight for a few drinks.

"Probably not," I say. "Just got called to the principal's office. I have to go see Kaladin, then I should get Gray home. She had a rough night."

I filled Kelsier in today on how I came clean to Gray last night about having her followed and about the perve who broke into her house.

"I'll text you where we end up in case you change your mind," he says. "Maybe Gray will want a drink after the last couple days."

"Maybe. Text me, and we'll see," I say as I hustle out of the locker room to head for Kaladin's office.

When I get up to the administrative floor a few minutes later, Kaladin's assistant sends me right in. I feel sorry for the woman. It's almost eleven o'clock at night, and she's still working.

I enter the office and head straight for the desk. Kaladin is seated behind it, but he stands when I enter.

"Ash, good to see you again," he says, but he's not smiling. "Thanks for joining us."

Us?

I glance at the other chair on this side of Kaladin's desk, only now noticing there's someone in it. My heart stops when I see Gray sitting there, looking as though she'd rather be anywhere else.

I whip my head back to Kaladin. "What is she doing here?"

343

Kaladin raises a brow at my demand, but I don't back down. If he thinks he's going to fire her because I can't keep my head on straight, he's got another thing coming.

"Why don't you have a seat," Kaladin says, gesturing to the empty chair next to me.

I glance at Gray, and she looks resigned.

We don't know for sure why Kaladin wants to see us, though, so I sit down before I jump to any conclusions that might get us in trouble.

"I just wanted to check in with you both to see how things are going," Kaladin says casually when we're both seated. "We didn't really have an opportunity to talk in depth the other night at the fundraiser."

Gray and I look at each other. Neither of us is buying his nonchalance. We're both here because I sucked tonight.

I open my mouth to speak, but Gray beats me to it.

"Mr. Gunnarsson and I are doing our best to find a solution that works for him," she says cooly.

Kaladin nods slowly. "And do you have any idea when a solution might present itself?" he asks, tenting his fingers in front of him.

Gray cocks her head. "No. As I warned both him and your lawyers when I took on this project, Mr. Kaladin, an intervention for trash talk doesn't yet exist, so it's going to take some time to figure things out. You're asking me to create something in months that often takes researchers years to develop."

She looks and sounds every bit like a professor explaining to a student that all the information for the exam was in the study guide, so if he failed, it was his own damn fault. It's so fucking hot, and I have to talk my dick down so I don't go full mast in the middle of Kaladin's office. I hope Gray feels better, because I need to be inside her when we get home.

I look at Kaladin and catch the brief look of surprise on his face at her reproach before he schools his expression.

"I see," Kaladin says, "Anything to add, Mr. Gunnarsson?" he turns to me, and I have to wipe away the smirk that's been slinking up my lips.

"I know my play tonight doesn't reflect it," I say seriously, "but we've made progress. Gra-…uh, Dr. Mackey has figured out why the trash talk gets under my skin, and we've been working on ways to help me ignore it, but it's been hit or miss."

Kaladin nods again slowly.

"Actually, I was able to pretty much ignore it all tonight," I say, filling the silence. "I was distracted because of a personal matter, but I feel like we're getting there."

Kaladin's gaze jumps between me and Gray, but I don't dare look at her for fear he'll see more than he needs to see between us.

"And how are the two of you getting along?" he asks. "How is the… fake relationship going?"

It takes everything I have not to react. I swear there's a knowing look on Kaladin's face, and that's a good indication we're fucked.

I shrug as indifferently as I can. "We're fine. Dr. Mackey is a great teacher, and she knows her stuff. I'm in good hands."

I didn't mean to say the last part like that, and I see Gray shift in her seat out of the corner of my eye. I keep my eyes fixed on Kaladin, who looks between us again.

"So you're not sleeping together then?" Kaladin asks, and I'm sure the color must drain from my face.

Gray handles the accusation far better. "Excuse me?" she says, and she's either genuinely indignant Kaladin would ask such a thing, or she's an amazing actress.

Kaladin turns his attention to her. "No offense meant, Dr. Mackey," he says calmly. "I've just been hearing some interesting rumors, and I'm trying to determine their veracity. For instance, word has it you spent the night at Mr. Gunnarsson's house last night."

How the fuck does he know that? Maybe Gray was right, and he is having us followed.

Gray's eyes widen and her mouth drops open. Her gaze darts to me, and I give her a look that hopefully says, *'Trust me.'*

The truth is about to set us free.

"She did spend the night at my place last night," I tell Kaladin. "Someone broke into Dr. Mackey's house a while ago, and she was afraid to be alone, so I invited her to stay with me for a while until things get sorted out."

Granted the break-in was weeks ago…

Kaladin's face instantly goes serious, his slightly smug look now gone. "Someone broke into your house?" he asks Gray, frowning deeply.

Her mouth works a bit, and I can almost see her trying to decide how much to tell him or how to spin it.

"Yes," she says finally. "At first I thought it was just my mother coming over to drop something off, but…new evidence suggests there was someone else there."

She glances at me, seeking reassurance, and I nod the barest amount.

"I did freak out a little last night," she goes on, "and Ash graciously offered to let me stay with him so I didn't have to be alone. Or stay with my parents," she adds. "I can get you a copy of the police report if-"

Kaladin waves a hand. "That won't be necessary. I believe you. Are you alright?"

Gray smiles sadly. "As alright as I can be knowing a stranger was wandering around my house."

Kaladin turns to me. "She's going to stay with you for a while?"

I see Gray's head whip to me in my periphery, but I don't look at her.

"For the near future," I say. "Until we can be sure it's safe for her to go home. I'm sorry. It's why I played like shit tonight. I've just been worried about the doc's safety."

Kaladin nods seriously. "I can imagine. That's very considerate of you to let her stay with you."

There's still a tone to his voice, but I just shrug. "I've got the space, plus a state-of-the-art security system."

I practically feel Gray's eyes boring holes in the side of my head, but I don't look at her. Not only does this get us out of hot water with

Kaladin, but now she has an excuse – and his blessing – to stay with me.

Kaladin turns to Gray. "Let me know if there's anything I can do to help," he tells her, and she nods. "Do you think it has to do with you working with Ash?" he adds.

Shit. This has the potential to backfire.

"I personally think it's her piece of shit ex," I say before Gray can answer. I turn to look at her finally, and her eyes are wide in an expression that I'm pretty sure means, '*You should stop talking now.*'

I never told her my theory about Drew, but it's something we should discuss later.

"Alright," Kaladin says, leaning back in his chair. "The two of you should get home and get some rest. Don't hesitate to reach out to me if there's anything I can do."

Gray and I rise, eager to be out of there. At least the last few minutes of panicked improvisation have fixed the situation in my pants.

"Thank you, Mr. Kaladin," Gray says. "I appreciate the offer."

We turn to head out, and I have to stop myself from putting a hand on the small of her back.

I open the door for Gray as we leave and look back at Kaladin. He meets my eyes, and I can tell from his expression that, while he may believe us about the break-in at Gray's, he still thinks there's something more going on between me and her.

I give him a reassuring nod. His nod back is full of warning. At least that's how I take it.

It's time for me and Gray to get back to work.

Chapter 43

Gray

When Ash doesn't come up to the locker room after practice two days later, I find him down on the ice still shooting pucks. I watch him for a few minutes as he uses his stick to guide the puck through a series of obstacles he's set up before he shoots it at the net. He makes every shot.

Far from making him happy, every shot he nets only seems to anger him more. I expect him to start hitting his stick on the ice or engaging in some other show of temper, but he doesn't. His swearing reaches me where I stand in the bench box, but he doesn't act out.

Finally, he looks up and notices me. He skates over, and we look at each other. I've never felt more helpless in my life. I want so badly to find a way to fix this issue for him, but so far we haven't found an intervention that works for more than a game or two.

I open my mouth to apologize for not finding the solution he needs, but before I can do so, he takes his helmet off, leans over, and lays his forehead on my shoulder. He wraps his arms around my waist, and his gloves dig into me lightly.

He's sweaty and smelly, and now I will be too, but I don't hesitate to wrap my arms around the top of his shoulders and thread my fingers through his wet hair.

"Are you okay?" I ask softly.

"I can do it," he says. "I can make goals in my sleep if I'm not thinking about it. The skills are still there, the muscle memory, but the second I let my brain get involved…" He trails off, shaking his head against my shoulder, and I hold him tighter.

"I'm sorry," I say. "I don't seem to be helping much."

He shakes his head again. "It's not your fault. You were honest from the start that you didn't know if you could do anything. No one can fault you for that."

"Still, at this point I feel like I'm just getting paid to have sex with you," I say. "I think there's a word for that."

He lifts his head, looking serious. "Are you saying you wouldn't let me fuck you if Kaladin stopped paying you?"

My mouth drops open, and my jaw works as I search for the right way to respond to his misinterpretation of my words. I haven't found it when his face cracks into a grin, and I realize he's kidding. It's a good thing I'm book smart, because I'm dumb as a stump when it comes to relationships.

He looks at my shoulder. "I got you all sweaty."

I look down as well to see the wet spot on my shirt where his forehead rested. I shrug. "I'll just make you do my laundry."

He chuckles. "I wonder if we have any skates in your size. You should come out and skate with me."

I hold up a hand and shake my head. "Oh no. I have no intention of re-enacting those cheesy scenes from movies where the guy pulls the woman out onto the ice and tries to help her skate, but she falls, and he catches her, and it's all romantic. Nope. Not my idea of fun."

He shrugs and opens the door to the bench area before he steps in.

"How about the scene where the hockey player picks up the woman and skates really fast around the ice with her in his arms?" he asks as he comes toward me.

I frown at him until it clicks into place what he wants to do. "Ash, no!" I yell as he scoops me up in his arms and turns to head back out onto the ice.

"Hold on tight," he says.

"Sweet Jesus, please don't drop me," I say as I wrap my arms around his neck in a death hold, ignoring the squish of sweat against my skin.

"Never," he says as he picks up speed and we swing around the back of the goal he was shooting at.

I feel his legs pump as he sprints down the straightaway, and I tuck my head against his shoulder, trying to pull my body in tight so my feet won't hit the plexiglass.

"I've got you," he says as we swing around the back of the other goal, and he puts on another burst of speed.

I know we're not even going as fast as we could if he used his arms to help him skate, but we're still going wickedly fast, or at least it feels that way. There's a mix of elation and abject terror coursing through my body right now, and I just hold on as tight as I can.

Instead of swinging around the goal again, he comes to a stop in front of it, spraying shaved ice into the net, and then we're skating backward. It's not nearly as fast, and I untuck my head and look over his shoulder so I can be his eyes, since he's not looking where he's going.

"Watch the goal," I say as we approach the far side again.

"Admit it, that was fun," he says, glancing back only a second to see where the goal is before he skates backward around it, then cuts across the ice toward the bench again.

Back at the side, he lifts me over the boards and sets me on my feet, then climbs over them himself. I sway a bit as I try to reacclimate to not shooting around at Mach 6 on the ice.

I look up at Ash and realize he's waiting for an answer.

"It was fun, in an '*I almost wet myself*' kind of way," I tell him.

He chuckles and ushers me into the tunnel toward the locker room.

"I'll meet you in the shower," Ash says when we get there. "It takes a while to get all this gear off."

"I'll wait until we get home to shower," I tell him. It hasn't taken me long to call his place 'home.'

He sits down on the bench and pulls his gloves off. "But I want to fuck you in the shower," he says.

The muscles between my legs tighten, but I ignore them. "I suspected as much," I say, "but I'm not taking the chance that one of the coaches or cleaning staff is still hanging around and will walk in on us."

He pulls off his shirt. "The risk of getting caught is part of the fun."

"Another time," I say. "My legs are already wobbly from our little free skate. I'm not sure I can handle the thrill of possibly getting caught having shower sex so soon."

He sighs and pulls me forward by my hips so I'm standing between his legs. "Fair enough," he says, "but you understand that if you deny me now, that's only going to carry over to what I do to you when we get home, right?"

My stomach flips. "Carry over how?"

He shrugs. "Maybe I'll tie your wrists to your ankles and fuck your ass tonight," he says.

I let out a long breath. I love how dirty he is, and I won't let myself think about *why* I love it so much.

"If that's the price I pay, so be it," I manage.

He grins at me. "Alright then. As long as you're willing to accept the consequences, we'll wait until we get home. Stay here, and I'll be out in a few minutes."

"I'll wait out in the hall," I say. "No offense, but this locker room smells like twenty sweaty men."

He chuckles. "Not gonna argue with you about that."

I head for the door. I briefly consider staying long enough to finish watching him undress, but if I see Ash naked, all my resolve about shower sex will go out the window.

I slip out into the cool, less-pungent air of the hall and take a deep breath. If people only knew the reality of how those locker rooms smell.

The sound of cart wheels on vinyl flooring draws my attention. One of the custodial staff is pushing a large laundry bin down the hall, and I feel a huge sense of relief at turning down shower sex. This guy almost certainly would've walked in on us.

I lean against the opposite wall to give him plenty of room to get by me or to go into the locker room, but he stops in front of me.

I'm lost in thought, so it takes me a second to realize he's just standing there. I look up, ready to apologize if I'm in his way, but the words freeze on my tongue. I know this guy from somewhere, but I blank on where. Maybe he's one of Ash's guys I've seen following me.

Then it clicks into place.

"Barry?" I ask, finally recognizing ManOfYourDreams89, the guy with whom I had my first InSync date. The one who tried to pick me up at home and who wanted to order the same thing I did.

"I didn't know you worked here," I say. I frown at his expression, which looks annoyed, even angry.

"Yeah, for several months now," he says. "Not that you'd notice."

I frown deeper. "When would I have seen you?"

He huffs a laugh. "I walked right between you and that hockey player when the two of you were having an argument in the hall one day," he says. "He grabbed you and shoved you into the equipment room."

I open my mouth to explain, but he cuts me off.

"I figured you'd be mad and come stalking out, but no." He shakes his head. "For some reason, you women seem to like the big neanderthal assholes that push you around."

I shake my own head, but he starts talking again before I can formulate an explanation.

"You all say you want a gentleman, someone who treats you right," he says, and I can hear his anger now. "But when you actually get someone like that, you reject them."

I know he's talking about himself. "Barry, it's more complicated-"

"It's really not," he interrupts. "But if that's what you want, a guy who's going to be aggressive, even violent with you, then fine. That's what you'll get."

He pulls something out of his pocket, and it takes me half a second too long to realize it's a taser. I try to step back from him, but he's too quick, and the scream that works up my throat is cut off as searing hot pain hits me in the chest like a baseball bat. Every one of my muscles convulses like I'm having a full-body cramp, and my teeth clack together as my jaw tenses shut.

The agony goes on for what feels like an eternity, but what's likely only seconds. I feel myself fall, and there's a sharp pain at the back of my head before everything goes dark.

Chapter 44

Gray

I wake up in the pitch black with a hum in my ear as my body vibrates. My head pounds, and I try to reach back to feel for a lump where the pain is more concentrated, but two things become immediately clear.

The first is that my whole body is in pain from being tased. I'm shaky, and every muscle is sore. My jaw hurts from clenching it shut, and I wonder if I wet myself, but I can't tell.

The second thing I realize is that I'm in a small, enclosed space. The humming and vibrating suddenly makes sense as it hits me I'm in the trunk of a car.

Instant panic grabs me. The first time I had an MRI, I started hyperventilating and the technician had to pull me out, then send me back in with my eyes closed so I didn't see the walls close in around me. Knowing that I'm shoved in the trunk of the car of a psycho who broke into my house and left flowers on my bed kicks that claustrophobia into high gear.

I can't breathe, and I take in big gasps. The air tastes stale and devoid of oxygen, and I let out a whimper as I push my limbs out to test the limits of my space. I don't have much room at all. Or at least, that's how it feels.

It's also cold. I left my jacket in my car in the parking garage, and while we've hit a relatively mild spell as far as New England winters go, the cold is settling in my body. If we have far to go, I'll freeze to death in this trunk.

I try to force myself to calm down. Having an anxiety attack isn't going to help. I inhale deeply, and the faint smell of Ash wraps me in its embrace. I was pressed up against him at the arena, and I've never been more grateful to be anointed in sweat. It makes my shirt smell like him, and I feel my heartrate come down as the reminder of him calms me.

Alright, Gray. Get it together and think.

I feel around for my phone, but it's not in my pockets. I can't call for help, but at least my hands and feet aren't bound. Maybe if I focus on the positives, I won't have a complete mental breakdown.

Ha! Look at me staying positive. If Celena could only see me now, she'd be so proud.

Then I remember that all cars made after a certain year have a release inside the trunk that will open it. I don't recall what kind of car Barry drives, but I'm banking it was new enough to have a trunk release.

I feel around but realize I'm facing toward the back and need to roll over. I'm not sure I have enough room to maneuver, so I swing my legs up and around carefully. The trunk is roomier than I expect, and soon I'm facing the right way.

I slide my hand forward, and it lands on something thin and metal. I pick it up and feel along the object. It's maybe an inch wide and a couple feet long with a plastic handle on one end.

My brain struggles to translate what I feel into an image, but it comes to me a few seconds later. It's a Slim Jim for unlocking cars. I'm at a loss for why Barry might need it until the answer hits me upside the head. My house has older windows, and the thin metal tool can be used to slip between the two parts of the window to pull the latch open from the inside. I even had to do it once a few years ago when I accidentally locked myself out. That's how the son of a bitch got into my house.

I start feeling around to find the trunk release, but I have no idea what I'm looking for. I've seen pictures of a plastic pull, but based on the car, I could be looking for a latch, switch, or button of some kind. I continue to fumble around in the dark when I finally feel something right in front of me in the center of the trunk. If I squint, it looks like it might be glowing a faint florescent green, and I remember that these release latches are supposed to glow in the dark so they're easier to find.

The car comes to a stop just as I put my fingers on the latch. It feels like a piece of plastic I need to pull to the side. The car shuts off, and the blood ramps up in my veins as fear grips me. Do I pull the latch now and run for it, or do I wait for Barry to open the trunk and try to fight him?

Instinct makes me pull the latch, and the trunk pops open. I squint now that there's more light, but it's night, so there's not much. I fight the soreness and jitteriness in my limbs and launch myself out into the cold air. I stumble but manage to stay on my feet as I start to run.

"Hey!" I hear Barry yell behind me, but I don't bother to look back. He didn't seem like he was in great shape. Let's see if he can catch me.

The ground near my feet explodes as a gunshot goes off, and I freeze.

"Move another inch, and the next one is in your back," Barry says.

I don't move. My entire body is shaking now, and I'm not sure how I'm managing to breathe. I've never been this scared in my life, but I have to calm down and get control of myself, or I'm a dead woman.

"Turn around and come back," Barry says.

I raise my hands and do as he says. I see we're pulled off on the side of the road with woods on both sides. Other than the occasional streetlight further down the road, there's nothing.

Barry motions into the woods with the gun, some kind of revolver. "Start walking."

"Where are we going?" I ask.

"Somewhere it will take them a while to find you," he says.

My stomach hits the ground. "You…you're going to kill me?"

"Walk," he says, ignoring the question.

I start walking into the woods as slowly as I can. I have to stall. I have to find an opportunity to run. I have to leave a trail.

I drag my toe in the dirt as casually as I can. If someone comes out this way in the near future, hopefully the scuff will still be there.

"Why are you doing this?" I ask. "What did I ever do to you?"

"I liked you," Barry says. "A lot. And I thought you felt it too."

"We had one date," I say in disbelief. "And honestly, I'm not sure how you thought we connected. It didn't feel awkward to you?"

"Maybe a little," he says. "But that's because you didn't give it a chance. You didn't give *me* a chance. No one does."

To be fair, he's right. I didn't give him much of a chance, but I also don't owe him anything, and certainly not my life.

"I thought maybe you just needed some time to get back into dating since you said you'd just started again," he says, "but then I followed you to that club a few weeks later and saw you practically having sex on the dancefloor. You crumpled up the note I left on your car that night without even reading it."

I recall the piece of paper I found on my windshield when Ash escorted me back to my car at the casino.

"I thought the note was one of those advertisements people leave on windshields. The last time I got one of those, it was for a psychic reader," I say as I nearly stumble over a rotted tree branch. Then something clicks into place. "Wait, you were at the club? Were you the one who took the video of me and Ash?"

"Yeah," he says, disgust in his voice. "I uploaded it to one of the discussion boards I'm on for other guys like me who've been unfairly passed over by women, and someone sent it to the media. I just wanted to show people what a slut you were."

My anger spikes, but I rein it in. Fuck what this asshole thinks of me.

"You refused to let me pick you up for our date, but you let *him* pick you up," Barry says. "I saw it on the news a couple days later. Were the two of you already together when you went out with me?"

"Of course not," I say. "I knew Ash already, but we weren't dating yet. It…we didn't exactly plan to get together."

"And the rose petals and note I left for you meant nothing?" he asks.

"You mean the rose petals you broke into my house to leave?" I snap back at him as we walk. "What made you think I'd like that? That I wouldn't find it completely creepy?"

He scoffs. "Isn't that women's thing nowadays? I watch BookTok.

You all want your own personal stalker."

I glance back at him. I'm shivering, both from fear and cold, but that observation sends more hot anger down my spine.

"Are you serious? Do you really not understand the difference between fiction and reality?" I ask as I nearly trip again. I take the opportunity to leave another long scuff in the dirt. "Books are an opportunity for people to safely experience something extreme. My friend loves horror as a genre, but that doesn't mean she wants to be hacked to death by an axe murderer or hunted by a monster wielding a chainsaw."

There's silence behind me, and I look around desperately. We're surrounded by trees, but I'm not sure they're dense enough to provide cover from gunfire if I run for it. Still, I can't let Barry push me too far into the woods. The further we get from the road, the more screwed I am.

I make a decision and turn to face him.

"Turn around and walk!" he yells, waving the gun at me.

I shake my head. "No. You want to kill me, do it here. I'm not going to save you the trouble of dragging my body further into the woods."

He raises the gun more, but his hand shakes, and I dare to hope he doesn't have it in him to pull the trigger.

"Did you even think about contacting me when you saw the note and rose petals?" he asks.

"I never saw them," I say. "Ash found them first and got rid of them."

He makes a noise of disgust and drops the gun a little so it's no longer pointed at my chest. "Of course he did."

"How would I have known they were from you anyway?" I ask.

"I signed the note," he says.

I frown as I think back. "Ash showed me the note later on. There was no name on it."

He pauses. "Yeah, I initialed it."

I shake my head. "No initials."

There's another pause before he lets out a growl of frustration.

"You used the Slim Jim to get my kitchen window open," I say. I need to keep him talking as long as possible until I figure out a plan. "Ash had someone watching the house. How did you keep from being seen?"

He starts laughing. "People don't notice me. I'm invisible," he says. "I sat in on your Communication class one day last semester, and you didn't look at me once. I waited for you to see me, to react, but you didn't. I thought maybe you were different, that I'd give you a second chance to prove you weren't like the others, but no."

My mouth drops open. He must mean my large lecture class. In fairness, there were three hundred students in it, and I only vaguely recognized most of them. I remembered those who sat in the first few rows, but my memory got murkier the further up in the lecture hall I went. If he sat up near the back...

I remember the quiz without a name on it. I never found its owner.

"What's wrong with you women?" he asks in exasperation. "Do you know how many dates I've gone on lately? I can't get past a first date. I try to be polite and respectful, but it's the same story with all of you. 'Sorry, I didn't feel a connection.' But that guy, the hockey player, spends his nights getting paid to get into fights, and you think that's great. Then you're surprised when guys like that turn around and hit you."

"Ash would never hurt me," I say vehemently. I know that without a doubt. "Ash has done nothing but try to protect me since I met him. Protect me from *you*. That's what a real man does, protects what's his."

And yes, I am Ash's. I have been for a while. Mind, body, and soul.

Barry makes a face like he just put something bitter in his mouth. "It's not enough that he gets to have all the really hot women," he says. "He has to take the regular-looking ones away from the rest of us as well?"

Of all the things Barry's said tonight, that one hits the hardest. He doesn't even find me attractive. I'm just 'regular-looking' enough that he feels he has a shot, and I'm ashamed to realize that's what breaks me.

Were the times Ash told me I was beautiful a lie? He said I needed to start believing he found me attractive, but even Barry is settling. It knocks the air from my lungs in a way not even the cold and the fear do.

"Way to make a girl feel special," I say, when I rally enough to speak. "Did you ever think maybe that's why you're single?"

I shouldn't have said it, but I couldn't help it, and Barry's face contorts in anger.

"Shut up!" he says. "Women have it so easy. If you want to have sex, all you have to do is open your legs and some guy will fall into your pussy. It doesn't matter what you look like. Do you know what you need if you want to get laid as a man? You have to be tall. You have to be hot and have a great job. You need a nice car, and apparently you need to grunt like a cave man and drag a woman off by her hair."

I really want to tell him how hard it was to get Drew to come fuck me, but I refrain. I'm not going to bare that part of my soul to this asshole.

"Having a personality and not blaming your problems on everyone else helps as well," I snap, because I'm fucked anyway.

Barry growls again, then raises the pistol at me and pulls the trigger.

I flinch at the click and nearly vomit as my stomach heaves, but nothing happens, and we both look at the gun. We realize at the same time he needs to cock it again, and I launch myself at him on instinct.

I grab his gun hand and try to shove him into a tree, hoping to dislodge it. I succeed in pushing him against the tree, but he swings the hand with the gun and cold cocks me. I see the gun go flying from the impact just before stars pop in my vision.

Barry doesn't try to retrieve it. He wraps his hands around my throat and falls on top of me while I'm still dazed. More stars swim before my eyes as my air is cut off, and I scratch and claw at Barry as I buck beneath him, desperate to dislodge him enough to suck in a breath.

In a last-ditch effort, I swing my fist up and clock him in the side of the head. Barry grunts in pain, and his hands ease from around my neck just enough for me to gasp in a sweet breath of air.

I'm about to hit him again when something barrels into him like a charging bull, and he's knocked completely off me. I cough as I try to sit up, but I jump in surprise as a man drops down in a kneel next to me.

"You okay, ma'am?" he asks.

I look up at the man, but I don't recognize him. Wait, yes I do. He's the man from the gym that I later saw when I had dinner with my mother.

"Who are you?" I ask.

He doesn't answer but looks past me and swears. He jumps up and runs over to where Ash is straddling Barry, punching him repeatedly.

"Mr. Gunnarsson!" the man says, trying to pull Ash off Barry. "Stop! He's unconscious!"

He wraps himself around Ash's arm to stay it, but it's a few seconds more before Ash stops fighting the hold and lowers his arm.

"He's down," the man says. "Go check on your woman."

Ash's head jerks to me where I'm still lying on the ground. He throws himself off Barry and crawls over to me. He pulls me across his lap and wraps his arms around me, squeezing me so hard I almost can't breathe.

"Fuck, Gray," he whispers, his voice cracking, as he cradles me against him. "Are you okay? Did he hurt you? I'll fucking kill him."

I can't answer past the lump in my throat. At some point in the near future, I'll break down in tears, and once I start, I doubt I'll stop, but for now my eyes are bone dry.

Ash grabs my face in his hands. "Baby, tell me you're okay, or I swear to God, I'll kill that fucker with my bare hands."

I swallow. "I'm okay." My voice is scratchy and barely a whisper, but I get the words out. I start to shake, partially from the cold, but mostly as the reality of what just happened sinks in.

"Jesus, you must be freezing," Ash says.

He pulls his coat off and wraps it around me before pulling me back against him and rocking me in his lap. "Do you know him?"

I nod against Ash's chest. "We went on a date. The night you gave me the shoulder massage."

Ash stops rocking. "Why did he take you? What did he want?"

A humorless laugh jumps up my throat. "Revenge on womankind for his involuntary celibacy?"

Ash tenses. "He's an incel?"

I nod.

"Boss, I gave the police our location," the other man calls to Ash. "They should be here any minute."

"Who's that?" I ask Ash.

"That's Sully," Ash says. "He's one of the guys I had following you the last few weeks."

I frown. "You still had him following me?"

"Sort of," Ash says. "I'd already paid him through tonight, so he was in the parking garage watching your car when this fucker came down with the laundry cart. Sully didn't think anything of it at first, and he wasn't watching too closely until he looked up and saw this guy pull you out of the cart and dump you in his trunk. He tried to stop him, but the guy got in his car and took off."

"Barry didn't notice him in the garage?" I ask. "Barry is the guy's name," I explain at Ash's questioning look.

"Tinted windows," Ash says. "Sully gets paid to stay hidden. Anyway, he tried to tail the guy, but he lost him, so Sully called a friend who's…um, handy with computers, and he tracked your phone. The guy, Barry, must've brought it with him, which is just dumb."

We hear shouts in the distance and a dog barking.

"Sully called the police to tell them what he'd seen and to give them the car's license plate. Then he called me, and I was able to catch up to him," Ash goes on.

I'm still sitting across his lap on the ground, and he reaches up to stroke the side of my face as he nuzzles his nose into my hair.

"If I'd lost you, Gray…" I hear the choke in his voice as he trails off.

His own break snaps the thin tether of my control, and I start to cry.

And then I cry, and I cry, and I cry.

Chapter 45

Two nights later, Ash receives a standing ovation from the sold-out crowd when he takes the ice at the Hydra's next home game. News of my kidnapping and his rescue of me hit the news not long after I was taken, and thanks to Cedric's efforts, Ash is being hailed as a hero. The guys have started calling him Captain America, an apparent promotion from Gunnery Sergeant.

For his own part, Ash insists to anyone who will listen that I was fighting off Barry when he got there and that I all-but rescued myself – a bit of a stretch – but his insistence on being the 'humble hero' has only stoked the media frenzy even more. Kaladin and Cedric, of course, are milking every last drop of publicity out of it they can, hence the Hydra's first-ever sold-out crowd.

Apparently, near-tragedy is as good for business as a winning team.

I stand and clap along with the crowd. I don't particularly want to be out in public right now, but Cedric pleaded with me to make an appearance, and Kaladin gently reminded me how much he's paid me thus far, so here I am. Although not alone.

Sully is on my left and Celena is on my right. Next to her sits Dean, the security guy I saw in the grocery store. Ash decided to keep Sully and Dean on a little longer, if only to keep the media away from me, and I didn't have any desire to protest. Ash only found me that night because Sully happened to be in the garage and saw Barry dump me in his car.

I try not to think about what would've happened if they hadn't found me. I've woken with nightmares the last couple nights. Ash just gathers me in his arms, kisses the top of my head, and holds me until I fall asleep again, only to do it all over hours later.

I tried to slip out of bed and sleep on the couch once so I didn't disturb him, but he only came out, picked me up without a word and put me back in bed with him.

I'm on leave from the university at the moment. They'll have an adjunct covering my classes, and I'm not sure yet if I plan to go back.

Kaladin offered me a permanent place on his staff so I can study trash talk fulltime and work with his players. Ostensibly, my job would be to continue to help Ash and others who might be susceptible to chirping, but Kaladin also 'joked' that he wouldn't be sorry if I developed a guide for weaponizing the practice.

Ash and I finally came clean to him that we're really dating, and so far there haven't been any consequences. Kaladin said he guessed as much, but he doesn't care as long as I fix Ash. I suspect he's afraid that making Ash and I stop working together will only have a detrimental effect on Ash's game. Or at least, that's what Ash hinted to him when we confessed.

I'm taking a few days to collect myself, and then I have my first therapy session early next week. Ash offered to attend with me if I need him. I appreciate the offer, but I can do this on my own.

Inside the arena, the crowd roars as Ash takes a quick circuit on the Hydra's side of the ice. He gives a couple nods to acknowledge the adoration and lifts his stick briefly before he stops in front of me.

My heart picks up its pace. He pulls his glove off and presses his hand to the glass. I press my hand against his through the barrier. I'm wearing his jersey, and the crowd explodes in cheers as cameras click around us.

The moment is a hundred percent scripted by Cedric, who is evidently a huge romantic, but the feelings that pass between me and Ash as we look at each other have never felt so real. I still haven't told him I love him, and it's well past time I do so. I wanted to say it the other night when he held me in his arms on the ground as I sobbed, but I didn't want him to think the words were trauma-induced.

As if reading my mind, Ash's lips move the barest amount. *'I love you.'*

The words aren't meant for the crowd or the media, but for me alone.

I don't want the first time I tell him I love him to be when we're separated by plexiglass in the middle of sixteen thousand people, but I also can't leave him hanging again. I mouth the words back, moving my lips as little as possible. *'I love you too.'*

The smile that splits his face makes my body tingle all the way down to my toes, and I want to dive into his dimples. Seeing me say those words makes him happy, and that's all that matters.

He turns and skates away, and I have to sit down as my feelings for him overwhelm me.

"That was so stinking sweet," Celena says as she sits along with the rest of the crowd.

"Shut up," I say, but I'm smiling.

Celena's eyes dip to my neck where the bruises from Barry's hands are just fading. I wanted to cover them up, but Cedric and Kaladin convinced me to leave them visible to the media. I only agreed so they're out there for potential jurors to see.

I'm sure a good lawyer would argue we're poisoning the jury pool or something like that, but showing people what Barry did seems important regardless. He felt entitled to my attention and affection, and when he didn't get it, he resorted to violence. I want to send a message that there are consequences to that kind of bullshit thinking.

"How are you doing?" Celena asks.

I pop open my can of wine and pour it into a plastic cup. If settling for canned concession-stand wine at games doesn't prove my love for Ash, I don't know what does.

I shrug. "I'm alive. I know that sounds flippant, but you have no idea how grateful I am for that simple fact."

Celena reaches for my hand and squeezes it. "Me too." She clears her throat to hide the break in her voice. "And how is Ash?"

I glance at the two bodyguards flanking us. "Paranoid to leave me alone. He says he only plans to keep Sully and Dean on for another week or two, but I'm not sure I'll ever be rid of them." I look at Sully, who I know can hear me. "No offense."

His mouth turns up in a small smile. "None taken, ma'am."

I like Sully. He's in his mid-forties and has a dry wit that catches me off-guard sometimes. I associate him with my rescue, so I think I imprinted on him or something. I'll miss him when Ash finally ends this job, but chances are I'll see him around. Sully and my dad already have plans to go golfing together, since Ash introduced my parents to my security detail the day after I was taken as proof he was keeping me safe.

Having Ash meet my mother went well enough. As expected, she fell instantly in love with him, and my calls with her now involve a deluge of questions about him, half of which I have to evade since they're about our sex life. I have no intention of divulging any of that to my mother.

Unsurprisingly, her reaction to the kidnapping ordeal in general was to take up Judo, kickboxing, and Krav Maga.

Dean, the other security guy, is nice too. I just haven't quite connected with him the way I have with Sully. I associate him too much with stalking me and car chases, but he doesn't seem to have taken my preference for Sully personally.

"Any news on Barry?" Celena asks.

"Denied bail," I say. "I think I have Kaladin to thank for that. The man seems to know a lot of judges."

Celena gives me a look that says that doesn't surprise her.

"I'm getting a restraining order in the meantime, just in case," I say.

"Can't hurt," Celena says. She pauses, then says, "And you're sure-"

"No gun," I tell her. "Although I wouldn't mind getting a taser."

She sighs. "I suppose that's a start."

"Uh, ma'am," Dean says from next to Celena. "I think someone wants your attention."

Celena and I turn toward the ice, and we both jolt to find Kingston, mask on, looking at us through the glass. Well, looking at Celena. It's clear his attention is on her.

Kingston slams a large, gloved hand on the glass in a dark imitation of Ash's gesture. I look at Celena, but she just crosses her arms as she scowls at him, refusing to engage in whatever game he's playing.

He cocks his head slowly at her, then reaches down to pull up his shirt a little. I catch a flash of something red that looks like it's pinned to the inside of his pants.

I'm about to ask Celena what it is when she launches out of her seat and throws herself against the glass to bang on it.

"You fucking bastard!" she yells at him.

I look at Sully and Dean, but they're just as shocked as I am.

Kingston puts his shirt down, and I swear I see him smile behind his mask before he skates away.

Celena growls and throws herself back into her seat.

"What the hell was that about?" I ask her. "What was that red thing?"

"Those were my panties," Celena bites out under her breath. "He won't give them back."

I stare at her. "How the fuck did he get them in the first place?"

She glances at Sully and Dean. "I'll tell you later."

I want to press her, but the game is getting ready to start, and we have to stand for the anthem. I turn to her when we're seated again, intent on getting an answer, but Celena points out onto the ice. "Look!"

I look where she's pointing, and my heart leaps.

Ash is at center ice for the faceoff. He's starting for the first time this season.

Chapter 46

I should be nervous. It's been a long time since I've started and most other players would be worried about making sure they don't screw up, but I'm strangely calm as I wait for the puck drop.

I'm almost certain I have Kaladin to thank for the start. He's been trying to ride the media attention surrounding what happened to Gray to promote the team, and I'm pretty sure he told Coach Davis to get me on the ice early. I'm still officially second line, but I intend to change that.

Ideally, I want to see me, Cote, and Bouchard promoted to first line together. They've put up with a lot from me this season, and they should be rewarded for that alone. All things considered, the three of us play really well together when I have my head on straight, like we're reading each other's minds. It's only been my consistency that was the issue, so if I play well tonight, maybe Coach will try starting us again.

I glance over at Gray and relax to see her in her seat with Sully and Dean keeping an eye on her. I know at some point she'll reject having bodyguards around her at all times, but for now she's not fighting it.

I clench my teeth every time I see the bruises on her neck, and I wish I'd gotten a few more punches in on the fucker who gave them to her before Sully pulled me off him. My hand still hurts from hitting Barry, but it was worth it.

Gray has a long road to feel safe again – if that's even possible – but I have my own demons to deal with. When Sully called to tell me what he'd seen, I freaked the fuck out. Losing Gray was unthinkable, and it'll be a long time before I'm able to let her out of my sight without fearing

I'll never see her again. Getting Barry behind bars permanently will be a good start, but there are more men like him out there. Too many.

I just know one thing with certainty. Gray is the woman I plan to marry. Now isn't the right time to tell her that, of course. We both need to heal first, but one of these days, she'll wear my ring, and knowing that makes everything alright for now.

I turn my attention back as the ref gets ready to drop the puck. Across from me, Lapoint eyes me like he wants to eat my liver. I haven't seen him since that preseason game when he put the tampon down my jersey, and I know the standing ovation I got pissed him off. He'll start chirping at me as soon as he can, but I'm not worried about it. Gray is safe, and I've come to some realizations lately. I'm ready to play.

The puck hits the ice, and I swipe it back to Cote who takes off and slaloms between defenders like he's an Olympic skier. He and Bouchard are feeding off my energy. They don't care how we got to the starting spot, but the three of us are determined to keep it.

We score our first goal less than a minute into the game, and I feel vindicated for having bumped Nilsen, Aasgaard, and Fig from this first shift. The honor of the goal goes to Bouchard, but I get the assist, and the crowd surges to their feet.

The chirping starts on my next shift, but it doesn't bother me anymore. I learned something important in this whole ordeal with Gray.

As much as I wanted to believe the misogynistic comments bothered me because I was so 'enlightened about feminism,' I had to face the fact I still held some deeply ingrained beliefs about how women were weaker and more limited in certain things.

When I ran toward Gray that night and saw her fighting off Barry, saw her trying to hit and buck off a man bigger than her who was holding her down as he tried to kill her, I had nothing but awe for her. She'd ultimately needed my help, but she'd fought until Sully and I could get there. She bought us time to get to her, and she's alive because of it.

Maybe I'm stretching things, but it's kind of like BDSM. Just because the submissive looks weak doesn't mean they are. They're actually the one with all the power in the dynamic.

In any case, once I allowed myself to truly believe how strong women are – how strong my sisters and my mother and the love of my life are – it made letting go of the trash talk easy. It has no power over me anymore, and hearing guys use it to get under my skin just seems pathetic.

Lapoint's frustration and that of the other Ducks is apparent as the game goes on and we take them apart piece by piece. Nothing they say riles me in the least, and the crowd turns practically feral as we pull ahead by three goals in the third period, two of which are mine.

Lapoint slams into Kingston with four minutes left under the guise of not being able to stop in time, and we're instantly on him, me in the lead. I get two minutes in the box for my trouble, but it's worth it. Kingston may be an asshole, but he's *our* asshole, and if you fuck with him, you fuck with us all.

The game ends just before things get really ugly, and we win 5-2. The chances that Cote, Bouchard, and I have secured our starting spot in the lineup moving forward are good.

Whether the crowds will continue to come once the media frenzy dies down remains to be seen, but we have a winning record at the moment, and we get better with every game. We're in the running for a wild card spot, and Kaladin's hopes of getting to the playoffs are not out of reach.

And for the first time this season, I believe we can make it too.

Ash

Gray's face lights up when I exit the locker room after the game. Celena has apparently left, but Sully and Dean stand in the hall next to my woman. I ignore them and pull her into my arms before slanting my mouth across hers for a deep kiss. Her moan of pleasure goes straight to my cock.

"Ugh," Kelsier groans as he exits behind me. He turns and calls back into the locker room. "Warning, guys. Captain America and the doc have excessive amounts of PDA going on out here."

I shoot him a glare, but Gray smiles and says, "Hi, Kels," before he gives her a wink and heads out. We'll meet him and a few of the guys out shortly.

Fig and The Don leave next, followed by Kingston, who stops to look around when he sees Gray.

"Your little friend still hiding from me?" he asks her.

Gray holds out her hand to him. "Give me her panties back," she says, ignoring his question.

My gaze shoots to her. "What? Why does he have her panties?"

"No idea," she says, "but he needs to give them back."

Kingston just grins down at her. "Convince Celena to come out tonight, and maybe I'll make a trade."

Gray narrows her eyes. "What kind of trade?"

"That's between me and her," Kingston says as he turns and heads down the hall.

We both stare after him, but I decide I'd rather not know.

"Ready to go, baby?" I ask Gray. She looks at me hesitantly, and I frown. "Something wrong?"

She glances at Sully and Dean, then looks back at me. "I need to tell you something before we go."

"Okay. What is it?" She looks so serious, and now I'm nervous.

"Not here," she says. She grabs my hand and pulls me down the hall until we get to the equipment room. I look behind to see Sully and Dean following at a safe distance.

"We'll just be a minute," I tell them as Gray drags me into the equipment room.

I'm not sure what to think. This room has some good memories, and my dick reacts accordingly as she turns to me, but the look on her face doesn't suggest she has sex on her mind.

"I love you," Gray says without preamble.

I blink. That was the last thing I expected her to say, and I have to reset my brain before her words sink in. Even so, my immediate reaction is, "...What?"

"I love you," she repeats, a shy smile adorning her face. "I should've told you a long time ago, back when you first said it to me, but I was afraid. I wish my first time telling you wasn't from the other side of the glass in front of all those people, but recent events made me realize I shouldn't wait to express how I feel. Hence the reason I'm telling you again now rather than waiting for a more romantic moment."

I pull her into what's likely a bone-crunching hug. "Fuck, Gray. I love you too. I love you so much."

My lips descend on hers again to kiss her deeply, and it's nearly a minute before we pull apart.

Then something she said hits me. "What were you afraid of? I already told you I loved you. Did you not believe me?"

She shrugs. "It's hard to explain," she says. "I mean, you're this big hockey star, and you're so..." She lets her eyes run over my body quickly. "Pretty," she decides on, making me almost laugh. "It's like Barry said. I'm just regular, and I didn't think-"

"He said *what*?" I interrupt, red rage filling my mind at the thought of that incel motherfucker.

She looks taken aback at the ferocity of my question. "It...It's nothing," she says. "He was just saying guys like you get all the actresses and supermodels, so he was mad you were also taking the regular women like me, and-"

"Stop," I interrupt her, closing my eyes against the desire to do violence in response to the utter fucking bullshit that jackass was filling her head with before I got there.

I open my eyes. "First of all, Gray, there's nothing regular about you, and I'm surprised at you for letting that piece of shit convince you otherwise."

Her mouth works as if she wants to argue, but it's a second or two before she says, "He just meant…I mean…well, compared to your last girlfriend-"

I put a finger on her lips to make her stop talking, and I wish that fucker was here so I could beat the shit out of him all over again. Sully should've let me put him in a coma.

"You need to listen to me carefully," I say, "because this is the last time we're going to have this conversation. Understand?"

She nods, my finger still on her lips.

I push her back toward the wall until she's pressed against it, and I grind my hips into hers so she can feel the erection straining against my pants. She groans.

"You are fucking gorgeous," I whisper to her. "Grace couldn't hold a candle to you."

She opens her mouth, and I already hear the argument on her tongue, so I bring my lips down on hers to stopper the words before she can speak them. I kiss her until her body goes limp against me.

"Fuck, baby. Don't you feel how God damn hard I am for you?" I ask. I push my groin into her, and she moans. "Grace never made me this hard. I'm fucking mad about you, Gray, and I don't fall for just 'regular' women. You're not just gorgeous. You're smart and fierce and brave, and if I could spend the rest of my life just breathing the same air you breathe, I'd be a happy man."

A small breath punches out of her. "Alright," she says.

"I don't believe you," I say. "I'm not sure you've gotten the message yet, so I think I have to take you home, strap you to the bed, and make you come until you understand."

"I…," she starts, then trails off.

I smile. She wants to argue that she understands, but she doesn't want to take being tied to the bed and given multiple orgasms off the table.

Gray swallows. "I thought we were going out with the guys tonight."

"We are," I say. I reach down and start undoing her pants.

She grabs for my hands. "What are you doing?" she whisper-hisses.

"If I'm going to make it the next few hours until I can get you home, I need to fuck you now."

Her eyes widen. "Now? Sully and Dean are right outside the door. They'll know-"

"Let them know," I say. "And if they're doing their jobs, they'll keep us from being interrupted."

As if on cue, we hear voices outside the door, and I distinctly here Dean say, "You can't go in right now." Give that man a fucking raise.

I finish undoing Gray's pants and pull them down her hips. She sighs as she kicks off her shoes, then takes her jeans and panties the rest of the way off as I pull out my cock and open my wallet to grab a condom. When I open the pocket, though…It's empty.

"Fuck!" I say. "I forgot to reload my wallet."

Gray shakes her head. "We don't need a condom. I have an IUD, and I just got my test results this morning. I'm clear. Come inside me."

Her words go straight to my balls.

"Fuuck, Gray," I say, drawing out the word. "Are you sure?"

She nods. "I'm sure."

I push my jeans further down my hips and lift her up, pinning her between me and the wall. She reaches down and lines me up, and I slide her down onto my cock as she wraps her legs around my waist. We both groan as her pussy swallows me up. I've never gone in bare before, and doing it for the first time with Gray is a religious experience.

"God damn it, baby," I whisper against her ear as I start to thrust. "My fucking angel."

She smiles. "My naughty demon."

I drive deeper as her body thuds softly against the wall. Gray clamps a hand over her mouth to stifle her cry, but I pull it away.

"Let them hear you. I want everyone to know you're fucking mine."

"I'm yours," she says, half delirious with rapture.

"Yes, you are," I say with a smile.

And I prove to her just how extraordinary she is.

Epilogue

A Little Over Four Months Later

Gray

There's a package for Ash on the front porch when I get back from shopping, and I pick it up on my way in. We leave tomorrow for the first game of the Stanley Cup, and I was out buying a new outfit for good luck. I rarely buy myself new clothes unless I need them for a special occasion, or unless Celena forces me to buy something for myself, but I decided that the Hydra playing for the Cup on their second season in existence counted as a special occasion.

"Something came for you," I tell Ash as I put the box on the counter.

He's getting ready to make dinner, but he drops what he's doing to come look at the package.

"Yes, perfect!" he says, picking it up. "Just in time."

"What is it?" I ask.

He steals an arm around me and pulls me close for a kiss. "A new toy. Do you want to test it now or after dinner?"

I eye him warily. "What kind of toy exactly?"

He grins. "Can't tell you. I need your answer first."

I survey the box, trying to decide what's inside. It's not terribly big. I guess there's room for a new dildo in it maybe, but Ash's excitement suggests it's not that simple.

I decide I'm not hungry yet, and I'm way too curious to wait until after dinner to find out what it is.

"Now," I say.

He grins and takes the package over to the junk drawer where he pulls out a box cutter and slices it open. Then he grabs my hand and pulls me down the hall into the bedroom where he hands me the package.

I give him a '*What are you up to?*' look and put the box on a dresser to open it. There's another box inside, and I pull it out to look at the picture on the front. My eyes meet his.

"A strap-on?" I say as he grins at me.

I try to imagine the logistics of what he wants to do, and only one thing comes to mind.

"You're going to use this to fuck my ass and my pussy at the same time," I guess.

He makes a face that seems to say, '*That's not a bad idea.*'

"Not what I had in mind," he says, "but that's definitely another use for it. We'll save that for after we win the Cup."

I frown. "What *did* you have in mind then?"

The grin is back on his face. "It's for you to wear…and use on me."

It takes a few seconds for that to sink in as I look at the picture on the box, then my head snaps up. "Wait, what?"

"I want you to peg me," he says.

I just stare at him, mouth hanging open.

"You know what that is, right?" he asks.

The question snaps me out of my stupor. "Yeah, I know what it is," I say. "And I'm not usually one to question someone's kinks but…why?"

"You remember how a few months ago I had to figure out how to deal with chirping that attacked my masculinity, right?" he says, and I nod. "Well, I decided that one way to get a sense for the female experience was for me to be the receiver."

He grins at me like he's figured out the secret to the universe.

"But you haven't had a problem with trash talk in months," I say.

"Yeah, but this is the Stanley Cup finals," he says. "I want to make sure I'm chirp-proof."

"And you think having me fuck you in the ass is the way to do that?"

He shrugs. "It can't hurt to try."

I resist the urge to tell him it can in fact hurt a lot if we don't do it right, but I ask instead, "Don't you think you might be taking this whole method acting thing a bit too far?"

He shrugs again. "Maybe, but I still want to try it. You seem to enjoy it when I fuck your ass."

Heat rises to my cheeks. I do enjoy it. More than I thought I would.

"Okay, but we can't just pull this thing out of the box and use it today," I argue. "You prepared me for weeks before we tried anal."

He only grins wider. "I've been wearing plugs all week," he says.

My mouth drops open again. "What? How did I not know that?"

"Just around the house," he says. "Not at practice. That's all I need is for one of those things to pop out onto the ice if I get checked. Or worse, get sucked up the other way."

I narrow my eyes. "You said that couldn't happen."

"Normally, no," he says, "but all bets are off when Mack checks you."

I give him a *'Fair enough'* nod. I cringe whenever I see Mack check someone. The man is like a wrecking ball.

"So will you do this?" he asks. "It has a mini vibrator for you."

I raise a brow, then sigh. "Fine," I say. "It's your ass."

He chuckles. "That's the spirit."

Ash pulls me to him and kisses me as I find the hem of his shirt to lift it over his head. He's too tall for me to fully reach, so he pulls it the rest of the way as I run my hands over his chest. I love touching him, and I trace some of the lines of his armor tattoo before I trail a finger down his torso to the fly of his jeans.

We don't break eye contact as I unbuckle his belt, then unbutton his jeans. His breathing is already heavy, and his hard cock presses against the fabric as I unzip him with fumbling fingers. It doesn't take much to get either of us going.

He gets his jeans the rest of the way off as I discard my shirt and bra, but he stops me before I can get to my own pants.

"Against the wall," he says.

"I thought I get to be in charge this time," I say.

He smiles. "Not yet."

I move to the wall and put my hands against it with my legs spread. Ash often has me start out in this position. It's convenient for undressing me, inserting a plug, spanking me, or any number of other things he likes to do. It also reminds me of that time in the equipment room.

He takes my pants off, and I step out of them, keeping my hands on the wall. I sense him walk away and hear him open the box to the strap-on as I wait patiently.

"Let's see how wet you are," he says as he returns and presses his chest to my back.

Ash slips a finger between my legs and pushes it inside me. I moan as it slides in easily, and Ash lets out a deep breath.

"Are you ever not wet for me, baby?" he asks huskily, thrusting his finger in an out a few times. All I can do is shake my head.

He bends to lift my foot and slips it through one of the loops for the strap-on before pulling the toy up my leg. The thing has two dildos attached, one that juts out in front, and one on the inside of the strap that fits inside me. Ash lines the second smaller dildo up with my entrance and pushes it in. I stick my ass out and moan again as it slides in. Ash pumps it a few times before pushing it all the way in and fastening the clip to secure the apparatus on my hips.

"How does that feel?" he asks.

I look down at the bright pink cock hanging from the apex of my thighs. "Really weird," I say. It's odd to feel a weight in front like that.

Ash chuckles. "Come strap my wrists," he says, and I take my hands off the wall as he climbs onto the bed.

It's not the first time he's let me strap him down. He doesn't allow it often, but twice before he's let me strap him spreadeagle to the bed so I could ride him. The only thing it does is make him feral to touch me, and our sex when I finally release him is intense, to say the least.

I teased him a little too much the last time, taking the opportunity to edge him a bit, and I was walking gingerly the next day by the time he was done with me after that. It was great sex, but…damn.

Ash gets on his hands and knees on the bed, and I secure the leather cuffs near the headboard around his wrists, giving him just enough leeway so he can rest on his elbows. I give him the remote control for the vibrator between my legs and go get the bottle of lube.

The vibrator goes on suddenly, and I double over and cry out. "Ash!"

The vibrator turns off.

"Sounds like it works," he says, chuckling.

"I advise you not to turn it on that high when I'm inside you, or I may puncture your colon," I tell him. "Are you sure this is a good idea? What if you get hurt and can't play?"

"I trust you," he says over his shoulder, "but I hear you about keeping the vibrator on low."

I sigh and climb onto the bed with the bottle of lube in my hand.

"Just juice that thing up good," Ash says.

I look between his legs. His cock hangs long and thick as usual, but he's only semi-hard. It occurs to me this might be better if he was harder.

I shift so I'm on my back, and I shimmy my head up between his legs.

"What are you doing?" he asks, looking down at me.

"Getting you started," I say.

Ash grunts as I lean up on my elbows and close my lips over his cock.

"Fuck," he hisses out. "You're so God damn good at that."

I pump my mouth over him and feel him thicken between my lips. I get my tongue involved, using it to trace the large vein on the underside of his cock before swirling it around his crown.

Ash swears and pumps his hips a little. I stay still and allow him to fuck my mouth, letting him push deeper and deeper into my throat as I relax my muscles to take him. I still can't quite take all of him, but I'm working on it.

I put a hand on Ash's stomach and pull my head back to stop his thrusting before I scoot out from under him. He swears again as I leave him hard and unsatiated, but he leans back, presenting me with his ass.

I slather the dildo part of the strap-on with the lube and notice for the first time it's on the smaller side.

"So you bought the small strap-on for yourself, but I get to take your thick cock up my ass?" I say with mock annoyance. "If you wanted the *real* female experience, you should've bought one as big as you are."

"I'm adventurous, not insane," he throws back over his shoulder. "Besides, you like my thick cock in your ass."

I snort and position myself behind him. I see the head of his plug and pull it out. He grunts as it pops free, and I toss it onto the floor.

I squirt some extra lube on his puckered hole, then run my hands over his beautiful, muscled ass cheeks. I wrap one hand around his left hip and use the other to line up the dildo.

"Are you ready?" I ask.

"Yeah, I'm ready. Give it to me good, baby."

He yelps as I give his ass a sharp slap.

"You'll pay for that later," he promises over his shoulder, and I will, but it was worth it.

I press forward with the tip of the dildo slowly, and Ash exhales a deep breath.

"Color?" I ask.

"Green," he says.

I push forward some more, and the bright pink head pops past his outer ring of muscle.

He grunts, and I stop.

"Keep going," he says, and I push slowly in some more.

I withdraw then press in, then withdraw and press in again until the strap-on is fully seated inside him before I stop to let him adjust.

Ash lets out another long breath. "Go ahead and move," he says a few seconds later.

I pull out about halfway, then push slowly back in. When I'm just about in, the vibrator buzzes to life, and I jerk forward in surprise.

"Oh fuck!" he groans.

"Are you okay?" I ask in panic. I'm about to pull out when he answers.

"I'm fine. I think you hit my prostate," he says.

I pause, trying to gather what I know about male anatomy. "That's… good, right?"

"Very good," he says breathily. "Keep going."

I start to move again, and Ash groans.

"Definitely my prostate," he says.

I gasp as he clicks the vibrator up a notch, and I pump a little faster.

"Holy fuck," he says.

I take long, controlled strokes, despite being nearly doubled over with my own pleasure as the vibrator sends shivers all over my body. Pressing into Ash also puts friction on my clit, and I feel my climax build as I fuck him. There's something strangely satisfying about pumping my hips this way, and his grunts at each thrust only arouse me more. I force myself not to get overzealous.

I hold onto Ash's hips as I move, and I have to admit, there's a certain power in governing another person's body this way. I understand why men enjoy it. I lean further over him so I can grab his shoulder with one hand as I press my hips into his ass. I thrust a bit harder, and Ash groans.

"You like that, baby?" I purr.

Ash grunts a laugh. "Don't get too used to this. It's only for Stanley Cup playoff time."

"Then you better make the playoffs every year, because this is fun."

The vibrator kicks up higher, and I cry out again as I thrust faster. Seconds later, Ash swears loudly and lets out a grunt as milky jets of cum shoot from his cock onto the duvet.

We probably should have planned that better and put a towel down, but as I understand it, only a certain percentage of men come that way during anal. Apparently, Ash is one.

The vibrator stops between my legs, leaving me short of a release. I whimper but stop moving as Ash lays his forehead on the mattress, and his body eases from the last throes of his orgasm.

"Undo my hands," he orders.

I carefully pull out of him and get off the bed to release the metal clasps that tether the wrist cuffs to the straps. He sits back to flex his shoulders before he goes into the bathroom and comes back with a hand towel that he uses to wipe the cum off the duvet.

I start to unfasten the strap-on, but Ash grabs my waist and throws me down on the bed so I'm lying flat on my back. He finishes unfastening the strap-on, helps me pull it off, then tosses it aside.

"Did you come?" he asks.

I shake my head. "No."

"Good. We're going to play a little game," he says as he pushes my thighs open, then sinks down on the bed with his head between them. "We need to win four games to take the Stanley Cup."

I nod at him, not sure where he's going with this.

"The number of times I make you come tonight is the number of games we're going to win," he says.

My eyes widen. "No!" I try to sit up, but he pushes me back down. "Ash, please, don't make me responsible for your Stanley Cup hopes."

Athletes are a superstitious bunch, and if I can't get my body to come enough times...

Ash looks up at me from between my legs. "You need to trust me, baby," he says. "I know your body, and I know what I'm doing. Can you trust me?"

The whole thing is ridiculous, but he's not going to let this go. I've learned that much about him.

"I trust you," I say as I lie back on the bed.

His mouth closes over my already-swollen clit, and I cry out as I undulate my hips, trying to ride his face. I was already close to coming, and within a minute or so, I've had my first orgasm.

"One," Ash says, and I wait for him to laugh like the Count on Sesame Street. Instead, he slips two fingers inside me and starts to work me again.

I arch back against the bed and brace for what's likely to be an intense few hours.

Gray

Two hours and fifteen minutes later, Ash and I lay sated and barely moving on the bed. His head is still between my legs, and he kisses my clit as I lay panting from my fourth orgasm.

We're exhausted, but we've secured the Stanley Cup for the Hartford Hydra. Or so he insists.

"Good job, baby," he says, smiling up at me.

I look down at him between my legs. "I just hope the team appreciates our effort."

He chuckles. "Unfortunately, they'll never know about your hard work behind the scenes," he says as he moves up to lie next to me.

"You were the one who did all the work," I tell him.

"Right, but that third orgasm was a big one. I didn't think you had another one in you after that."

I shiver, remembering how hard Ash made me come half an hour ago when he fucked me on the floor in the living room after we'd played a chasing game. He's right. I didn't think I'd be able to come again after that, but I'd underestimated the magic of his tongue and how well he knows my body.

Ash leans over me and kisses me deeply. I taste myself on him, and I savor it. He loves going down on me, and I love letting him.

"You know you still have to play good hockey the next couple weeks, right?" I tease when he lifts his head. "As talented as your dick and your tongue are, they aren't going to win you the Cup."

He laughs. "I know. But thinking of you makes me play better, and thinking of that look of ecstasy on your face the last time I made you come is going to make me play some of the best hockey of my career."

I slap his shoulder playfully. "You're incorrigible."

His face goes serious, and he runs a finger gently down my cheek before it traces along my jawline. "Whatever happens these next couple weeks," he says, "I've already won, Gray, because I have you."

I smile and roll my eyes. His words hit deep, but I've never handled sentimentality well, and I have to bite back a snarky remark. This man is everything I ever could've wanted and more, and I'm overwhelmed by my love for him. I swallow back the emotion and meet his eyes.

"You're going to win," I tell him. "I know it."

He smiles. "And how do you know that?"

I shrug one shoulder against the bed. "You just aced the oral exam. After that, I have a feeling the field test will be a piece of cake for you."

He chuckles. "So I passed then, huh, teach?"

I lean up and kiss him. "A+."

Did you like this book?
Indie authors very much appreciate your help spreading the word about their books. Please consider rating or reviewing the book on Amazon, Goodreads, or the platform of your choice. You can also share the book on social media or recommend it to others.

Thank you so much for reading!

Acknowledgements

First and foremost, I want to acknowledge the unwavering love and support of my husband, Patrick McDermott. It takes a special kind of man to not only let his wife write smut about fictional men, but to actively try to sell that smut to everyone he knows and meets. How many other men would sell their wife's book to two women they met on a golf course or ask the bartender at the airport bar if they can leave some cards on the counter? I love you, Patrick. (And I will consider adding dragons to the next Romantasy series. Also, Fred is fine. I swear.)

I'm new to hockey, and while I've learned a lot on my own in the last few months, I'd like to acknowledge and thank my hockey consultant on this book, Jason Phillips. I'm especially grateful for his nuanced explanation of the difference between lines and shifts, as well as his suggestions for hockey-specific language like "buzzing." Thanks so much for taking a look at an early draft of this book and making sure I had my terminology right!

Big thanks to my Icelandic culture and language consulting team, Alma Líf Þorsteinsdóttir, Anna Karen Amin Kolbeins, and Fjóla Heiðdal. I truly appreciate all your support for my books, and I'm grateful for your help in making sure that I accurately represented Icelandic culture in this story. I've loved learning about it from you!

Special thanks to Alma for providing the MP3 file for my narrators to demonstrate the Icelandic accent and word pronunciations for the audio version of the book. And thank you for being my very first ARC reader for *The Last Triumvirate*, then for sharing the book with your friends so I was able to meet such a wonderful group of women!

Thanks as always to my cover designer, Mick Estabrook, who also designed the Hartford Hydra logo. I thought we had an easy one this time around, but of course, you knew better. Sorry for the extra stairs.

Thank you to my alpha reader, Karen Pasquale, who continues to take the rough, rough drafts I give her and find ways to make my stories better. And to my trusty beta readers – Liza Boritz, Mindy Petruck, Emily Rice, Heather Lee, Erin Estabrook, Lana Zadrosny, and (new!) Jennifer Butler – for their keen eyes and great feedback. Each one of you brings a unique perspective to your critique and helps catch different things that need to be fixed. Special thanks to Heather for helping with the 'trunk test' and for providing entertainment and confidence boosting in her early-morning comments on the beta drafts of my books. You are truly a gem.

Finally, as an FYI, the information presented in the early half of the book about how trash talk works is absolutely true. It's based on a study I did for my graduate program that was published in its short form by the academic journal, *Communication Studies*. (The gender-specific results are currently unpublished.) You can also read my original comments to *ESPN* about Scottie Pippen's line to Karl "The Mailman" Malone at https://www.espn.com/nba/story/_/id/29166548/before-last-dance-scottie-pippen-delivered-six-words-trash-talk-changed-nba-history. How Ash deals with his trash talk issue in the book is made up, but the social science information about the shame-rage connection, and much of the other theory is accurate.

Finally, thanks to Emily Rath for introducing me to the joys of hockey romance. I didn't see that coming, but I love that I got here.

www.ingramcontent.com/pod-product-compliance
Lightning Source LLC
Chambersburg PA
CBHW020346010826
48973CB00005B/1295